John Smith grew up on the south coast of England close to Brighton. After leaving school, he moved to London and began a career in the Meteorological Office. At the age of 32, John contracted a debilitating muscle-wasting illness that led to him taking early retirement in 2004. He kept up his interest in the weather, though, regularly producing small articles for websites, but the lockdown during the COVID-19 pandemic provided the time needed to complete a book. His disabilities meant the novel was typed on the computer using only the index finger knuckle on his left hand.

John Smith

BECAUSE OF YE BLEEDIN' SPANNER

AUSTIN MACAULEY PUBLISHERS™
LONDON * CAMBRIDGE * NEW YORK * SHARJAH

Copyright © John Smith 2023

The right of John Smith to be identified as author of this work has been asserted by the author in accordance with sections 77 and 78 of the Copyright, Designs and Patents Act 1988.

All rights reserved. No part of this publication may be reproduced, stored in a retrieval system, or transmitted in any form or by any means, electronic, mechanical, photocopying, recording, or otherwise, without the prior permission of the publishers.

Any person who commits any unauthorised act in relation to this publication may be liable to criminal prosecution and civil claims for damages.

This is a work of fiction. Names, characters, businesses, places, events, locales, and incidents are either the products of the author's imagination or used in a fictitious manner. Any resemblance to actual persons, living or dead, or actual events is purely coincidental.

A CIP catalogue record for this title is available from the British Library.

ISBN 9781398495043 (Paperback)
ISBN 9781398495050 (ePub e-book)

www.austinmacauley.com

First Published 2023
Austin Macauley Publishers Ltd®
1 Canada Square
Canary Wharf
London
E14 5AA

Thanks to my wife, Kirsten, who suffered my many emotions as the story evolved. And to Laura, our neighbour, for her meticulous dissection of my grammar and spelling in the original manuscript.

Table of Contents

Prologue 9
Chapter 1 10
Chapter 2 16
Chapter 3 20
Chapter 4 25
Chapter 5 30
Chapter 6 36
Chapter 7 42
Chapter 8 47
Chapter 9 52
Chapter 10 58
Chapter 11 62
Chapter 12 71
Chapter 13 82
Chapter 14 91
Chapter 15 96
Chapter 16 105
Chapter 17 112
Chapter 18 117
Chapter 19 128

Chapter 20	134
Chapter 21	140
Chapter 22	147
Chapter 23	152
Chapter 24	158
Chapter 25	165
Chapter 26	170
Chapter 27	182
Chapter 28	187
Chapter 29	192
Chapter 30	197
Chapter 31	203
Chapter 32	211
Chapter 33	220
Chapter 34	225
Chapter 35	236
Chapter 36	245
Chapter 37	250
Chapter 38	253

Prologue

The sound of measured steps echoed along the corridor as they had done on countless occasions during the last five months or more. Could this be the day, or will it be another day of monotony in this fly-infested cell? A day when food is thrust through a trap door at regular intervals, or a day when Benyon appears, or could it be a day far worse?

Chapter 1

My introduction to this world occurred thirty-six years ago, almost to the day, in my grandparents' cramped bedroom on an estate in Finglas, a northern suburb of Dublin. It was just a short walk from St Canice's church where my parents had married seven months before. I was christened Sean, and this was coupled with Boateng, the family name obtained from Ghanaian ancestry a couple of generations back. My father was, in fact, Jamaican from a middle-class Kingston family who had pushed their son through medical school. He found his way to Europe and was a junior doctor at the National Orthopaedic hospital when he bumped into my mother, who was then a trainee nurse.

Their relationship was, and probably still is, stormy. By all accounts, it was worse in the early days when they lived with my grandparents. I was not close to my grandparents, they appeared to be deeply religious, but immensely prejudiced people, and because of their daughter's marriage, their twice-daily walk to church became a source of embarrassment rather than pride. These are words my mother used to express this to me later in life. It wasn't long before my parents uprooted to London, to a leafy lane in Highgate, and for the rest of my upbringing it was the place I called home. The house itself was in one of those late Victorian terraces, typical of the area. They rented it for many years, but then the landlord wanted to sell and they were given the first option to buy, which was gratefully accepted. The property was far too large for our small family, but there was an expectation that I should have siblings, however, that was not to be.

To say my childhood was happy would be an exaggeration, but to say it was unhappy would be an injustice to the efforts my mother, in particular, made to raise me. The arguments between my parents were almost a daily occurrence, yet hostility was never long lasting. Curiously, for an orthopaedic consultant, my father had not got a practical bone in his body. This riled my mother who, in her best Dublin slang, would berate the poor fellow calling him a 'bleedin' spanner'.

He would respond in Jamaican patois until eventually a truce was declared. I found the language they used on these occasions difficult to understand, but it was probable that they equally faced the same problem of comprehension. These rows, however, produced an interesting, and probably life-changing, side effect for me.

From an early age, I learnt to mimic the accent of my parents, and initial amusement turned to a realisation that this was a talent that could be exploited. I was encouraged to explore foreign languages in local library books, and my voracious appetite for learning led to me being sent to a boarding preparatory school near Worcester at the age of seven. Perhaps surprisingly, I didn't find the experience too depressing. On the contrary, there was a new group of boys, far more interested in learning than was the case at my previous school. There were no playground gangs, and no unpleasant parents standing at school gates ready to escort their precious children back to disparate family nests.

By the age of thirteen, I was fluent in French and had a good knowledge of Spanish. It helped that we had lengthy summer holidays in France, usually at campsites on the Atlantic coast, where many nationalities congregated, and of course there is the common language of play. How the green Morris Marina managed to complete a round trip from Highgate to Benodet every summer was beyond my understanding, but it did, and the three weeks spent with friends from France, Germany and the Netherlands was my highlight of the year. We did have other holidays, usually with my Irish grandmother, either in Dublin, or at a little cottage in Slade, a delightful little fishing village in County Wexford.

At school, the teachers gave us comfort and security, as well as education, and the self-belief instilled in me aided my ability to pass exams fairly effortlessly. The passing of the last exam at prep. school enabled me to enter a nearby Independent co-educational school which specialised in languages. I was probably regarded as a swot by my classmates, but apart from one person, I was left alone to indulge in my love of languages. That one person was George Spence.

From the very first day he seemed to take a dislike to me. His parents were very rich, and brash with it. They drove to open days in their black Lamborghini, and although it wasn't the most expensive car in the car park, it did offer a marked contrast to my father's green Marina. George had this slow cultured accent, probably attained by spending several hours in front of a mirror monitoring his facial movements. Despite several years in prep. school my default accent was still that of north London, a legacy of the formative years spent in the hurly-burly of kindergarten. The perceived class difference, combined with my linguistic prowess, seemed to produce a festering hatred in George, and although no physical confrontation occurred, even at that young age, I was very wary when he was close by.

Apart from the George problem, my time at the school was largely unexciting. I studied languages assiduously and emerged from the sixth form as a fluent speaker of French, German and Spanish, and with a passable knowledge of Russian, thanks to excellent tuition in the upper sixth. Of course, there were other activities at the school, and I enjoyed playing contact sports, as well as cricket and athletics. Although I had good stamina, pole-vault was the sport I excelled at, but overall, I probably disappointed my parents when it came to sport. Socially, I tended to shun the extra-curricular activities, and while many trysts were made and broken, my studies came first and no young romance came my way.

There was one occasion when I briefly became a focus of attention. It was while I was in the lower sixth. There was a general election, and although too young to vote, I was interested in the event, probably partly because of the increasing moans of my parents foisted on me at every opportunity. The school had a mock election and I stood as a candidate for the Socialist Workers' Party. George Spence was the Conservative Party candidate, and above all it was my wish to beat him. My passionate delivery of the manifesto seemed to astound the teachers, and to everyone's surprise, especially my own, I won at the ballot box. A few odd glances from teachers occurred, and there was brief adulation from pupils, but in this case the expression 'famous for 15 minutes' definitely applied, and I soon resumed my studies in anonymity.

'A'-level results, although not perfect, were good enough to get me into Cambridge on a modern languages course. The first two years were a struggle, and at times I thought I was sinking in a mire of studies, whilst those around me were swimming. Fortunately, I passed the exams and even found a little time to play cricket and go to parties, but social gatherings were few and far between. In the third year, I was attached to the language faculty at the University of Malaga in southern Spain and stayed with a Spanish farming family on the outskirts of Alora, a small town about forty kilometres northwest of the city of Malaga.

It was probably the most rewarding year of my life. Matias and Maria, my hosts in Alora, along with their daughters Marta and Dolores, were very welcoming, although from the very beginning I had misgivings about Matias. At the time I didn't know why, but after a while the reasons for my apprehensions emerged. As part of the course, I had to teach some older pupils at a school in west Malaga, a number 15 bus ride away from Malaga station, but Maria worked there, teaching English, and she would usually give me a lift to the school in her hatchback. The work helped to pay for my lodgings, as well as giving me a little pocket money. It was only part-time, with some of the week spent in the university researching philology as part of my degree course. It was in the library that I met Youssef, a Moroccan in his late twenties who was lecturing in, and studying, Arabic languages. We hit it off immediately. He taught me basic Arabic, an onerous task in itself, and I helped him with some of the nuances of the English language.

He was my entry point into the Malaga social life. Andalusian Spanish is difficult to understand, and Andalucians are difficult to get to know. However, they relish debate and over a few bottles of locally brewed Victoria beer we discussed everything political, from the Spanish Civil War to the future of the Spanish enclaves in North Africa. There was a problem, though. The last train to Alora was at half past nine, and at that hour of the evening Malaga was only just beginning to open its bars and nightclubs. A floor at Youssef's flat was the answer, but although I was approaching twenty-one, my hosts felt protective towards me and obviously disapproved of my lifestyle. They offered their own form of entertainment, and with Marta involved, some of it was very acceptable.

Firstly, I learnt to ride a horse, which, for me, was challenging. It came as a surprise to me how high up one is when one is mounted, but it was fun, and a joy for my tutor, Marta. She was two years my junior and embarking on a career in medicine. She had the *joie de vivre* of a spoilt teenager from a wealthy family, but there was also compassion, a trait probably inherited from her mother. We got along very well, but there was no hint of romance from either side.

My second form of entertainment was offered by Matias. He tried his best to be a father to a son he had never had, but our relationship was awkward. He was elitist, patronising, misogynistic and probably prejudiced against the colour of my skin, although perhaps I'm doing him an injustice. He was keen on shooting animals, a past time I find repugnant now, but at the time I was curious as to what went on at these hunts, the *monteria*, the organised hunting with dogs and beaters. I was not invited to them, but we occasionally visited an estate west of Cordoba, where a friend of Matias was host to small shooting parties at weekends. Having never seen a gun before, let alone having used one, I was not permitted to carry a rifle in the beginning, but Matias was keen to teach me his craft, and on warm evenings in a fallow field on the banks of the gently trickling River Guadalhorce I learnt to kill, but the victims, for the time being, were rabbits.

There was so much to do in southern Spain, and so little time, that my parents were largely neglected, apart from a brief, but only occasional, weekend telephone conversation. I had a week at home around Christmas, but my mother spent most of the time at work, and my father, along with my visiting Jamaican grandfather, spent the holiday period alternating between bouts of eating, and domino marathons. Neither of these pursuits grabbed my attention for many minutes, and I was left to my hobby of the moment, listening to, and learning, Arabic from the linguaphone.

On one evening, I went to The Flask, in Hampstead, a Young's Pub with plenty of history but not too many seats. I met an old school friend there, but it was too crowded for chat, and we adjourned to a pizzeria around the corner. There is a period in one's life when one branches off in a new direction, and for me that time had been reached. I never saw that old friend again.

With great reluctance, at the end of my third study year I left Spain to continue my education in Cambridge. I had new lodgings close to the college in an ageing and musty building. The attic room offered plenty of light from above, but no distracting views of city life, a bonus in this stressful year. My housemates, two girls and two boys, were distantly friendly, but each was involved in her or his circle of acquaintances and we didn't socialise as a group.

It had been decided that I was to write a dissertation on Mozarabic, a Latin-based language of southern Spain, spoken during the early middle ages by the non-Muslim population. It was a subject that intrigued me, and to be able to write about it, pleased me considerably. My supervisor, a small man with an infinite knowledge of medieval Spain, and the worst taste in clothes known to the human race, embraced my subject with gusto, and the last year of college flew by.

My social life was limited to a few political meetings, although I never became a member of any party. Cynicism grew as the unworkable enthusiasm of youth was drowned by the so-called pragmatism of mainstream politics. There were few that shared my views, and as such, self-imposed isolation often seemed the best option. On three, or maybe four, occasions, Youssef came to visit me and we renewed debate on many subjects whilst enjoying the sights of Cambridge, as well as the tourist attractions offered by London. At the Tower of London, he pointed out that as William the Conqueror was beginning the construction of his austere fortress in the Capital, the Golden Age of Islam was beginning to wane in southern Spain, a period that saw major advances in mathematics, medicine and other sciences. Christians, Jews and Muslims lived in harmony, but as prosperity grew, so did decadence, and in the late eleventh century a stricter form of Islam became established in Andalusia and the newly imposed strictures led to disharmony in the majority Christian population. In 1085, Alfonso the Sixth took control of Toledo, and this marked the beginning of the reconquest of Spain, although it wasn't until the end of the fifteenth century that the Muslim rulers were finally driven out of Spain, and all Muslims were brutally forced to either convert to Christianity or go into exile.

Even between terms, my visits to Highgate were rare, but I remained appreciative of my father's financial contribution to my education, and an added bonus was his funding of driving lessons, these carried out on the streets of Cambridge. I fortuitously passed my test at the first attempt on a rainy day just after Easter and following a few beers in The Eagle I went home without a worry in the world. My degree was expected to be a formality, and a career in academia beckoned, but on the following day there was a knock on the door. It was the College Porter and he had an envelope in his hand.

Chapter 2

'Mister Boateng' he said, with the emphasis on 'Bo', 'I have been told to deliver this letter to you in person, I hope it isn't bad news.' I thanked him, took the letter and hurriedly shut the door. I could see from the markings that it was from the College Master's office, and a hundred thoughts raced through my brain. Firstly, what had I done wrong? Okay, I had had a few beers the previous night and the discussion with fellow students who had attended the earlier debate about the Green Party became a little heated, but I wasn't drunk, and the walk back to the lodgings in the cool April night air was, as far as I knew, uneventful. Was there anything else I should have done, or didn't do? The guilt level was high as I fumbled my way through the envelope in search of its contents.

The letter was terse and offered more questions than answers. I was to attend an interview in the Small Lecture Theatre on the following Tuesday at half past two, where I would be met by two Government representatives. As it was only Thursday, I decided to take the train home and discuss the contents of the letter with my parents. My mother's reaction was negative. What had I done wrong? What people have you been associating with? What have you written? And even more absurd postulates. Whereas my father took a more reasoned and benevolent view. After much debate, it was decided that the interviewers were probably from the Foreign Office and, if I performed well, they may give me a job. With renewed confidence, I returned to Cambridge to await the fateful day.

At precisely two thirty, I knocked on the door of the Small Theatre, and without waiting for a response I entered. There were three people present. The College Master was standing talking to two men who were seated. When the master caught sight of me he smiled, said goodbye to the other two and left by a side door. The men then stood and beckoned me over. The taller one, dressed in a grey suit and wearing a bland tie, introduced himself as Peter. There was no handshake, and his manner of speaking suggested smiling and a sense of humour were not on his curriculum vitae. The other man, much shorter and well fed, did smile, although it was bordering on a nervous twitch from someone who looked ill at ease in his ageing brown suit and crumpled tie. He said he was called Michael and they were both Civil Servants and were interested to find out more about me with the view of possibly offering me employment.

Peter ushered me to a seat and I sat down much relieved that I wasn't there to be reprimanded for some unknown misdemeanour. The interview was a curious affair. I likened it at the time to an interrogation. Peter sat close to me, perhaps too close, I could smell his breath every time he spoke. His questions were wide-ranging, from my family history in Ireland, to my social life in Cambridge. The questioning was staccato with little reference to notes, although he did write down a few observations in a small leather-bound notebook. Meanwhile, Michael sat about two rows away and interjected with banal comments and trivial questions. It was unnerving and perplexing, and to this day I don't understand the purpose of conducting an interview in this way, but a week later I received a large brown envelope with application forms to join the Civil Service.

The branch of the Civil Service I was advised to apply for was the Foreign and Commonwealth Office, which appeared to offer many opportunities to travel and interesting work within the field of languages. Two more interviews later, and three months after graduating, I found myself walking through a long corridor in central London to my first proper job in the wide world. The six-month probationary period passed quickly by as courses and assessments were interspersed with placements in language teams dealing with many aspects of international affairs.

During this time, I was living at home and it was convenient to take the tube from Highgate to Embankment, and then there was just a short walk to the office. Rent was low, and on many days there was dinner awaiting me when I arrived home. However, as ideal as it seemed, I needed my independence, and the constant bickering between my parents became an increasing source of irritation to me. Also, my social life was becoming centred south of the river, and although I became the proud owner of a second-hand VW Golf, negotiating the traffic of central London became tiresome. That social life consisted of Karate lessons at a club in Balham on Wednesday evenings, and tennis in Southfields, usually on Fridays. And there were parties. Many young people worked in the Foreign Office and it wasn't long before I was included in the fun-filled weekends. Much of the partying was centred around a house in the Surrey countryside near

Mogador. In reality, it was a large bungalow with stables and a swimming pool set in a sizable garden of trees, shrubs and grass. The building had been sequestrated from an African dictator, who had since died. Although the property was quite old, there was doubt whether it was legally built. As a result, several court cases were pending, and litigation had been going on for a number of years. At some stage, and I'm not sure when and how, a notice went up on the board in the office, offering rented accommodation for up to five persons at a house in Surrey for an unspecified period. Four of my colleagues jumped at the opportunity, and they had been living there in luxury for the previous three years. It was fully furnished, and there was even a full-sized snooker table.

The first party I went to there was a real eye-opener for me. I wasn't really a party animal but now and again I ventured into nightlife. I went with Terry, a friend from work who was probably the most cynical and miserable person I knew, yet he had this unassuming charisma that girls found attractive and line managers intensely irritating. He was a specialist in the German language, and he was also fluent in Russian and Slovene, with a working knowledge of other Slavic languages. Apart from a bookish interest in languages, his other main interest revolved around eating and drinking. He had no interest in healthy eating, and the idea of partaking in sport horrified him, although he did seem to be an expert when it came to rugby and football results.

We stopped off for a drink or two at the Sportsman in Mogador. It was packed and drinks were hard fought for, but then around nine we left and drove down a narrow tree-lined lane to the evening's entertainment. We parked on the large gravel area next to the stables and walked to the bungalow. It was already very lively and the sweet smell of cannabis reached us well before we arrived at the open front door. Around forty people were gyrating to the music, or leaning against walls and doorframes, clutching drinks. Most of the partygoers seemed to know each other, and for me there were several recognisable faces. It was interesting to see work colleagues in this environment.

Young people who were working to better their country in the eyes of the world by day, were illegally getting stoned in the evening. To make matters worse, it was a serving police officer who was supplying the cannabis. Terry appeared to have the same views on drugs as I did, but he wasn't averse to an occasional beer, although on that evening the interlude between occasions was very short.

At some stage as a teenager, I learnt it was a good policy to stay sober if one wanted to meet a young lady, and at a party like that, where drink and drugs were in abundance, the idea was wise. Her name was Julia and she was German, working as a nurse in Hammersmith. Apparently, she was a friend of a friend and didn't really know anybody particularly well. She was from Berlin and her parents lived in the east of the City and were both in the East German civil service prior to the toppling of the Wall. She was good company and we had an enjoyable time, but the relationship wasn't going to progress, and at the end of the evening she joined the other single girls in the attic. The ladder was hauled up by the last girl and that was that. Terry had disappeared somewhere, but most of the remaining males bedded down on cushions and sofas, or just slept in a drunken slumber where their legs had given way under them.

No one stirred until after nine o'clock in the morning, then a few bleary-eyed girls descended from above and began preparing a cooked breakfast. The lads slowly appeared, including Terry, who ignored me as he walked past clutching a bedraggled girl in a pink dress. Not much was said, at breakfast, as many appeared to be nursing hangovers. However, someone decided it would be a good idea to have a game of rugby. To me, this seemed a very bad idea, but egged on by the girls, a majority decided to play. The rules seemed rather obscure, and as there were only thirteen males on show, a six-a-side version was played with a myopic teacher as referee. The score has been lost in the mists of time, but everyone emerged unscathed, and we slowly meandered back to our homes.

I gave miserable Terry a lift back to Wimbledon, although he was surprisingly buoyant; *a temporary condition*, I thought. That party, and others, mainly centred around Putney and Wandsworth, helped me to decide to flee the nest, and with generous help from my father, I purchased a two-bedroomed flat in Tooting.

I was beginning to stagnate in my job, and I felt it was now time to look for a new challenge away from translations and pro-British promotions and propaganda. I made my views known at the routine annual review and I managed to alleviate the tedium by going on two courses, as a preliminary to serving abroad. A couple of months after the courses had finished I was invited for an interview, and it turned out to be a very surprising experience indeed.

Chapter 3

The venue for the interview was one of those anonymous ageing buildings in Victoria which constantly teeter on the brink of demolition or having a preservation order imposed on it. The middle-aged receptionist inspected my security pass, read my letter of invitation, and then peered at me over her rimless glasses for an uncomfortable fifteen seconds before taking me to the lift and inserting a key into the third-floor button. The lift was slow and creaky, but the door opened at the third floor and I was ushered into a small room which appeared to double as an office and a soundproof studio. There was a coffee dispenser and I took the opportunity to lubricate my larynx before the interview commenced.

At precisely ten o'clock the door opened, and to my great surprise, Peter, the po-faced interviewer from my Cambridge days, entered the room. This time he was alone, and with the merest hint of a smile he moved behind the desk and sat down. With his left arm, he beckoned me to sit and there was an awkward silence as his eyes bore into mine. He looked at the green file he had brought with him, and then at me again.

'Have you heard of the S.I.S?' He seemed pleased that he had negotiated the sentence.

'Yes.' I replied quizzically, and then the words flowed as he gave me a precis of the work of the Secret Intelligence Service, commonly known as MI6.

At the end of the monologue, he said, 'Semper Occultus' and smiled, as if he had just come across the bureau motto, 'always secret'. He asked me about my abilities in Arabic and Russian languages, and then on to lighter subjects such as hobbies. He was intrigued to hear that I enjoyed learning new languages, and he seemed uninterested when I said that I had joined a martial arts club and was awaiting approval to enrol as a member of a rifle club in Carshalton. At the conclusion of the interview, I was given the chance to ask a few questions, and from the answers Peter provided, it seemed that the work required of me would use my language skills and introduce me to a more interesting and challenging job.

A month later I cleared my desk at the Foreign and Commonwealth Office and started to learn a new trade, although in many ways it was similar to my previous job. The work during the first year was as far removed from the images portrayed in James Bond films as it could possibly be. Sifting through files, memorising profiles, and courses, many courses. The protection of the nation was paramount, but was it the nation? Or was it the people running the country? There seemed to be undertones of elitism, and definitely a feeling of racism. Understandably, terrorism was public enemy number one, but while weapon caches were being confiscated from so-called jihadists, arms were being exported from Britain to countries that harboured men, and women, with similar opposing views of western democracies.

The hypocrisy was plain to see but increasingly my interests turned to drugs, particularly cannabis. Plenty of crime involved drug abuse, and there seemed to be a burgeoning use of arms to obtain the smallest quantities of cannabis. Even in Tooting, which was rapidly becoming gentrified, there were small-time dealers on street corners almost within sight of the local police station. Nothing appeared to be done about the problem and my line manager just smiled when I had my occasional moan about the situation. That was until one day in October, a few years ago now, when he came up to me with a surprising new project and, at the time, I thought it was exactly what I was looking for.

The Government of the United Kingdom had become concerned about the influx of cannabis from North Africa. Too much was coming into the country, according to the minister, and it had to be stopped. By coincidence, my knowledge of southern Spain obtained during my university placement, 'could prove invaluable' according to my line manager, and after receiving comprehensive background information I was dispatched to the British Consulate in Malaga.

The posting was open-ended, so before I left I put a note on the office noticeboard to try and temporarily let my flat. To my surprise there was plenty of interest, and a girl named Amelia took the keys a week before I was due to depart for Spain. Commuting from Highgate to work, and a return in the evening to my bickering parents became tedious after a mere four days, and I was relieved, and somewhat excited, when I made way to Heathrow for a business class flight to Malaga.

It had been decided that I should find my own way to the Consulate, which, as it happened, consisted of an easy walk to the station at the Airport, the more difficult task of obtaining a ticket, and the short stroll from the main-line station to the modern building where the Consulate was housed. Even though it was late October, the air was still warm, too warm for someone carrying a large rucksack, but the spacious air-conditioned reception area offered welcomed relief. I was directed to the lift and told to go to the second floor, where another reception desk awaited me at the end of a small queue of elderly people with a distinct look of British about them. After close on twenty minutes, my turn came and I presented a letter of introduction which was checked on the computer.

A middle-aged woman emerged from one of the side rooms a minute or two later, and warmly greeted me before ushering me into her office. She was a no-nonsense type, and in a short flurry of words conveyed to me that I would need a bike, which was at the flat, a fishing rod, which was also at the flat, and the keys to the flat, which was situated in Huelin, a western suburb of Malaga. The address was on the keys, and as she proffered a hand to say goodbye she said, 'And by the way, you'll be fishing with Jose on the jetty, at the western end of the *paseo* at nine thirty tomorrow morning. Don't be late.' She said, with a smile in her eyes, and after a meeting which had lasted barely two minutes, I left.

The flat was within walking distance, just. It was about a kilometre away in Calle Mendoza. An ugly street with a hotchpotch of buildings, many resembling prison accommodation, while others were edifices from the nineteen sixties, some with air conditioning units precariously stuck to the walls. These buildings had ground-floor shop space, some bricked up with breezeblocks, but with most housing small bars or mini-supermarkets. My flat was on the first floor above a tiny kebab restaurant. It was closed when I arrived and I hoped it would remain that way. There was no lift, just a set of dark marble stairs that appeared to go ever upwards past a series of anonymous front doors.

On entering the flat, I was greeted by a rusting dark green bicycle, with a D-lock and key sitting on the saddle. Across the handlebars there was a long, thin cloth bag, which, I assumed, contained a fishing rod, and on that there was a fishing licence, complete with my photograph, just awaiting my signature. The small entrance hall branched off into an even smaller kitchen with a cooker, powered by a large orange butane cylinder. The fridge freezer seemed overly big, but had been well stocked with milk, butter and cheese. There was a fresh-looking loaf on the table along with a six-pack of sparkling water. So far I was impressed. The next room was the bedroom with just enough space for a double bed and a wardrobe with sliding doors. Next there was the bathroom with a small bath-cum-shower. These three rooms each had small windows of frosted glass. They could open, but with no air conditioning, the rooms were decidedly stuffy, although the bedroom had an old-fashioned fan, and extractor fans were installed in the kitchen and bathroom. The lounge was decked with dark furniture and colourful cushions. There were two sets of French windows, one with a full-length *reja,* and the other with an ornate Juliet balcony about one metre high.

The floor was tiled, with a small mat under a coffee table separating two comfortable looking chairs from a double sofa. There was a small ageing television in the corner and a couple of obscure posters on the white painted wall, these probably purchased in Ikea. I thought it was a warm and relaxing room, only offset by the constant street noise and the seemingly endless convoy of high-revving mopeds.

I was surprised that so much had been done to accommodate me, and by whom? To this day I have no idea who prepared my welcoming package of food and drink, as well as the bike and fishing rod. Oh yes, the fishing rod. I had never been fishing before and my knowledge of the sport was rudimentary to say the least. I decided to stroll down to the beach and see if there were any fishermen. Fortunately, there were, but I had limited expectations that I would be able to cast a line in an efficient manner the following morning. And what about bait? In Ireland, as a youngster, I had watched the anglers in their galoshes digging in the sand near Slade for worms, but in the Mediterranean there was very little tide, so it was impossible to dig for bait. I casually looked to see what the fishermen were using, but they had something hidden away in tins, and I was unwilling to draw attention to myself, so I decided that any fish that visited my line would have bread, and if they rejected it that was alright by me.

A Chinese take-away sufficed for an evening meal, and I had hoped for an early night. But firstly, the Chinese restaurant didn't open until nine o'clock, and secondly, the cacophony of Spanish street life continued until close to midnight. The last moped and the last barking dog probably fell silent much later, but for me the day had already finished, and on the following morning my job was to begin in earnest with a trip on my bike with a fishing rod slung over my shoulder.

After a good night's sleep, I made my way showered, but unshaven, to the meeting place. The jetty was easy to find. It consisted of a wide, but rough, track out into the sea with huge rocks deposited on either side of it to prevent erosion.

At the end of the jetty, there was a rusting and decaying platform with pieces of jagged metal rising from the seabed. There were three or four anglers already positioned on the left-hand side, and as there was a gentle swell splashing on the right-hand side, it seemed sensible to keep left. The jetty was almost two hundred metres long, so there was plenty of distance available between the fishermen, and I found a spot on the rocks about two thirds of the way towards the end and proceeded to cast a fishing line for the first time ever.

The bait I used, hidden in an opaque plastic box from the fridge, consisted of damp bread and pate. It seemed to stick to the hook fairly securely, and maybe an undiscerning fish would find it intriguing. Secretly, I had hoped that no fish would come anywhere near the hook. The water was very clear and probably about three metres deep. The seabed was easy to see, and there were fish swimming around. They were probably mullet, and I had heard they were difficult to catch, so I was hopeful that my quest for fish would fail. Apart from the handful of fellow anglers, the jetty was quiet.

A couple of female joggers puffed by before turning back as the surface became rougher. Two middle-aged men, with tourists written all over them, ambled to the end of the jetty, sat down for a while, and then sauntered back towards Malaga. A huge cruise ship was berthed in the port, and I wondered where those thousands of passengers were spending their day. It was very peaceful.

I looked at my watch. It showed half past ten and I realised that I had been sitting on an uncomfortable rock for over an hour. There was one man who was slowly edging in my direction. He had engaged in conversation with two or three other fishermen on his journey and he didn't seem like someone I should get to know. Eventually, he reached me and we exchanged a few pleasantries before he moved slowly up the jetty to a position about thirty metres away. He unsuccessfully fished for about twenty minutes before moving to the end of the jetty where he spoke to two more anglers. After another twenty minutes or so, he approached me again and asked if I had any bait. Of all life's embarrassing moments, this rated pretty highly, as I removed the lid from my plastic pot and exposed its contents of liver pate and bread.

Without batting an eyelid, he said, 'I hope your children are not going hungry, Sean. My name is Jose.'

Chapter 4

In typical Spanish style, the conversation covered subjects from all angles, and my lack of fishing skills, in particular, were thoroughly analysed. I didn't like the man, not because of his criticisms, but his eyes hinted at a ruthless streak, and from the beginning I was very wary of him. He was about one metre seventy tall, slightly overweight, and, I would guess, in his mid-fifties. He was an officer in the *Guardia Civil,* 'Just a simple policeman' as he put it. He talked a lot, but it was difficult to get a real impression of him. He was from Madrid, the accent was noticeable, and he was definitely keen on fishing, a sport he had taken up after his posting to Malaga some twenty years before. Occasionally he interrupted his speech to ask me a question. He assumed that I was also a policeman and I didn't tell him otherwise. He was keen to find out where I was living, but that was something he was not going to find out, and when I just waved my arm in reply, he assumed that I was renting a flat at Sacaba Beach, an urbanisation not very far from the jetty.

When we started talking about corruption in the police force, he shuffled uneasily and glanced away as he said that there are bad officers in every force. It was obviously a subject he wanted to avoid and his monologue then ceased with conversation becoming stilted. He seemed relieved when I said that I had things to do, and we packed away our fishing gear. Neither of us had been successful in our quest for fish, although small crabs showed a passing interest in my bait. We exchanged phone numbers and walked back along the jetty, mostly in silence. I said, I needed to go to a cycle shop before it closed for lunch, and as that was in the opposite direction to Sacaba Beach, he wouldn't have been any wiser as to my address. He stopped at a worn 'B' registered Ford Fiesta and said, that was his car, and that was all he could afford with his salary. It was something I expected to hear, and I watched as he drove off along the service road towards Malaga. Why did I not like this man? It was playing on my mind as I cycled inland to buy a puncture repair kit for my ancient bicycle.

I had lunch at one of the many beachside *chiringuitos* that adorn the *paseo* along its five-kilometre length into Malaga. I thought I would give Youssef a ring to see if he was available during the afternoon. He wasn't, but we arranged to meet at a pizzeria close to the *Parque Mediterraneo* in the evening. In an empty corner of the restaurant, we talked about my mission, and his eyes widened as I laid out details of the plans to thwart the import of cannabis into the UK. We had been instructed not to speak about our work to anyone outside of our closest relations, but I trusted Youssef more than my immediate family, and it was good to have someone to talk over strategy with in the days ahead.

Jose called me several times to invite me fishing, and he seemed perturbed when I showed a lack of interest in my newfound sport. I suggested that we should meet for lunch or dinner, but he was reluctant to do that, so we made do with short conversations. I was unable to glean anything useful from Jose, and it was my impression that he was there to keep tabs on my movements rather than enter into an exchange of information. Youssef was providing plenty of ideas, and one of those involved visiting Morocco, and on the following Friday afternoon we took the bus to Algeciras to catch an evening ferry to Tangiers.

Youssef seemed to have family all over Morocco, but his older brother was an accountant in Tetouan, one of the larger cities in northern Morocco and my friend had invited us to stay there for the weekend. The ferry docked at Tangier Med, a huge newish port well outside the main city, and from there we used our pre-booked bus tickets to travel to Tetouan. The trip through the hills, enhanced by the setting sun, was very pretty, although there seemed to be plenty of rubbish lying around. Much of it consisted of plastic bottles and bags, but there was also a lot of builder's rubble to be seen. So, my first impression was that it was dirtier than on the European side, but the second impression was formed on the bus journey. It was slightly shorter than the trip from Malaga to Algeciras, but unlike on the Spanish bus, where the noisy babble of voices continued throughout the excursion, this bus was almost totally silent. The vast majority of passengers were male and elderly with a few women wearing mainly brown or blue *jalabibs*. There was no air conditioning on the bus, and although windows were open, the rushing wind could not hide the smell of stale sweat and cheap perfume.

After just over an hour, we reached Tetouan and we were met by Mohammad, Youssef's brother, in a bright red Renault Clio. He was a tall thin man with a full moustache topped by smiling friendly eyes. From the bus station we had a short trip to Mohammed's home at Martil on the coast. It was a large flat, tastefully decorated, mostly in blue and white, and with expensive looking rugs in the capacious lounge. A pile of toys had been swept into the corner, probably by the woman who emerged from the kitchen and introduced herself as Fatima, Mohammed's wife. The two children had gone to bed, but the table had been laid for four people, and we were served with couscous, which is traditionally served on Fridays.

It's the equivalent of Sunday roast in Britain, but unlike at home, there wasn't any wine, just four glasses of mint tea. I was surprised that Fatima was wearing modern western clothes, but she said that was normal in many households, although most women still wore the traditional *jilbab* overgarment when they went outside.

Mohammed's dialect made conversation in Arabic difficult for me, so we spoke in French, the second language of the country, and with most educated Moroccans speaking it fluently. It wasn't long before the subject of drugs arose, and Mohammed seemed to have more than a passing knowledge of cannabis cultivation. Apparently, one of his accountancy firm clients was a fig and olive farmer who was supplementing his income by growing cannabis. Mohammed was very relaxed about it, saying that many farmers were doing the same, and the authorities tolerated it as long as the cultivation and processing wasn't carried out too openly. That came as a bit of a surprise, but as he pointed out, some countries allowed cannabis to be smoked or cannabis oil to be used as medication. This seemed to be in total contrast to the views expressed by the *Guardia Civil* officer in Spain. We retired to the sofa area for coffee and biscuits, and, as is tradition, the guests, in this case Youssef, poured out the coffee. It was agreed that we should contact the fig farmer on Saturday morning and try and organise a visit to see for ourselves how the cannabis story begins. Mohammed said, 'You will have some surprises.' And it was with that statement we ended the evening and retired to our bedrooms.

The noise of young children playing brought a good night's sleep to a premature end, and I emerged from the bedroom to be confronted by a sea of chaos. Two boys had spread toys to all corners of the lounge, with one parent preparing breakfast as the other worked on his laptop. The children, Sami and Hachim, ignored me but friendly good mornings were forthcoming from Mohammed and Fatima. Youssef soon joined us and we had a breakfast of freshly baked *msemen*, a cross between bread and pancakes, served with a glass of fresh orange juice and some mint tea. On the bread we spread olive oil, as a substitute for butter, and there was feta cheese and jam. Sweet biscuits followed to cap a simple, but filling breakfast.

Mohammed called the farmer around nine o'clock, and he was very keen that we should visit him. That was my first surprise. I had always thought that the Rif mountains were potentially dangerous and unwelcoming to strangers, but maybe not.

Fatima was staying at home with the boys, so the three of us climbed into the Renault for our trip into the hills. The road was single carriageway, but mostly of good quality, certainly compared with the roads in south London, and as traffic was fairly light, we covered almost ninety kilometres in less than two hours. Most of the journey had been made under cloud cover, but the sun emerged when we reached the farm and it became very warm. Mohammed, the farmer, was a small thin weather-beaten man of indeterminate age, but probably in his sixties. His warm smile exposed an incomplete set of uneven teeth, as he beckoned us to enter the house. His wife, who was wearing a black *jilbab*, was not introduced to us, but she quickly produced a large teapot and four glasses, each of which contained a sprig of mint. Youssef's brother poured the tea from a great height, so the tea in the glass resembled *caffe latte*. Dishes of salad, pulses and pastes were brought from the kitchen, along with a large basket of fresh-smelling bread.

In French, the farmer told us his life history. The farm had been in his family for generations and although it had given them a reasonable standard of living in the past, that was not so anymore. In the nineteen sixties and seventies, hippies came to the area and set up encampments and sat on street corners in Derdara, the local town, completely stoned, or wandered around begging.

Since then, the internet had arrived, tourists arrived in hire cars and drug production had become a sophisticated industry. After lunch, we walked along a hillside track which opened out into a cultivated valley criss-crossed by a rudimentary watering system. Most of the crops had been harvested but there were still some patches of withering cannabis plants. Mohammad pointed out a couple of fields and said that they had Pakistani plants, whereas the others were solely Moroccan, but he also said, there was a certain amount of cross-pollination. I had read that around seventy percent of the world's cannabis production occurred in the Rif mountains and I wondered, as it was illegal, why the authorities had not stopped it. Mohammed smiled and said that it was a way of life, and although the taxes and bribes had become more expensive, they had largely been left alone. As there were now countries legalising cannabis use, the tourists were less inclined to visit the area for drugs, but rather they came to walk the stunning mountain trails and see the beautiful waterfalls.

We went back to the farm where even more mint tea was awaiting. Mohammad, the farmer, pulled me to one side, and with a serious look on his face, said, 'I know why you are here, and you would probably like to see me lose my livelihood, or at worst, have me imprisoned, but it's not people like me you should be after. There's something far worse going on now, and it's going to cost many, many young people their lives.'

Chapter 5

I was more than a little taken aback by the passion of Mohammed's statement and listened intently as he sought to clarify his words. The clients of the farmer were from many different countries and from various backgrounds, but the general thread was that a change was occurring in the drugs market. There was a new strain of cannabis taking over the market place, and it was highly addictive. People were killing to obtain it, or worse, killing to obtain the money to buy it. To make matters even more disagreeable, certain right-wing governments were condoning lawlessness to enhance their credentials as advocates of 'law and order'. The result was a crackdown by some governments on cannabis from Morocco while the import of the addictive drug had been left largely unchallenged. He went on to say, with bitterness in his voice, that Britain was one of the worst countries for this change in drug culture and he hoped that I would do something about it.

It was obviously something he had wanted to say for a long time, but he quickly resumed his friendly countenance. It seemed to be the appropriate moment to leave, and we thanked him for his hospitality and waved farewell to the farmer that had now given me so much to think about. On the way back, we took a detour to the ancient town of Chefchaouen and walked around the narrow, blue-walled streets. There was a smell of leather everywhere, as many of the shops were trying to sell leather products to the handful of mostly elderly tourists that were also strolling through the medieval lanes. There were many reservoirs on the route back to Martil, and all were desperately in need of replenishment, but Mohammed assured me that the rains would arrive, and presumably the following year would then see another bumper crop of cannabis.

We discussed the events of the day over dinner in the evening, but the children were centre stage, and after they had gone to bed, we felt too worn out to continue debating and we all had an early night. On Sunday, after breakfast, we went for a walk along the seafront. There was row upon row of low-rise mostly white and blue apartment blocks on one side of the road, with a broad promenade giving way to a wide sandy beach on the other side. It was breezy and there was drizzle in the air, so I wasn't impressed, but then Youssef suggested we head off to Marina Smir, a fashionable resort, twenty kilometres along the coast, for lunch. It was certainly much classier than Martil and the weather was better.

Mohammed explained that the purpose-built resort was constructed in the early nineteen nineties, aiming at the top end of the tourist market while maintaining relatively low costs. It was quiet on the streets, with some marina-side restaurants closed, although those that were open seemed to be reasonably full. We chose one that had tables in the sun but out of the breeze, and as we were off back to Spain later in the day, Youssef and I decided to have a full meal because we would be too late to eat in Malaga.

Naturally, our conversation soon turned to the drugs business that we had seen on the previous day, and the farmer's emotive words on the subject. Mohammed had a *laissez-faire* attitude to cannabis exporting, and the thought crossed my mind that he was more involved in the drugs world than he was letting on. Youssef continued to have a zero-tolerance attitude, and while I had a certain amount of sympathy for the farmer's plight, a world without harmful drugs still seemed a goal to aim for.

As we were eating a memorable *paella* we were looking across at the array of hugely expensive yachts and speedboats in the marina. Our attention was drawn to one extravagant grey monster that seemed like a hybrid between a speedboat and one of those super yachts. There were four men loading items onto the boat, and their dress and demeanour suggested criminals. They shiftily looked around them, and with their black clothes and sunglasses, even the casual observer would guess that they were up to no good. We asked Mohammed what he thought was going on. He smiled, and said, it could be anything from drugs, cigarettes, artefacts to counterfeit money. He said, there may even be a holding house somewhere full of migrants waiting to board the boat to seek their fortune in Europe. He went on to say that the new moon was due at the beginning of November, and under the cover of darkness was the time when most of these high-speed crossings took place.

After lunch, we returned to Martil and chatted for a while, drank the ubiquitous mint tea, and watched the children play. Mohammed offered us a lift to Tanger Med to catch the ferry, so we said our goodbyes to Fatima and the boys and left. The trip to the port seemed even prettier in the soft autumn light and everyone seemed jolly. Mohammed, because we were leaving, I thought, and Youssef and I because we were going back to the bustle of Malaga. We thanked Mohammed for his hospitality and also for all the new information he had provided, which had now left me with much to think about.

The sun was sinking into the sea as we left the port, and it was midnight before the bus reached the terminus in Malaga. I thanked Youssef for all his help and we went our separate ways. It was about a twenty minutes' walk back to the flat and on the way I picked up a kebab. For some reason, intuition maybe, I had left my mobile in the flat so that I couldn't be traced by anyone. It was something I remembered from my training. 'Trust no one and you live longer.' There had been several calls, mostly from the same number, and I smiled as it occurred to me that Jose had been ringing, and his calls had become increasingly frequent, but that was for another day.

The first call in the morning was before nine o'clock and, of course, it was Jose. He did his best to sound cool and collected, but there was a hint of concern in his voice. I jovially said that I had had an interesting and relaxed weekend and hoped that he had had the same. The tone of conversation seemed to placate him, and when I suggested that we should meet for fishing in a couple of hours he reverted to his usual relaxed manner. The bread was not fit for human consumption anymore but with a little work it could be made attractive to fish, and with the required paraphernalia, I set off for the jetty.

Jose was there before me, talking to a youngish man wearing red and black lycra, a helmet, sunglasses and leaning against an expensive looking bike. He quickly bade farewell to the cyclist when he spotted me, and he strolled along the jetty to the spot where we had been fishing together before. He was gushingly friendly, helped by the fact that he hooked a small bream on his very first cast. He then spent most of the morning telling me in great detail how heavily loaded he was with paperwork, and how grateful he was that he could take this opportunity to indulge in his favourite sport. Eventually, he asked me how my weekend had gone.

I wanted to choose my words carefully to see what his reaction would be to my travels. It was my intention to give him as few details as possible, but if he decided to check my story I didn't want him to think I was lying.

'I've been to Morocco for the weekend.' I said.

Firstly, he opened his mouth in astonishment, secondly his eyes flashed angrily, and thirdly he smiled and banally said, 'That's interesting.' I inwardly laughed at his response.

As I thought, he wanted to know my every move, and he was annoyed that I had absented myself without his knowledge, although he was professional enough not to say so. He questioned me like a police officer would a suspect, but I was vague in my replies and put an emphasis on the tourist sites I had visited rather than anything specifically to do with drugs. He became increasingly irritated, but he could see that he was getting nowhere and he fell into a sullen silence.

I broke the silence by saying that I had heard that a drugs run was planned for the following weekend. I actually had no knowledge of that, but with the new moon due early in November, it seemed like a possibility.

Jose stroked an imaginary beard and replied quietly but seriously, 'Yes, we believe a big shipment of cannabis will arrive in the *Guadalhorce* estuary next weekend.' He bit his lip, perhaps regretting he had told me, and he then concentrated on his fishing for a while.

The *Guadalhorce* estuary is a designated nature reserve of roughly seventy hectares and offers sanctuary to over two hundred species of bird. Although it is only about six kilometres from the centre of Malaga, it is one of the quietest coastal areas on the Costa del Sol, and for decades it has been a place where smugglers of goods from North Africa have made their landfall in Europe. The proximity of a motorway has made their getaways easier, and in recent years the trafficking of people from sub-Saharan Africa has been added to other illegal activities.

It had been a successful morning's fishing for Jose and at lunchtime we parted amicably with an arrangement that we would meet again on Wednesday morning. He appeared to have free rein to do what he liked, and it made me wonder what his role was in the prevention of illicit drug smuggling. As I cycled along the cycle lane at the back of the *paseo* I couldn't help but notice the man in red and black lycra that had been talking to Jose earlier in the morning. He was sitting on a bench talking on his phone with a half-read novel by his side. He might as well have had a blue flashing light on his head, it was so obvious that he was a policeman. I nonchalantly cycled past him humming the theme song to the Pink Panther films and settled on a bench some fifty metres further along the promenade. He cycled past and stopped a short distance away and fiddled with his saddle. This happened twice more and my thoughts were, how amateurish. It was a bit of a nuisance, though, as I didn't want him to know where I lived. So, I decided to cycle all the way into Malaga, and once there, went into a cafe on the harbour front where they served delicious *patatas bravas*. He positioned himself in the Argentinian restaurant next door, and it amused me that he would be paying considerably more for his lunch than I would.

 I sat and thought of a strategy, but his bike was more efficient than mine and he matched me in fitness, so when I left the cafe it was with the intention of losing him in some of the narrow alleys of the old town. As I glanced back, I could see him hurriedly settling his bill with a half-eaten steak left on his plate. In a fast, but seemingly casual, manner I cycled towards the lighthouse and then headed left along the *paseo* bordering the *Playa la Malagueta*. Pedestrians tend to share pavements with cyclists in this part of Spain, and although most pavements are broad, a speeding cyclist is at high risk of a collision. The one-way street was equally as hazardous, but I changed to that option when I caught sight of my pursuer rounding the corner by the lighthouse. A quick left turn, followed by a right, brought me outside the local supermarket, and there I had a stroke of fortune. A retractable garage door, serving flats above the supermarket, was automatically closing after a car had either left or arrived. I quickly ducked underneath and into the fetid atmosphere of the garage. The inside lighting had already switched off but a line of metal grids high on the wall towards the street allowed just enough light in for me to see the layout of the interior. There were not many cars there, and those that occupied the spaces appeared to be permanent fixtures. In the corner, there was an ageing Mercedes, and I wheeled the bike behind it and sat down on a child's tricycle to plan my next move.

 The best idea was to wait until nightfall in the hope that someone opened the garage door. There were not many ways back to the flat, and it seemed less likely that I would be spotted in the dark. I couldn't imagine that there would be lookouts on every corner, and I was beginning to think that maybe I was overreacting to being followed and my whereabouts were not really that significant to the authorities. However, it was important to me, for some reason, that my temporary address stayed private. With that thought in mind, I waited and waited. Eventually, two chatting employees of the supermarket entered the garage, jumped into a small hatchback and drove off. It took a little while to adjust to the lighting, but already the door was beginning to close, and without further ado I jumped on to the bike and cycled out into the late evening fresh air.

I left my cumbersome fishing accoutrements behind the old Mercedes just in case I had to take some more avoidance measures on the way back to the flat, but in the usual bustle of Malaga nightlife there were no signs of lurking policemen.

I took the back roads into the main part of Malaga and then felt free in the labyrinth of small shop-filled alleys that make up the greater part of the old city north of the cathedral. The streets were becoming quieter when I finally got back to the flat with a large, boxed pizza under my arm. It appeared I had outfoxed the policeman on this occasion, but if they were that interested in knowing where I was living, then I knew that a repeat of the pursuer and the pursued would happen again in the not-too-distant future.

Chapter 6

Thursday dawned clear and fresh with a strong northwest wind rattling doors or windows somewhere in the block. Not a pleasant day for fishing, and not a good day to cycle into the city to retrieve my abandoned tackle. So, after breakfast I wandered up to *Calle Ayala* and took the number 1 bus into the harbour area. I waited for a good half hour before the garage door opened and a young girl emerged riding a Vespa. She quickly disappeared round the corner and I nonchalantly walked into the garage before running to the corner to collect my fishing tackle. It was how I had left it, and within a minute I was outside again with the door steadily descending. I felt like a sneak thief as I walked along the street, but even though there were several people around the supermarket, no one showed any interest in me and I slowly relaxed. Rather than lug this unwieldy equipment around for the rest of the day, I took the bus back to the flat, and then spent a pleasant afternoon wandering around the Russian Art Museum, housed in a splendidly ornate old tobacco factory just a short stroll from the flat.

I was surprised that I hadn't heard from Jose, but I wasn't to be disappointed. He phoned in the early evening and suggested that we meet for an early lunch on Friday at one of the *Chiringuitos* close to the fishing jetty. He sounded cheery and I wondered what he had in mind, as there was no mention of fishing, and no questions about what I had been doing since we last met.

At around half past twelve on Friday, I walked into the almost empty *chiringuito*. The proprietor was busily skewing sardines ready for their traditional roasting above an old sand-filled rowing boat at the side of the restaurant. Jose was sitting alone at an outside table smoking a cigarette and peering into a steaming cup of cafe solo. His greeting was cordial, but there was something remote and vague about him. He stubbed out his cigarette and asked how things were, and I told him about my cultural afternoon in the museum, and as expected, he seemed totally uninterested. We ordered some food and made small talk, but after a small bowl of olives arrived, along with a couple of beers, he leant forward in his seat, and in a low voice, began to tell me the plans for the coming weekend in anticipation of the drug run from Morocco.

It surprised me how open he was about the plans considering his ill-disguised anger about my unregistered trip across to North Africa. Nevertheless, it was decided that we were to meet up outside the church in Guadalmar, a fairly modern coastal urbanisation bordering the Guadalhorce River, around dusk this evening, and then we were to proceed into the nature reserve to wait for events to unfold. No further details were forthcoming, and the rest of the meal was eaten in near silence. He suggested that I should get some sleep as it could be a long night, and his parting sentence was 'Don't forget to use mosquito repellent, they'll enjoy your blood.' It was said, as a joke, but with more than a hint of malice in his voice.

He walked over to his car and left, with no sign of anyone left behind to follow me. I cycled along the *paseo* with a certain exhilaration that now something was about to happen in the war on drugs. I wasn't sure what to bring with me for the night's adventure, but dark clothes seemed sensible, and I filled my small dark rucksack with muesli bars and two boxes of fruit juice. I thought it would be a good time to try out my expensive new nighttime field glasses that also had the ability to take photographs. Refreshed after a couple of hours of sleep, and plastered with mosquito repellent, I went down to the main road to hail a taxi.

One soon appeared driven by a small man who, it quickly emerged, had originated from Sierra Leone. His English was far better than his Spanish and in the twenty-minute trip I had a potted history of his life, with the exception of how he had arrived in Malaga. He was a very jolly fellow and positive about his future, and his ability to keep my mind free of trepidation for the night ahead, earned him a substantial tip when we arrived in Guadalmar.

Jose was already outside the church, sitting on the steps wearing camouflage fatigues with one of those long-lens cameras associated with bird spotters, slung over his shoulder. We must have looked like an odd couple as we walked past the long line of eucalyptus trees on the approach to the river. One was dressed for military combat, the other resembled a cat burglar. It was very quiet in the street, and on the rough track leading to the nature reserve there were no people but an increasing number of mosquitoes.

Instead of crossing the river into the reserve we turned left by the bridge and took a small path that led under the motorway. We walked on, and eventually

Jose pointed to an almost completely overgrown track through the reeds. It was just a short path to the river's edge, but a large lump of concrete, probably the remains of an old irrigation channel, bordered the river, and with reeds on three sides, it was the perfect hidden spot for viewing the river, as well as the busy road that ran parallel to the motorway about two hundred metres northwest of us.

A nearby coot shrieked in alarm, and rapidly splashed across the river, encouraging a flock of seagulls to gently rise in unison before relocating a hundred metres down the river. Otherwise, all was silent apart from the constant low hum of traffic noise from the two main roads and the occasional high-pitched whine from an eager mosquito. The daylight had faded away, although enough light remained to see local outlines, and the well-lit road was near enough to offer a little more illumination. Jose sat on the lump of concrete and lit a cigarette. He hadn't said a word since we had left the street to walk to the river, but a monologue then ensued giving details of what to expect for the coming night.

Much of what he had to say was quite surprising. Firstly, very little was expected to happen, as this was going to be a dry run before the big night on Saturday. I wondered how he knew that, but I let him go on. Secondly, there were only four other police officers following the proceedings, so as not to heighten the risk of the drug smugglers stumbling across something that would make them abandon the main show. So, all we were to do was observe what was going on in preparation for Saturday night. It was a bit of an anti-climax, but probably they knew a lot more about these operations than I did.

It was crushingly boring sitting there by the river with a man of limited conversational ability. I had already had a potted history of Jose's life and he had no interest in my past. Cricket was a sport alien to this man, and though he had a passing interest in football, it didn't extend much beyond Malaga FC, a club whose supporters always seemed to languish in the depths of despond. The monotony was occasionally broken by a splash from the nocturnal wildlife, and as the land breeze slowly increased in strength the reeds rustled, drowning out the noise of the decreasing traffic flow. At around one o'clock, I retrieved the muesli bars and a box of juice from my rucksack, and at the same time I put the binoculars around my neck. Jose had a small old-fashioned radio with an earplug and he was listening to some form of popular music, although it was barely audible to me sitting just a metre away from him.

After the snack, I began toying with the binoculars and I was really impressed by the clarity of the night vision. A rodent was silently swimming across the river disturbing some of the roosting birds. A fox was prowling on the far bank. The traffic was much clearer too, with a considerably reduced glare from the streetlights. A broken-down lorry was at the side of the road just before the bridge and two men were looking thoughtfully at one of the wheels. I zoomed in and took a picture, and again the quality was good.

At around two in the morning, the low hum of a powerful speedboat could be heard, and I nudged Jose, who had fallen asleep. We instinctively lowered ourselves behind the concrete wall and watched as a low, dark boat glided up the river. Not one, but three boats, passed by our look-out spot and stopped mid-stream about fifty metres from us. The first one pulled into the side and several boxes were unloaded. The boat then chugged quietly back towards the mouth of the river. The same process took place with the other two boats and then there was silence again. The whole episode lasted less than fifteen minutes. Meanwhile, the broken-down lorry, which I had completely forgotten about, sprang into life and reversed down the narrow track to where the boxes were. It disappeared from our sight, but we assumed they were loading the boxes onto the lorry. About ten minutes later, it was driven off in the direction of Malaga with no trace of any wheel or engine malfunction.

So, that was that. A bit of an anti-climax I thought, but Jose seemed very pleased with the night's work and on the way back to the church where we had met he chatted amicably about the dry run that had gone so well, and the night ahead when 'these criminals' would be 'nailed'. There were no other people to be seen, and throughout the evening I had not seen one other person who could have been a policeman engaged on this spying mission. Jose offered me a lift home, which I was very grateful for, but I was not going to reveal my address to him, so I asked him to drop me at some traffic lights on the main road a couple of hundred metres from the flat. He didn't show any interest in where I lived and bade me a jovial 'goodnight' with the arrangement that we would meet at our hideout around dusk. I waited for him to disappear from sight and then walked back to the flat feeling that the evening had posed many questions and yielded very few answers.

My brain was racing, but I knew sleep was needed before any cohesive thoughts could emerge. The alarm was set for ten o'clock and I slept soundly for about five hours. After a shower and breakfast, I tried to make sense of the previous night. It seemed to me that this was no 'dry run' it was the real thing, and where were the other police officers? And that broken-down lorry, I'm sure

I had seen it somewhere before, but where? I was becoming increasingly suspicious of the whole affair, and with that in mind, I decided to rent a car to take me to the nature reserve, and a sixth sense told me to take an overnight bag as well.

Late in the afternoon, I had a hearty meal of Russian salad, pork stew and ice cream at a little restaurant round the corner from the flat. It was from the set menu and very cheap, a far cry from some of the pricey tourist restaurants close to the cathedral. I had an overnight bag with me as well as my rucksack, when I took a taxi to one of the many off-airport car hire centres in St Julian. A shuttle bus had just arrived with a handful of German tourists aboard, and it took a good forty minutes before my car hire was processed. I drove the small hatchback to waste ground close to the *Canal Sur* television station and left my overnight bag in the boot. I liberally covered myself with mosquito repellent and set off down the track. Jose was not there when I arrived and it was almost dark when a rustling of the reeds revealed his presence.

He was in a buoyant mood and he talked at length about the need to be rid of these criminals. His enthusiasm made me begin to doubt my suspicions about him. We had an uncharacteristically cosy conversation that made time pass quickly. He revealed that it was not always easy for drug runners.

Last year the river had dried up due to lack of rainfall, and the year before thunderstorms prevented the landings, and in a laconic way he said, 'They had to go elsewhere.' I asked him why the criminals hadn't been caught, and this question seemed to take him off guard, and without an answer he lapsed into silence, and I felt the good atmosphere had been soured.

At two in the morning, there was no sign of any boats and no broken-down lorry by the roadside. In fact, I was beginning to think that nothing was going to happen, at least on the smuggling front. However, the weather was changing. There was not a breath of wind and it felt sultry, and an orange glow in the sky above Malaga suggested plenty of clouds. In the distance, towards the southeast, there were some flashes of lightning, and they appeared to be getting closer.

Eventually, the occasional boom of thunder could be heard, and then Jose said, 'I can hear boats.'

I listened intently but heard nothing except the low rumble of distant thunder.

Then suddenly, from somewhere closer to the river mouth several shots rang out and there was the sound of splashing water as a flock of seagulls lifted into the air in front of us. Another two distant shots pierced the silence and then Jose said, 'And now it's your turn Mister Boateng.' There was a vivid flash and a deafening bang, and then silence.

Chapter 7

My sixth sense told me that something was seriously wrong and I ducked down a moment before a bullet whizzed harmlessly over my head. In an instant, I dived towards Jose's legs and before he had the chance to fire again I had brought him down, grabbed his hair and slammed his head on to the concrete block. He must have dropped his gun, because no further shots ensued and the only noise was his groans of pain and confusion. The adrenalin was running fast and mixed with extreme fear. I grabbed his head again and threw it at the concrete, and twice more, until the only sound was my heavy breathing, but there was a new sound. The *splish-splash* of rain on the reeds.

I had never killed a man before, I hadn't even been in a serious fight before, but Jose was dead and lying at my feet. What's more, he was a policeman. There were some quick decisions to make and my life could depend on it. I located Jose's gun, and along with his binoculars quietly lowered them into the river. I then dragged his body deep into the reed bed. It was squelchy, smelly and very unpleasant, but at least a casual observer would not be able to see him without wading into the reeds.

All of these actions took less than five minutes, but that was a long time, and those that fired the other shots could soon arrive on the scene. I grabbed my rucksack and dashed towards my car expecting to hear a call to halt at any moment, or worse still, hear another shot, and a thud as the bullet hit my back. To make matters even worse, the rain became torrential and the thunderstorm came ever closer. I reached the car breathless and shaking with fear. The simple task of putting the key into the ignition was almost beyond me but I managed it and the car purred into life.

Almost immediately, car headlights appeared in my rear-view mirror. I thought it must be the police, but it was just a car emerging onto the service road, probably a late worker at the television station. He sped past, and the road was empty again. It was the most foul night. The rain was bouncing off the road and lightning was streaking across the sky, but I let out the clutch and drove off, heading towards Malaga. The best option was to put as much distance as possible between me and the scene of the crime. To that end, I drove along the motorway and took the route to the north, signposted to Granada and Cordoba. The winding road, that follows the *Guadalmedina* river into the hills, is fast but tortuous with many tunnels and several speed traps. On one occasion, I saw a police car parked in a lay-by, but it made no attempt to follow me and I slowly began to relax. I ruefully smiled at the thought that James Bond would have been tucked up in bed with some exotic beauty by now, but I was no double o seven, and I was in a real pickle.

The road eventually flattened out and where it forked I took the Granada route. It was around four in the morning and the roads were almost empty, and as the rain had ceased soon after leaving Malaga, driving became very easy. For the first time in over an hour, I could begin to think coherently. The heavy rain had probably helped to cover my tracks, and as far as I knew, no one knew that I had rented a car. No doubt enquiries would become extensive once the body had been found, and when the connection between me and the killing had been made, there would be intense scrutiny of airports and ports. With that in mind, I decided to aim for Alicante as quickly as possible and seek out the British Consulate. First of all, though, I needed to wash and change clothes. A twenty-four-hour service station west of Baza, halfway between Granada and Murcia solved that problem. On the side of the service station shop, there was a toilet and washroom to which I took my overnight bag. Ten minutes later I was clean and fresh, and confidence was returning, and just maybe I could succeed in keeping clear of the trouble that was inevitably brewing.

I topped up the petrol tank and purchased some snacks, but hunger was not my main concern. Although there were CCTV cameras trained on the petrol pumps and shop, the side door to the toilets appeared to have no surveillance so I felt sure that my previously dishevelled state had not been observed. I took the precaution of paying in cash and the very sleepy Latin American who was manning the petrol station hardly raised his eyes from the desk when I paid.

My next task was to dispose of the dank and bloodied clothes. I was in one of the least populated parts of Spain where the weather can be harsh and living off the land can be a struggle. Since tourism began to flourish in the nineteen sixties more and more people abandoned their rural life for the better opportunities to be found on the coast. This left many farmsteads deserted and crumbling and one of those was my intended target as a place to dispose of my clothes. I turned off the motorway on to a narrow road running through untended olive groves. Fortunately, I quickly came across a small, abandoned house with rusted corrugated iron on the windows and a sagging lichen-covered tiled roof. In the car headlights, I could see that the door to the single-storey building was missing.

I had hoped that a well may be somewhere close by but there was no sign of one. Using the torch on my mobile, I could see that one corner of the roof had partially collapsed, and it would probably not be too long before the rest of the roof caved in. There was a cavity under the tiles and rotting wood, and I threw my overnight bag as far as I could under the debris. Satisfied that it would be a long time, if ever, before the bag would be discovered I returned to the car.

No vehicle had passed along the road while I had been disposing of the bag and there was very little traffic on the motorway. A few large lorries, probably laden with citrus fruit, were beginning their long journeys to northern Europe and the occasional camper van was heading for a similar destination, but as I passed Lorca, dawn began to break and local traffic slowly increased. By the time I reached Murcia, it was the start of the rush hour and busy car drivers were weaving from lane to lane. The road to Alicante was bumper to bumper, and with a low sun in front, it was a most unpleasant final stage into Alicante. I was very tired and my driving was bordering on dangerous at times, but I managed to park the car in a multi-storey car park close to *Corte Ingles,* and using the phone for navigation, I walked the few hundred metres to the British Consulate.

I produced a security pass at the reception desk and asked to see a senior consular official. A young man quickly appeared and ushered me past several unhappy looking people in the waiting area to a lift, and then into a small sun-lit room on the sixth floor with a couple of chairs and a desk for company. I felt more relaxed, but with each passing minute the likelihood of the body being discovered was increasing. I took the opportunity to send a coded message on the mobile to my line manager, as events could suddenly move fast and I wanted certain people to become aware of my plight without giving away too many details.

After about forty minutes, a casually dressed man of about thirty-five came into the room and introduced himself as Robin. He seemed somewhat irritated that I had disturbed his Sunday morning, but he unlocked a drawer in the desk and took out a laptop. He plugged it in, opened it up and muttered something about it being an old and slow piece of equipment. He then looked up, smiled frostily, and said, 'We don't have many visits from your sort.'

I was not quite sure how to take that, but I gave him a precis of the night's events, without the gruesome details, and told him that I needed to leave for England as soon as possible and could he arrange a flight ticket for me. It was easy to see that he didn't want to do that but felt duty-bound to do so. Of course, there were many forms to fill in. The flat in Malaga needed to be sorted out and the rented car had to be returned. The question was, could I get out of Spain before an arrest warrant was issued for me?

Robin left the room with my passport and my apprehension increased as he took many minutes to return. Eventually, he came back with a bundle of papers to sign and a single boarding card for an evening flight to Luton.

I would have preferred a flight to Heathrow or Gatwick but none was available, and anyway with the situation I was in, a flight to Glasgow would have sufficed. The aircraft was delayed for two hours and my nerves became increasingly frayed as I visualised a police force scouring the country for the murderer of one of their own. The sun had set by the time we taxied down the runway and lifted off from Alicante airport. I was seated next to an elderly couple who were very friendly in a patronising kind of way, and by the time we were flying over the Pyrenees I knew just about everything there was to know about their one-bedroomed holiday home in Villajoyosa. They had had the flat for thirty years, and each year for the last thirty years they had spent their holiday in it. In a way, I envied the simplicity of their happiness. Since the age of fifteen he had worked in the paint shop at Vauxhall Motors and now he was eighty-two.

She had worked in the canteen after the children had grown up, and between them they had saved enough money to buy a time-share property, and then they managed to buy-out the other part owners. The one-way conversation continued until the seat belt sign came on heralding our approach to Luton Airport. I felt a tremendous relief as the plane touched down on the tarmac but shivered at the thought of the explanations I needed to give to my manager on why my mission ended the way it did.

There was the usual rush to leave the aircraft as if every minute was vital. For some reason, all semblance of decorum seems to vanish when tourists arrive at their destination, whether it be going abroad or arriving home. Trolley cases come crashing down from overhead lockers, followed closely by folded raincoats, and then of course everyone is facing the front when the stewardess announces that passengers should disembark from the rear of the aircraft. I let my two elderly flight companions push through into the melee and they bade me a cheery farewell as they were swept towards the back of the plane.

I was one of the last to leave the plane and emerged into the cold Bedfordshire night. I was inadequately dressed for the season and regretted not having packed something more suitable in my overnight bag. It was warm enough in the terminal building, and as I had decided to take a taxi home, I wasn't unduly worried. There was a shortage of staff, probably because of the late arrival of the flight, so a long queue built up at Passport Control.

It slowly snaked forward, but it took a good half hour before it was my turn to present my passport to the tired-looking official in the booth. He looked at the passport, typed something into the computer, looked up at me, looked again at the passport, and then turned and nodded at two men who had been lounging against a wall on the other side of the control booth.

They approached me, and the taller of the two men stepped forward, took my passport from the border control officer, looked at it quickly and said, 'Mr Boateng, we would like you to come along with us, please.'

Chapter 8

The whole of the previous night's events flashed through my mind as I followed the men down a wide corridor towards the baggage conveyor belts. They did not speak, but it was obvious to me, and obvious to my fellow passengers, that these men were policemen, and I was stared at with a mixture of curiosity and malice as we strode forward. I caught up with the taller man, who was carrying a briefcase, and pointed out that I had no hold luggage, but he just looked at me with blank eyes and continued walking. Next to the red customs channel by the exit there was a door and after it was opened I was beckoned to go in. It led into a fairly narrow corridor with several numbered doors. The one chosen for me was number three. We entered the small, air-conditioned room, and the shorter of the two men put the light on and gestured towards a functional, but uncomfortable, chair.

I tried to read the body language of the men, but they betrayed no emotions, and there was continuing silence as the taller man took a small laptop from his briefcase. He then put out his hand, smiled wanly, shook hands and introduced himself as Detective Chief Inspector Stephen Noon.

He turned to his colleague and said, 'This is Detective Sergeant John McNamee.'

Sergeant McNamee then said, 'Have you got anything to say?'

I must have looked extremely puzzled because I had many things to say and I was not sure what they had in mind when they brought me to this uninspiring room.

First of all, I enquired about my status. 'Was I under arrest?'

The hackneyed reply was 'No, you are just helping us with our enquiries.' The conversation became very stilted. They didn't seem to know what they wanted me for, and I didn't know what to say to them. The silence was broken by the chief inspector who, in a mildly condescending voice, suggested that as I had sent a very high priority coded message to London, I should write, in as much detail as possible, what had occurred in Spain, and had resulted in him being kept from his bed on a Sunday night.

I ignored his hint of sarcasm and began to write a report of the events that took place on that fateful Saturday night. It was a relief to be able to elucidate the jumbled thoughts that had wracked my brain for almost twenty-four hours. So much seemed to have occurred in such a short space of time that it took almost two hours before I had completed the report. The chief inspector scanned through the pages on the computer and frowned. He could see that this was going to be a long night. I asked to use the bathroom and was accompanied to the toilet by the detective sergeant. It was then that the gravity of the situation I found myself in really hit me. I had killed a man, albeit in self-defence, and I had confessed to it. There would be a trial, and what if the jury didn't believe my version? Could I be found guilty? I shuddered at the thought of being incarcerated as a murderer with a career in ruins and not much chance of ever attaining gainful employment.

The chief inspector left room three when we returned from the toilet and I was left alone with the rather sullen sergeant. I tried friendly small talk to pass the time, but although he wasn't hostile, he was unwilling to engage in conversation. After about twenty minutes, the chief inspector returned with a much-improved demeanour and stated that we were heading off to London and that I would be able to get some sleep. The computer was packed into the briefcase, and bypassing the customs control we headed towards a Vauxhall that was parked outside the terminal building.

I was introduced to Rob the driver, and we all set off down the MI towards London. As we drove, I wondered aloud whether I should call a solicitor. 'No, no,' was the jovial reply from the chief inspector, who could now see an end to his role in this affair.

'We're taking you to an address in Wimbledon. It's a sort of safe house, but it's very luxurious. You'll enjoy it.'

So, I was under arrest in all but name. I asked how long I was expected to be there, but I knew I would get a non-committal answer, and that's what I got. The house was, in fact, one of those anonymous Edwardian terraced maisonettes that are common across south London. A stairway led straight up to the expansive first floor which consisted of three bedrooms, a living room, a kitchen diner and a small bathroom. It occurred to me that I had had no food for several hours, and I was now also very short of clothes. Toiletries were provided, and on enquiring, I was told that there would be food arriving later.

I was desperately tired and the food could wait, so I expressed a wish to sleep. The chief inspector almost looked sympathetic, but then said, 'In these situations we have to relieve you of any means you could use to communicate with the outside world. Nothing personal, you know, it's just a precaution until everything's cleared up.'

It hadn't really occurred to me that I would be held incommunicado, but it seemed logical, so I accepted the chief inspector's statement without question.

'By the way,' said the sergeant, 'There is a landline in the lounge for emergencies. It will directly put you in touch with a call centre.'

'But you're not going to have any emergencies.' The chief inspector added dryly.

The doorbell then rang, and before we had reacted, a young man came bounding up the stairs and planted himself in front of us. I looked bemused, but the others seemed to know the man, and he turned to me and introduced himself as detective constable Mohammad Khan. He described himself as my slave, but in reality, of course, he was my minder. Without further ado, the two detectives who had accompanied me from Luton politely said goodbye, and I was left with Mo who seemed enthusiastic about the idea of catering for my needs, the first of which was sleep. It was heading towards mid-morning when I finally shed my clothes, had a wash and climbed into bed. Sleep came instantaneously, and daylight was fading quickly when I awakened some seven hours later.

I wasn't sure if I had been locked in the house while I slept, but the kitchen was now brimming over with food. Plenty of fresh fruit and vegetables, milk, cheese and various tins of processed food. Mo was humming as he busily filled the fridge and freezer, but for me it was a rather depressing sight, because it looked as if my stay in Wimbledon could be lengthy. I decided that a phlegmatic approach to my confinement would be best and engaged in a cheery conversation with Mo.

I picked up an apple and began to eat it, and when Mo asked me what else I would like, I inappropriately said, that 'I could murder a take-away curry.'

Mo seemed rather disappointed that he wasn't going to show me his culinary skills, but he soon regained his good humour, and added that he knew a really good local curry house. It was too early to order food in, so I attempted to ascertain from Mo what my immediate future was likely to be. He seemed to know nothing about me, and as far my prospects were concerned, he had no idea.

'Sometimes, people moved on quickly, while others stayed for weeks,' was his almost scripted reply.

I was getting frustrated, but it didn't help, so I switched the television on to distract me from my current predicament. The usual array of banal programmes were being broadcast, and even the early evening news was short of drama. It occurred to me that there may be some Spanish news programmes available, but the television was old and only the standard four channels were available. Apart from a mention of flash flooding in southeast Spain, there was no other news from Iberia, so at least my Saturday night activities had not become internationally newsworthy.

The curry was as good as Mo said it would be and it raised my spirits considerably. I spent the rest of the evening chatting with the amiable Mo and watching more television before another good night's sleep. I was up early on Monday morning, but Mo was earlier and two cups of tea were gently steaming on the breakfast table. Mo asked me what I wanted to eat, and it was then that I decided he was not going to be my servant, and thereafter we prepared food together. The rest of the day was spent trying to relieve the boredom by reading, listening to the radio, watching the television, and absorbing as many news reports as possible. I thought it quite probable that the death of a policeman in southern Spain would not be worthy of news coverage in the UK, so I was not expecting to see or hear anything. I didn't discuss the issue with Mo, and if he was meant to be monitoring me in any way, then he was doing a very good job at disguising it.

Another day passed, but on Thursday Mo told me that a couple of gentlemen were coming to visit me at eleven o'clock. I felt even more like a prisoner, or even a patient in an asylum. It was a strange feeling, but Mo had no further information and he cheerily went about his business while I sat and read. At precisely eleven o'clock, the doorbell rang and Mo rushed downstairs to open the door. I stood at the top of the stairs waiting to see who was there. One of the men was my line manager, and that was no surprise. The other man was a corpulent, balding man, maybe in his mid-fifties. Both men were wearing dark raincoats and carrying briefcases.

I stood to one side as Mo showed the men into the lounge and offered to take their raincoats. My line manager looked nervous and twitchy. I hadn't seen him like this before and it put me somewhat on edge. He introduced me to the other man who was looking at me suspiciously, with piercing blue eyes. He had overdone the aftershave that morning, and apart from that, there was an arrogant air about his manner. Oliver Legg was his name, and from the very start I did not like this man.

We sat in the lounge, Mo offered us tea or coffee and for a while we spoke awkwardly about the accommodation, the food, the weather and anything else small talk could produce. All the time, Oliver was staring into my eyes as if he was trying to read my soul. Mo came in with three coffees and a few biscuits and then left, shutting the door behind him.

My line manager then leant forward, and with a serious look on his face said, 'We have read your report, and it's very comprehensive. It certainly had us running around.' His injection of a hint of humour into the discourse was met by a scowl from Oliver who was staring at me.

'The fact is Sean,' he continued, 'we have contacted the authorities in Spain, and as far as we know, a body hasn't been discovered, and no police officers have been reported missing.'

Chapter 9

There was the faint sound of music from a neighbouring house, otherwise there was a prolonged silence. My emotions were in turmoil. Firstly, relief that I wasn't sitting there being accused of murder, and then anger that my account was probably being questioned. 'Am I being accused of lying?' was my impulsive remark. 'Not at all,' my line manager replied. I had always thought of him as being a fair man, and as far as I knew he had never had reasons to doubt my commitment to the job.

Oliver then spoke. 'The national police in Spain have told us that the area you have written about has been used for drug-running in the past, but so far this year nothing untoward has occurred. They had been expecting someone from British Intelligence to assist them in the prevention of drug trafficking but no assistance had been forthcoming. Can you explain this?'

For me, this was like a bad dream. Had I been duped? It would appear so, and my confidence was ebbing away as I envisaged an ignominious exit from my chosen career. But no, the hypnotic stare from Oliver was not going to make me veer from the truth of what had happened and I made a robust defence of my actions. My line manager looked pleased by my explanation, but not Oliver.

He sat tight-lipped and pondered for some while about my statement. 'No shots, no body, no boats, no drugs; in fact, nothing. No evidence that you were ever there.' He jutted out his chin and looked smug.

'Why do you think I would lie?' I said. It was now time to go on to the attack.

'I was sent on a mission, and I've achieved plenty; perhaps you should question some of the statements you've received?' It was my turn to jut out my chin.

My line manager looked embarrassed and Oliver flushed with inner anger. Oliver continued to stare at me with his penetrating gaze, whilst my line manager dropped his head and turned away.

After what seemed a prolonged silence, Oliver spoke in a calm and measured voice. 'We will make further inquiries, and of course, as there has been no crime reported, it would be improper to keep you here. Go home and think about what you have told us.' He turned to my line manager and nodded. I followed his eyes as he focused on my immediate boss who was fiddling with his coffee cup. 'I leave Mister Boateng in your capable hands.' And without as much as a goodbye, he picked up his briefcase, opened the door, called for his coat and left.

My line manager looked very relieved and his eyes were friendly when he turned to me and said, 'A bit of a mess Sean, but we'll get there. Don't worry, go home and have a long weekend's rest and I'll see you in the office on Monday morning.'

Thoroughly decent, I thought, and as I said a warm goodbye to him at the front door my spirits were raised, but for how long? There were plenty of things that just did not add up.

My laptop and mobile phone were still held by the police, and as Amelia was still in my flat, 'home' for a while would have to be in Highgate where my parents lived. I asked Mo for the use of his phone and then tried to contact my parents, but to no avail. Presumably they were working, but I was sure that they would see the text message I had sent to them before I arrived unexpectedly on their doorstep. Mo was busy tidying the maisonette, and I wondered where all the food was going to go, but without giving details, he said there was a routine to be followed, and sometime in the near future a new houseguest would arrive. He was well suited to his job, and his cheerful disposition would undoubtedly lift the spirits of anyone having to spend time in this form of imprisonment.

I picked up my few possessions, stuffed them in my rucksack, thanked Mo warmly for his help and strode off towards Wimbledon Park underground station. It was one of those mild and soft autumn days, with fleeting glimpses of weak sunshine. It was good to be free again, and even standing on the almost deserted station for half an hour was pleasurable. I changed trains at Embankment for the final leg to Highgate and the train north was crowded with schoolchildren, harassed mothers and office workers. I smiled inwardly at the normality of this snapshot of late afternoon life in London.

My mother was there to welcome me when I arrived, my father was working late. For the first time in my adult life, it was the one place that I wanted to be, and in my confused mind, to be with the only two people in the world I could really trust. Both parents had eaten lunch at the hospital, but my mother insisted that she should cook my favourite spaghetti bolognese for dinner. At seven o'clock, our small family sat down to eat and there was much fun and laughter, and to anyone that had seen us, these were three people without a worry in the world.

After dinner, we sat and chatted for a while, but I carefully avoided my Spanish problems. The oldies were working on the following day and excused themselves before going to bed. I went to my old room, unchanged from the last time I stayed, with my trusty ancient Sony computer still in position on the desk. I surfed the net for a while, catching up on the latest news, but nothing grabbed my attention and then I too slept, a deep sleep, full of strange dreams.

I awoke to the sound of raised voices interspersed with wicked laughter. They hadn't changed, my parents were having one of their 'discussion' sessions. By the time I emerged from the bedroom, they had gone off to work, but a scribbled note pointed me in the direction of the fridge where a large bowl of yoghurt, cereal and fruit was awaiting my attention. It was so relaxing. I listened to the *Today* programme on the radio, not with great interest, but with my ears alert for any news from southern Spain. After breakfast, I unpacked my rucksack, and of course my night vision camera was there.

I had completely forgotten about it and I quickly took the SD card out and attached it to my laptop. The quality of the film was good and I realised how important this could be in my quest to get my version of events in Malaga believed. There was film of Jose, there was film of the boats slowly making their way up the river on Friday night. And there was a film of the lorry. Yes, the lorry; there was something about it that seemed familiar. I had thought about that briefly on Friday, but then I went on to think of other things, but now I was focused. It was something about the dent on the wheel arch. I zoomed in on it and I wondered what had made it and how it could possibly have got there, and then suddenly I remembered. I had had the same thought several years ago on the farm I had stayed on in Alora. This lorry was from that farm.

Slowly, the pieces from the jigsaw were beginning to fit, but there were still many questions that needed answering. At least, there was some concrete proof that my statement was factual. The thought of concrete made me shiver, and of course, that was the biggest question. Why had the body not been discovered? Or had it? If so, would the death of a policeman not make news headlines? It was very baffling, but the SD card sitting in my computer might hold the key to me keeping my job. I scanned through the photographs I had taken during my stay in Alora, but although there were distant images of lorries at the packing warehouse, there was no sign of the one that I saw on Friday. I also looked at the photos from Marina Smir, but there were no speedboats matching those that chugged up the estuary on Friday night. I wracked my brain for more clues to what may have happened, but none were forthcoming. Next, I decided to scan the local Spanish newspapers for information, but again nothing. The main story was still about the storms east of Malaga on Friday night which led to much flooding and some loss of life.

It was a little depressing that the answers had not been found, but I was cheered up in the evening by my parents putting on their best show of hospitality. Good food and good wine followed by an old-fashioned game of cards. On Saturday, the weather was mild and sunny so we made sandwiches, and with a flask of coffee and three mugs we set off for Hampstead and spent most of the day wandering around the Heath admiring the splendour of the trees and their autumn colours. On Sunday, I went alone to Brick Lane market and for some reason enjoyed the teeming throng of people intent on finding an imaginary bargain, or just sampling the many outlets of exotic food. It had been a very good weekend and an escape from reality, but Monday was approaching and the return to work.

Walking to Highgate Station, picking up a free newspaper and sitting on an ever-more crowded tube train used to be a regular occurrence, and although the trip to work from Highgate to the City had ceased several years ago, it occurred to me that this journey had been undertaken just before I had gone to Spain less than a month ago.

There was a new person on the reception desk at work, and she inspected my pass even more thoroughly than the previous incumbent. Eventually, she nodded approval and I then entered the lift for the slow journey to the third floor. The creaky lift was an old friend and it raised my spirits by the time the doors carefully opened into my workplace. The smell of fresh coffee pervaded the open-plan section of the office, and there were familiar faces already poring over their computer screens. One of those faces belonged to Ray, the office fount of all knowledge.

'Enjoy your paid leave?' He said sarcastically, and I wondered how much he, or anyone else in the office, knew about my activities.

I could see my line manager was already in his little side office, and I hadn't been at my desk long before he called me, shut the door and beckoned for me to sit down. After the usual pleasantries, his brow furrowed and he looked at me with something bordering on sadness.

'We have looked for the man you knew as Jose, and I must say, the *Policia Local* and *Guardia Civil* have been very helpful. It was a pity you didn't get his surname, but the Spanish have given us some names and photographs, and perhaps one of those could be the man. Otherwise, it's going to be difficult for us to, let us say, connect your story to reality.' He paused, and I could see that he was now awaiting a contribution from me.

I produced the SD card from my pocket and told him about the night-vision binoculars. Although my line manager had appeared to support me all along, he seemed palpably relieved that progress was being made. I had not edited any of the film on the SD card and much of it was of me exploring the capabilities of my binoculars. Actual evidence from the Friday and Saturday nights, however trivial, could be crucial when, or if, this episode was to be cleared up. I mentioned the similarity between the lorry that was used to transport the boxes unloaded from boats to the lorry I had remembered from Alora, but disappointingly for me that was not viewed as important.

I was asked to go through the police photographs while my boss viewed the film. Two of the photos provided possibilities. One was of a young Jose Ibarra from San Sebastian who was with the local police in Fuengirola for seventeen years, but had resigned and, as far as was known, had moved to France. The other was of another young man, Jose Fernandez, who had spent five years in the *Guardia Civil* but had resigned around fourteen years ago. He was now a self-employed painter and decorator living in Malaga.

A lot of imagination was needed to equate the man in the image to the Jose I knew, but he seemed to be the only person anywhere near matching the profile. I tried to see if he was on face-book, but his name was common, and the added complication was that most Spaniards use their mother's surname as part of their own, so I soon realised that I would make little progress in that particular search.

My line manager had left his office and apparently he wouldn't be back until after lunch, so I busied myself with some unrelated work that had built up in my in tray while I had been away. It was not until mid-afternoon when he returned, that I was then summoned to his office. It surprised me that his demeanour hadn't really changed. Somehow I was expecting, perhaps not an apology, but an admission that my statement was probably accurate.

Instead, he said, 'This is becoming more and more unusual.'

I thought it odd, his choice of the word 'unusual' and I immediately asked for an explanation. Returning to a more genial manner, he went on to tell me about his trip to see Oliver Legg, and how Oliver, on viewing my footage from Malaga, had got irritated and went on about a lack of substantive evidence. I almost laughed aloud. If this was not substantive evidence, then it could prove to be very difficult to verify my account.

'For what it's worth Sean, I believe what you say.' My line manager's vote of confidence made me feel better, and I returned to my desk buoyed up by the knowledge that my career was probably still intact.

During the rest of the week, I carried on with other work, but the events in Spain continued to gnaw at me. On Wednesday, I sent an email to my friend Youssef, and without going into detail I suggested that he should do a bit of bird spotting alongside the Guadalhorce River. It would be best for him to take his bike and I told him the exact spot where best to view the rare white-headed duck. He knew the nature of my work and I was relying on him to understand my message, rather than to think I'd taken leave of my senses. I almost had second thoughts, maybe it would put his life in danger, but no, I couldn't imagine anything would happen to him there in broad daylight, assuming he would go there in broad daylight.

My phone and laptop were returned to me and it appeared the matter was closed as far as management were concerned. I strongly resented it, and each evening I scanned the Spanish newspapers for any new developments which could restore my reputation. On Friday morning, I gave Amelia a month's notice to leave my flat. She was disappointed to have to leave, but already, I was beginning to feel irritated by the bickering in my parent's house, and in a month's time it would be intolerable. On Friday evening, I had an email from Youssef. He had been over to the Nature Reserve and had failed to observe the white-headed duck. He did say that he thought several people had been there to look for the duck as the reeds were well trodden down and there were boot marks everywhere.

What's more they had left behind rubbish that included a plastic box, a drink's carton and many cigarette ends. Youssef continued to appear full of indignation, and I silently thanked him for going along with the little charade that I had enticed him into playing. Later that evening I was scanning the Spanish papers when I came across an article about a fishing boat tragedy, and there, peering out of a page from *Sur* was a picture of Jose.

Chapter 10

It was an old photo of Jose taken when he was much thinner, but there was no doubt it was him. Another man, unbeknown to me, was alongside him in the picture. The article was short, just a few lines of text, but it stated that two men had taken a boat out fishing on Saturday night and hadn't returned in the morning. The weather had been stormy, and after a search, no trace of a boat or the two men was found. However, a body was washed up on the beach, and has been identified as that of Jose Sanchez Fernandez, a keen Malaga fisherman. The other missing man had yet to be found.

This was an interesting and unexpected development and I had the whole weekend to think about what possibly could have happened. My line manager had taken the day off on Monday, so I spent a frustrating day on other work, as I did not want to mention my discovery to anybody else. Ray asked if I wanted to go for a drink with him after work, but I said, no, much to his surprise. This new unearthing of information had become all consuming. On Tuesday morning, I was called into my line manager's office, and I thought he was looking like a worried man. Immediately I told him what I had read in the Spanish newspaper, but he seemed to be far away and I was a little disappointed by his reaction. After a pause in which he muttered a reluctant thank you, I decided to tell him my theory as to what could have happened.

After the distant shooting started on Saturday night maybe someone was killed and that person was taken out to sea and dumped, although if that person had a bullet embedded in them it would have been discovered. Maybe the shooting was just a signal for Jose to then kill me, but why would he want to do that? In any case, it would appear that possibly two bodies were taken out to sea and one was conveniently washed up along the coast several days later and it was made to look like an accident, but why? I was beginning to run out of postulates, and all this time my line manager sat in silence with a look of disinterest.

'Have you any ideas?' I eventually asked.

'None,' he replied. 'And by the way, Oliver has kept your SD card, some sort of evidence he said.'

There was an awkward silence, and then I asked, 'If that is all?'

To which my line manager replied in the affirmative, and I then left for my desk, but not before I saw a sigh of relief that this interview was over.

My suspicious mind wondered why Oliver Legg had kept my SD card as there now seemed to be a general lack of interest in what happened down in Spain. Maybe I was becoming paranoid, but I knew it was now time to go for a drink with miserable Terry. We went to the Mitre in Holborn, a pub that produced a good pint of Fuller's ESB. I knew it would be a place that would make Terry less miserable, especially as the evening wore on. That indeed was the case, and by the third pint he was almost talkative. It was probably helped by the fact that he now had a steady girlfriend, although as she lived in Liverpool, it made it less steady than some relationships. The golden rule about not talking about our work was not broken, but I did ask Terry if he knew of Oliver Legg.

He laughed dryly. 'He's a good man to have on your side, but so was Attila the Hun.' He offered no other words on the subject and I was left with that cryptic statement. We talked politics for the remainder of the evening, a subject where we shared common ground, and at the end of the fourth pint we went our separate ways.

Amelia left my flat well before the month's notice had expired, and it was good to move back to Tooting. I celebrated by going for a curry at Samrat, and my routine life resumed, both at home and at work, as if the Spanish episode had never occurred. Occasionally I wondered what it had been about, but gradually the graphic details of that Saturday night in Malaga faded from my memory. Youssef came to stay for a few days before Christmas and we discussed the events of late October long into the nights with days spent Christmas shopping or walking the South Bank, but wherever we went there were crowds of busy people.

Christmas and New Year came and went. My parents spent the festive period in Jamaica and I was left alone in my flat. However, I wasn't lonely. Ever since the Spanish problem I had needed time to reflect. Maybe I wasn't cut out for this type of work. Was I too sensitive? Was I expecting more from the job than it could provide? These and similar questions occupied my mind while others were over-indulging on wine and food. Yes, there was a social life of sorts. I had been accepted at the rifle club and I spent time there, as well as at the martial arts club, although I was disinclined to build up my body to the extent that some of the club members had done with theirs.

After New Year the return to work was welcomed, but the tasks presented to me were fairly uninspiring. I wondered if I was being sidelined from more interesting jobs because of the circumstances of my last assignment abroad. Ray had departed on some overseas mission, and two or three others had also vacated their desks to be replaced by more youngsters helping the country to combat international crime. There was a regular turnover of Staff, and that was also not particularly good for my social life. One chap I got on reasonably well with was Thadeus, or Thad as he wished to be called. He was from Preston and very much a working-class lad complete with cloth cap. He was very bright, though, and there wasn't much about football that he didn't know. Like the rest of us, he did not talk about his work, but the rumour mill suggested he was involved in counterterrorism. At that stage in my career, I was unaware of anyone else in the office working in the field of drugs, and it was my grim task to match so-called foreign students who had overstayed their welcome with drug trafficking. I was just trying to provide the link while others followed up the leads. It was almost boring, but not quite, and I persevered with it through the remainder of the winter. Then one day in early March I was invited into my line manager's office.

I had just had my job appraisal review, and it had gone surprisingly well, so I wasn't expecting anything bad, but now a formal meeting, this was intriguing. He proffered a chair and shut the door behind me, sat at his desk and leant forward. He looked nervous, and I detected something bordering on sorrow in his eyes.

'We have another assignment for you. It could be risky, and after your last, er… job abroad, you can say no, but we think it is something that may interest you.'

I raised my eyebrows in curiosity as he went on.

'It's in Slovenia, at least to start with, and it's to do with drugs again. Are you interested?'

'Most definitely.' I replied enthusiastically.

'Then I will carry on.' He didn't, because at that moment Freddie, one of the new chaps, knocked on the door asking for urgent advice. My boss logged out from his laptop and strode off into the main office where he remained for the following twenty minutes. When he returned, he seemed more relaxed and he continued to give me details of my assignment.

I was to meet a Slovenian agent in Ljubljana, which prompted me to say, 'Do you think he might want to kill me?'

It resulted in an icy stare and a prolonged silence before he went on, 'I know you are very discrete, Sean, but please tell no one at all about this mission, not even your close family.'

'Why?' I asked.

'Because,' my line manager replied, 'the last chap we sent out to Ljubljana has disappeared, and we presume he is dead.'

Chapter 11

After the Spanish issues, the ability to be surprised by events had been much reduced, but why Ljubljana? I had heard of it, and I knew where Slovenia was, roughly, but why was that a hub for drug smuggling. If I remembered correctly, it barely had a coastline. The instructions I was given for this trip were much more comprehensive, and this time they did not include any mention of the British consulate. That was interesting in itself, because in Malaga, the person who dealt with me at the consulate knew all about the flat and the bike, and the fishing tackle, but Jose never knew my address. It just didn't add up.

'You are to buy some sauerkraut at the open-air market by the station.' I suddenly regained full attention.

'Pardon?'

'The person you are meeting has been fully vetted and will make herself known to you somehow or other.'

'Herself?' I asked.

'Apparently so,' my line manager replied almost apologetically, before re-emphasising the need for secrecy. With great relief, I heard that the alert code would remain the same if I ended up in a very difficult situation, although no one had mentioned if I had been correct to use it in Spain.

I had a few days leave before my departure, and this time I decided not to let my flat. I was less naive than before the Spanish expedition, and I wondered if my sojourn would be shorter than anticipated. However, at lunchtime on the following Monday, with a packed trolley case and a rucksack containing my trusted night-vision binoculars, complete with a new SD card, I made my way to Gatwick for a late afternoon flight to Ljubljana. I had found on *Booking.com* a cheap apartment just north of the station. It had good reviews and was meant to be quiet. It certainly looked very modern in the photographs and there was free Wi-Fi. I booked it until the end of the week as I had no idea what to expect.

The journey on the almost half-empty flight was uneventful but it was very cold when I emerged from the terminal building into the mid evening air of Slovenia. I was going to catch the bus into the city, but the icy wind made me decide on a taxi instead. It cost me thirty euros, and that was almost as much as the flight, but it was comfortably warm in the car. I thought it best to be cautious, so I paid off the taxi driver at the station and left him with the impression that I was going to take a train somewhere. Fortunately, it was just a short walk to the apartment, but it was so cold. There was no snow on the ground except for a few small piles of grey frozen slush mixed with grit.

At the apartment block, there was an intercom and according to the instructions agreed through Booking.com I was to press the top button. There were labels next to the column of buttons, but the writing was all in Slovene, and although some names were familiar, most were unrecognisable to me. The button clearly buzzed, I'm not sure what I would have done if it hadn't, and a few seconds later there was a 'ja' coming out of the box.

I said my name through chattering teeth and then there was silence. It seemed many minutes before a light appeared inside the corridor and a large, jovial-looking, breathless, middle-aged man appeared in the doorway. He beckoned to me to follow and muttered 'kaput' as we passed the lift. Further along the corridor there was a flight of stairs and I followed the man up to the third floor. He unlocked a door and smiled and said, 'potni list'. I smiled back and he repeated 'potni list', but this time he drew an imaginary rectangle on the door and held out his arms as if he was flying.

'Passport?' I said, and the smile widened. I had learnt my first two words of the Slovene language.

He gave me a tour of the apartment which had already been heated, and I was pleased to see sachets of tea and coffee as well as capsules of milk in the kitchen. It was approaching ten o'clock and I hadn't eaten, so as soon I politely could, I thanked the man, ushered him out of the door, grabbed an extra jumper from my case and followed close behind him to the stairs. He went up and I went down. I wrapped up as much as I could against the cold and strode off back to the station. I had noticed a Turkish kiosk by the station selling food and I had hoped it would still be open. It was, and the smell emanating from the place was very inviting, although the appearance of this food outlet was less so. I bought a simple pizza for the evening meal, and a couple of pasties for breakfast. I scurried back to the apartment, by which time the pizza was cold. A microwave solved that problem, and for the remainder of the evening I scanned the google maps to familiarise myself with this capital city I had landed up in.

The following morning was sunny and the apartment was bright and warm. The view was not one you would mention on a postcard, but I was in high spirits and looking forward to the mission ahead. I could see from an icicle hanging from a pipe on the opposite apartment that the temperature had not risen overnight, and by the time I was ready to leave for the market, I was well protected against the cold.

The market by the station was not big, in fact it only consisted of a few stalls, these mostly selling fresh vegetables and some less fresh fruit. My attention was drawn to one stall which had plastic tubs piled high with limp, what appeared to be, shredded cabbage. It looked decidedly unattractive, but trade seemed brisk and there was much banter between the customers and the two women dishing out the produce into polystyrene containers. The women were wearing white coats and elasticated plastic hats, attire more suited to an operating theatre than a market stall. One was aged about fifty, rather plump and with a weather-beaten face.

The other looked as if she should still be at school and I judged her to be around seventeen or eighteen years old. Neither of them looked like agents, but perhaps that was good. I waited until there was a lull in the flow of customers and boldly strode across to the stall and asked in English for half a kilo of sauerkraut. Immediately I felt stupid, as the stall was only selling sauerkraut.

The young girl stared at me with dull eyes and said, '*Sprechen sie Deutsch?*'

This threw me completely and I replied in French '*Oui, un petit peu.*'

The merest hint of a smile showed in her eyes as I felt acutely embarrassed. In mumbled and jumbled German, I repeated my request for half a kilo of sauerkraut, and she quickly turned, picked up a loose box, shovelled in the sauerkraut, weighed it and said, '*Zwei euros.*'

I paid and without saying thank you, I shuffled away and disconsolately returned to the apartment. It doesn't happen like this in films I thought, not for the first time in my life.

As the latest venture had fallen flat at the start I thought I would take the opportunity to see some of the culture offered by Ljubljana, but first some food. In the excitement to get to the market, I had missed breakfast apart from a hastily drunk cup of coffee, and I thought it a good idea to eat something substantial before embarking on my afternoon as a tourist. I tasted the sauerkraut, and it was surprisingly pleasant, so lunch consisted of two quite large meat and vegetable pasties plus half a kilo of fermented cabbage, if I could manage it. I microwaved the pasties and poured the contents of the polystyrene container onto a plate. On top of the sauerkraut, after I had poured it out, was a small rectangular clear plastic wallet, and in that, there was what looked like a note. My heart beat faster as I wiped the cabbage from the wallet and extracted the note. The microwave went 'ding' but I ignored it. I unfolded the note and in clear English it read 'Meet me in the cafe at the museum of contemporary arts at 1500 hours. I will flirt with you.'

Many interesting thoughts went through my brain whilst I negotiated my pasties with sauerkraut. The first was that sauerkraut didn't taste too bad at all, and the second was, which one of the two women at the market stall was going to flirt with me. I had already intended to see the cultural sights of Ljubljana before deciding on my next move, so after the early lunch I set off for Metalkova. I had read that this area of the capital was bohemian in its outlook, and after less than twenty minutes' walk I was in an area where graffiti had become street art, with walls and buildings adorned with colourful depictions of daily life. I had plenty of time to wander around the area, but it was still very cold, and I was numb with cold by the time I entered the museum.

There was a temporary exhibition of poster art from the nineteen sixties and seventies which was fairly uninteresting, but it did give me the opportunity to warm up. At five minutes to three, I queued up to buy a cup of coffee and a doughnut in the cafe, but there were many other people, mostly youngsters, who had decided that this was a good place to stay warm, and there were no free tables. I looked around for any familiar faces, but saw none, so when I had paid for my coffee I grabbed one of the few remaining seats and waited. On my table, there was an elderly gentleman sipping what looked like hot apple juice. He was deep into his own thoughts and barely noticed my arrival. There was also a young couple, in animated discussion about something, and they only briefly paused, when I asked if the seat was taken. In fact, there were two seats, and on one of them I quickly placed my scarf and topcoat.

I continued to look around the cafe for one of the two women I had seen at the market stall, and of course, I wondered which one was going to arrive at the table. I assumed it would be the younger one, but I laughed inwardly at the thought of her fifty-year-old companion flirting with me. And what form would this flirtation take? I could honestly say that I was unaware that any girl had ever flirted with me and would I be aware this time?

I waited and waited. The doughnut had been eaten long ago and the remains of the coffee were cold. The young couple continued their heated debate but the elderly gentleman had left and the customers in the cafe were thinning out. There was no queue at the till anymore and I took the opportunity to buy another cup of coffee, and then moved to an empty table in the corner so I could keep an eye on anyone arriving at the cafe. One of the waitresses was busying herself clearing the tables, and I was becoming increasingly worried that the cafe was about to close. Five o'clock was approaching when the door flung open and five noisy youngsters made their entrance. My heart missed a beat as I saw that one of the new arrivals was the girl from the market stall. She looked very different without her plastic hat as she now had straight light brown hair flowing down to her shoulders. She hadn't noticed me and continued chatting and laughing with the others as she took a plate with a cream cake on it from one of the coolers and ordered a drink.

They had trouble deciding where to sit and it was the girl from the market that pointed to a vacant table quite close to mine. A cacophony arose from the table when they sat down, as their debate, about who knows what, continued. It was loud enough to drive an elderly couple out of the cafe, and I could see they made some disapproving comments to the waitress as they left.

The girl from the market was sitting opposite me, albeit two tables and about four metres away. I stared at her, but she continued to engage in deep conversation with the young man next to her and no eye contact was made. The girl sitting next to her at the round table did make eye contact, but mainly because she seemed to have been left out of the debate and was becoming bored. I continued to stare at sauerkraut Sarah, a name I had come up with in the long wait for her appearance. I guessed she was about twenty-one, and probably a student, maybe studying languages, although almost all the conversation was unintelligible to me.

The talking slowed and I noticed the girl who had seemed bored nudge sauerkraut Sarah and said something. Sarah briefly looked in my direction before the two girls continued to converse in lowered voices. I continued to stare. It hadn't occurred to me that I was being rude, but no one seemed to notice my intense interest in the girl opposite, so everything was fine. That was until Sarah picked up the cream cake, took a bite from it, and cream exploded all over her face. The girl next to her burst into laughter, as did the others on the table in sequence as they realised what had happened, and so, unfortunately, did I.

She looked across at me with anger in her eyes and shouted something through a froth of cream. I felt highly embarrassed as four other faces turned and looked at me. The staff in the cafe, as well as the remaining customers, also turned in my direction.

I felt a small voice say, 'I'm sorry, I'm English' and I realised it was my voice and I was then lost for words. One of the young men asked me where in England I came from, and when I replied 'London' a series of questions began and I was invited to join them at their table. English was not a problem, they all spoke the language very well, but they were not studying languages, in fact they were enrolled on an ethnology and cultural anthropology course at Ljubljana University, and that sounded very interesting. I almost forgot my reason for being in the cafe as I became absorbed in their conversation.

Sauerkraut Sarah was not the main contributor to the discourse, that was Jan who had the ability to talk the loudest. I knew his name was Jan by the number of times he was told to shut up, but slowly, without being introduced to them, I found out their names. The girl from the market was called Anja, although everyone seemed to call her Annie. She was the most serious one in the group, but I liked her, in fact I liked her a lot.

Our increasingly heated discussion was brought to an abrupt halt by the elder of the two cafe workers coming over to tell us they were closing. We had finished our drink and snacks long ago so we just had to dress up to face the cold evening air. It was Jan that suggested we continue our evening in a quiet restaurant he knew not too far from the river. Two of the group said, thank you, no, it was too expensive, but Anja thought it was a good idea and so did Jan's girlfriend Zala, so off we went. Anja and I dropped in behind the other two as we walked briskly towards the restaurant but as the post sunset cold intensified, we said little to each other.

Much of the architecture in Ljubljana consisted of solid looking edifices typical of much of Eastern Europe, but as we neared the river the buildings became older and smaller with a mixture of single-storey terraces, and loftier ones with first-floor dormer windows. I remarked on that to Anja and she said that an earthquake in eighteen ninety-five had destroyed most of the city, and the reconstruction that had followed was modelled on the buildings in Vienna at the time. The houses looked quite attractive, but everywhere there was graffiti and as in London, it was a blight on this part of the capital.

The restaurant was one of those small cosy corner places with small wooden chairs and tables adorned with red and white checked tablecloths. Jan had not reserved a table but the proprietor, a small dark man with an extravagant moustache, smiled warmly, and showed us to a table close to a stove which was throwing out some welcomed heat. We decided to have two pizzas between four, and although I had hoped to try the local wine, the others wanted beer and I followed suit. For dessert, I had strudel and ice cream while the others finished with cups of coffee. We lingered in the restaurant until after ten o'clock, but we were the only customers that evening, and eventually the proprietor hovered around our table long enough for us to take the hint and we asked for the bill. I thought it was inappropriate for me to offer to pay, and they didn't seem to expect me to do so. We had had the same food except for my strudel, and as that was more expensive than the coffee, my offer to pay the tip was accepted.

It was a shock to leave the warmth of the restaurant, and while we had been in there a flurry of powdery snow had fallen. It was swirling around on the road and pavements and had formed small drifts in the gutter. A keen wind blew in our faces as we walked back towards Metalkova and the intense cold encouraged us to keep silent. Just before we reached the museum Jan turned to Anja and in English offered to walk her home. Somewhat to my surprise she said, 'I'm in the capable hands of a gallant Englishman, and he will walk me home.' Anja turned and smiled at me and the others laughed. I thanked Jan and Zala for a lovely evening and followed Anja as she headed off down a side road.

I had difficulty believing that Anja was a government agent, but now we were almost alone on the quiet dimly lit streets of Ljubljana, I wondered what was to happen next. It was no more than two hundred metres to the austere block of flats where Anja had an apartment. We stopped at the entrance, it was an awkward moment, probably for both of us, so I just said, 'The next move is yours.'

The phrase seemed to clear the air, and Anja then said, a lot very quickly.

'Tomorrow,' she said, 'I am working at the stall in the morning and having a lecture in the afternoon, and in the evening I will be busy, but on Thursday I have a free afternoon. Would you like a tourist guide?'

That seemed like a very good idea, and we agreed to meet outside the restaurant that we had just eaten in at quarter to three. I felt like asking her not to be two hours late but I refrained from doing so.

There was a short silence and I then thanked her for a super evening, to which she replied. 'It was good, very good.' She then blew a kiss in my direction, opened the door, slid through, and shut it gently behind her.

I wasn't quite sure how the evening was going to end and in some ways it was a relief that nothing further occurred to advance our relationship. There was much to think about on the walk back to the apartment, but my main thought was, could I trust her? My instinct was to be wary, but she appeared to be such an innocent young girl. Of course, these were the very girls we had been trained to be careful of. It was with that thought in mind I reached the apartment and returned to some semblance of warmth. I switched on the television and zapped from channel to channel, not really wanting to settle, but just to clear my head of the many emotions that were running through it. Was Anja really a government agent? She seemed like an ordinary student, and her friends? They spoke warmly to her as if she was 'one of us'. Not for the first time I was confused. And did I like her more than I professionally should do? She was much younger than me and cradle snatching was not for me, but her face and those deep blue eyes kept reappearing. I found a German news programme and tried to concentrate on world affairs and eventually managed to hear and see what was emanating from the screen.

Sleep that night was intermittent and in the morning I felt tired and grouchy, not helped by the fact that I had forgotten to buy any food for breakfast. There was still a sachet of coffee and a little milk, so I made do with that before making preparations to go out. The day was sunny, but the icicle hanging from the apartment opposite showed no signs of thawing. I ventured out wearing most of my available clothes, but the wind had dropped and under cloudless skies it felt quite pleasant in the sunshine. Before heading towards *Hofer,* one of the local supermarkets, I decided to make a short detour and see how Anja was getting along. It was quite busy, and I leant against a wall and observed what was happening. I was a long way away and somewhat behind her so I was sure she wouldn't see me. I felt a little guilty spying on her in this way, but I put sentiment aside and thought about my reason for being in Slovenia.

The flow of mainly elderly people to the stall was almost continuous and it was obvious that both Anja and her older companion worked hard for their money. Nothing unusual occurred, except for one man who spent several minutes talking to Anja. It was ridiculous, I felt pangs of jealousy seeing this man and Anja together, and he was old enough to be my father. Perhaps he was her spymaster, perhaps a relative. Anyway, after about fifteen minutes he left and I resumed my journey to the supermarket. I purchased enough food to last me for three days and without thinking I bought two bottles of Slovenian red wine.

Foreign supermarkets had always fascinated me, and although this was a sister shop to Aldi, it was still intriguingly different. I had spent over an hour in the supermarket and the bill was almost eighty euros, but I was now well stocked for the immediate future. That afternoon I was going to send in a report to my boss in London, and I thought maybe a photograph of Anja should be included. I went back to my almost concealed position some distance from the market stall and used my mobile phone to take a few pictures. Just as I was about to return to the apartment, I noticed the middle-aged man from earlier in the day had come back to the stall and was once again in earnest conversation with Anja.

Chapter 12

The man left after about fifteen minutes with a large container of sauerkraut, and I decided that there were enough photographs and it was time to return to the apartment. I needed to file a report to my line manager and I wanted to send a photograph of Anja and the man who visited her twice at the stall. Most of the day was taken up by composing the report, and the remainder of it was spent online, reading about Ljubljana and its many attractions.

On Thursday morning, there was no response to my report sent to London so I just pottered around readying myself for an afternoon as a tourist. It was interesting that my reason for being in Slovenia had not been discussed with Anja yet, and she had not shown the slightest sign that our first meeting had been anything other than random, except for, of course, that carefully packaged note under the sauerkraut.

I set off at two for the walk down to the restaurant close to the river. I didn't want to be late. The weather had changed. It was still cold, but not that icy cold of the previous days. The wind had changed direction and clouds were increasing, but I hardly noticed as I strode through the city. To my surprise, Anja was only about five minutes late for our rendezvous. She was smiling and radiant, and immediately grabbed hold of my arm before kissing me on both cheeks. It was as if we had known each other for years and conversation flowed unfettered. To anyone that was observing us we were just two people in love, and just maybe we were.

Our trip started by the *Ljubljanica*, the small river that flows through the capital, and then on into the bigger *Sava, which* merges with the Danube in Belgrade. There was some ice along the edge of the waterway, otherwise the gentle flow was unhindered on its way to the Black Sea. Anja provided an interesting commentary as we walked through the older part of the city and then on to the castle via the Cathedral of St Nicholas. The baroque building, mostly constructed during the first decade of the eighteenth century, replaced several wooden structures that had succumbed to fire since the first church had been built on the site during the Middle Ages. The impact of the 1895 earthquake had been immense, but the castle remained largely intact.

We had coffee and a light lunch before we undertook the climb through the woods to the castle. There is a funicular railway that runs from the city to the castle and the trip takes less than a minute, but Anja insisted that we walk, both because it was healthy and because of the views *en route.* The path we took was wide and well maintained, but totally deserted. I thought it was the right time to spoil the occasion and bring up the subject of work.

It was difficult to know how to begin, so I started by saying, 'And how long have you been a spy?' It was a weak opening, and it got the reply it deserved.

'Longer than you think. I noticed your attempts to spy on me yesterday.' It was said, as a mild chastisement and I felt blood flowing into my cheeks.

'Would you have not done the same?' I retorted.

'Probably, but better.' She laughed, grabbed hold of my arm and pulled me along the path.

It took a long time to reach the castle, mainly because at each viewing point Anja continued with her thoroughly interesting history lesson. It was difficult, and probably rude, to ask Anja any personal questions, so I just waited to see if she would become curious about me. The castle proved to be somewhat disappointing. Although it dated back to Roman times, and probably earlier, very little remained of anything prior to the fifteenth century. Unlike the Norman fortifications familiar to the British, the material used in construction was wood rather than stone, and for a variety of reasons the structure had become derelict by the end of the fourteenth century. An overhaul took place during the fifteenth century with further significant modifications taking place in the eighteenth and nineteenth centuries, but its use as a prison, military garrison, and a refuge for the poor, had not endeared it to the local population. So rather than a tourist attraction to be proud of, it had been mostly used as a conference centre. Anja said that the main reason for visiting the castle was to enjoy the sunset, but there was an exhibition to see, and coffee to drink in the castle cafe before that happened.

The view from the castle was quite spectacular, helped by the excellent visibility. Distant snow-capped mountains and green countryside seemed to arch around the city in the foreground. The sunset was very good, with the pinks and yellows of sunlight on the extensive cloud cover adding to the beauty.

We lingered until the last colours of sunset had disappeared and then took the funicular railway down the hill. It had been my intention to invite Anja to my apartment for dinner, but before I had the chance she said, 'Would the amateur detective like to have dinner at my flat? Or has he got someone else to follow this evening?'

Anyone else, and I would probably have felt offended, but it was said, with a smile, and of course I said, yes.

As we walked arm in arm to her flat I thought how confident and trusting she was. I was still suspicious, especially after my close encounter in Spain, but hopefully it didn't show. Why was she not suspicious? A man she had only just met, a government agent working for a foreign power. Was she just very, very good and had she almost lulled me into a false sense of security? That was what I was thinking when we arrived at the grubby door to her apartment complex. Once inside, a light flickered into life revealing a long corridor with mail boxes on either side, and stairs at the end with a row of bikes underneath neatly arranged. There was a smell of boiled cabbage and the faint sound of pop music coming from one of the flats. Anja strode up the stairs two steps at a time. On the third floor, she turned right and lighting automatically came on in another corridor with doors either side and what looked like a fire escape at the end. About half way along, Anja stopped outside number four hundred and thirteen with a small plaque on the door which read *A Vasylenko*.

'That's an interesting name.' I ventured.

'Yes.' She replied, 'My father is from Ukraine.'

I waited for her to say more, but she didn't and quickly unlocking the door she pulled me inside.

The flat appeared cramped, but neat, with clean parquet floors supporting some worn, but tasteful, furnishings. It looked as if some rapid tidying had recently taken place, but my first impression was that this was a typical student's flat. She asked me to make some coffee and she disappeared into another room. The kitchen was small but well laid out with labelled tins containing food or spices of some kind. The well-used tin with *Kava* inscribed on it was obviously not sparkling wine, and seemed the best bet for coffee, and so it proved. It was instant coffee, fortunately, as apparatus for more sophisticated forms of coffee making were not apparent. A few minutes later, Anja appeared and she had changed clothes for dinner.

She looked ravishing in a simple blue dress and wearing neither make up nor jewellery. My first thought was that she had dressed to kill, which made me think that maybe I was being slowly lured into the centre of the spider's web. I genuinely complimented her on her attire and she smiled self-consciously.

I then mused, 'Are you going to cook looking like that?'

She must have read my thoughts and said, 'I was delayed at the market this afternoon and I didn't want to be late meeting you, so I had no time to come back here to change.'

'I'm impressed.' I said.

'Thank you,' she replied, 'and now you can help me with the cooking.'

I liked her directness and sense of humour. That humour became apparent when she revealed the menu for the evening. It was Carniolan Sausage served with sauerkraut, mustard and salad. The sausages came from the freezer and Anja said she preferred the sauerkraut hot and mixed with the mustard. It was traditional food, but she emphasised that it was not what she normally ate, and it was just for me. It tasted better than it looked, but this was more about getting to know Anja than the food.

When we sat down to eat I said, 'Shouldn't we talk about work?' She immediately put a finger on her lips and quietly went 'shh' before dragging me to the kitchen. I was somewhat startled by her reaction but she wrote on the whiteboard, 'The walls have ears.'

She looked to make sure I understood and then erased the writing. As an afterthought she asked if I would like a beer, but I declined and settled for a glass of mineral water. Anja had the same, as she had another early start in the morning and she said, beer tended to give her a hangover.

Slowly, I began to find out about her and her family. She was an only child and her mother had been a nurse in Maribor, the city where Anja was raised. Her father was a salesman for a large manufacturing company and spent much of his time out of the country. Anja became tearful when I asked her about her mother. She had been killed in a car crash when Anja was just fifteen. The driver of the other car had been under the influence of drugs and he had survived unscathed. A trial ensued but his defence lawyer had been clever enough to prevent him from having a custodial sentence. I felt very sorry for her and we clung to each other until her sobbing ceased. Then a smile brightened her tear-stained face, and she said, but that was thirteen years ago.

So, she was twenty-eight, and there was me thinking she was barely out of her teens. A dessert came out of the freezer, but somehow it never got eaten. There were other things that seemed much more important, and if those walls did have ears, let's hope our frolics did not make them go too red.

At some time after midnight, Anja decided it was time for me to go. I had hoped to stay the night, but she said she desperately needed sleep. We exchanged details and arranged to meet on the following evening, this time at my apartment. I left with a buzz in my head and hardly noticed the steady drizzle as I sauntered back to my own bed. It had been a fantastic day and I could hardly wait for the following evening.

Immediately I unlocked the door to my apartment. I knew someone had been there. A faint smell of aftershave and stale sweat greeted my arrival. I tensed up, wondering whether the person, or persons were still there. I quickly established that I was alone, and on the face of it, I could see no change. My laptop was sitting open on the dining room table as I had left it, and fortunately, from force of habit, I had taken the SD card with me in the afternoon. My rucksack was on the floor beside my bed, also as I had left it, except the fastening zip was in a different position, and that confirmed to me that someone had been in the apartment. I rummaged around in my rucksack to see if my expensive binoculars were there. They were, and once again I had had the foresight to take the SD card with me.

The bathroom appeared to have been thoroughly searched. The contents of my toilet bag had been removed and replaced. I knew that because there was no sign of the disintegrated paracetamols that had lain at the bottom of the bag for many months. The toilet seat had dirt on it suggesting the cistern cover had been removed. I stood on a chair and looked at the top of the bathroom cabinet, and yes, fingers had recently run along the top of it, presumably looking for something. The kitchen hadn't escaped attention, and although nothing seemed to be missing, everything had been inspected, including a tin of mustard, the top of which I had failed to remove, but the intruder, or intruders, had managed to loosen and gain entry to.

I concluded that nothing had been stolen, and I admired the professional way that the apartment had been searched. A layman probably would not have been aware of the search, but whether it was instinct or training, I was aware, and my first reaction was one of anger. Anger because the one girl I thought I could trust had let me down, and anger because I was stupid enough to let emotions rule my head. I could see what had happened. When Anja went to change clothes, she must have sent a message to say that I was safely detained, and when I left she sent a warning to say I was on my way back to the apartment. I was livid, I felt betrayed. It must have been the way it had happened, and I was helpless. I couldn't go to the police, I couldn't go to the caretaker, because I'm sure he wouldn't say anything, and somehow if it was mentioned in the Booking.com review, it would have been met with extreme puzzlement.

I sat down on the sofa deflated, and pondered, and after a while those thoughts turned to what would I have done in her situation. Probably the same, and why was it I suspected her immediately when I entered the apartment? It was because I didn't trust her. I felt depressed that one of the happiest days of my life had turned so sour, but had it? If I had taken the same course of action, what right had I got to think that I was better than her? That was arrogance, and I was now beginning to see events in a more positive light.

It took me a while to fall asleep as imaginary voices weighed in on either side of the argument regarding Anja. Eventually, the dark thoughts were cast aside. On the following morning, it was dull and drizzly, but I could see from the persistence of the icicle opposite that it was still cold. I was still somewhat upset, but I had a job to do and it was best to set emotions aside. So far, I had found out no information that could be useful to my government, and that had to change.

I had had no answer from London regarding the man I had seen her talking to at the market stall, and with that in mind I decided to visit the area around the market stall and do some more observation work, and this time I would try to stay hidden. After breakfast I went out, and indeed it was a dank morning. I took up a position in a doorway of a disused shop and I had purposefully dressed to look like a person who had fallen on hard times, and I had already noticed that there were several of those in Ljubljana. It was just before ten o'clock that I noticed that man again. He was having another long and serious conversation with Anja. He was doing most of the talking, and she was nodding. Giving instructions I thought. I took some photographs, and then decided to follow him.

He spent around twenty minutes talking to Anja and came away with a large carton of sauerkraut. I wondered if he had a message at the bottom of his carton. He walked past me and I was able to have a good look at him. I judged him to be fifty-five years old, fairly short and slightly stooping with a careworn face. He was carrying a *Hofer* supermarket bag which contained more than the carton of sauerkraut. He took the road under the railway and headed north. He passed close to my apartment before turning into a side street. He stopped in front of a low, but large, gated building with a garden, unlocked the gate and entered. I took some photographs and returned to my apartment, happy with my morning's work.

Friday was meant to be my last full day at the apartment but more time was needed in Ljubljana, much more time, so I tried to arrange for an extension to my stay. It was not a busy time of year and it was surprisingly easy to book another week. There was no reply to my request for information from London, and so I just let my line manager know that I was staying for another week. Then, I thought it was time to send a message to Anja. We needed to clarify a few things, and if we met in the evening at my apartment she would probably play 'the walls have ears' card and many questions would remain unanswered.

We agreed to meet by her market stall at half past five, and that gave me time during the afternoon to prepare food. I wasn't sure whether she would still want to join me for dinner after we had completed our discussion, but I optimistically readied my version of a cottage pie which would need only a little extra cooking in the evening. It was overcast but dry when I left the apartment to meet Anja, and to my surprise she was there waiting for me. There was apprehension in her eyes but she hugged me warmly, took my arm and led me along the pavement. We stopped at the edge of a little park opposite the railway station and sat down on a low stone wall that surrounded a statue of a man on a horse.

Huddled together against the cold, she told me about the horseman, a General Maister, who liberated Maribor from the Austrians towards the end of the First World War.

'I would have been Austrian, if it wasn't for him.' She smiled weakly and said, 'You're not happy.'

I had been thinking how I should open my speech, and after looking around to make sure that we were alone, I blurted out, 'My apartment was searched yesterday evening. What do you know about it?'

She neither looked surprised nor angry. In fact, she looked sad. 'You know the business we're in Sean. You would have done the same, and before you say it, yes I trust you, as much as you trust me.'

There was a long pause before I said, 'Did I pass the test?'

'Yes, I think so,' Anja replied, 'but you'll have to look after your paracetamols better.' This broke the film of ice that had developed between us and we embraced before strolling slowly back to my apartment.

I opened a bottle of wine, and although Anja said, she only drank alcohol occasionally, she was not slow in emptying her glass, and the second bottle was uncorked before we started dinner. The cottage pie was well received but the dessert of pastry and yoghurt had to wait until breakfast time. I was not sure if Anja had expected to stay the night, but she hadn't dressed up for dinner, and in the morning the clothes she was wearing would not have looked out of place behind a market stall. She asked if it was okay to come and see me after work on Saturday, just after two, and of course it was.

After she had left, I hummed around the kitchen doing the washing up, thinking to myself how radically emotions can change in twenty-four hours, and what will this roller-coaster relationship produce next.

At twenty past two, Anja arrived looking flustered and waving two tickets. 'We're going to my uncle's house in Bled and the bus leaves in forty minutes.'

'Do I need to pack?' I said.

'Yes.' She looked at me quizzically.

'How long for?' I asked.

'Two nights,' she said, smiling mischievously.

We boarded the bus at ten minutes to three and at precisely three o'clock it departed. It was a full bus and I asked Anja how long she had been planning this trip as I thought the tickets must have been purchased several days earlier. I was surprised to hear that she had ordered them online after our very first meeting at the market stall.

'You can call it love at first sight if you like.' I did like, but I wasn't sure if she was being serious or not.

The trip to Bled took about an hour and twenty minutes, and when we left the bus it felt noticeably colder than it had been in Ljubljana. It was misty with snowy drizzle in the air, and grey slush, mixed with gravel, coated some of the roads and pavements. Anja set off enthusiastically along the street. 'It's quite a long walk, and we're stopping at the supermarket on the way.' She said, over her shoulder, and I just followed.

It was around a twenty-minute walk to the supermarket, and there she stocked up with enough food to last a week, and at my insistence we added red wine to the trolley. Fortunately, our destination was less than ten minutes' walk away from the supermarket, although it was uphill. The property was on a quiet narrow road lined with imposing Swiss chalet-style houses. The one we went into was smaller than most, but nevertheless it had three floors and nestled in quite a big garden. Patches of slushy snow lay on the brown grass and to me it looked unoccupied. Anja took a key out of her pocket and unlocked the heavy looking wooden door.

'Is your uncle here?'

Although I think I already knew the answer.

'No.' Anja replied. 'But he will be at the end of the month. He lets the place from Easter until October. Nice isn't it?'

I had to agree.

It was cold and dark inside, but Anja turned on the electricity and ignited the boiler, and slowly it warmed up. Anja told me that this was her favourite place and she often visited it in the winter months with friends, or alone if she needed to concentrate on writing an essay for her college work. I felt a pang of jealousy at the thought that she might have been here with past boyfriends. She must have read my thoughts because she said, 'You're the first proper boyfriend I've taken here.'

I then silently wondered what a proper boyfriend was.

We had a cosy dinner and talked about our common dislike of illegal drugs and its impact on society. I spoke about my trip to Morocco and my meeting with Mohammed the farmer. Anja listened intently. Of course, I refrained from mentioning the days that followed in Spain, but I could see from Anja's reactions that she liked what she had heard. We limited ourselves to one bottle of wine but we were jolly and laughed a lot as we exchanged more anecdotes from our formative years. By the time the evening had ended, I felt that I could trust Anja, and I believed that she trusted me.

A night of blissful sleep ended abruptly around nine o'clock with Anja shouting 'It's snowing.' We had neglected to close the curtains on the previous evening and from the bed you could see big white flakes gently floating down.

'Get up.' She said, throwing the duvet on the floor. 'We must walk around the lake; it should be so beautiful.'

I tried to think of an excuse not to, but in vain, so after a hurried breakfast we set off on our walk.

There was no wind and the snow clung to the trees with about ten centimetres of crispy snow, the type that makes good snowballs, on the roads and pavements with no signs of thawing. We saw no one as we walked to the lake, and the main road had very few tyre tracks in the snow. The stroll through the woods in the snow was magical. The lake was partially frozen and it was silent apart from the gentle crunch of snow as we walked along the well-marked path. Anja said that the circuit was about six kilometres, and halfway there were some cafes, but we were in no hurry. After about a kilometre we sat on a bench by the lake where the view to the island, which Lake Bled is famous for, was at its most stunning. Anja gave me a potted history of the church which, with its fifty-two metre tower and spire, is the centrepiece of the island.

After the history lesson, there was a brief silence, then Anja turned to me with a serious look in her eyes and said, 'Do you know Sir Oliver Legg?' I was completely taken aback.

'Yes, sort of,' I stammered.

'Is he your boss?' she continued.

I laughed dryly. 'No, no, not at all. I'm not even sure he's my bosses' boss.'

'But you do know him?' Anja continued.

'Yes, we've met once or twice.'

'Did you like him?'

I folded my arms; I was beginning to feel defensive. 'Why do you ask all these questions?'

'I have to know if I can trust you.' Anja replied.

There was a long silence while I thought, and I watched as the snowflakes gathered on the sleeves of my jacket. Finally, I said, 'No, I didn't like him, and yes you can trust me.'

To my surprise she said, 'I'm happy that you said that, because we believe he is not working for the best interests of western democracies.'

'Really?' I replied, not quite believing what I was hearing.

'Go on.' Anja looked around. The muffled sound of a car cautiously travelling along the road some thirty metres behind us was the only sound I could hear and there were no people to be seen. She held my gaze and proceeded to explain about this new mind-bending strain of cannabis that was flooding the markets in Europe, and that some powers were welcoming this for their own political ends. She paused to allow me to take in this new information and continued, 'The British Government, or at least elements of the British Government, are trying to undermine our attempts to eradicate this new drug.'

'How do you know this?' I interjected.

Anja appeared to think hard about what to say next. 'Our agency has been working with those of other countries to try and arrest the criminals, that's stating the obvious, but we make little progress because powerful people want us to fail.'

I had heard something similar from Mohammed in Morocco. It was getting interesting. 'Why do you think our government is involved?' I said.

'Because Kevin told me.' Anja replied.

I looked bemused 'Who's Kevin?'

'You don't know him?'

I shook my head.

'He was the agent that the British had working in Slovenia before you arrived.' Anja continued.

There was a pause before I spoke. 'I had heard he was missing, presumed dead; I didn't know his name though.'

'He is dead.' Anja responded.

'How do you know that?' I said.

Another pause ensued before Anja said, quietly, 'Because I killed him.'

Chapter 13

The snow continued to fall thickly and the island was barely visible. 'Am I next?' I tried to make light of what I had just heard.

'I hope not,' replied Anja without a hint of a smile.

I said, 'Shall we walk?'

I felt that Anja regretted telling me about the killing, but I respected her for it, and in a way it increased my trust in her. 'Do you want to tell me more?' I said.

'No, not now.' She replied.

We walked on, arm in arm, almost in silence. I thought about Oliver Legg and the encounter I had had with him. I thought about the mysterious duo of Peter and Michael and wondered if they were working for, or against, the Government. It was heavy stuff I was thinking, and we were walking through enchanting woods with the leafless branches bending under the weight of snow; but the thoughts wouldn't leave me.

'That man you earnestly talk to every day at the market stall, is he your spymaster?'

To my surprise, Anja burst into laughter, and I thought she would never stop. Eventually she turned to me and said, 'That was Franc.' After another bout of laughter, she continued 'His wife runs a home for elderly people, and nearly every day she sends him out to buy our sauerkraut. He's our best customer.'

I continued, 'You'll be amused to hear that I followed him home on Friday and took photographs of the building he entered.'

'Have you thought of changing your career?' Anja said it in a way that was just gently mocking and I wasn't offended. We walked on, the first crisis in our relationship was over, but I did think, I must do better.

Halfway round the lake there were several cafes and they were very busy. Not many cars were in the car parks, so like us, the people must have walked from somewhere, but we certainly hadn't seen them. We had no luck in finding seats in the cafes and bars, and similar to many customers, we had to make do with sitting on a bench outside. There was no sign of any outdoor service and only two overworked youngsters manned the bar inside. The snow had almost stopped falling by the time Anja emerged from the bar with two piping hot espresso coffees and two large cream cakes. I mentioned the cream cake incident which preceded our first meeting, and Anja admitted the exploding cream cake was staged. Apparently, though, it is well known in Slovenia that the unwary can make those cakes disintegrate spectacularly. On this occasion, we were both careful.

It was late afternoon before we completed the circuit of Lake Bled, by which time a pale sun had appeared with the snow sparkling in this winter wonderland. We lingered for a while watching ice skaters on the lake, but the temperature was dipping rapidly and we were glad to get back to the house. We were both hungry after our day's exertions and together we prepared a simple meal. We were eager to talk about what we were going to do next in our assignments.

Anja knew a lot more than I did, and perhaps my government did, about the drugs entering Europe, but neither of us knew the source. I wondered why Anja was working with sauerkraut rather than tracking criminals, but she said her assignment was to observe and report back, and she was undercover. What's more she would have a degree in her favourite subject at the end of it.

She said that over the two and a half years that she had been working on the task she had found out much about the drug culture at the university. Mister Big had yet to be found but from her market stall close to the railway and bus stations she had identified three leading players in the supply of drugs to Europe.

I was intrigued, this was obviously the information I had been looking for. Anja continued to provide details. One of the men was a Hungarian named Sandor Horvath. He was living in Koprivnica, a small city in northern Croatia, less than twenty kilometres from the Hungarian border as the crow flies, but considerably further by road. He was a talented artist with a studio in Hlebine, a village at the centre of naive art in Croatia lying about fifteen kilometres east of Koprivnica. Despite his talent, his lifestyle was not compatible with the money he earned from selling paintings.

He was very difficult to pin down for any length of time, and as yet the authorities had not been able to link him with any criminal activities. However, he had met several known drug dealers and Anja regarded him as someone fairly high up in the empire being built around this new addictive drug.

The second man that Anja was monitoring was an Englishman, or at least a man who appeared to have English as his first language. He spoke good Slovene too, and it was thought that he lived in Maribor, although so far he had managed to elude all those that had tried to follow him. In fact, it had been suggested that he resided across the border in Austria. Anja said that this person also met with small-time criminals but he was adept at changing his appearance and changing his mode of transport.

The third was an Australian who answered to the name of Greg. Anja had met him and found him sexy, much to my chagrin, but she was reluctant to trust him. He was far too flippant, and although he worked for the Australian secret service, that much had been verified, she was not sure if he was not part of the drug smuggling empire. He was a regular visitor to Slovenia, always smiling, always positive, and meeting people in high places, but as Anja pointed out, with some anger in her voice 'He also meets people in low places.'

I was pleased with the information that Anja had provided, and I decided that I would not withhold from her any new leads that I managed to get. She was a little concerned that I intended to send a precis of what she had said, about these three men to my line manager, but I assured her that I trusted him, even though I had begun to have doubts about all my colleagues working in the British government security machine.

Monday was a free day for Anja and we managed to postpone the inevitable talk about work until late morning. The sun was shining and we decided to walk into Bled and sit by the lake. Clumps of snow were falling from the laden branches, and the roads and pavements were wet, but the snow in the small lakeside park was glistening and largely undisturbed by footprints. Few people were out walking and we could talk freely and there was one point I wanted to clear up.

'Are you going to tell me what happened to Kevin?' Anja was expecting the question.

She looked around and said, 'Let's walk.' We found a bench on the south side of the lake with the most beautiful views of the island and the snowy peaks near the Austrian border as a backdrop. It was probably not the most appropriate place to speak of a murder but Anja proceeded to tell me about Kevin and his demise.

He had been sent to Slovenia by Oliver Legg to investigate the blockage in the flow of drugs through Europe to the UK. That was what Anja had managed to glean from him after several weeks of getting to know him. I winced at the thought of what Anja meant about getting to know him, but in the beginning he had appeared to be an agent keen on tackling the drugs problem, but slowly she had gathered information which would not only thwart the operation to prevent drug trafficking but would also put the lives of agents at risk.

Eventually her boss said to her, 'You know what you have to do.'

I listened intently as she told me about how she had managed to wheedle the names of contacts from him, and how she had eventually feared for own life as he tried to recruit her into the sordid drugs empire.

The death occurred just before Christmas. It was snowing heavily and Anja was staying with Kevin at her uncle's house, just as I was. Anja suggested that they went for a walk in the snow in the hills north of Bled. There were some ski slopes near the top of the hill, and Anja knew of a short cut through the woods. It was a long walk but Anja knew the area well as she had visited it regularly since her childhood. In what she considered was the remotest part of the woods, she led him unknowingly away from the path and shot him.

'The heavy snow probably muffled the gunshots,' she said, 'and anyway, occasionally people go to the woods and shoot deer or boar.'

'Did you just leave him there?' I said, with more than a hint of surprise in my voice.

'Yes,' Anja replied. 'It was at the bottom of a little cliff with many leaves, and I threw some over him, and a bit of snow, and walked back to the town.'

'Did you not feel any compassion?' It was an instinctive question and immediately I wished I hadn't posed it.

She looked at me quizzically and with a hint of irritation before replying. 'He was evil and many people will die before we stop these drug barons. His death will save lives and I hope that if you were in my position you would have done the same.' She jutted out her chin and stared at me with tears in her eyes. 'Anyway,' she said, after a while, 'the wolves or bears will have eaten him by now.'

'Bears!' I said.

'Yes.' She said, looking surprised by my ignorance. 'There are plenty of bears and wolves about, too many, the government says, they've started to cull them.' Anja assured me that it was safe to walk around the lake. Although attacks on humans had occurred, they were very rare and generally both animals avoided people if at all possible.

We walked a little further alongside the lake, but as the sun lowered in the sky, it started to freeze again and the path became slippery so we slowly headed back to the house. 'Why did you think you could trust me, Anja?' I said, after a few minutes walking.

'Because you're naive, Sean, and always will be. You see the good in people. You listen to reason. You're not ruthless. Do you want to hear more?' She looked at me smiling. I thought about telling her of the Spanish assignment, but I hadn't sorted it out in my own mind, so I stayed quiet. We reached the house and cooked a meal together before clearing up and packing ready to catch the last bus back to Ljubljana. It was a light and cheery evening, but I was slightly apprehensive as I planned my next course of action.

Anja was working on Tuesday morning, so we parted at the bus stop in Ljubljana and I walked back to the apartment. There was no snow on the ground but it was very cold and I was glad to return to my temporary home. After a good night's sleep, I set about writing a report to my boss asking for information about the three individuals that Anja had spoken about. I waited for a speedy reply, but it didn't arrive, and as the icicle outside the window was thawing quickly, and a great tit was chirping enthusiastically in a nearby tree, I thought a stroll outside would be good for clarifying my plans. I passed the sauerkraut stall where Anja was very busy. I blew her a kiss and she waved back cheerfully.

I then went into the railway station to check on trains to Zagreb. I decided that I wanted to find out more about Sandor the Hungarian and a trip to Koprivnica might be worthwhile. As I looked at the timetables I realised it would be much more sensible to take a car. The journey by train would take between four and five hours, and, as I found out later, the car trip was just over three hours. There was a car rental company at the station and within half an hour I drove away in a brand-new Renault Clio.

Back at the apartment, I tried to book a hotel in Koprivnica for Wednesday night, but I had no luck. There appeared to be only one good-sized hotel in the town, and after phoning the hotel directly I found out that there was a big football match on Wednesday evening and all the rooms were booked. That upset my itinerary a little, but I hoped it would mean extra time spent with Anja. I did manage to obtain a booking for Thursday night, plus a further two nights just in case I uncovered something of interest. I told Anja of my plans, and we agreed to meet for dinner around her flat in the evening. She was somewhat stressed by her workload, and I could see she wanted an early night so I returned to the apartment after dinner having made an arrangement to meet in *Smartinski* Park at three o'clock on Wednesday afternoon.

I spent Wednesday morning looking around Koprivnica on google maps, just to get a feel for the place before my arrival. Halfway through the morning a message arrived from London with some information on the names supplied by Anja. Sandor, the Hungarian, was very much on the radar of the authorities in London and they were keen to learn more about his activities. The Australian, Greg, was meant to be on the side of law and order, but I was given a reminder to be extra careful if I met him because he had a fearsome reputation. The Englishman they didn't know, but they said, further investigations would take place. Once again, I was told to be as discreet as possible.

On Wednesday afternoon, I went to the park and sat on a bench wondering why this area had become a park. It wasn't pretty and was criss-crossed by electricity cables emanating from a substation on the other side of the road. It was a beautiful afternoon with strong sunshine and it had become pleasantly warm. A few people were strolling along the paths with prams, or young children, and there were some groups of people sitting on the grass.

Anja appeared soon after three, and to my surprise she was accompanied by an older man. She was smiling, and so was the man with her. I judged the man to be about forty, a little taller than me, with a set of very white teeth and cold blue eyes that sent a shiver down my spine. His hair was quite long and unkempt and he was wearing a safari jacket and jeans. I could only think this must be Greg, and indeed it was. He put out a very large hand and introduced himself, and if it wasn't for those eyes I thought he was a very affable person. We walked for a while along the path engaging in small talk, and then, at Anja's suggestion, we ambled across the grass and from a bag she was carrying Anja produced a blanket, some sandwiches and three beers. We probably looked like three friends who had met up in the park for the first spring-like day of the year, but our ensuing conversation was far removed from those normally taking place on a warm and sunny afternoon.

Greg allowed Anja to do most of the talking while he quietly observed my reactions. I found him difficult to read and I felt that he did not trust me, and he was not going to divulge any sensitive information. However, he did talk about Sandor Horvath. Greg reckoned that Sandor, despite his appearance as a hippy artist, was a shrewd businessman and a lynchpin in the organisation transporting drugs from Hungary to Croatia, and onwards to Slovenia and beyond. He had no hard evidence, but he believed the crossing point from Hungary was somewhere close to Zakany where thick woodlands covered either side of the border.

Unfortunately, his attempts at gaining information had been thwarted, probably by officials on Sandor's payroll, and without going into details, he thought he was lucky to escape Croatia alive. He suggested that I learn about naive art in a hurry, because any foreigner arriving in a small town like Koprivnica in March would arouse suspicions, if they were not there for a specified purpose. That seemed to be good advice, but when the picnic party broke up, I felt that I was being used by both Anja and Greg for the purpose of achieving important information for their respective governments.

I watched as Greg slowly disappeared across the other side of the park. He had patted me on the arm as he left, and there was a hint of sadness in his eyes, but during the two hours we had spent in his company I had found out very little about the man himself. Why did he walk away in the opposite direction to the bus and train stations? Perhaps he had a car; but then he arrived on foot, with Anja, from the other direction. I asked Anja if he lived in Ljubljana.

'No, no,' she replied.

'How did you know he was coming today?' I said.

'He just sent me a text message.' Anja was not saying much. 'Do you trust him?' I asked.

'Yes, I think so.' She replied.

I realised after a couple more minutes of walking that I was probably worried that he was Anja's lover. 'Have you ever had an affair with him?' I blurted out.

Her eyes briefly flashed with annoyance. 'No, and no I don't want to either.' After a prolonged silence she said, 'He's a business colleague, no more, stop sulking.'

I felt he had some hold on her, but I couldn't determine what, so I let it rest. The evening was spent in my apartment and we had a carefree dinner followed by a passionate dessert. We were loath to part, but Anja had an early start on Thursday, and I had to do my homework on naive art before I departed for Koprivnica. As it happened, I surfed the net until three in the morning, and by the time I left for Croatia at eleven o'clock, I had become something of an expert in the unusual art of naive painting.

I took the scenic northern roads to Koprivnica to avoid Zagreb. It was slightly slower than the main route, but in Slovenia it was mostly on the motorway, and in Croatia the roads were good, but mainly single carriageways. The road crossed, and in places followed, the mighty *Drava* river, a wide and fast-flowing tributary of the *Danube*. The river rises in the southern Tyrol of Italy before flowing eastwards for over seven hundred kilometres before joining the *Danube* on the Serbian border east of Osinek. The hotel in Koprivnica was clean, but basic, a characterless block from the era when Croatia was part of Yugoslavia. I made a point of mentioning my interest in naive art and praised the paintings hanging behind the reception desk.

I had the address of Sandor Horvath and it was only about six hundred metres from the hotel, so I took a stroll in the warm sunshine and passed by his house on my trip round the centre of the town. Sandor's house was a corner plot close to a church. It was big and quite dilapidated, and I actually wondered if it was being lived in. The tour of the town did not take long. Although the centre by the park was quite open and attractive, it was a much smaller place than Ljubljana and didn't appear to have sufficient discernible history to attract tourism. I bought an ice cream from a kiosk and sat in the park and thought about my next move.

Maybe I should visit Mr Horvath posing as a buyer of art, and perhaps that would be the best way to find out about him. Having made that decision, I returned to the hotel and learnt some more about local art before going out for dinner. Greg had mentioned a restaurant that I should visit but it was a long walk. Instead, I wandered into the centre and found a bar that cooked a passable beef stroganoff. On the way back to the hotel, I took a detour and was pleased to see a downstairs light on in Sandor's house. At least, that meant there was a good chance of finding someone at home during my stay in the town. The rest of the evening was spent in my room at the hotel watching television.

The following morning I had a very good breakfast at the hotel before striding off towards Sandor's house. I had a hunch that his description as 'a hippy type' might mean that he wasn't one for rushing out of the door at eight in the morning. I arrived just after half past nine and moved the decrepit gate into an open position and walked up to his front door. Green paint was peeling from the woodwork and the brass doorknocker, showing the face of a lion, was badly corroded. The door was slightly ajar, and when I knocked there was an echo from within. I waited, but there was no response, I was more determined with my second rat-a-tat-tat on the door, but still no response.

I looked around the corner into the garden, but it was a tangled mass of brown undergrowth and bare fruit trees, and I guessed it hadn't been visited for a while.

I went back to the door and pushed it a little, and then noticed that the light was still on. It was probably the same light that I had seen on my way back to the hotel on the previous evening. I ventured into the hallway, and was met by a damp, musty smell. The black and white checked floor tiles were in need of a wash, so was the brown mat that covered several of them. Off to the right was a sunlit kitchen and to the left a lounge.

I stopped and called 'Sandor, is anyone home?' I thought maybe he couldn't understand English, but at least he would have heard that there was someone in his house. I called again, and then went forward to what looked like an office. There was a laptop on the desk and a mobile phone next to it. On the other side of the desk, there was a small cup with what looked like coffee in it, and a patterned plate with a half-eaten pastry on. Alongside the desk there was a white wastepaper bin, and draped over the edge of this was a hand.

Chapter 14

Why I was not surprised to find a body in that house I will never know, but from the moment I saw the front door open and the garden empty my suspicions had been aroused. Sandor, I assumed it was him by his appearance, had been bludgeoned to death, and although I was no expert in the decomposition of humans, my guess was that the murder had taken place the previous evening. I instinctively listened for any noises but assumed that the murderer had long gone. Strangely, there was no sign of a struggle, and it didn't look as if anything had been taken. Sandor was dressed in jeans and a red sweatshirt, and I smiled wryly at the thought that he had chosen to wear red on the day of his bloody death.

Using a tissue to avoid leaving fingerprints, I opened one of the desk drawers, and I was pleased to see a wallet, along with SD cards and several flash drives lying there. I made a decision to fill my pockets with as many useful articles as possible and hoped the police would not suddenly appear. I switched the light off, carefully shut the front door, and within five minutes of entering the house I was back on the street again. I quickly looked up and down the road and saw no one. I was confident that I entered and left the house unseen.

Obviously I was not going to call the police about the murder, there would have been too many questions and I would probably have been detained as the prime suspect. The short time I had spent in the house was enough to suggest to me that he had lived alone, and if I was lucky, his body would not be discovered for some while. Nevertheless, it was imperative that I should work quickly to find out more about this man and his business. With that in mind, I walked briskly back to the hotel, and in the room looked through the contents of his wallet. There was nothing of great interest except his business cards that contained the address of his studio in Hlebine. That would be the starting point for my investigations.

The trip to Hlebine in the car only took twenty minutes across flat farming country with the single-carriageway road lined with small one-storey houses. There were few signs of wealth, and Hlebine, the centre of naive art in Croatia, seemed equally poor, and although I expected to see indications of bohemian lifestyles, there were none on view. Apart from a fairly new-looking museum with grounds dotted with sculptures, the village seemed like any other deeply rural community. A couple of tractors had recently deposited mud on the road, otherwise the place appeared to be deserted. Fortunately, I had located my destination on a google map and the village was small enough for me to memorise the road network and recognise the house that I was looking for.

I was not sure what to expect at the house, but it looked very neat and tidy outside, and from what I had seen of Sandor and his property, this place was under the influence of somebody else. I rang the doorbell, and if it was to be answered I had a plan to account for my appearance. It was answered, and by a small very elderly woman wearing dark old-fashioned clothes. I asked after Sandor in English.

I said I had an appointment to meet him with the intention of buying some paintings of his. She didn't understand English, so I tried German with the same result. I then had a go at Russian and her face lit up. My Russian language skills were rudimentary but she understood the purpose of my visit, and immediately invited me inside. To my surprise, she offered me a beer. I refused but accepted an orange juice. She then proceeded to tell me her life story. Her parents were Russians who had fled the country in the nineteen twenties and had settled in Croatia. She had married a Croatian farmer, settled in Hlebine and raised five children. Her husband had died many years ago but she was proud to say that she still drove a tractor and helped to maintain the fields she shared with an adjoining farm.

The kindly old lady was keen to show me around her garden, and she seemed to have forgotten that I was there to meet Sandor. The first part of the garden was enclosed and used for growing vegetables, she told me. Chickens were running freely, but, if I understood her correctly, they were housed every night to prevent foxes from killing them. Further down the very long and narrow garden there was an orchard, and beyond that some open fields, already ploughed and ready for planting. In between the orchard and the vegetable garden, there were some buildings. One housed the tractor and agricultural equipment, another appeared to house the chickens, and yet another, which appeared to be converted stables, had a large sign outside which read 'Sandor Horvath Slikar.'

The elderly lady pointed to the sign and beckoned me to follow. The door to the studio was unlocked and I followed her into a large, bright room warmed by the afternoon sunshine. She waved her hand around and more than hinted that the place should be tidied. It was filled with paintings in various stages of completion. Some finished ones had been framed and were hanging on the walls, and there was a well-thumbed folder lying open on a paint-splattered desk. I was asked if I would like to have a look around the studio, and when I replied in the affirmative, she said that she had to go back to the house as she was expecting a call from her son. A stroke of fortune, I thought, as I watched her disappear up the garden path into the house.

Ignoring the array of brightly coloured paintings around me, I went straight to the desk, and using a cloth to avoid leaving fingerprints I went through the contents of the unlocked drawers. There were some surprisingly well-ordered files with lists of clients and suppliers and some accounts, but the top drawer proved to be the most interesting. It held a map, a small book, and a set of olive wood rosary beads. With my heart beating a little faster, I scooped up the three items and concealed them in my jacket pocket. I then examined the rest of the studio, but I really knew that there was little else to interest me, and after ten or so minutes I went back to the house.

'I have tried to call Sandor,' I lied, 'but he's not answering his phone.' I knew he wouldn't of course, and I had seen his mobile on his desk in Koprivnica, so I knew if anyone rang his phone it would ring but not be answered. 'I do hope he hasn't had an accident.'

The old lady said. 'He's so dangerous on that motor-bike.' I had thought of saying that maybe his car had broken down, and I let out a silent phew of relief when she mentioned the motorbike. I said that I would continue to try and contact him, and the old lady left it at that. Fortunately, she didn't want to get involved and when I left she smiled and waved goodbye without even asking for my name or mobile number. I felt sorry for her. She was probably eking out a precarious living by having a steady income from letting out the studio. She was very trusting too, and I had deceived her; but then she had unknowingly been helping a criminal. I felt better, but only slightly.

At the hotel, I asked the receptionist to book me a table at the restaurant Greg had recommended. It was a long walk, but the evening was fine and I wanted to clear my head regarding the events of the last day. Was it a coincidence that we spoke at length in the park about Sandor on Wednesday, and he was dead by Friday, but why would either Anja or Greg want to kill him, or have him killed?

It didn't make sense. If anyone should have been killed, it should have been me. And with that thought in my mind I reached the restaurant.

I was shown to a table by a rotund middle-aged woman with dyed black hair. I assumed that she was the owner. She brought me an English menu card and then left to attend another table where two couples sat, and who were ready to order. Apart from those four, there was one young couple who were already eating. After a few minutes, the proprietress came back to my table and stood poised with a pencil and notepad. The restaurant had a good reputation for home cooking, and I asked what she would recommend.

Instantly she said, '*Pasticada*', which, on the menu card, had been translated to beef stew. I said, yes to the *pasticada* and in passable English she asked what I would like to drink. I decided on a local red wine, and both my choices were met with approval as she broke into a smile.

As I sat waiting for my food, a police siren sounded and a car rushed past. I shuddered at the thought that they may have discovered the body of Sandor. A couple of minutes later an ambulance went past, siren wailing, and I relaxed thinking it was probably just a traffic accident. My meal arrived and it was truly delicious. A piping hot stew, somewhat similar to Lancashire Hotpot but with beef instead of lamb. It was served with a little side salad and, what looked like, dumplings.

Just as I was finishing my first course, two fire engines went past, with sirens blazing and I joked to the restaurant owner that I hoped my hotel wasn't on fire. I took my time with the dessert, a homemade almond tart, topped by a generous amount of liquor. By the time I had finished, I was the only one left in the restaurant, and the owner came over to me for a chat. She seemed to be in no hurry to close and appeared to be pleased to be speaking English.

I asked her if she had many British customers, and she said, 'No, but one comes in occasionally. An Englishman, very quiet, you know, but he does speak a little Croat. A businessman, I think. And last week an Australian came here,' she continued.

'Really,' I said, 'And can you tell me what he looked like?'

It was a very good description of Greg, and I wondered what he had been doing in Koprivnica. He had not mentioned the visit on the picnic afternoon although he had recommended the restaurant.

'Do you know him?' asked the owner.

'No, no.' I lied. 'I might know the Englishman, though.' I said, flippantly.

'I think he has been living around here for many years,' the owner said, 'He has lots of business friends.'

'What is his line of business?' I asked.

'Something to do with furniture making.' She said, 'They lay drawings of cupboards and tables and chairs, all sorts of things, out on the tables. It makes the place look very untidy.' She obviously didn't like this man and I had no interest in him, so the conversation moved on to art. I enthused about naive art, but her eyes glazed over, so I politely asked for my bill. The chef, presumably her husband, emerged from the kitchen to say goodbye, and after saying that I hoped to visit again I left having had an enjoyable evening.

It was a cool, clear and starlit night, a rarity in polluted London, but one I had become accustomed to in this part of Europe. In front of me, on the walk back to the hotel, was a glow low in the sky, and as I approached the hotel I realised that it was a fire. I couldn't see where the fire was, it certainly wasn't at the hotel, but I was curious to see where it was, so I walked past the hotel and into the centre of the town. A smell of smoke hung over the centre and I could see flames shooting upwards close to the church. I walked along the street towards the fire and many others were milling around talking and watching as hoses from several fire engines were sending out cascades of water and foam to try and quell the intense fire. As I got closer to the fire I drew a sudden intake of breath. I knew the house that was on fire. It was the one where Sandor Horvath had met his grisly end.

Chapter 15

I stood and gazed vacantly at the efforts made by the fire service to extinguish the blaze. Not for the first time, unexpected events had occurred to thwart my plans. In more ways than one, it had become too hot in Koprivnica and I decided to leave a day early. I wondered if the ambulance that had passed the restaurant a couple of hours before had been summoned to pick up the dead body, but no, he was so obviously dead that there would have been no need for speed. It was probably just a precautionary measure, although I couldn't see an ambulance in the area. There were a couple of police cars, and officers were endeavouring to keep the locals at a safe distance from the fire. The blaze was fierce, and Sandor must have been well and truly cremated, but forensics are very good these days, and undoubtedly the professionals would arrive to ascertain whether the fire had been started deliberately.

After a while, the fire began to die down and sightseers returned home. I ambled back to the hotel to find it full of noisy teenagers. The receptionist said, there was a youth football tournament taking place on Saturday and the hotel was full of youngsters and their coaches. The noise went on for much of the night and when I checked out a day early, showing feigned indignation, the receptionist apologised profusely and gave me a ten percent reduction to my bill. As I left the car park next to the hotel I smiled to myself at the excuse I had used for leaving, but I had no plan. It was probably prudent to leave Croatia, and maybe I should leave the area, and with that in mind I drove back to Ljubljana to pack.

My thoughts turned to Anja. I didn't contact her on Friday night, I was too worried about my own predicament, but when I arrived back at my apartment, instead of packing, I grabbed a shopping bag and headed off to the market. Anja was there, and when she saw me she beamed with delight. I had wondered what her reaction would be and I was pleased to see that I hadn't been forgotten.

The stall was very busy, but I queued for some sauerkraut and when I paid Anja she just said, 'Six o'clock at my flat.' and then went on to the next customer.

I was a little disappointed that we couldn't spend the afternoon together, but it gave me time to look at what I had acquired in Croatia.

A further examination of the wallet revealed little of interest. There were a few banknotes of Croatian Kuna, and some more of Hungarian Forint. In fact, there were more Forint than Kuna and one of the credit cards was from OTP Bank of Hungary.

There was a passport-sized photograph of a woman. An identity card and a number of receipts. I thumbed through them, and most were from a supermarket or hardware store, but four were from restaurants. Two stood out. They were from the restaurant that I had visited the previous night. One of the bills was quite large and suggested that three or four people had been present. The other was smaller, but it looked as if he had not been alone in the restaurant. The other two receipts were more intriguing.

One was from a restaurant named *'Csulok Csarda'*. I typed the name into google search and came up with three restaurants, all of them in Hungary. One was in the Capital, Budapest, the other two were in Esztergom and Miskolc. The other bill was in a language that I did not recognise. It looked a bit like a Southeast Asian script, perhaps Thai or Lao, but the bill was faded. However, on the back of it there was what appeared to be a telephone number and a name above *'Nino'*.

I had known someone in Spain called Nino, a waiter in a cafe I used to go to with Youssef. I think it was just a shortened version of Antonio or something like that. I took a photograph of Sandor's identity card and the bill with the unusual script and then put most of the items back in the wallet. It was my intention to dispose of the wallet at the earliest opportunity.

The SD cards had records of paintings, to whom they were sold to, and other data associated with the art world. The two memory sticks were more interesting. They contained usernames and passwords which may have some use, but there were also some photo albums. Many pictures were of the woman whose photograph I had discovered in his wallet. She seemed happy, and there was a little girl in many of the pictures and I assumed they were of his wife and daughter, or at the very least part of his family. I felt sorry for them, but from what I had found out about Sandor, I was less than sorry for him.

What fascinated me most was the language used on restaurants, boats and road signs in the photos. Unfortunately, there were no directions or road number pictures, but one sign showed the mystery script with a very English 'no parking' underneath. There was a restaurant called 'Lighthouse' and a tugboat in a harbour was called 'Tamara 1'. Palm trees were in some of the photos, but other people in the pictures did not look like Asians. It was truly a mystery.

Next on my list was the diary which seemed to double as an address book. There were many names, and I was encouraged by the slips of paper that were protruding from the pages, many of which had names, addresses and telephone numbers. It would be a lengthy task to examine all the diary entries so I decided to file a report to London and to ask for information on the mystery language.

My next dilemma was what to say to Anja. Could I trust her? The perennial question not helped by the death of Sandor. Anyway, at six o'clock I arrived outside the main door to Anja's apartment block and I was let in. She seemed to be pleased to see me and there was no sign of tension. Pop music was coming from the lounge and the smell of cooking pervaded the flat. I felt relaxed, and when she casually asked me how it had gone, I just smiled and put a finger to my lips and whispered, 'Walls have ears'.

Anja said that she had been invited to a birthday party that evening and she couldn't really miss it and would I like to come along. I didn't want to, but the right answer was to say yes, so after a hurried dinner we went along to a flat some hundred metres up the road. It was a small flat and twenty or more people were already packing the rooms, with the lounge offering the semblance of a dance floor. The four youngsters from the first afternoon when I met Anja were there, and we spent another evening hotly debating world affairs. It was a refreshing diversion from the reality of the previous few days.

The party broke up relatively early and Anja and I went back to her flat where I stayed until mid-morning on Sunday. I decided that I was going to tell her about Sandor and judge her reaction. I said that I had something important to say to her and she suggested that we should have a walk in the forest, a couple of kilometres west of Ljubljana. It was cloudy, with a hint of rain in the air, so we took the car to the edge of the forest and set off along one of the well-signposted tracks. A carpet of crocuses made the walk very pretty, but I was aware that Anja was apprehensive, and as soon as we were away from the car park she asked what was troubling me. I told her the whole story, just leaving out the fact that I had acquired some of his effects. She did seem to be genuinely surprised by the events that had taken place and I could tell that she had now become a doubter of Greg's integrity.

We sat on a bench in silence as the latest disclosures sank into Anja's head. She looked worried, and eventually she asked what I was going to do. As I was meant to leave the apartment on Monday, I thought that maybe a trip to a certain restaurant in Budapest might be useful and wondered if Anja would like to join me there. It was unfair really, because although she would like to have gone, there was much work to be done in Ljubljana, and at such short notice it could not be done. We walked in the forest until sunset and then ate in a nearby cosy Mexican restaurant. We both felt a bit sad as this was our last evening together for a while, and I wondered if this relationship would endure the tribulations that could arise in the weeks ahead as I tried to uncover more about the life of Sandor Horvath.

Anja wasn't working on Monday so she stayed at my apartment overnight and helped me to pack in the morning. I found the '*Csulok Csarda*' restaurant in Budapest on google maps and booked a hotel for two nights. Only the expensive hotels had parking available and the hotel I eventually found was over two kilometres from the restaurant and charged, what I thought, was an unreasonable fee for parking. My next problem was taking the car to Hungary. I had to go to the office and fill in forms as well as paying a cross-border fee. I suppose I should have thought of these obstacles in advance, but I didn't, and by the time I arrived back at the apartment there was a bucket and mop lying next to the door.

Anja was quite tearful through the morning and we were both emotional when it came to saying goodbye, and the first few kilometres on the motorway towards Maribor I felt numb and empty, but I now realised I completely trusted her.

The first part of the journey was pretty, with rolling hills, woods and mixed farming and the day was cloudy, dry and good for driving. There was plenty of traffic on the motorways but hold ups at the tollbooths were minimal. In Hungary, the countryside was mostly flat and almost entirely used for agriculture. The route skirted the south side of Lake Balaton, but much of the road was constructed in a shallow cutting lined with trees and glimpses of the lake were rare. Unsurprisingly, the last leg of the trip into Budapest was difficult as it coincided with the rush hour.

A series of route changes because of roadworks upset the GPS system in the car and it was almost six o'clock before I located the hotel and parked the car in the underground car park.

I felt a little uneasy about the walk to the restaurant in the gathering dusk, but the last kilometre was on a busy road next to the magnificent mainline railway station. I found out later that the facade of the station was adorned with statues of the British railway pioneers, George Stevenson and James Watt. It was almost eight o'clock by the time I reached the restaurant housed under one of the many edifices that abound in Budapest and, as I expected, it was almost empty. I was shown to a table by an attentive but dispassionate waiter. Beef stew looked enticing on the menu card, and I settled for that, washed down with fifty centilitres of red wine. I tried to engage the waiter in conversation but he was reluctant to speak English, and I didn't think it was wise to try Russian. After a large ice cream dessert, I had another unsuccessful attempt at communicating with the waiter. I then asked for the manager.

The young waiter looked shocked and rather irritated, but in less than two minutes he returned with an older man who asked in very good English how he could help me. I showed him the photograph of Sandor on my mobile and asked if he recognised him. He looked puzzled. 'No, I do not remember seeing this man.' was his response. He then asked for his name. I was reluctant to tell him, in case he really did know Sandor, and would warn others that I was enquiring about him, but I had no choice.

He then said, 'I can look through our booking diary. When do you think he was here?'

That threw me a bit, but I said, 'Probably sometime during the last six months.'

He looked at me as if I had just asked him to stand on his head. 'You are very welcome to look through the diary yourself,' he said, after a few seconds thought, and he came to the table with a tome and planted it in front of me. The waiter eyed me suspiciously but the manager seemed keen to help. Over a cup of strong coffee, I thumbed through the neatly laid out book, and there were several 'Horvath' entries. When I pointed them out to the manager he said, they were regular customers and none of them were Sandor. He was very open and I concluded that he was an honest man, but I had found out nothing more about Sandor in Budapest.

As a last resort I asked if it was possible to find out if he had visited the sister restaurants in Esztergom and Miskolc. His eyes lit up, 'A friend of mine manages the restaurant in Miskolc. I will call him and see if he can help.'

Immediately the manager disappeared at the other end of the restaurant. The waiter pointed to the tome with the bookings, and I said he could take it away. He then dealt with the bill for the last remaining customers. It took another twenty minutes before the manager returned to my table and he looked glum. His friend had a computerised bookings form, and although he knew one Sandor Horvath, he was sure that he was not the person that I was looking for. I thanked him for his help and left a generous tip when I paid my bill. It was after eleven when I left the restaurant and although it was Monday, the streets were still full of people. I made my way to the station, and from there took a taxi back to the hotel. I was fairly certain that Sandor Horvath had not visited the restaurant in Budapest. He may have been to the one in Miskolc, but in my mind the favourite was in Esztergom.

After a good night's sleep, and another substantial breakfast, I planned the day ahead. A mail had arrived from London with an answer to the mystery language. It was Georgian, and the location of the photographs appeared to be Batumi on the Black Sea coast just north of the Turkish border. It was an interesting new development, but that had to wait. First of all, I had to dispose of Sandor's wallet. If for any reason, the police stopped and searched me I would have had difficulty explaining why I had all these credit cards and an identity card belonging to Sandor Horvath.

My intention was for the wallet to end up at the bottom of the Danube but it needed some assistance. Although the wallet would eventually sink, someone might see it floating along the river first and hook it out. I couldn't think of a practical solution to this problem, but I took everything from the wallet and put the contents in one pocket and had the empty wallet in another pocket ready for throwing away.

The weather was cloudy, windy and cold, and as it was still quite early in the year, there were not crowds of tourists. Despite the cloud, the riverfront and the backdrop of churches and other historic buildings offered a magnificent panorama. I must have walked over ten kilometres, and it was very enjoyable, but uppermost in my mind was the disposal of all traces of Sandor Horvath. The wallet went into a large bin next to the central market, but I found the perfect place to rid myself of the cards. I went into St Stephen's Basilica, paid my thousand forints and wandered around the large church. It was close to lunchtime and there were few people around. At the side of the statue of Saint Rita, there were two marble columns, one of which had very slightly come away from the main wall of the church. I pretended to study the guidebook while I looked around for CCTV cameras. The niche that contained the statue was in a camera blind spot, and after making sure no one was in sight, I quickly slipped the credit cards and identity card down the crack between the column and the main wall. I expected them to remain there for decades, if not for centuries.

I then resumed my tourist day with more vigour. The view from the top of the ninety-six metre basilica was stunning, and before leaving I lit a candle, even though I wasn't religious. I found out later that St Rita was the patron saint of lost and impossible causes. The sun appeared after I left the church, and after a late lunch at *Running Sushi* I resumed my walking and finished with a stroll to the Hapsburg fortress that offered splendid views of the city, and in this case, enhanced by the setting sun. I then bought some snacks from a convenience store and took a taxi back to the hotel. It had been a very interesting day, and a break from work, although with a little help from St Rita, one of my immediate work problems had been solved.

The following day I checked out of the hotel and made my way to Esztergom. The route wound through a largely unpopulated area with dense woodlands covering low hills. The road was quiet and the weather was grey and drizzly but the journey only took just over an hour so the monotony of the scenery was acceptable. By way of contrast, Esztergom was a fascinating town. Quite small and compact, but even on a gloomy day, the old buildings and winding streets were attractive. I found a travel agency that doubled as a tourist office, and after booking a night at a guesthouse, I set about exploring the town with guidebook in hand.

Apparently large sections of the town were destroyed during the Second World War but much of the old town was restored. The imposing nineteenth century hilltop basilica next to the river was the highlight. The interior was stunningly beautiful, and outside the views along the Danube and across to Slovakia were also impressive. Momentarily I forgot my reason for visiting Esztergom, but evening approached and there was a restaurant to visit. First of all, I checked into the small guesthouse. It was spotlessly clean and there was just enough room to park the car in the courtyard. The restaurant was on the other side of town, but it didn't seem like a place where dangers lurked for those walking alone after dark.

The welcome at the restaurant was warm and it was popular, with several nations represented by the customers. Most of the tables were widely spaced, and

I thought how ideal they were for people wanting a private business meeting. The table I was shown to was small and next to the bar with a large speaker adjacent to my left ear. The young manager was of a cheerful disposition and spoke good English. Alongside him was an even younger man who appeared to be learning the trade as a waiter. He seemed to be frightened of his boss, but he was left to deal with me and I managed to get him to relax.

After my main course, which inevitably ended up as goulash, I called the young waiter over and showed him the photograph of Sandor. Did I detect a look of fear in his eyes? He told me that the boss might know him and quickly walked off to fetch him. I could see them having, what looked like, a rather heated discussion at the other end of the restaurant, but eventually, the waiter returned with the manager who asked politely how he could help me. I went through the same procedure and showed him the photograph. Quicker than I expected he told me that it was not someone he recognised.

He then asked me, not 'Who was he?' but rather, 'Why was I looking for him?'

'Are you sure you don't recognise him?' I said, in a friendly manner, that I could barely muster.

He shook his head and went on 'Would sir like anything for dessert?'

I ignored the question and said, 'Do you think you could look at the book for reserving tables to see if my friend has been here recently?'

He smugly replied. 'Our customers would not like their details given to others. It is not good for the reputation of the restaurant.'

He turned to the young waiter, smiling falsely, and said, in English 'Can you see if this customer wants anything else.' He then turned and left. At no time did he ask for the name of the person I was looking for, and nor did I offer that name.

The young waiter seemed even more frightened than before, and it was noticeable when the dessert bowl of ice cream arrived it was rattling in the saucer. I gently asked if he enjoyed working in the restaurant and he just replied weakly 'It's okay.' He avoided eye contact and looked awkward, so I just said, 'thank you.' and he left.

The customer numbers were quickly dwindling, and by the time I had finished coffee I was the last one left in the restaurant. The young waiter had his coat on the next time he emerged from the kitchen and he waved and mouthed a weak goodbye as he departed. That just left the manager in the restaurant, who arrived at the table soon after with the bill. The food was excellent, and so was the service, and I did not hesitate to praise the manager. The flattery seemed to work and he appeared to have a genuine smile when I left or was it a smile of relief that I hadn't asked any more awkward questions.

As I walked along the road back towards the guesthouse I thought about the evening, and I was convinced that the manager had been lying and that he knew exactly who Sandor Horvath was, but could I prove it? I let the subject go and just enjoyed the stroll through the deserted streets. It was calm and clear, but mist rose from the river and my footfall echoing through the quiet roads made me think of Victorian England alongside the Thames. I stopped at an antique shop and looked through the dimly lit window at the bric-a-brac on display. I then became aware of someone else in the thickening mist some fifty metres back along the road. He, or she, was also looking into a shop window. A coincidence I thought, or was I being followed.

I ambled along the road, occasionally stopping to look into shops, and after a while I was indeed sure that I was being followed. Just to make sure, I took a narrow lane and partially doubled back on myself, and to keep up the outward appearance that I was oblivious of my pursuer, I continued to look into shop windows until I almost reached the river, by which time the mist had thickened into fog. Because of the fog, the person following me had become closer so as not to lose me, and as I turned another corner, I caught the briefest of glimpses of my pursuer. It looked like a young person of slight build and I decided to hide in the shadows and find out why I was being followed and by whom.

Chapter 16

I caught the faintest sound of footsteps edging towards me, and I could also hear the *thump, thump* as my heart beat faster. The person rounded the corner and I grabbed hold of the neck with one arm and put a hand across the mouth and said, in English 'Shout and I'll kill you, what do you want?' It was something I had never done before except in training. I'd seen the movies, where every foreigner could speak and understand English, and I just hoped that this would be the case in this situation.

The person had frozen instantly, and I was worried that I was going to kill him or her anyway. I slowly released my grip, and from the spluttering that followed I realised my pursuer was in fact male.

'So, what's going on?' I said, in a tone that strongly suggested I required an answer.

'I'm Tamas, the waiter from the restaurant, do you remember?'

'Yes.' I replied, relaxing my grip further. Tamas was shaking with fear, and I felt a little guilty at my heavy-handed reaction to being followed.

'Okay.' I said, sounding more conciliatory, 'Why do you want to see me?'

'You showed my manager a photograph of a man, I have seen him in the restaurant many times. He is a bad man.'

I let go of Tamas and said, 'Go on.'

'Are you a policeman?' He asked.

'Sort of,' I replied. 'Go on.'

'His name is Horvath, Sandor Horvath, and he brings guns into the country from Russia.'

'Guns.' I said, in total astonishment.

'Yes.' He said. 'My dad has a little farm by the river, and I go there sometimes, and I saw them unloading guns from a barge. I didn't say anything to anyone, but two of the men that I saw there come to the restaurant and they meet Horvath, and I heard them discussing the guns. I had to tell you.'

'Why me?' I asked. 'Why not go to the police?'

'Because one of the men is a policeman.' He said it as if it was something I should have known.

'You are putting yourself in great danger by telling me.' I said. 'I don't care. I think it's wrong, and I don't like my dad. He hit my mum and brother.'

'So, why do you still work in the restaurant?' I asked 'My dad knows the owner and got me the job when I left school. It is difficult to get a job here.' He was now much more relaxed and I asked him where the farm was. For the first time he smiled. 'If you have a car we can go there tomorrow, it's my day off.'

It was an adventure for this young man and probably quite dangerous. I told him so, but he just dismissed it. 'The *pap* said, "Do what is right," and my girlfriend hates guns.' I admired the moral stance of this youngster, and thought about how the media, often run by elderly people without morals, vilified the young who were seeking a better life for their generation.

Although I felt that our lives could be put in danger, I agreed to pick up Tamas in the morning and drive to the farm. We parted with a handshake and I made my way to the guesthouse. Breakfast was a raucous affair with lorry drivers and travelling salesmen in heated discussion about what, I had no idea, watched over by a timid host. There was no lack of food and the coffee was strong and freshly made. Before I left to meet Tamas I managed to book another night at the guesthouse. I had a feeling that it could be a long day.

Tamas arrived at our rendezvous in the car park next to the bridge across to Slovakia wearing combat fatigues and a red baseball cap. This worried me somewhat, especially as he had a shopping bag with him that I thought might contain a weapon. It was in fact a neatly prepared picnic lunch and a pair of binoculars. I almost regretted getting involved in this little escapade, but there was a chance that something useful could emerge from it.

We drove west out of Esztergom along a quiet road next to the railway and not far from the river. After several kilometres, Tamas pointed out a small track on the right which we turned on to. It wound through woodland with carpets of anemones, the occasional primrose and blackthorn bushes covered with blossom. I asked Tamas where we were going.

'To the mine.' He said, as if I should have known that.

There was no sign of a mine and having a mine next to the Danube seemed rather unlikely, but I drove on for another couple of minutes on the bumpy track towards the river.

He then pointed at a rusting crane and said, 'We park here.' I then realised that the 'mine' was in fact a gravel quarry. Tamas was keen to tell me exactly where the barges moored and where their illicit cargoes were stored. Although we were hidden from the main road, I felt we were rather exposed to anyone in the nearby farmhouse or outbuildings but Tamas was adamant that neither his father nor any farm workers would be in the area. We walked across a small grass field to an old brick shed.

'This,' said Tamas, 'is where they bring the guns.'

The door had a chain and lock hanging from it, but it wasn't even shut. The window had a rusty frame but no glass. It didn't look the best of storage places.

'How do you know they were guns?' I asked.

'There were not just guns, bombs as well.' I was beginning to think that he could be exaggerating, or even lying, but he seemed so enthusiastic I didn't want to dampen his eagerness. 'So, Tamas,' I said, trying not to sound dubious about his statement, 'What were the guns and bombs contained in?'

He looked unsure and asked me to repeat the question. I did.

'In boxes.' He replied, looking at me as if I was an idiot.

'And the bombs?' I said, trying hard to remain serious.

'Oh, they were in plastic.' And he proceeded to draw a large rectangle in the air.

'How did you know they were bombs?' I continued.

'What else could they be?'

'Exactly,' I replied quietly, thinking that those must be the drugs I had been searching for. 'I don't suppose you know where these guns and bombs go after they leave here?' I thought it highly unlikely that he knew any more than he had already told me, but it was worth a try.

'I don't know where the guns go but the bombs go to my uncle's farm.

I could hardly conceal my excitement. If my theory about the drugs was right then I may have got a really good lead. 'And where does your uncle live?'

'Near Zakany.'

'And where is that, then?'

'Oh,' Tamas said, 'It's a long way from here.'

I thought he was not going to actually tell me, but then he said, 'It's near the border with Hrvatska.'

My heartbeat quickened. 'Not far from Koprivnica?' I volunteered.

'Yes, you know it?' There was some respect returning in his voice.

'Yes, very well.' I replied. Tamas seemed to lose interest and we left the empty shed. He pointed to some more buildings on the other side of a larger field.

'That was my grandfather's farm. He's dead.' Tamas looked sullenly at the ground.

We strolled back to the car and Tamas continued to look gloomy, so I told him how useful the information would be, and that when the weapons smuggling has been stopped how many lives will be saved. It cheered him up immediately and I brightened him further by suggesting that we sit by the river and see what was in his picnic hamper. We collected the bag from the car and sat on a fallen tree by the river. I had Sandor's diary with me and I showed it to Tamas. He thought it was very interesting. There were stars on some dates in late May, with further stars in June and July, and he thought that they may be dates when guns would arrive. I thought this was a bit far-fetched. I asked him if he knew any of the names in the diary. A couple of names had addresses next to them, the rest just had telephone numbers.

The first one he pointed to and said, 'That's my dad,' and then he went through the list, 'and that's Uncle Balint; and that's the policeman I told you about.' Tamas seemed to know a large number of people mentioned in the diary, and I made notes as he continued to tell me about the people he knew. I was surprised how long this smuggling had been going on, and if each shipment had guns and drugs, who were the recipients?

When Tamas had finished talking about those known to Sandor, I produced the photograph of the woman that Sandor had kept in his wallet. Tamas looked at it and said, 'Yes, that's his wife; but I think they're not together anymore.'

I thought he definitely had that one right, they weren't together anymore.

'Do you know anything else about her?' I asked.

'She's not from here.' Tamas replied.

'Does that mean she's not from Esztergom?'

'No, no, she's not Hungarian.' Tamas was beginning to get bored, and it was necessary to obtain as much knowledge as I could from this young man.

I pressed on. 'Do you know where she is from?' There was a long pause.

'She didn't speak much Hungarian. I think they spoke to her in Russian. The English man spoke to her in English.' Tamas laughed. 'He always spoke English.'

That was an unexpected twist. 'An Englishman?' I looked him in the eyes.

'Yes, he was one of the big men, I think. He always wore a suit and my dad was afraid of him.'

'Do you know where he lives? Does he come over here from England?'

This was perhaps a breakthrough I was looking for. 'I don't know where he lives but I've seen him at Uncle Balint's.' Tamas had had enough of interrogation, and he became rather irritable and I felt enough information had been squeezed out of him.

A cool breeze blew in from the river as we packed the picnic things and returned to the car. We then drove back to Esztergom. Tamas had turned sullen, I didn't know why, but he said little more to me, and at the car park where I dropped him off he barely said goodbye even though I had thanked him profusely for his help.

That evening I ate at a pizzeria on the other side of town. I had much to think about, but what really kept going through my mind was the fact an Englishman appeared to be heavily involved in the operation in Hungary. Tamas did not know when the next barge was going to arrive and that was something I wanted to find out. Maybe I should pay Uncle Balint a visit. If I went to see Tamas' father, I would probably put Tamas in an awkward, and probably dangerous position, and although national security came first, I considered it wrong to put Tamas in danger if I could avoid it.

The following morning, I checked out and drove to Nagykanizsa, the nearest large town to Uncle Balint's farm. It was a three-hour journey, retracing the route I took a few days before when I left Koprivnica. Much had happened since then and I was still thinking about how to confront Balint. First of all, I found a hotel in Nagykanizsa, but as it was too early to check in, I went to the Fine Arts Museum, a tranquil place to put together a plan. I wandered around the town afterwards, but apart from a few interesting, mostly baroque, buildings, the town was uninspiring. The hotel was quite old, but clean with very friendly staff and it was reasonably priced. There was no private parking, but I was assured that the car would not be broken in to.

Having settled into the hotel, I decided to go and have a look at Balint's farm. It was only a short drive to the farm along a fairly straight road running through rolling wooded hills interspersed by ploughed fields already beginning to show green ahead of the summer harvest. I had viewed the farm on the google map, and I was pleased to see that there were trees around the farmhouse, some of which were conifers. I parked the car on what looked like a disused track through the woods and walked towards the farm. The thought did pass through my mind that he may be outside shooting rabbits, or other game, for supper, and a trespasser may be a fair target, but all was quiet. I approached from the side, and although there was little spring growth, the trees were close together and I could not easily be seen from the house. Smoke was rising from the one chimney in the centre of the roof which at least suggested that someone was living there even if the information from Tamas wasn't accurate.

A well-fed black and white cat appeared from behind a shed, sat down in the last sunny spot at the side of the house, but there was no sign of Balint. I wondered if there was a dog on the property, but again there was nothing to suggest a dog was present. I crept through the woods to observe the north-facing side of the house. An old grey Opel Corsa was parked in front of the door, and some way away from the house there was a garage or workshop. A rusting ploughshare was propped up against the outbuilding, but there was no tractor to be seen. Maybe Uncle Balint wasn't farming anymore and his fields had been let out or sold, and as Tamas had not mentioned an aunt to go with the uncle, I had begun to think that Balint was probably alone on the farm.

I waited in the woods until dusk and then made my way round to the more open south-facing aspect of the house. I was some fifty metres away from the house, when suddenly a light came on inside. I was so tense that I stepped back in alarm. A figure moved slowly across the window and appeared to be preparing food in a kitchen. I waited for another fifteen minutes, but no one else appeared, so before it became completely dark I returned to the car.

I thought long and hard on what my next course of action was going to be as I sat eating in yet another pizza restaurant and decided it would end with a return to London. I spoke with Anja after dinner and asked if I could stay with her the following night, and without hesitation she said yes, although I thought I probably wouldn't arrive until the early hours of the morning. I slept late on the following day and missed breakfast, but after checking out I walked into the centre of town, bought some snacks, and sat in a small park in the sunshine.

After that, I found a shop that had a sale of skiwear, and purchased goggles, gloves and a balaclava. I found another museum to visit in the afternoon, and in the cafe there I had a late lunch.

At around four o'clock I went to the car, still parked outside the hotel, and drove to a village about forty minutes' walk away from Balint's farm. I had looked at the map and plotted a shortcut through the woods to the farm, but by road I reckoned the walk would take well in excess of an hour. I parked behind an abandoned house, well out of sight from the main road, and walked through the back garden into the woods. The first part of the hike was difficult with the ground boggy in places, but eventually I found a rough, ill-marked path that wound its way towards the farm. The sun had set by the time I reached my destination, and to my annoyance his car was not there.

I moved round to a position quite close to the front door and donned my balaclava and gloves with goggles ready to put on. I kept well hidden just in case anyone was at home, but all was quiet. I waited, and waited, cursing myself for not having taken action the previous night, but just as I was beginning to despair I saw some headlights through the trees. The car was eased slowly onto the gravel outside the house and a PIR light came on and illuminated the man emerging from the vehicle.

He was older than I had expected, probably in his mid to late sixties, quite short and decidedly overweight. He was humming to himself and appeared to be drunk. When he reached the door of the house, I pulled my goggles into position, leapt out of the shadows, and in ten strides I had reached him.

With an arm around his throat and two knuckles in the small of his back, I said, 'Move and you're dead.'

Chapter 17

As I said those words, I thought he probably didn't understand English, but apart from gurgling something, presumably in Hungarian, he didn't move. Worried that I might strangle him, I relaxed my grip a little.

In an angry, but resigned, voice he said, something that I interpreted as 'What do you want?'

I replied by saying, 'Do you speak English?'

'Nem' was the reply, so I tried Russian. He let out his breath and squeaked a few words in Russian which gave me some optimism that we would be able to communicate.

I thought it likely that, as a farmer, he probably had a shotgun in the house, and if indeed he was smuggling weapons, then he may have had a handgun. I made it clear that he would suffer if he tried any tricks and he appeared to be acquiescent. I asked him if he had any rope. He nodded in the direction of the car. I marched him to the vehicle, aware that he could regard this as an opportunity to try and escape. He opened the boot, and just to the left of the spare wheel there was a monkey wrench. He made a grab for it, but I kicked him hard in the left calf and he let out a yelp of pain and missed his target. I picked up the monkey wrench and brought it crashing down on his left hand.

'Now, are you going to behave?' I said, in Russian. He whimpered, and I took that to be a yes. Without further trouble he extracted the rope from the car and I released the hold I had on his neck. I now had a weapon and my assessment was that Uncle Balint would not fare too well in a fair fight.

The next problem was what to tie him to. As we entered the house and put the hall light on, my eyes fell on a door to a loft space in the single storey dwelling. I asked if there was a ladder to the attic. He didn't seem to understand, but by jumping up with the wrench in my hand I was able to release the catch on the door, and it dropped open to reveal an aluminium ladder. I told Balint to sit on the floor. He did, but he was in obvious pain and for the time being I felt he posed no danger to me. I extended the ladder and invited him to lean back on it. I then proceeded to tie him to it. He made no protest and made no further attempt to escape.

Blood was gently dripping from his left hand and I was worried that he might die from a loss of blood. I thought it would probably be in my best interests to keep this man alive, so I looked around for a medicine cabinet. He began moaning, and it occurred to me that I had better relieve him of his mobile phone just in case he managed to extract it from his pocket and make a call. In the bathroom cabinet, I found a basic first aid kit and I set about patching up Balint. Administering first aid wearing gloves was a difficult and messy task, especially when the recipient is constantly snarling at you, but although there were no expressions of gratitude, there was a noticeable improvement to his hand. I then went for a look around the house.

There were two bedrooms. One was relatively tidy but dusty and appeared to be the guest room. The other was dirty, smelly and a complete mess with a half empty bottle of *palinka* on the table next to the single bed. A large 'still life' picture on the wall merely added to the disorder in the room. I looked into the wardrobe and without hesitation I left to try somewhere else. The large kitchen with an ancient oak table was cleaner and tidier than I had expected.

A shotgun was propped up next to the fridge, otherwise it looked like any other kitchen on any other farm. In the lounge there was a small television, which must have been at least thirty years old, a leather sofa that appeared to be even older and a newer chair in front of the television. In the corner, there was a writing desk with an open laptop on it. Two cupboards on the side of the desk were open and contained magazines and a few papers, but the drawer on the desk was locked.

I wondered how easy it would be to get the key from Balint. He was still securely tied to the ladder, head drooped. When he heard me come in, he looked up and uttered '*macska, macska.*'

I looked blank.

After a pause he said, '*Kot.*' I thought maybe he was tired, and I just ignored him. He then went 'Meow, meow.' and I was beginning to think he was losing his senses.

I asked him where the keys were and he indicated the rear. I then realised the keys were still attached to the front door. There were six keys on the key ring. Two were obviously for the car, another was the front door key, and one of the remaining three also looked like a front door key, perhaps for the garage or workshop building. I tried one of the other keys in the writing table drawer. It opened without a problem.

Inside the drawer there was a pack of playing cards, a silver cross attached to a string of beads, two wads of high denomination forint notes, and a grey revolver. I had a look through the playing cards to see if there were some hidden codes or something else of interest, but the pack seemed to be completely normal. The used banknotes had nothing unusual about them, but the gun did. It was an Iranian made nine-millimetre Zoaf pistol. I had learnt about them in training, but this was the first one that I had seen. I was puzzled.

There were two remaining keys on the key ring. I decided to search again for a wall safe. Of course, any wall safe was likely to have a combination lock, but there was a chance that there could be one with an ordinary key lock. I tried the spare bedroom first, but it didn't take long to establish that the wall in that room had not been interfered with, and apart from the almost empty wardrobe and a bedside shelf with an alarm clock on it, the room was bare. An old striped mattress was all that bedecked the wrought iron bed, and under the bed the layer of dust was even thicker than in the rest of the room. The other bedroom proved a challenge. The fitted wardrobe was crammed with all sorts of things. A jewellery box contained a couple of brooches, some hatpins and a pearl necklace. Jewels from a bygone era I thought, perhaps an inheritance. It made me think that there probably wasn't a safe, but I continued to examine the wardrobe, making sure there was no removable back to it.

As I stood at the door to leave the room, I turned, just to see if I had missed anything. I looked at the ugly still life painting on the wall and walked over to it and lifted the side a little. The paint had peeled away, and I smiled at the idea of covering a paint blemish with a picture, and the number of pictures I would need to buy to make my bedroom in Tooting more presentable. I lifted the painting a little more, and there was what looked like a metal plate. I gently took the painting off the wall and it revealed quite a large grey metal rectangle flush with the wall. No effort had been made to redecorate after the safe had been installed.

I felt a tingle of excitement as I tried to insert the key into the lock. It was reluctant to turn and I tried the other key. It was soon obvious that the first key was the most likely one to be right and I persevered. Eventually there was a click and I was able to pull open the heavy door. I was amazed to see that it was completely stuffed with banknotes. There must have been tens of thousands of

Forints in that safe. A few of the wads were in a bag. I took it out for an examination. It was made of some kind of heavy-duty plastic, and on the sides there was a stamp which read 'S*outhern Polypropylene, Victoria, Australia.*' I immediately thought of Greg and wondered if he knew anything about this development.

I took a photograph of the label, and I also photographed a box which contained several nine millimetres bullets. I removed the money and the box of bullets from the safe and ran my gloved hand around the inside, but there was nothing else. I left the contents on the floor. I wasn't going to take anything for myself even though I was sure the money had been obtained by nefarious activities.

Balint looked thoroughly dejected, his head slumped forward and his face grey from the trauma of the evening. His bandaged hand looked alright, but the other one was whiter than I would have liked. He mumbled something as I approached him but fortunately he didn't appear to be offering any resistance. I asked him where all the money had come from.

'You know that.' He replied with contempt.

'He owed it to me.'

'Who?' I asked, somewhat surprised.

'Horvath, of course.'

'Did you kill him?' I asked, as the jigsaw pieces began to fit together.

'He wanted to leave the organisation and the Englishman told my friend that I would die if I didn't get rid of him. It's all over for me now anyway,' and his limited Russian gave way to a monologue of self-pity in Hungarian. I left him for a moment and returned to his bedroom and looked at the wads of money scattered over the floor. I picked up one bundle and the banknotes were not Forints, they were Euros.

I went back to the hall where Balint was now gently weeping. 'Who is your friend that told you about the Englishman?'

He looked up and sneered. I moved back as I thought he was going to spit, but he didn't.

'Okay, you're not going to tell me.' I said, lightly. 'But you are going to tell me where the drugs and guns are from.'

He looked baffled. 'What guns?'

'The guns you get from your brother.' I said.

'I don't get any guns.' He was getting his fighting spirit back.

'That pistol in the drawer, and the bullets in your safe, where did they come from?'

'I have had them for years; my brother gave them to me. I've never used a gun.' He said, defiantly.

I believed him, 'but where do the drugs come from?'

'Turkey, I suppose.' Balint seemed happy that the conversation about guns was over, and I felt hopeful of making some progress on where the drugs arrived from, but I was wrong.

I threatened him, by saying that I would go to the police and mention the murder of Sandor. That did frighten him a bit, but he appeared to know little about the drugs, other than that they were stored on his farm for a while before being smuggled across the border into Croatia. I asked why he thought the drugs originated from Turkey.

'Sandor used to say he went there to meet the smugglers. He thought he was an important man.' Balint said, bitterly, 'But he was nobody.'

'Didn't Sandor have a wife?' I asked.

Balint looked up. 'Yes.'

'Did you meet her at all?'

'No, she didn't want to come here, to Hungary, I mean.'

'Where did she live?' He regarded me suspiciously.

'Who are you? Why are you asking all these questions?'

'We're just trying to stop the drug smuggling.' I replied.

'You won't,' he said, assertively 'It's a very big business, too big for you, whoever you are.'

'Can you answer just one more question for me?' I asked hopefully.

He just stared at me. I asked the question anyway. 'Where does Sandor's wife live?'

He thought about the question and replied, 'Batumi in Georgia, satisfied?'

Chapter 18

I could not think of any more questions relevant to the smuggling and it was then up to me to make my escape back to Ljubljana. I explained to Balint what I intended to do and he seemed surprised that I wasn't going to kill him. I did threaten to punish him, though, if he didn't adhere to my strict terms for his release. I asked him if he had any more mobile phones other than the one I had found in his pocket.

He hesitated, and said, 'No.'

I could tell he was lying, and I said. 'Try again.' He didn't quite understand, but after a short silence he responded by saying there was a mobile on the table in the workshop, and I could find a torch in the kitchen.

I took the keys and walked across the gravel drive to the workshop. Unsurprisingly, the workshop was as untidy as most of the house. Disused farming implements, covered in dust and the webs of long dead spiders were propped up against the breeze blocked walls with old household goods that were never quite discarded. The mobile phone was on the table, along with a tablet. Interestingly, there were piles of the polypropylene bags, similar to the one that I had found in the safe. I went through them one by one, wondering about their original use. I smelt one and thought I detected the odour of marijuana, but it could have been my imagination. At the bottom of one of the last bags that I looked at there was a fragment of paper. It was faded and curled up but the script intrigued me. A few words were in English but the majority were in what looked like Arabic. I pocketed the piece of paper and carrying the tablet and phone I returned to the house.

A cat was sitting at Balint's feet looking up and meowing. I surmised that the cat needed food, and that was why Balint had been behaving strangely earlier in the evening. I took the mobile phones, laptop, tablet, the gun and ammunition and put them in the boot of the car. I also took the landline telephone out of the wall socket and put that in Balint's car. I then showed him the piece of paper which contained a rough map of where I was going to park the car. After that, I took a knife from the kitchen and wheeled the chair from in front of the writing desk into the hall. Balint looked mystified, especially when I untied the ropes fastening his legs to the ladder and asked him to sit in the chair. He complied meekly after implying that plan B was to knock him out. I then untied his hands before securing them to the arms of the chair. I felt that this was a dangerous moment, but his hands appeared numb and he offered no resistance.

The last part of my plan to keep Balint out of circulation for a couple of hours, involved pushing the chair outside and attaching the remains of the tow rope to the car with the other end attached securely to the chair. The idea was to drag the chair and Balint some distance up the drive and then release his hands so he could crawl back to the house and free himself. Unfortunately, I hadn't factored in the inability of wheeled chairs to move freely over gravel. The chair toppled over almost immediately and Balint let out a yelp of pain. I looked at the position of the chair and Balint and concluded that I could still drag the combination along without causing him unnecessary pain. I began the tow at a very slow speed, and for a while it worked, but after about fifty metres there was a scream of pain.

I investigated and found one of the arms had become detached from the chair with Balint's arm ready to become detached from his body. Light from the hall illuminated a shallow trench in the gravel, ending where the farmer was moaning on the ground. I untied the towrope from the car and freed Balint's hands.

I was fairly sure he would need a knife to undo the remainder of the ropes securing him and I took the kitchen knife and left it on the doormat. I made sure that Balint was able to crawl with the remains of the chair on his back, and I reckoned it would take him a minimum of half an hour to get back to the house, with another few minutes to free himself.

There were no parting words as I drove away, but I felt certain he would be able to separate himself from the chair and I thought it unlikely that he had now had the means to contact anyone from the farm. If he set off for the village as soon as he freed himself, it would allow me about an hour and a half to flee the area, and by that time I should be back in Slovenia. I had no compassion for Balint. He knew what he was doing, and his actions, combined with those of his fellow criminals, had led to countless deaths, and misery for many others.

It was almost midnight by the time I arrived in the village where the car was parked. Nearly everyone appeared to be sleeping with only two houses showing lights. I parked the Corsa at the back of the deserted house and transferred to the Clio. It was a great relief when I left the village, but there was a long way to go.

It was after one in the morning, when I reached Slovenia. I stopped at the service station just across the border, filled the car with petrol and called Anja. I thought she may be irritated by the lateness of the call, but I had forgotten that it was Saturday night, and in fact she had only just returned home after an evening out with friends, so there was no problem. I bought a chocolate bar and a soft drink from the shop to sustain me for the rest of the journey and set off for Ljubljana. It was a good feeling to be back in Slovenia even though there was another two hours driving ahead of me. A police car followed me for a while after the Lendava exit, otherwise the trip back was uneventful. It was difficult to find a parking space anywhere close to Anja's flat, and it was almost four in the morning by the time I pressed the button on the intercom to be let in.

We had a long lie-in on Sunday morning, followed by a large brunch. As the day was fine and pleasantly warm, we decided to go for a walk in the woods. Even though there were many people out walking, it was easy to find some empty tracks, and as we walked I told her much of what had occurred in my life since we had last met. She was surprised to hear about the gun smuggling operation, but otherwise she absorbed the information without comment. While I had been away Anja had led a mundane existence of study, selling sauerkraut and mingling with students.

No large consignment of drugs had appeared on the campus, and Greg had not been in the city as far as she knew. There was a two-day security course she had to attend, and the lecturer amused Anja by saying it was the time to be especially vigilant when dealing with British people. She implied that there was a deep distrust of the British security services among the counterparts in her own intelligence organisation.

We then went on to lighter subjects before having dinner in a cosy restaurant close to the woods. It was time to make some difficult decisions. Both Anja and I were aware that it would be hard to justify to my employer a continuance of my stay in Slovenia. I tried to persuade Anja to come and live with me in London, but I knew the answer would be no, and I felt guilty that I was trying to entice her away from a mission that she was pursuing with the same fervour that I was. She tried to persuade me to remain in Ljubljana but visions of spending my working life, at best translating in the university, or at worst selling sauerkraut in the market, was a prospect I wasn't willing to face. I knew that this was more than a holiday romance but the impasse was profound.

We returned to Anja's flat after dinner, opened a bottle of wine and listened to music. It cheered us both up and the rest of the evening, and much of the night, was spent blissfully, with the future blanked out of our minds. Anja wasn't working on Monday and had no lectures, so we had the day to ourselves, but first I had to file a report for London to let my boss know I was returning home, and then to book a flight to Gatwick. I had hoped there would be a morning flight on Tuesday, but the earliest seat available was not until Wednesday afternoon. It would mean more time with Anja, but once the decision to leave had been made I would have preferred not to prolong the pain.

Monday was one of those rare soft Spring days with no clouds and no wind. Anja suggested that we go to the beach. I hadn't realised that Ljubljana was so close to the tiny Slovenian coastline that is less than fifty kilometres long, stretching from the Italian border in the north to the Croatian border in the south. It took less than ninety minutes to reach Koper, the largest coastal town. Originally, there were two small islands with fishing communities surrounded by shallow water and marshlands, but over the centuries land reclamation had taken place and the islands have been absorbed into a town of twenty-five thousand people. We walked around the old town and the Italian influence was very noticeable with the twelfth century cathedral and the fifteenth century palace both showing a remarkable resemblance to buildings in Venice.

We had lunch at an expensive restaurant next to the marina, and Anja told me about the port. Tourism was flourishing and the massive cruise liners often visited. It was also a major container port, and she wondered if the drugs were leaving on container ships. I had almost forgotten about the drug smuggling, but the reality was that we had no idea yet how the drugs were being distributed through Europe. A cold mist rolled in from the sea after lunch, and Anja suggested that we should drive back towards Ljubljana and visit Predjama Castle on the way.

It was an excellent place to spend the remainder of the day. The stunning castle, built in, and around, limestone caves, and set in a beautiful park looked at its best under the clear blue sky, and away from the coast it was pleasantly warm again. We arrived back at Anja's flat as night fell, and while she was preparing food for us I checked my messages. There was one from London and it was marked 'Very Urgent'.

It read, 'Your work has been exemplary, but we insist that you do not return to England at this time. We believe that you have other leads to follow. It is necessary that we close this channel of communication but of course the emergency code will remain operational. *Bonne chance.*'

I felt I had been cut loose, that my own security had been compromised. I didn't understand it. Yes, I had several leads, but I would have liked guidance or encouragement towards the direction I was taking. It was as if my boss was absolving himself of responsibility. There was nothing to say that I was in immediate danger, but also nothing to say what I should do next.

Over dinner, we ignored the future and talked of our time together, the time, albeit short, that we had spent talking, discussing, learning and above all laughing. We kept up the pretence that it wasn't going to end, but deep down there was this tightness in the stomach as impending sorrow tried to fight its way to the surface. I had not shared the message from London with Anja, partly because we had this rule about not talking about work in the flat, and partly because I was filled with uncertainty about how to react to the text. As it happened, the evening went well, and we had an early night, mainly because Anja was working the next day.

It was six in the morning when I prepared breakfast for us and before seven Anja bade me a cheery farewell and swished out of the door. Firstly, I cancelled my Wednesday flight to Gatwick and then sat for a long while deciding what to do next. I concluded it was time to pay Nino a visit, and I tried to book a flight to Georgia. It was easier than I thought it would be. There was a flight to Tbilisi, via Warsaw, leaving early that afternoon, and the next one was not until Friday, so I somewhat reluctantly booked the afternoon flight, and found a hotel for the night in the Georgian Capital.

I felt quite upset about leaving a day early, although in some ways it was probably an easier parting. Nevertheless, I felt guilty, and I knew how unhappy she would be when she came home. I had an hour before I needed to leave for the airport, so I went out and bought a big bunch of flowers and a box of Anja's favourite chocolate biscuits. At least, it made me feel better. Just before I left, I rang her to tell her of my plans, but the phone was switched off. I sent a short text and hoped that she would be able to view it, and then left a brief message next to the flowers and biscuits. I put the spare key back in the pot in the kitchen, took my luggage and left. It was a sad moment, but if destiny decides that we should meet again, then so be it. Those were my thoughts as I walked round the corner to the car.

The flight to Tbilisi was via Warsaw, but the first part of the trip was short, less than an hour and a half and there was plenty of time to catch the connecting flight. There was a delay leaving Warsaw, and the weather *en route* was poor with plenty of turbulence. By the time we reached Tbilisi airport, it was after two in the morning local time. I had read that I needed Georgian currency, as dollars and euros were not accepted in shops. Of course, I had credit cards, but I wasn't sure if taxi drivers accepted them. I changed money at the ATM, but as it happened the taxi driver took card payment. It was after three before a bleary-eyed receptionist handed me a key to the room. I was very tired, but alert enough to ask if there was a room available for the following night as well. There was, and I fell into a deep sleep safe in the knowledge that I didn't need to rush out of the hotel later that morning.

I just managed to beat the time deadline for breakfast, but the staff were so friendly, I would have been surprised if I had been thrown out of the breakfast room even if it had been the middle of the afternoon. The sky was clear and the view from the hillside hotel was inviting me to spend a day exploring the city. Firstly, I had to make a phone call to Batumi. Tamas had told me that Nino was the name of Sandor's wife, and not the shortened name of an Italian waiter, as I had previously supposed. It occurred to me that she may have changed her number, or perhaps she only spoke Georgian or Hungarian. I called the number. It was answered by a woman in an unintelligible language.

I tried English. 'Yes, I'm Nino, what do you want?'

She replied in clear English. I had a strategy to try and get her to meet with me, but I wasn't confident it would work. 'I would like to talk to you about Sandor.'

There was a long pause. 'He's dead, isn't he?'

'Yes.' I replied, trying to sound as compassionate as I could.

There was another long pause. 'Can I come and talk to you about him?'

'Who are you? Are you a friend?' She said, with a hint of aggression in her voice.

'No.' I said.

'I work for an agency trying to eliminate illegal drugs.'

'Do you?' She said, but not expecting an answer.

I thought that the hints from both Tamas and Balint that she wasn't keen on drugs might help my cause.

'I don't know.' she said, vaguely. 'Are you in Batumi?' Her voice sounded more affable.

'No, but I will be tomorrow.'

Another pause 'After three o'clock, then.'

'Can you tell me where you live, then? Please.' I said, after another lengthy silence.

I vaguely understood the address she gave me and hoped the road signs would be in a script that I understood. The conversation ended there and my next task was to book a rail ticket to Batumi. That was easily done online, and then I looked on a google map to see where the address was and booked a week in a nearby apartment block. It had been a problem-free morning and that left me plenty of time to explore Tbilisi.

The hotel was situated near the top of a steep hill with an uneven pavement down to the river, but once there, the exploration began. Interesting churches, one supposedly dating back to the fifth century, were the main attractions, especially with the mesmeric Gregorian chants used in the religious services. A fortress, again with origins from the fifth century, was atop a very steep hill, and ancient sulphur baths, around which the city was allegedly founded in the fifth century.

Finally, I visited the unexpectedly pretty waterfall that fell from a vertical cliff a mere ten minutes' walk from the bustle of city life. Many of the signs were in English, and in the shops and restaurants English was widely spoken. Despite it being early in the season, there were quite a few tourists in the city, and many of them were speaking Russian. Having had a large breakfast, I skipped lunch and stayed in the centre for dinner. I had *Kachapuri,* a dish not too dissimilar to a pizza, and the Ossetian version that I had contained potato. The bread, plenty of cheese and potato was very filling, but the homemade ice cream was too tempting to miss. At the end of the evening, I walked over the spectacular floodlit 'Bridge of Peace' and across the park towards the hotel. The park was poorly lit and many couples were walking or sitting on the benches, but strangely I didn't feel there was a risk of being mugged. Perhaps I was wrong to think that, but my main thought was of Anja, and how I wished we were walking together through this park.

It was an early start on the following morning with the train scheduled to leave the central station at eight. The receptionist advised me to leave extra early as the traffic during the mornings was particularly heavy. She was right. I had allowed nearly an hour to get to the station just three kilometres away, but to catch the train I felt the need to walk the last four hundred metres. It was a good decision. I was still searching for my allotted seat when the modern double-decker train began pulling out of the station for the five-hour trip to Batumi. A young Spanish couple on their honeymoon sat opposite me, and when they found out that I understood Spanish, their life history tumbled out.

The time passed quickly, although there was plenty of interest outside as the train sped through the Georgian countryside. The last leg of the trip was along the Black Sea coast, and although the beaches and sea looked uninviting, there was some stunning scenery. The modern station at Batumi was some way out of the centre by the coast, and I decided to walk into the city along the path by the sea. A brisk wind was coming in off the sea and compared to Tbilisi it was decidedly chilly. It took longer than expected to find my apartment which was situated on the fifth floor of a modern high-rise block. It was very light and spacious, and also remarkably good value for money when compared to some apartments I had stayed in across central and western Europe. A concierge relieved me of my passport, apparently a normal practice in Georgia, and I was left to unpack my trolley suitcase.

It was after four in the afternoon before I found Nino's flat on the first floor of an old Soviet era block. There was no intercom outside, just a door that led on to a staircase that appeared to go forever upwards. On door two hundred and five, there was a hand-written nameplate which read 'Glonti.' I knocked gently and the door was almost immediately opened.

'Nino?' I asked.

She nodded and pushed the door wide open to let me in. I introduced myself, automatically went to shake her hand but she was unresponsive. She seemed to float around the flat and so far she hadn't said a word. I eyed her with curiosity. She was tall and thin with long dark brown hair containing natural looking flecks of grey. I guessed she was in her late thirties and had once been very attractive, but she was not wearing well. Her big brown eyes were lustreless, and the red rims suggested she had been crying, or was suffering from sleepless nights. She was wearing a long, mainly black, dress and round her neck was a string of orange beads.

In very good English she said, 'Would you like a cup of tea?' I replied in the affirmative and at that moment noticed a child sitting cross-legged on a chair in a room off to the left playing on an iPad.

'Is that your daughter?' I said, nodding in the direction of the room. I knew the answer, but it was a way to break the ice.

'Yes.' She responded with a hint of a smile.

'She's called Tamar. Sandor was her father, you know.'

'Yes, I know.' I replied awkwardly. Nino removed two Lipton's tea bags from a box in the kitchen and placed them in white mugs with the black inscription in English.

'Say no.'

'Say no to what?' I asked, pointing at the mugs. It produced another half-smile.

'We say no to many things in Georgia. It's a national pastime.'

'And you said, no to drugs I hear.'

She looked at me intently. 'Who are you?'

There was an emphasis on each word, and I could see that she was still suspicious of me. I realised that there was a risk involved if I told her too much about my mission, but it was important that Nino trusted me. We sat down in the lounge.

After I had finished explaining the purpose of my visit, she sat for a while in silence. There was a clock ticking somewhere in the flat, and an occasional noise came from the game that Tamar was playing on the computer.

'How did Sandor die?'

I had been expecting that question, and in the circumstances I thought it best to lie. 'There was a fire in his house.'

Nino absorbed the statement. 'He was probably completely stoned,' she said and went on.

'He told me he wanted to get away from these criminals and just paint. He was doing quite well, you know.'

And she pointed at a colourful naive painting on the wall. 'He sold several paintings last year, and he had some exhibited in Zagreb.'

After another pause she said, 'I still love him, you know.' And then tears welled up in her eyes. 'But not now, no, not anymore, he's dead.' The full realisation of his death hit her and she burst into a flood of tears.

Tamar put her iPad aside and looked accusingly at me with big round eyes as she hugged her mother. It took several minutes before she composed herself. I asked if I should leave, but she said, 'no.' I offered to make her another cup of tea, but gently pushing Tamar aside she stood up and glided into the kitchen. Tamar sat glowering at me while I desperately tried to think of something to say to her. I asked her what game she was playing on the iPad, but that resulted in no change to her demeanour.

I was rescued by the return of Nino with two fresh cups of tea. She quietly guided Tamar back to her seat in the corner and she resumed her game but with occasional pauses to glare menacingly at me.

'How did you meet Sandor?' I asked, feeling that she was now ready to talk more about her late husband.

'We met here in Batumi. I was training to become a teacher and he was running an export business in Hopa.'

'Where's Hopa?' I asked.

'It's in Turkey.' Nino replied.

'And what was he exporting?' I asked.

'Rice,' was the reply.

'Rice!' I was taken aback. 'Why rice?'

She said, 'It was a special rice that was popular in certain parts of Europe.' *I bet it was*, I thought to myself.

'Did you see any of the rice yourself?'

'Yes,' Nino replied, 'Sandor took me to Hopa once and showed me the containers.'

'Did you know where they came from?' I asked. This was now becoming very interesting.

'No, not exactly.' She answered, 'but I remember he had a big problem with one of the containers, and that was in Tabriz.'

'That's in Iran, isn't it?' I interrupted.

'Yes.' She replied. 'Quite close to the Turkish border.'

We talked for a little longer, but it was becoming like a cross examination and it was obvious that Nino was tiring. It was coming up to Easter and Nino had promised Tamar a trip to the park for a picnic on the following day and to my surprise, Nino asked if I would like to join them. I accepted and left the dingy flat in the hope that more useful information would be forthcoming in the park.

It was dusk, and there were plenty of people around, but for some reason I felt very foreign in Batumi. At one stage, I thought I was being followed, but decided it was paranoia. A casual look behind me when I reached my apartment block confirmed that no one was trailing me. I spoke to Anja for a while on messenger and I was pleased that she wasn't upset by my hurried exit from Ljubljana. I felt she was the only one that I could trust, and apart from her, no other person knew of my whereabouts. There was then a knock on the door.

Chapter 19

I thought it was probably the concierge, so I was not unduly alarmed, but when I opened the door I was faced with a very odd-looking gentleman. He was quite tall, with unruly greying hair, a prominent dark moustache above a row of white teeth that were smiling at me. What made him appear odd, though, were his eyes, which seemed to have been placed either side of his nose as an afterthought. 'Ahmet Sahin,' the man said, 'I think you were expecting me.' He stuck out a hand for me to shake, but in my confused state I ignored it.

His English was good, but the accent was a cross between Eton and Essex. I said nothing and just stared.

'Mister Boateng. Here is my calling card.' He reached into his jacket and produced a rectangular piece of cardboard. I looked at it.

My eyebrows rose as I read, 'Sandor Horvath, Import and Export, Hopa.'

'Where did you get this?' I said.

'I made it last week.' Ahmet replied. The teeth smiled at me again. 'You had better come in,' I said.

'Thank you.' He bounded in, produced a gadget from his pocket and proceeded to stride round the apartment pointing the laser-type implement at various objects. I looked on totally bemused. I had hardly unpacked, so I wasn't too concerned about anything being stolen, but I did wonder what this peculiar man was doing.

After three or four minutes he returned to where I was standing by the door to the hall and said, 'All clear, can't be too careful these days.'

Another smile. I was beginning to like him. His persona was that of the village idiot, but his button-like eyes exuded intelligence and I felt that he was someone who should not be crossed.

'Are you going out to eat? Would you like me to take you to a good restaurant?' Ahmet was in full flow.

'How do I know you're not going to take me up a dark alley and put a knife in my back?' I retorted.

'You English are so funny Seen. Can I call you Seen?' A reappearance of the teeth.

'Firstly, I'm not English, try Irish and Jamaican, secondly I'm not being funny, and thirdly my name is Sean not Seen.' I peered into the buttons and the mouth briefly shut.

'Okay, I'm sorry,' and then Ahmet spoke to me in Arabic.

From the time spent with Youssef, I had learnt much Arabic, but apart from self-consciously using it on rare occasions in Morocco, I had not engaged in Arabic conversation. I was slow to react, but I followed his lead and we had a trivial chat before he reverted to English again.

'Who are you working for?' I asked.

'The common good.' He replied.

'You're Turkish, yes?' I was intrigued by this man.

'In part, but other parts are from elsewhere.' He laughed.

'Why should I trust you?' I was aware they were words I had used on several occasions during this assignment, but important words, nevertheless.

'And why should I trust you, Sean?' The emphasis was on Sean, and there was obvious relief that he had managed to negotiate my first name. For some reason, I hadn't expected him to question my trust and I just weakly said,

'But you do, don't you?' He nodded and without a smile just said, 'The common good.'

Weighing up the risks, I decided that a walk through the dimly lit streets of Batumi with Ahmet would probably not cost me my life, and so it proved. He took me to a restaurant with a very French-sounding name that served very typical Georgian food. It was cheap, the food was good, and as Easter was approaching, it was fairly full. I tried to elicit some information about Ahmet's reasons for latching on to me but he remained evasive. I reciprocated, but nevertheless we had a pleasurable evening talking about the world in general, and by the time the bill arrived I felt I understood more of the personality behind that toothy grin.

I told him that I was meeting Sandor's ex-wife for a picnic lunch, but Ahmet expressed no surprise at that statement and that left me feeling that maybe I had been followed back to the apartment from Nino's flat on the previous afternoon. Ahmet and I arranged to meet by the bamboo grove in Batumi Boulevard, a park by the coast, at lunchtime on Saturday. Outside the restaurant we went our separate ways, and for me it was just a short walk back to the apartment block.

There was some bottled water in the fridge, but apart from two tea bags and two sachets of coffee there was nothing, so in the morning I hastily visited the local supermarket, which just happened to be a well-stocked Carrefour. It was a fine and warm morning, and at that moment I felt just like a holidaymaker. After breakfast, I unpacked and prepared for the picnic lunch. I wanted to make a generous contribution as I felt sorry for Nino and the child that would never see her father again. With two bags of food and soft drinks, I walked round to Nino's flat. A knock on the door was answered by Tamar.

I smiled and said, 'hello,' and there was the merest hint of a smile in return before she skipped off into the lounge. She pulled another girl from the room and Tamar addressed me in Georgian, or at least I presumed it was Georgian.

When she had finished I said, 'Hello,' to the other girl and she was brave enough to say 'Hello,' in English before they both ran off into the lounge.

A few moments later Nino emerged from the bedroom. She looked as if she had dressed for the theatre, rather than the park, and there was a strong smell of perfume. My clothing was necessarily more modest, but she was warm in her greeting and to my surprise she immediately came up and kissed me on the cheek. It took a while to collect everything together, but with arms laden we strolled off towards the park.

We went into a crowded area with a big lake, but Nino said that was not our destination and we carried on to another park closer to the sea. Nino spread out a blanket under a tree between, what looked like a set of Doric columns, and a children's playground. Before we had even set up our little picnic area the girls had run off to the playground and the two of us sat down on the simple chairs we had brought with us and prepared lunch. We had far too much food, but it was an experience that was making Nino happy, and she was very chatty.

While we waited for the girls to arrive for lunch, I gently turned the subject to Sandor.

They had married ten years ago after Nino had realised that she was pregnant and Sandor was pleased to move from Hopa across the border to Batumi. The first few years were good, but then drugs became an issue. Both of them had smoked cannabis, but Nino had given up when she found out that she was pregnant. Sandor continued smoking and that irritated Nino, but the relationship was still sound, until one day he left his mobile at home and a message arrived.

Nino read it in good faith, thinking it may be something she could convey to his office in Hopa. The SMS was in some form of code and Nino immediately suspected that Sandor was having an affair. She confronted him on his return home and he pleaded innocent. A big row developed and then he told her about the drug smuggling.

At first, it placated her and on a couple of occasions she and Sandor had dinner with a fellow smuggler and his wife. At this stage, I asked if she knew much about the couple. She said she didn't. They were Turkish and she didn't like them. It was nothing to do with the country they came from. She said she knew Turkish people in Batumi who were friendly enough, but even so, I suspected that there was an underlying prejudice. I questioned her further on the Turkish couple, but apparently the evenings ended with the men talking together in one room, whilst she was left with Feray, the wife, to do the clearing up, and engage in banal chat.

The girls then came running back from the playground and serious conversation ceased as the picnic lunch began. The adults were largely ignored, but while I was keen to extract more information from Nino, I had to hold back until lunch was over. It was Nino who restarted the subject spoken about before the meal by saying. 'There was something I remember about the evenings. They talked about the Englishman, and it seems they were both afraid of him.'

'Do you know him?'

'No.' I replied, 'I have heard of him, but I was hoping that you may know a little more than me.'

'Sandor and this man, sorry, I've forgotten his name, had met him. I think he was the boss.'

'Do you know where he lives?' I asked gently.

'Not in England.' Nino responded, 'Something went wrong once and Sandor flew in a hurry to Budapest, that's all I know.'

It made me think that he may have been flying off for a meeting at the restaurant in Esztergom.

The conversation dwindled and the girls were urging Nino to take them to the beach and she gave in to them. The beach was only a couple of hundred metres away, but it was almost deserted. The grey, stony foreshore looked singularly uninviting, but the girls trotted down to the water's edge and seemed content building towers and walls from the flat stones. I changed tack with Nino and asked why they had split up. She said that he spent more time away, and although plenty of money was coming in, she wasn't happy that it was probably illegally gained. They had rows, and eventually he left. They had stayed married, and he had always supported Tamar financially. She began to cry as she said, 'He told me he was selling his paintings and that he wanted to get out of the business he was in. I hoped we might get together again.'

While Nino wept, the girls continued to laugh and chatter around their pile of stones.

After a while, I asked Nino why she thought Sandor had moved to Koprivnica. She didn't really know, but he was quite happy there because it was close to his studio. Which came first, the house or the studio she didn't know. The sea breeze brought a sudden drop in temperature to the beach and the girls rapidly lost interest in building dry stone walls. We went back into the park for the remainder of the afternoon and then returned to Nino's flat. There was still plenty of food, and Nino asked me to stay for dinner. She managed to make a passable cooked meal from the picnic scraps and produced a bottle of red wine to wash them down with. The wine was Georgian and extremely good, and I wondered why I had never seen any in the shops at home. At the end of the meal, Tamar and her friend went off to bed and Nino and I tidied the kitchen.

It came as no great surprise to me that she asked if I wanted to stay the night, but I felt that Nino was vulnerable at this moment in her life, and I didn't want to complicate it further for her. Above all, though, I had this loyalty to Anja, and call it old-fashioned, but I didn't want to be unfaithful to her. I didn't make excuses, so I let her think that I was just prudish, and the rest of the evening went by in a distantly relaxed way. We arranged to meet in the park on Sunday afternoon, but already I thought there was little more to gain from questioning her.

On Saturday, I met Ahmet by the bamboo grove at the appointed time. He was all smiles and said that he was taking me on a guided walking tour of the city. I was very appreciative of a personalised tour, but I was also sure that he expected something back from me. As in most cities, there was a marked contrast between the richer and poorer areas. Modern skyscrapers, some with extravagant designs, were built alongside crumbling blocks of flats from the Soviet era. Some of the older houses appeared Germanic, but it was certainly a city on the move, with plenty of building work taking place. It was another warm and sunny day and there were crowds of people promenading, or sitting, in the parks.

Ahmet informed me that Batumi was the wettest city in the whole of the Caucasus region with over two thousand millimetres of rain a year, and that was why a sunny day enticed so many people onto the streets. I made a quick calculation and worked out it was more than three times wetter than London. Ahmet joked, that was the reason the British only stayed in Batumi for two years. Up until then I had been unaware they had been there at all, but apparently for a brief time after the First World War, British troops occupied the area, and there was a memorial to those that had lost their lives defending the city.

We stopped at a large cafe next to the harbour for a late lunch, and as expected Ahmet asked me a few questions about Nino. I told him as much as I knew and then asked him why he hadn't questioned her. He replied by saying that they had tried but she seemed to distrust policemen and Turks. I tried to corner him by asking if he was either a Turk or a policeman, but with the broadest of toothy grins. He said, 'A bit of both my friend, just a bit of both.'

It suddenly occurred to me that as he had spoken fluent Arabic to me the last time we had met, maybe he could make something of the piece of paper I had found on Balint's farm. It was in my heavy coat back in the apartment, but I had a photograph of it on my mobile. I took it out and showed it to him. For the first time, his reaction didn't include a smile.

'Where did you get this?' He said, hurriedly in a low voice.

'It was in a discarded bag on a farm in western Hungary.' I replied.

'Why, what is it?'

'It's part of a customs declaration form.' Ahmet sounded excited.

'Do you know where it is from?' I asked.

'No, but I'll be able to find out.' Ahmet responded, 'It has a number on the top and that identifies where it comes from.'

He took out his mobile and typed away for a few minutes. Eventually he said, 'Got it.'

'I thought you would.' I said, 'I can speak a bit of Arabic but not read it.'

He looked at me, and in a condescending voice said, 'It's not Arabic my friend, it's Farsi, or to you, Persian, and the form you showed me was from Bandar Abbas on the Strait of Hormuz. Time for us to take a trip to the desert.'

Chapter 20

I continued to be intrigued by Ahmet. Nothing seemed to faze him, but I knew little more about the jolly Middle Eastern man than when he knocked on my door earlier in the week. 'Are you saying that we are both going to Iran?' I said.

'What about visas and that sort of thing?'

'No problem, Mister Boateng, we'll have a holiday, you'll enjoy it.'

I gave Ahmet a strange look. While we were eating lunch, the clouds were building and people were looking skyward. Ahmet paid for the meal, and as we left the cafe a rumble of thunder came from the direction of the mountains.

'I have things to do.' Ahmet said. 'I'll be in contact.' And with a wave of his hand, he was gone. A cool breeze accompanied the downward turn in the weather and the streets quickly emptied.

I made my way back towards the apartment, but before I got there the rain started and I was drenched before I fumbled in my pockets for the door key.

The remainder of the afternoon I sat by the window watching the rain tumble down. I sent a text to Anja, but she was in a panic about an essay she was writing, and at that moment I felt alone in the world. My thoughts then turned to Bandar Abbas and I looked at the google maps to see where I might be sometime in the future. What worried me most was the weather in that part of Iran. Temperatures regularly rose into the forties from late Spring until early Autumn. It didn't look inviting.

Sunday dawned grey in Batumi and the rain poured down relentlessly. I called Nino, and she agreed that our trip to the park should be cancelled. The conversation was stilted, and it probably came through in my voice that I had gained as much information as I could from her, and further meetings would not be beneficial. In a way, I felt guilty that I had used her, but I thanked her for talking to me and wished her well for the future. We had spoken earlier about Sandor's paintings, and as she was still married to him at the time of his death, she should be able to inherit his art. I hoped so, because she was a decent woman, and her stance on drugs deserved some reward.

On Monday, I managed to add an extra week to my stay at the apartment and then went to Carrefour to shop. It was another miserable day with mist clinging to the tops of the taller buildings. It was a day for museums, and the Art and Archaeological museums provided the entertainment. Both were small, but very interesting and the exhibits were labelled in English. I spoke to a young New Zealander in the art museum and he suggested that I might enjoy a visit to the Botanic Gardens, but that was for another day. During the rest of Monday, I wandered around aimlessly, and in the evening, after cooking a meal I watched television.

There was no knock at the door from Ahmet, and on Tuesday the weather was sunny again and I took a taxi to the botanic garden. It was a few kilometres out of Batumi on a coastal hillside. The entrance was at the top of the hill and wide well-maintained paths wound their way down through plants and trees from all of the continents. The site was the idea of a Russian botanist and was constructed over a period of twenty to thirty years beginning in the late nineteenth century. It was the largest botanic garden in the former Soviet Union. All the information within the garden was written in English as well as Georgian and Russian. Plant names were in Latin and I was particularly impressed with their *Camellia japonica* which was in full bloom. Even though the garden was showing many spring colours, there were surprisingly few people in the grounds to appreciate them. I spent over four hours, either walking the paths, or sitting on the benches overlooking the sea. To the left, the high-rise buildings of Batumi stood out like a mini Manhattan skyline. It was very uplifting, but back at the apartment there was still no sign of Ahmet, and when I went to bed after another evening of watching television, I wondered if he would return.

The next morning was cloudy again and I was becoming bored, but at eleven o'clock there was a knock on the door and the ebullient Ahmet stood outside waving a couple of, what looked like, airline tickets.

'Good morning, Rachid,' he beamed at me and the button eyes moved slightly up his face.

I looked at him awaiting his next move. 'Can I come in, please?' And without an invitation he stepped inside. 'You are now a Moroccan and your name is Rachid Alami.'

I stared silently and let him continue. From the pocket on the inside of his jacket, he produced a worn looking green passport with Arabic, French and English writing on it. I opened it and there was a fairly recent photograph of me on a page that didn't look very different from my British passport.

'Where is your passport?' Ahmet asked. I remembered that it was still with the concierge.

'I think the caretaker has it.' I replied.

'Hmm,' Ahmet scowled. 'I need it,' he said sharply.

'Why?' I asked, feeling the situation was beginning to get out of control.

'Because it's not a good idea to travel into countries with two passports. The security people don't like it.' He said, sarcastically.

'Do you really think I'm going to give you my passport?' I said.

'Yes,' replied Ahmet, 'and your driving licence, and your mummy's telephone number.'

'Okay, and what will happen to my personal stuff?'

'It will be destroyed of course. Sorry, only joking. It will be well looked after and returned to you when the mission has been completed.'

'I'm not sure I like this very much,' I replied hesitantly.

'Do you get well paid? Would you rather be a bricklayer, not that I have anything against bricklayers.'

I thought about his words, and perhaps I was being something of a wimp. 'What about my laptop, my mobile, and my camera. Where are they going?'

'Same place.' Ahmet replied.

'Have you done this sort of thing before?' I asked.

'All the time, my friend, all the time.'

I could see that Ahmet was getting a bit irritated and I just said, 'Okay, when do we start.'

'Early on Thursday. It will be a long day; or two.' His toothy grin returned.

He reached inside his pocket again and produced a wallet. From another pocket came a mobile. 'Remember who you are, Rachid, and memorise the contents of your wallet. You're a lecturer in modern languages taking time out to travel. You can work out your own CV. Any questions?'

'Presumably I can't make any phone calls to let the folks know where I'm going?'

'That's right.'

'And what about you Ahmet, do you not have a family? A wife, children maybe?'

'Maybe.' Another smile, but no more personal information was forthcoming. Ahmet then busied himself going through my clothes, checking, or removing, labels and placing the articles into two piles. He produced a plastic holdall from another of his magical pockets and proceeded to stuff one of the piles of clothes into it. I just looked on, lost for words, while this was going on, and when he had finished he said, 'Could you get your passport from the caretaker and tell him that you'll be leaving early on Thursday.'

Like an obedient schoolboy I did as I was told and located the concierge who was washing the floor near the entrance to the block. He halted his work and went to a locker and retrieved my passport. He asked me to leave the key on the kitchen table on Thursday morning and shut the door, no inspection would be necessary. That went well, and I returned to the apartment.

Ahmet had made himself a strong cup of coffee and was sitting patiently surfing the net on my laptop which he was about to confiscate. I handed him the passport: he ran through it before putting it in his pocket. 'There is just one more thing, my friend,' Ahmet began, 'we have to teach you how to pray.'

'Pardon.' I said, 'This is getting ridiculous.'

'When in Rome, do as the Romans do.' Ahmet responded.

'A good Christian proverb, I believe.' He patted me on the shoulder.

I remembered Youssef saying that Moroccans were Sunni Muslims and that Iran was a mainly Shia country. I put that point to Ahmet. 'No problem, my friend. We pray together when we have to.'

'Are you Sunni or Shia?' I asked.

'Oh, a bit of this and that.' he replied.

'I have to go now.' Ahmet said, after a few moments. 'See you at the main bus station at half past six.' After a pause he said, 'In the morning.' He then proceeded to gather up my property that he had confiscated and left.

I found a pen in my jacket and I wondered if he had missed that or he had left it for me. It made me focus on my isolation, and I made my mind up not to disappear without letting someone know where I was going. The only person I had been in contact with was Anja, and although I now trusted her, I thought I might jeopardise the whole operation if I contacted her through my new mobile. So, off to Carrefour I went in search of writing paper and envelopes. I found them in the schools section, and with some snacks to sustain me I went and sat by the lake in one of the parks. It was breezy, cool and cloudy but I didn't mind, I felt like a naughty schoolboy as I wrote the letter revealing my new identity and the proposed destination.

It was written in a way that would be understood by Anja, but to anyone else it would appear like an ordinary letter from a friend. I felt relief when it was finished and I strode off in search of a stamp. It was more difficult than I thought it would be. I tried a couple of hotels without success and then a newsagent. Apparently I could only obtain stamps from the post office. The Turkish manager of the newsagents showed me how to get to the nearest post office and I joined the end of the queue for service. It took a very long time and it cost me twenty-eight Lari, which was the equivalent of six pounds Sterling.

Early on Thursday morning I left the apartment with the little luggage I had retained and walked the short distance to the bus station. Ahmet was sitting there wearing a bright red baseball hat with a huge rucksack standing in front of him. He looked ready for a holiday and I had to smile at the thought of this man being my travel companion.

When he saw me he immediately rose and hugged me saying 'Peace be upon you,' in Arabic. He then gave me an idea of what to expect in the day ahead. We caught a bus going to Hopa, the small Turkish port city about eighteen kilometres from the border, and from there we were to take a car to Trabzon. Firstly, though, we had to navigate the border. Leaving Georgia wasn't a problem, but at the Turkish customs post we had to take our luggage from the bus and queue at the border whilst the luggage was checked and we were processed. As it happened, everything went smoothly, but some passengers had to empty their suitcases, and it was nearly an hour before we re-entered the bus and continued on our way to Hopa. In Hopa, Ahmet picked up a car from a small hire company and we continued along the north coast road towards Trabzon.

The day was bright and sunny, the roads were good, and the scenery was often spectacular. There were many impressive, mostly white-walled, mosques, and we stopped to see one at Findikli, a small market town crammed between the hills and the motorway. Apart from the mosque at the end of the cobbled street, it was much like a small town anywhere in Europe, except for the women, who were very conservatively dressed. Ahmet said, we were lucky to have warm sunshine, because the north coast is normally cloudy and often wet.

Apparently ideal weather for growing tea, a crop, along with hazelnuts, which featured highly in the economy of the area. We went and had tea in a tea house, a strictly male establishment, and that morning populated by a large group of elderly men. Ahmet greeted the men, I nodded, and they resumed their cheery discussion. I was getting used to being called Rachid, and with Ahmet speaking to me in Arabic, rather than English, I was beginning to feel confident with my new identity.

We continued along the coast, and most of the time we were right next to the sea. The shoreline was mainly rocky and inaccessible, but occasionally there was a sandy cove fed by a footbridge across the motorway. Ahmet said that people didn't go to the beach because of the bad weather, but somehow I didn't believe him. He started to open up about what his plans were for us over the next few days. First of all, we were to take an evening flight from Trabzon to Istanbul, and then an overnight flight to Tabriz in Iran. I asked why the convoluted route, and he assured me it was the easiest way to get to Tabriz. It was mid-afternoon when we reached Trabzon. The airport was right by the coast before we entered the city, but as we had time to spare, Ahmet suggested that we had a look around the city itself. It was a busy place and it was noticeable that many of the young women in particular had forsaken the traditional attire and were wearing jeans and T-shirts. The shops in the pedestrianised streets were similar to those encountered in any big western town, and to the disappointment of Ahmet, I found the city uninspiring. We had a meal, then backtracked to the airport. As Ahmet was keen to point out, the holiday was yet to begin.

Chapter 21

The short evening flight to Istanbul was problem-free with the official at Trabzon Airport barely looking up when he examined my passport. After my experience on the Georgian border, I had now become less nervous about my new identity. Istanbul Airport was very busy with faces from all continents rushing through the spacious and beautifully designed terminal building for flights they were sure they were going to miss. We had a meal and waited for the overnight flight which was due to arrive around dawn on Friday. Although I managed some sleep on the journey, the flight proved to be quite bumpy, and a wailing child made deep sleep impossible. Tabriz Airport offered another tastefully constructed terminal. It, too, was busy at that early hour, and as Ahmet pointed out, it served a population of one and a half million, a city larger than Birmingham.

Just as I was becoming confident in the shell of Rachid Alami, a problem arose at Tabriz Airport. Ahmet had made a visa-on-arrival application on-line, he had thought of everything, and it had been accepted, but at the security control I was asked to fill in another form which involved another payment. The form was in Iranian only and I had no idea what it was about. The kindly official produced another form in Arabic which again proved to be difficult to understand. Ahmet stepped in and began speaking rapidly and occasionally pointing at me. After a discussion to and fro, the official gave the form to Ahmet, he filled it in and my passport was reluctantly stamped.

As we left the terminal building I asked Ahmet how he managed to negotiate my entry into Iran. He said that he spoke to the official in Azerbaijani, which endeared him to the man as that was his first language.

Ahmet went on, 'When he offered you the form in Arabic I told him you were a Berber and although you spoke Arabic, you could only understand the written Berber language. I thought it unlikely that he would have a form in Berber and he didn't.'

I thanked Ahmet for his quick thinking and wondered how many more times he would have to bail me out in this so, so different country.

To my surprise, instead of heading out of the airport to find a taxi, Ahmet joined a queue at a car hire desk. It took a while, but eventually he came over to where I was sitting with a bundle of paperwork and a set of keys. We found the car, but instead of following the signs to the city centre he drove in the opposite direction. I questioned him about it and he said, the hotel we were going to was some way out of the city because the traffic in the centre was heavy and the air very polluted. It was barely nine o'clock when we reached the hotel, but after protracted negotiations and plenty of smiles we were let into our room early.

After a much-needed sleep we took a taxi into the centre of the city, and I could understand why Ahmet had avoided this part of Tabriz as a base. A blue haze of fumes hung over the area and there was a sea of people and cars. I insisted that we went to the main railway station as this was probably where the containers from Bandar Abbas were transferred to lorries for their journey to Hopa. I was not sure what I was looking for, but Ahmet humoured me by letting me wander around the impressive nineteen-fifties-built station. There was no sign of a container terminal, and outside Ahmet pointed along the road to where the industrial area could be seen.

I suggested we went to have a look at the container area and he just said, 'Why? If you want to kill the snake you don't bite off the tail, that makes it angry. You go for the head.' He smiled.

I think I understood what he meant, and I just let him resume control. We went to the Grand Bazaar and Tarbiat Street, an ancient thoroughfare dating back to the days when the Silk Road was the main method of exchanging goods between China and Western Europe. It was Friday, and many of the shops were closed, but cafes and restaurants were packed as the locals enjoyed their traditional day off.

Although there were some interesting buildings in Tabriz, it was not a place I would go back to, and Ahmet agreed, but he said, there would be many much more interesting cities to visit in the days ahead. He was right, with Isfahan and the desert city of Yazd particular highlights of this holiday in Iran. It was hard to justify the tour and getting paid to do it, but Ahmet assured me that it was important to get a feel for the country before we reached the far south. My impression was of a country that was modern in many respects and full of friendly people, but the inequality between men and women was very noticeable.

In fact, in many places we travelled to, women were seldom seen. There were areas where poverty was apparent, but Ahmet was keen to tell me that there was a higher percentage of poor people in Spain than in Iran. As we travelled further south, however, we noticed an increasing number of poor people, and when we finally reached Bandar Abbas we came across a large section of the population living in absolute poverty. Ahmet, as usual, had planned ahead and he drove us into the backstreets of the sprawling city and stopped in front of a seedy looking tenement block. 'Look at this my friend,' he said, 'this is your new home,' and he burst out laughing.

We then drove towards the city centre and Ahmet said, 'Take a good look at the car. You won't be in one of these for a while.' We gathered our luggage, which didn't amount to much, and Ahmet went into the car rental office to drop off the car. We walked the two kilometres back to the apartment block, negotiated the maze of corridors and found the grey door which marked the entrance to our new home. I wasn't impressed. Ahmet must have caught my downcast look.

'Don't worry,' said Ahmet, 'there's air conditioning and internet, and that's more than many people have got around here.'

I wandered into the rooms. The floors were of polished stone or tiles and there were mats covering them, and in the lounge a threadbare carpet. An ancient electric cooker graced the kitchen, and although attempts had been made to clean it, residue from many dinners had become a permanent feature of this, the sole means of producing hot food. The fridge was of a similar vintage and omitted a continuous whirr of protest. The sink was large and deep with sizeable built-in drainage areas on either side. The bathroom was special. There was a squat toilet in one corner and a tiled box in another corner with a low-level shower hose attached to a tap between the two. There was no washbasin, bath or proper shower, but it was spotlessly clean. Curiously, just inside the door, there were two pairs of new flip-flops, one pink and one blue. I wailed to Ahmet, 'but there's no shower.'

'Don't worry my friend, there are several bathhouses in the city.' The windows throughout the flat were covered with thick curtains and the rooms were stuffy, but all the windows seemed to look out onto the windows of neighbouring apartments. At least, there were two bedrooms. They were identical with iron bedsteads, thin mattresses, a folded spread and a couple of cushions. A cockroach scuttled across the floor. I wasn't happy.

'Do you think this place might be bugged?' I asked.

Ahmet bellowed out, 'Not a chance, we could plot a coup here if we wanted to.' He laughed.

I was not sure why he laughed, but for me the holiday was rapidly turning sour.

'Yes, Rachid,' Ahmet was looking serious. 'I can see you do not like the new hotel, but there is a reason for it, and you will be grateful to me one day, but for now there are two very important things. The water should be okay to drink from the taps but you should boil it until your gut gets used to it. And here,' He waved a sachet of pink tablets at me. 'Malaria tablets. Don't forget to take them. Any questions?'

'Yes, plenty.' I said, 'What exactly are we going to do?'

'I hoped you wouldn't ask. Only joking.' Ahmet replied after noticing the despondent look on my face. 'We are going to find the containers with the drugs and then find out where they come from. No problem. You do the easy part. Get to know the container port, do a little work here and there, and I track the incoming and outgoing ships and find out what cargoes they carry. And, because I'll be here for most of the day, I'll do the cooking and the housework and all the other things. Does that sound like a good deal?' On the face of it did sound like a good deal, but how wrong I was.

The idea was to go to the port gates at dawn and get picked for a day's labour, but first of all I had to look more like a labourer than a tourist. This involved growing several days' stubble, wearing unwashed clothes and generally looking in a woebegone state. Thanks to the bathroom in the flat, it was quite easily accomplished, and on the following Saturday, the start of the working week, I walked to the port gates. I had no idea what to expect, but when I arrived, several men were already milling around the entrance. A few were talking to each other, but most were just standing with vacant looks on their faces. I felt a bit self-conscious, especially as I was several centimetres taller than most of the men. Looking around I was surprised to see quite a few faces that suggested roots in sub Saharan Africa.

Others appeared to be from the Indian subcontinent, but the common thread was that they looked desperately poor. The sun shimmered as it rose above the horizon into a cloudless sky, and soon after, a minibus arrived and a moustached man got out and observed the small crowd that had gathered. I was one of the first to be picked out, and when about nine of us had been put to one side we were directed to enter the minibus. The stench of unwashed bodies was almost unbearable, but we were driven through the gates towards the containers, and for me it was my first day at work.

Ahmet had provided me with some paperwork to pass any inspection and knowing the thoroughness with which he carried out his duties, I was confident everything would be alright. We were taken to an area where containers were being unloaded onto the quayside, and prior to stacking they were being randomly opened, presumably to track any illicit goods. My job, and those of my colleagues, was to remove boxes, sacks and other packaging to allow officials to scrutinise them. It was hot work. Late morning was the worst, not a breath of wind, not a cloud in the sky and a shade temperature nudging forty. The afternoon sea breeze was a relief but it was uncomfortably humid. We were paid a daily rate which was way below the official minimum wage. My colleagues were obviously grateful to receive the wage, and I was aware that any dissent would result in being overlooked for work.

The first few days were the worst. I was picked from the crowd to work on each of the first four days, and I remember looking behind when the minibus departed and seeing envy on the faces of those left behind. I was the only regular over the early days except for one man. He was a small wiry chap called Khalid. He lived in the shantytown with his wife and four children and had been working in the port for about ten years. He was the only one I had met who spoke Arabic. He had fled Sudan, but when I tried to find out why, he was reluctant to talk. Generally, talking was discouraged by our overseers, and it was a fact that just chatting used up much needed energy.

For some reason, I wasn't picked to work on Wednesday, and I was a bit concerned that I may have inadvertently broken one of the rules. I joined the rest of the group and milled around for a while until it was clear no more work was available, and then they slowly dispersed and wandered off to their homes. It was actually a relief not to work, and I looked forward to a day in the air conditioned flat. Ahmet was out when I arrived back home, but he returned soon afterwards carrying two bags full of shopping. He looked worried when he saw me and shared with me the concern that I may have done something wrong.

There had been little time for us to talk since our arrival in Bandar Abbas, as I left the flat early each morning and it was evening before I returned home. Ahmet had kept his side of the bargain by providing breakfast and dinner each day and replenishing my knapsack with water and some basic snacks. I had a cold shower every evening and that was followed by an early night. It was an exhausting time. So, on Wednesday afternoon we sat down and talked of our progress. I had begun to get some idea as to how the container port was laid out, and the tagging system that was being used.

There was a hub where the customs declaration forms were being processed, and there were small offices where accounts appeared to be filed in cupboards rather than on computers. As yet, I had failed to find anything remotely connected to the smuggling of drugs. Ahmet had tracked many ships during the week, and four had transported containers from Pakistan and India that he suspected had contained rice, but whether that was significant, it was too early to tell.

I felt cut off from the world in this corner of Iran, but I continued to labour on most days through the increasingly torrid heat of summer. I was beginning to think my task was a waste of time, but I persevered and Ahmet continued to check the shipping. In early August, we were told to unload some sacks of rice from a container that had recently arrived from Pakistan. I looked at the officials to see if there was any nervousness and my heart raced as Khalid and I entered the container. We were told to be quick as the rice was temperature sensitive, but it was noticeable that the jute bags containing the rice were different from the polypropylene bags I had discovered on Balint's farm. The bags also had 'made in Pakistan' inscribed on them in English. It was a disappointment, but there was nothing to suggest that the drugs were smuggled in from Pakistan.

I don't know how it started, but one day Khalid started talking about drugs and asked if I smoked cannabis. Naturally, I said, no, and Khalid agreed that it was not desirable to do so, but he said, many people in the shantytown smoked it and seemed to go into trances from which they didn't emerge. I wondered if I had understood his words properly. My knowledge of Arabic was still fairly rudimentary, but when I challenged him about the so-called trances he was adamant that was what he had said and backed it up by saying that he had seen people high on cannabis in the past and they behaved in a very different manner. I asked where this cannabis came from and in a matter-of-fact way he said, 'Off the ships.'

I felt this could be the breakthrough I had been looking for, but rather than risk making Khalid suspicious, I left the subject. I mentioned it to Ahmet over dinner in the evening. 'You'll have to get yourself invited to the Shantytown.' He said, with one of those rare serious looks, but it never happened, because the following day destiny took over and the changes for both of us were going to be profound.

Chapter 22

The morning started the same as all the others. Breakfast before dawn had broken, and then a walk to the port in the still morning air with the yellow green sky of a desert sunrise just beginning. At the port gates, both Khalid and I were picked for a day's work and the minibus took us to the same place that we had been two days before. As it happened, it was another container filled with sacks of rice, and this time it was well advertised that everything was grown, or manufactured, in India. It was a custom that when the contents of the containers were being inspected we would either go for a walk or, more often, find a shady spot to sit and rest. It occurred to me that there may be more rice containers in the area, so I ambled around to see if there were. There were none, and the one from Pakistan I had been involved with a couple of days before had already gone.

What I did discover, though, was a numbering system on the site where the containers were inspected, and one of those numbers was two thousand and ninety-four. That was the number on the fragment of the declaration form found in Balint's garage. I casually asked Khalid whether he had unloaded anything at twenty ninety-four.

'No' he replied, 'but sometimes there's a container there.'

'Any idea why it's not inspected?' I asked.

'Don't know if it isn't,' he shrugged his shoulders, 'but I know I haven't touched it at all.'

I went home in the evening and talked over the new information with Ahmet. We decided that it was now time to try and find out more about the origins of the containers that were collected from twenty ninety-four, and to get those details we needed to raid the office.

'No problem,' said Ahmet. For Ahmet nothing was a problem. 'We just have to go there one night, tie up the security guard, grab the documents and leave.' I laughed inwardly at his naivety.

'There's a small matter of security cameras. The place is brightly lit at night, and there's a big fence around the whole port.' I replied.

'Not the whole port, my friend,' Ahmet's teeth gleamed at me. 'There's not a fence on the seaward side.'

'So, we swim in and out. Come on Ahmet, be realistic.' The smile disappeared and we both sat glumly thinking of a way to achieve our aims.

'We have to become security guards.' I said, after a while. 'It's the only way. How are you at making uniforms?' It was my turn to smile.

Over the following few weeks, I continued to work, but on fewer days than before. I told Khalid that I was exhausted, and I could see he was genuinely concerned about me, but I couldn't see the point of risking heatstroke now that plans were evolving to end our sojourn in this overcrowded oven of southern Iran. I made mental notes of the positions of surveillance cameras, found out about the time that shift changes occurred amongst the security guards, and kept an eye on unloading Bay 2094 to see if it became occupied.

It was a Monday in the middle of September that a bright blue container with no obvious markings had been set out on the site ready for onward transport. I had been working further along the same street dealing with agricultural products from India but could not fail to notice the new arrival. Whether it was the container we had been looking for I didn't know, but in the evening Ahmet decided that we would put our master plan into action.

What I had noticed was that the little offices each had something similar to a notice board with rows of bulldog clips on hooks holding notes from the daily inspections. On Sundays, the notice boards were empty, and I surmised that the notes were either filed in cabinets or, more likely, stored away on computers. We decided that Thursday night would be the best time to enter the port. Operations largely ceased ahead of the Iranian weekend, and it appeared that only a handful of security personnel were manning the offices. So, on Thursday, we slept through the afternoon, and after a substantial late evening meal we prepared ourselves for the adventure ahead.

At around three in the morning, we wished each other the best of luck, and Ahmet left to walk to the port. I followed about half an hour later. Apart from a few stray cats, the city was quiet. A couple of taxis went past, one slowing down briefly, but the driver probably thought I was a local vagrant and quickly sped off. I reached the port gates and noticed that the first part of the plan had worked. Ahmet was sitting in the office at the entrance looking every inch the security guard that he had now become. I smiled at him as I passed by and he responded with his usual toothy grin. I pulled the hood from my light jacket down over my face and bent forward as I came within range of the cameras, just in case Ahmet had failed to disable them.

I strode towards the little office that housed the paperwork for the containers that we were interested in. I had to take a circuitous route to avoid the cameras, but it only took ten minutes. I was dismayed to see that there was a low light on in the office and a man was sitting there staring at the computer screen. I thought he was probably watching a film as he seemed totally transfixed. I walked up to the office, the door was open, and I stepped inside. He lazily looked round and began to smile, but quickly realised it wasn't someone he knew and a look of apprehension spread across his face.

I wasn't sure whether he was armed and did not know if he had an alarm button so I had to act quickly. I produced a knife and told him in my best Arabic, complete with arm movements, to go and stand against the wall with his arms raised. I'm sure he didn't understand what I had said, but he did appreciate the situation and slowly rose from his chair with raised arms. I looked at the man in front of me. He was young, probably no more than twenty-five and short but wiry. I reckoned he, or his ancestors, were from India.

It appeared that he wasn't armed and his jacket, hanging limply from the chair, was quickly checked and contained nothing but a wallet and a few coins. Attached to his trousers there was a set of keys, and I was worried that there could have been an alarm activator among them. I carefully removed the keys from his trousers, expecting that he would take the opportunity to attack me, but he was shaking with fear, and obeyed my every command. I noticed that there was a door on one side of the office and I suspected that it was full of filing cabinets, but I was surprised to find that it was a toilet. I told the security guard to go into the toilet but he just stood facing the wall and said, nothing.

I forcefully said, 'Hey.' and he turned his head to look at me. I pointed to the toilet and he quickly got the message and shuffled dejectedly into the stuffy little room. There was a small window that seemed to be fixed in a half open position, but it was far too small for him to get through. I drew my hand across my throat and then put a finger to my mouth to suggest silence. He understood immediately and nodded. I shut the door, and as an afterthought, wondered whether any of the keys fitted the lock in the toilet door. My luck was in. One of the bigger keys in the lock turned and there was a gentle click. The guard was now secured and I could return to my mission.

The film was still running on the computer. It looked like one of those Bollywood blockbusters and just as I glanced at it I saw what looked like a security guard fighting with a criminal. I smiled wryly and turned off the film.

I had managed to learn a little Iranian since my arrival in the country, but it took a while, with the help of an Iranian translation tool, to find the files I wanted to view. Fortunately, the container arrivals were stored on a simple spreadsheet and I didn't even need a username or password to access the information. I wasn't sure what I could use, and as I wanted to spend as little time in the office as possible, I copied most of the spreadsheet to my USB flash drive. Once the job was done, I searched through the row of bulldog clips and found the one relating to the twenty ninety-four loading position. I stuffed it in my pocket and re-arranged the bulldog clips on the wall. I smiled at the thought of the confusion it may cause. I then left the office.

I had only spent around fifteen minutes in the office, and with the walk to and fro from the main gate, I was hoping to be back with Ahmet in just over half an hour. I took the shadowy route back again, and just as I was rounding the last container my heart sank. At the main gate, alongside the reception building there was a car, and on its front door panel it read 'Police.' I could see three or four men in the office. Two appeared to be in police uniform, one was Ahmet, and the other one was a young man who seemed to be very agitated.

I waited, and waited, but the discussion continued, and even though it was Friday, the coming of dawn would expose my location and some workers were bound to arrive at the port and I could be in trouble. I tried to think of a way to exit the port without being spotted, but with a brightly lit entrance and the police just a few metres away I thought my chances of escape were minimal. Suddenly, there was the sound of a gun being fired. I counted three, possibly four, shots, but immediately it alerted me to the possibility of escape. The door of the office flung open and Ahmet came bursting out. He fired a gun at the car twice and petrol came pouring out of the tank. He then went sprinting up the road towards the city. He was some fifty metres away when a policeman emerged from the door, looked at the petrol flooding from the car, and then ran off in hot pursuit of Ahmet.

I walked towards the entrance appearing as relaxed as I possibly could. I didn't glance towards the reception office, and I felt my heart pumping faster and faster as I neared the port exit. The barrier was only to prevent vehicles passing through, with pedestrians free to walk through on the pavement. There was a strong smell of petrol as the contents of the tank continued to spill along the gutter. I walked out of the port without being challenged and inhaled deeply, but then a voice sounded from the direction of the reception. I don't know what he said, but I assumed he was addressing me. It was quiet at first, but got louder, until eventually I heard 'stop'. That was the cue for me to start running.

I sprinted in the direction of the shantytown, my thinking was that if Ahmet had taken one policeman towards the city, I would stand a better chance if I went in almost the opposite direction. Where I would hide, and for how long, were not thoughts that were passing through my brain at that time. From a greater distance there came the command 'stop.' And then the sound of gunfire. I felt a sharp pain in my left shoulder, and then a stinging pain on the right side of my head. I was dodging from side to side and then I reached the tightly packed rows of shacks. Dawn was just beginning to break, but it was difficult to keep my footing in this dimly lit area. I continued running, but my head was throbbing, and everything appeared to be moving into slow motion.

I remember reading about a red mist rising when you are about to lapse into unconsciousness, but my legs continued to run, until my head fell forward, then nothing.

Chapter 23

I awoke to the sound of a rooster repeatedly crowing and a child, probably aged about three, staring down at me with big brown eyes. I probably looked as surprised as she did as she quickly ran off shouting something in a language that I did not understand. A young, dark-skinned woman, presumably the girl's mother, came and looked down at me with a concerned look in her eyes, but said nothing. I tried to get up but it felt as if my limbs were encased in concrete. I slowly became accustomed to the semi darkness and discovered that I was lying down close to the floor under a low corrugated iron roof. The curtains were drawn and it was hard to make out any furnishings as I seemed to drift in and out of consciousness and felt incredibly weak.

At some time during the day, I heard 'Rachid, Rachid.'

It took a little while before I opened my eyes and realised it was me that was being addressed. A kindly looking middle-aged man smiled benignly and said, in Arabic, 'Peace be upon you.'

I weakly said, 'Thank you' in reply.

'I am Doctor Samir. You have had a nasty accident.' He waited to see if I would say anything. I didn't, so he carried on. 'You were found in the street and taken into one of the shacks. They could see that you had been shot and your passport was from Morocco. That's not a good combination.'

The doctor smiled. 'You know the police are looking for you.' He said, softly.

I nodded.

'You need to rest.' The doctor said, 'We can talk later.' The doctor turned to leave.

'Can I ask a question?' I said, and before he replied I went on, 'Am I in a hospital?'

'No, you are not in a hospital, but you are in a place where you are being cared for.' At that point, I fell asleep.

I awoke to the feeling that I was being lifted from the bed. I automatically resisted as much as I could, but the two people that were lifting me urged me to be calm. It was then that I realised that a drip was attached to my arm. I relaxed as I took in the seriousness of my situation. I felt very weak but my brain was beginning to clear and it allowed me to take in more of my surroundings. I knew a little about medicine from overhearing the conversations my parents occasionally had between their bickering.

I had an intravenous line attached from the lower part of my arm to a bottle that was suspended from an upturned coat hanger attached to an ancient hat stand next to my bed. It was at that stage I became aware that I had no clothes on and I was being lifted on to a commode. My time at boarding school had ironed out any embarrassment about nudity and bodily functions, but this was altogether a new experience for me. I muttered 'Doctor,' and the young, kind looking man pointed to his watch, and I assumed that meant later. I occasionally glanced up and noted that the bottle of yellow liquid was slowly emptying into my veins. It felt slightly cool, otherwise I didn't notice anything. Before the bottle had emptied, I fell asleep again.

The next time I awoke I felt much better. I had been returned to the bed and was propped up and could see in front of me into what looked like the kitchen. A woman was preparing food and a spicy smell was drifting towards me from that direction. A child was playing on the floor and a radio was quietly playing some eastern music. It was a pleasant rural scene and I almost wondered if I was dreaming. I heard a door open and then a man spoke English.

I suddenly felt very apprehensive but knew there was nothing that I could do to protect myself if danger arose as I could barely lift my hand to my face. The man was the one who had earlier lifted me from the bed. He was greeting the woman in a mixture of Arabic and English. He came into the room where I was propped up and greeted me warmly in Arabic. He asked me if I would like something to eat, but when I pointed at my cannula he frowned, said, 'okay,' in English, and left to help his wife in the kitchen.

It was agonising to hear the sound of a meal being eaten, which made me think that I must be recovering. Sometime after the meal the doctor arrived. I had no idea what time it was, but the child was awake and the sun was shining, so I assumed it was probably late afternoon. The doctor checked me over and seemed to be pleased with my progress. I had many questions to ask but he stopped me, and instead started to question me.

'I am not a policeman, Mister Alami,' he began, 'but we believe that you are not a Moroccan. Can you explain?'

It took me aback. Had I spoken English in my sleep? What happened after I had run away from the port? I looked into the eyes of the doctor. They showed curiosity rather than anger.

'Why do you think that?' I replied, desperately trying to think of a way to allay his suspicions, 'and you are not Iranian, is that correct?'

He laughed at the comment. 'Yes, you are right; I'm from Oman.'

There was a short silence. 'But where are you from Rachid?' The doctor was insistent.

'I have a Moroccan passport, or at least I did have.' I replied.

'You still have,' the doctor muttered softly. 'And you also have trainers from London, and a shirt from Turkey. Shall I go on? But you don't appear to have anything from Morocco.'

'I have been out of the country for a long while.' I countered weakly. I didn't want to lie to this mild-mannered man who had probably saved my life, but should I tell him about my mission? It was a difficult one.

'I will answer more of your questions when you have told me where I am and what is happening to me.' I said, defiantly.

The doctor looked thoughtful before replying. 'You are in a village in the hills not far from Bandar. The family you are staying with are taking a big risk by having you here, and I'm taking a risk too.'

'Why did you help me?' I asked.

The doctor looked surprised. 'We try to help anyone in the slum area, because the authorities do not, and to save a person that has been shot is regarded as a victory. You were found with bullet wounds in a pile of rubbish. The one that found you thought you were dead, but you weren't. I was summoned and you were moved into one of the shacks.'

'Why wasn't I taken to hospital?' I asked. The doctor laughed bitterly. 'You were in the wrong part of the city. You would have been cast out for the dogs. Anyway, the shack you were taken to was often searched by the police and the family that lived there were worried that they would be punished if you were found. The following night I brought you here in my car.'

'Thank you.' I interjected.

'You are welcome.' He replied drily 'Now it's your turn to say something.' He seemed resigned to the fact that I would say nothing, but I felt that he was owed a full explanation and I decided to give it to him in English.

I started speaking and his head jerked backwards as I told him my name and nationality. I went on to outline my reason for being in southern Iran. I waited for his reaction, and fortunately it was positive.

'It is good that we found you, your cause is worthy,' were the doctor's opening words. He then went on to talk about the drug problem in Bandar Abbas, especially amongst the poor and migrant communities. He agreed that governments could be complicit in encouraging drug use in those that would otherwise be on the streets protesting about authoritarian governments. He then went on to tell me about my injuries which could have been far worse. He had judged that no bones were broken, but I had lost a lot of blood and there were wounds, both in my left shoulder and just below the ear on the right side. He told me that I was in a safe house, which was actually a small grain-growing farm in the hills with a date grove. I wondered why local people were not suspicious of strangers coming and going, but he smiled and said, 'Most people here are immigrants. Some from Pakistan, others from India and Oman. There are many different religions here as well; mostly Sunnis, but a few Christians and there is even a family of Jews from Tehran. You see, people in this area are poor but happy and they don't want that to change. They pay their taxes, and probably a little more, and the authorities leave them alone.'

'Why are you here?' I asked.

'It's a long story, but many years ago I met a girl at medical school in Muscat, you know, in Oman. She was from Tehran, and after a while she decided that we should move to Iran to work. She was a Shia Muslim, and for her it was easy to find work, but for me, as a foreigner, and nominally an Ibadi Muslim, it was much more difficult, and we just drifted apart. I think you use the expression; the rest is history.'

After a long silence I said, 'I feel very weak. How long will it take before I'm back to normal?' Relieved that the conversation was focused elsewhere, the doctor told me that it would be weeks rather than months, but that I should make a full recovery. He helped me to the seat next to the bed and removed my cannula. My legs were stiff and could barely support me and it was almost impossible to lift my left arm, but for me this was point zero, and for each day ahead there would be a target, until I was fit enough to move on.

My hours were taken up with exercise, eating, sleeping and trying to keep clean, but it didn't take long before I started thinking about the outside world. My mobile and wallet had disappeared, but my jacket pocket still contained the flash drive that I had used to obtain information from the port computer, as well as the crumpled piece of paper from the bulldog clip with the heading twenty ninety-four, but a jacket was not an item of clothing I needed in this part of Iran. Even in the hills, the days were hot, although the nights were much cooler than on the coast.

Work on the farm generally ceased during the afternoon heat, but resumed in the evening, and again very early in the morning. There were a few animals to feed, but the grain had been harvested in late spring and the fields were bare and dusty. It was the time of year for the dates to be collected, and although the grove was small, there were many bunches, and their sale provided a reasonable living for the young farmers. It was my job, along with several villagers, to cut the bunches from the trees, select the ripe dates and put them into crates to be taken to the processing centre on the way to the coast. It was hard work, but the villagers, mostly Arabic speaking immigrants, were friendly and the time on the farm passed quickly.

I had regained full fitness by the late autumn and I was ready to leave, but how, and to where, I had no idea. I discussed my dilemma with the doctor, and he came up with an idea. There were many small fishing villages along the coast and there was often an exchange of fish between Iranian and Omani ports. The authorities allowed this to happen without much red tape, and the doctor thought that I might like to try and return home via Oman as it could prove easier, and less risky, than travelling back through Iran. I agreed to this course of action and the doctor made some discreet enquiries to see if it was possible to be smuggled into Oman. I asked whether there had been any news about Ahmet, but although the local media reported that an incident had occurred at the port, details were sketchy, and the story was quickly forgotten. I wondered if he had got away or had that engaging smile been finally wiped from his face. I thought about the flat we had shared. Was it as we had left it on that fateful evening or, more likely, it had been cleared of our effects, and been re-let.

I had almost given up hope of leaving Iran, but one December evening, after a tiring day helping with wheat seed planting, the doctor arrived to say that we were going to a little fishing village where a dhow was waiting to take me to

Oman. I asked about payment, to which the good doctor replied, 'You give me the Iranian Rials you earned here, and I'll give you some Omani Rials.'

I made a point of thanking my generous hosts profusely, and I felt quite emotional as I left the farmer and his wife who had helped to nurse me back to health, but unless I had been given up for dead by my employer, there was a job to be done, and I was ready to carry on fighting the war against illegal drugs. I felt reinvigorated by the challenge ahead, and as we drove down towards the coast I pondered on my next move as a British citizen in a country I had never been to before and travelling with a Moroccan passport. It could be interesting.

Chapter 24

It was dusk when we reached the harbour and the western sky had that deep orange red hue of a desert sunset. There was no wind and the fishing boats stood motionless in the water. There were few people around, although an old car was on the quayside alongside one of the traditional dhows which looked like a smaller version of a war galley from the era of the Spanish Armada. It was painted bright blue and white and my first impression was that it would topple over if there was even a hint of a breeze. *No*, I thought, we can't be heading towards that boat, but alas we were. The doctor jumped out of the car, shook the hand of the car driver and warmly embraced the other men, who perhaps numbered twelve or more. I remained in the doctor's car, but after the other vehicle drove off, I was invited to join the men alongside the boat.

I was introduced to a tall man wearing a white collarless gown and on his head there was something resembling a turban. He was wizened but I estimated he was about fifty years old and assumed he was the captain. The others busied themselves with loading crates, but cheerfully acknowledged my presence. I immediately felt at ease with these pleasant fishermen. I had very few possessions with me and just stood, with my knapsack on my back, waiting for the loading to finish. There was no effort to hide me, so I just assumed people smuggling wasn't a problem in this part of the world. The doctor was in a deep conversation with the captain. But after a while they embraced again and the doctor came over to me. He said, in Arabic 'May Allah bless you' and I embraced him and thanked him for all his help. I was in tears when he drove off, it had been such a wonderful experience to know such a decent human being.

The captain could see that I was upset. 'He's a good man, Samir, he's my brother,' the captain said, proudly.

As I boarded the boat I asked how long we would take and was pleasantly surprised to hear 'Three hours.' I asked if I could help in any way and was shown to the galley. A small round man, beads of sweat on his bald head, was grilling some fish while a large saucepan full of a thick liquid gently simmered on the stove. A pile of prepared rice was lying in a trough on the worktop. He introduced himself as 'Butrus,' and quickly had me chopping up fresh-looking cucumbers that he had retrieved from a crate on the floor. Overhead, there was the noise of men at work, and a glance through the hatch revealed a sail being hoisted. It seemed hard to believe that a sail would be of any use as there was no wind, but a few minutes later there was the clank, clank of an engine bursting into life followed by the smell of diesel fumes.

I asked Butrus why the sail was needed, and he said that the wind would start blowing from the land in an hour's time and we should make good progress out to sea. I was sceptical, but in less than an hour, I could hear the sail rustling, and with help from the engine we left the small harbour. It was a cooling breeze and it made working in the galley more bearable, but the dhow was in open waters, and although the sea was not rough, it was bobbing around and I had to fight against seasickness. Butrus noticed that I was suffering and suggested that I had a break up on the deck. The moon shone brightly and it was easy to make out the horizon. In the distance, there were flashes of lightning, otherwise the sky was clear and starlit. The captain noticed me from the open bridge and called me over. He was steering the boat while a couple of the crew were sitting behind him listening to a radio. He told me it was easy to navigate in these waters at night as long as the moon shone. It was better than during the day because the heat of the sun made it very uncomfortable on deck.

'There are hazards,' he said, and pointed towards the long black outline of an oil tanker heading north. 'We can use the engine to keep out of trouble, but we prefer using the sails, they're cheaper.' He was a jolly fellow and said he had spent his life at sea. Unlike his brother, he had had no formal education, but he didn't mind, Allah had been kind to him.

After a while, I went back to the galley where Butrus had finished preparing a meal. From every corner of the vessel, men emerged to partake of the food. Not all the crew ate, and Butrus said, some were sleeping ready to take over the navigation later in the night. The food was unusual, but very edible. It could best be described as a sweet sardine curry washed down with strong coffee. Following the meal, I made enquiries about the toilet and was shown to the back of the boat where a squatting area opened directly out onto the sea. I had no problem with this primitive, but effective, toilet, but I was beginning to wish for the flush toilet in my Tooting flat.

It was obvious that the trip was going to take more than three hours, and as I helped Butrus to clear up, I asked him about our travel plans. When I told him that I understood the journey would last three hours, he laughed uncontrollably and spluttered some comments about having jet engines fitted. When he had sufficiently recovered, he informed me that it would take three days to reach home, and the destination wasn't the mainland of Oman, it was a little island several kilometres from the coast called Masirah.

He smiled. 'You'll like it there, it's very quiet at this time of year, apart from the warplanes.'

'Warplanes?' I repeated.

'Yes, there's an airbase on the island and it gets noisy sometimes.'

'What else happens there?' It was a place I had never heard of, and I was somewhat perturbed by the thought that I was sailing towards a place that was even more remote from my comfortable flat in London than southern Iran was.

Butrus suggested that we slept for a while because it would be an early start in the morning. He threw a rolled length of thin foam mattress towards me and pointed to the back of the galley. He must have noticed my doubting look.

'Don't worry,' he said, 'you'll sleep well.'

And I did. The gentle motion of the boat was beneficial, and the thoughts of seasickness were consigned to history. It was around dawn that I felt Butrus shaking me out of a deep sleep. Unlike me, he was jolly and very much awake and was already preparing breakfast. I had a quick look on deck. It was quiet apart from the gentle thud, thud of the diesel engine. The sea was calm and the sky cloudless and the only person I could see was a fairly young man on the bridge in front of the ship's steering wheel. He was heading obliquely towards a range of mountains lit by the early morning sunshine. The heavy-looking sail hung limply, and I wondered whether it was hindering our passage through the sea, but an irritated call from the galley refocused my mind.

Breakfast was a cross between bread and pancake, infused with pureed dates. It was a messy and sticky job making the meal, but the crew ate it with relish and that was pleasing. As usual, strong coffee was in abundance, and that was a good awakener for the day ahead. The heat in the galley increased rapidly during the morning, and both Butrus and I were quick to clear up so we could emerge onto the deck. Many of the crew were sitting quietly repairing fishing nets and other activities were minimal in the increasing warmth. We had moved to within a couple of kilometres of the Omani coast, and in the late morning a breeze developed which helped us on our way and the sail took over from the engine as our means of propulsion.

Lunch was similar to breakfast, but with less bread and more coffee, and in the evening, when the wind had died away, there were sardines again for dinner. Another electric storm occurred over the mountains in the evening, but this time we were nearer and the long, low rumbles of thunder were audible. The captain assured me that it was a good thing, because it would mean a stronger land breeze and would help to propel us forward quicker. He was right. Just as the storms were dying away over the land, a rustle occurred in the sail, and within minutes we were bouncing along over the waves with spray showering the deck.

The same pattern of work and sleep followed overnight and during the next day, but towards evening on the third day, land appeared on our port side. Butrus had abandoned the galley and said, there would be no evening meal as we would all have food with our families when we arrived home. The place we were heading towards looked inhospitable. To our starboard side, there was a sea of sand, punctuated by a few flat-roofed beige buildings. To our port side, there was a hint of colour with more substantial buildings and as we neared the coast, scattered palm trees appeared. Butrus pointed out the harbour and the mosque, and even a hotel, but he said that the harbour we were aiming for was over an hour further to the south.

It was dark when we docked, but there was enough light on the rustic quayside for us to unload our supplies. Many willing hands appeared to help us with the task, and in a very short time the dhow had been emptied, and the quayside cleared. The crew drifted off in different directions, some with family members, others alone. Butrus was met by his equally rotund wife wearing traditional black and a niqab. She said nothing to me, and just a few words to Butrus before she followed him up the street. The captain had told me during the trip that I would stay with him and his family until I had decided what to do next.

The walk to the captain's house was lengthy, but after a while we arrived at a low, walled property. Without ringing a bell, the captain just opened the door and we entered a courtyard containing one date palm and several potted shrubs. The sprawling one-storey house appeared to be quite modern but the courtyard was much older with worn stone slabs, stone benches, and what looked like a capped well in the middle. Although it was late, children were running around, and several adults, mostly dressed in western clothes, were sitting on cushions on the ground finishing a meal. I was introduced to the family as Rachid, and I wondered just how much Samir, the doctor, had told the captain about my past life. The children just stared at me wide-eyed, but the adults were warm and friendly in their greetings, they all seemed in awe of the patriarch of the family, a tall, thin and very elderly looking man. He stared at me intently and beckoned me over.

He welcomed me to his house and asked if I would like to eat. The captain was already eating. There was no cutlery, just a pile of meat, I was not sure whether it was goat or lamb, and a smaller pile of rice. I observed how the rice and meat were deftly interwoven before being stuffed into the mouth. I had noticed there was also a certain way of sitting and I did my best to emulate the captain and the remaining diners, but my attempts at combining the meat and rice were woeful. My struggles didn't go unnoticed, and rather than ignore my plight, it caused much undisguised merriment. I was hungry, though, and eventually I managed to master the art of eating in rural Oman. It was late, and the house quietened down quickly. I was shown to a bare room, but with a bed and the luxury of an adjoining bathroom, although the toilet was the same as the ones I had experienced in Iran. Nevertheless, after cleaning myself thoroughly, I enjoyed the best sleep I had had for weeks.

Breakfast was similar to the one that I had prepared on the dhow, but coffee with cardamom was the early morning drink served, embarrassingly for me, in my honour as a guest. The elderly patriarch did not arrive for breakfast, but he appeared later and requested that I go for a walk with him. The weather was perfect. No wind, no cloud, and with a temperature in the low twenties, but the landscape was unable to match the weather in perfection. When we left the house, and then the village, there was sand, and much of it. There were no trees, and just the occasional small Limonium plant. In the distance were some hills of a darker hue.

For an old man, the patriarch walked briskly and we strode off towards the beach and a square lump of concrete that was jutting out of the sand. He sat, and uninvited, I sat beside him. He said nothing for a long time, but just looked out to sea.

After a while he said, 'You're English?'

I was taken aback as he had said his opening words in English. Without wanting to explain my somewhat more complex origins, I just said, 'Yes.'

'How is Samir?' the old man asked, his eyes still riveted on the sea ahead.

'He's well.' I said and went on to give him a quick summary of my meetings with him in Iran.

'You speak English.' I said after another lengthy pause.

'Yes,' he replied, 'I worked in the British camp on Masirah.'

I was intrigued. 'What camp was that?' I proffered.

'In the sixties and seventies, the British helped the Oman government to prevent communist insurgents from entering the country from South Yemen. There was an air force base here in the north of the island. Much of the year it was quiet, but in the monsoon season—'

'Monsoon season?' I interrupted.

He smiled. 'Yes. In July and August, we have strong southwest winds but no rain, in Salalah, though, that's in the south of the country near the Yemen border, they have days of low cloud and drizzle. The communist fighters used to gather in the mist-shrouded hills above Salalah and start bombing the town, and especially the airport. That was when the British fighter jets were called on to help locate and destroy the insurgents.'

'I never knew that.' I said, matter-of-factly.

He went on, 'No, it was kept very quiet, I believe.' After a pause, he resumed, 'I managed to get a job at the base, cleaning mostly, looking after the golf course, and laundry—'

I interrupted. 'Did you say golf course?' I gave him an incredulous look.

He grinned. 'Yes, there was an eighteen-hole golf course on the hills at the side of the camp. There was no grass, just sand and a few rocks, but there were greens, called browns.'

I looked confused. 'They were flat areas with a hole somewhere near the middle, and a flag, and they were made of oiled sand and salt, and were rolled flat. My job was to make sure the camels or sand lizards had not dug up the browns overnight.' I laughed. I didn't know much about golf, but the vision of a camel molesting a golf course seemed amusing.

The old man let me have my moment of glee before resuming. 'I then went on to the power station, and while there, learnt to read and write and absorbed a lot of English, but above all it paid well, and I was able to send my sons to school.'

'And one of your sons became a doctor. You must be a proud man.'

'Yes, I am.' He appeared wistful, 'We lived in a small village by the base. It was poor, we were all quite poor, even though we were better off than many on the island. Our house only had two rooms and was not well built, but it was home.' There was a long pause, then tears welled up in his eyes. 'In the mid nineteen seventies the British left Masirah and American personnel took over. It was a hard period. We lost our jobs and we had difficulty feeding ourselves and educating the children, and then the storm came.'

He burst into tears and wept for several minutes while I just sat and felt very awkward. I did not know how to comfort this austere patriarch who, a few hours before, appeared to strike fear into his family members. After a few minutes, without apologising, he went on, 'In June ninety seventy-seven, I can't remember what date, a cyclone hit the island. It was very, very bad. It rained, and the whole island was flooded, and the wind blew everything away. We lost our home, we lost our village, I lost my wife and daughter. They never found my daughter, but my wife.' He was now inconsolable. I put an arm across his shoulder but he said nothing. It was as if he had been waiting to say this for decades, and the moment had been too much for him.

Eventually he began speaking again, 'We had some help from Saudi Arabia and other countries in the area, and I was able to build a house, he waved his arm behind him, but I was also able to get education for my boys. Samir was seven when he lost his mother, and I remember him saying that if he had been a doctor, then he would have made mama well.' He turned and looked at me. 'You know the rest.'

'What about your other son?' I asked gently.

'He was in shock for months, no, years. He wouldn't speak. We could not teach him anything. He wasn't badly behaved, he just seemed immensely sad. Can one so young be that sad?' He looked at me for a reply.

'I suppose so.' I replied. 'It must have been awful.' I said, immediately feeling the words were banal. He looked at the ground and said, nothing. I looked at the wavelets silently breaking on to the sand in front of me.

'Do you have a family?' He said, without raising his head.

'Yes,' I replied. 'My mother and father, no brothers or sisters, though.'

'Do you not have a wife?' He seemed surprised.

'No.' After a while I added, 'I have a girlfriend that I'm very fond of.'

He grabbed my hand lightly. 'Cherish her, because one day Allah may take her from you.'

Chapter 25

Anja had been in my thoughts many times over the past few weeks, but I didn't want to compromise our mission, and after my injury, the opportunity did not arise. Since our arrival in Masirah, however, I was determined to contact her. I wondered whether she had found a lover amongst her student friends, and at times it was difficult to quell pangs of jealousy, but I was realistic enough to think that her life had probably moved on.

The old man had finished his tale, and he looked better for it. It was as if the years of anguish had been cleansed from his mind, and I felt a certain satisfaction that by listening to him I had made his life less burdensome. He got up, made a gesture and said that we should return to the house to eat. On the way back, I said, 'I have been wanting to contact my girlfriend for weeks. I was unable to do it in Iran. Can you help please?' I was not sure what his reaction would be, or what the mobile phone coverage was like in Oman.

He smiled benignly and said, 'In Oman, the number of telephone subscribers exceeds the population, and of course you can make calls. I will lend you a phone while you stay with us.'

The streets were deserted, but as soon as we passed through the gate into the courtyard of the house, the bustle of daily life was apparent. Women were preparing lunch under an awning in one corner, several men were sitting in another corner discussing something loudly, and children were running around playing some form of tag. It was difficult to work out who was related to whom, and I wondered if the fishing boat captain had several wives, but I thought it would be rude to ask and I waited, in vain as it happened, for an introduction to all the family members.

Lunch was a chaotic affair, presided over by the old man who had regained his authoritative manner after his earlier emotional outbursts. Although I sat next to him again, I was ignored and he ate in silence. I spoke with his son, the captain, who was preparing for another fishing trip to Iran. He said, the fish, and particularly the shellfish he was able to drag up from the shallow waters, fetched a much better price in Iran, and with the money they received, they could bring some cheap supplies back to Masirah. He and his crew had been fishing in that way for many years and he was pleased with that way of life.

After a while, the captain asked me a few questions and I tried to be vague without lying, but Samir had told him a few things and he whispered, 'I know you are not Moroccan.' There was no resentment in his voice, and I didn't deny the fact.

'Do you know the Englishman?' He said nonchalantly as he struggled to consume a large piece of rice-covered fish. It was a question I wasn't expecting, and it was one I perhaps didn't understand, so I asked, 'What Englishman?'

The captain went on, 'Samir spends a lot of time in the poorer parts of Bandar and he told me about the big drug problem they have, and he told me the big boss of the drug importation is English.'

'Really,' I said. 'He didn't tell me that.' I felt a little aggrieved that I hadn't been told earlier. 'What do you know about him?' I continued.

'Have you met him?' The captain smiled and immediately said, 'No, I have no interest in drugs, my holy book says no drugs or alcohol.'

Just on the off chance I asked if he knew where the Englishman came from. I expected either a blank look or a simple reply from England, but no, he said, 'I heard that he lives in a big house in Austria and has servants and eats from silver plates.'

I had visions of a stately home in Vienna and a man sitting in a baronial hall with a queue of waiters bringing food to the table, but I quickly remembered this man was peddling misery to thousands of people.

'How did you find this out?' I asked. 'I had a friend in the village where we unload our catch, you know, where you boarded the boat.'

I nodded.

'He used to work in the port at Bandar and told me about drug smuggling that was going on and he mentioned the Englishman, that's all.'

'Do you think I could contact this man?' I asked.

'No, no,' the captain suddenly looked unhappy. 'He died the week before last in a road accident.'

I doubted whether this man died in an accident, but I said nothing to the captain. It just made me even more resolute in my quest to bring an end to these criminal activities.

After lunch, the elderly man took me to one side and produced an old iPhone. He said, 'It's best if you go to your room to make the call. I trust my family, but the less they know the less they can tell. You understand?'

'Of course.' I replied. I was going to my room anyway, but I thanked him for his concern and left. There was a two-hour time difference between Oman and Slovenia, and I assumed that Anja would be working. I left a short message to say that I would call at seven and then went back to the courtyard. It was quiet. The children had disappeared and even the kitchen was empty. I decided to walk down to the beach and along to the harbour. I needed to think of a plan to get out of the country. No one had asked me what I wanted to do, but I knew there must be a limit to their hospitality. Another thing was that the fishing vessel was leaving for Iranian waters on the following day.

By walking along the beach, I learnt several things about Masirah. There were land crabs everywhere. They stood in front of their holes in the sand staring at me until I was within three or four metres, then scuttled back into their homes. To avoid upsetting them I removed my sandals and walked through the shallow waters. The water was warm but wavelets disturbed the fine sand and it was not clear. I had been warned not to bathe by the captain. He said he had known someone who had been eaten by a shark. There were also stonefish with their venomous spines, but I trod on a small bivalve, and red-hot pain shot up my leg. Fortunately, the pain was short-lived and I was able to continue my walk to the harbour, but this time back on the dry sand.

At the harbour, the crew from the dhow were making the final repairs to the nets, while Butrus was loading some fresh supplies. I received a cheery greeting, and they asked if I was going to sea with them again. It was almost tempting, but I hoped for another way out, even so, the walk along the beach had not helped me find an answer to that conundrum.

In the evening, after dinner, I excused myself and went to my room to make a phone call to Anja. I wasn't sure what to say. It had been a long time and I had become unusually nervous.

She answered the phone, and I said, 'It's Rachid.'

There was a brief pause, and then, in a jolly voice she replied. 'Hello, Rachid, are you enjoying your holiday?'

I assumed that she was in her flat and she was enacting her 'walls have ears' theory.

I played the game by responding, 'Super holiday, I learned a lot, but it's a bit hot. How are you getting on?'

After another pause she replied, 'Missing you, when are you coming home?'

I was so pleased to hear those words, that it was me that paused for a long while. I took for granted that 'home' meant Ljubljana and after some thought I said. 'As soon as possible, but it's not easy to travel with a Moroccan passport, it's alright for you Europeans.'

I began to feel more relaxed.

'Where are you at the moment?' Anja asked, and I then realised that she probably had no idea that I was in Oman, although she was quick-witted enough to know from the telephone number that it wasn't Iran.

'Still in Oman, a lovely country, the people are so friendly.' I said, casually, 'but I reckon it's soon time to leave.' There was a sharp intake of breath when I mentioned Oman, so maybe she hadn't noticed the difference between the nine eight and nine six eight of her received call. 'It's at times like this I wish I wasn't Moroccan.' I said, hoping that she understood my predicament with regards to my passport.

'That's not a problem.' Anja said, enthusiastically. 'Just think, you might have been an Englishman, and you wouldn't want to be that, would you?'

That was a very enigmatic sentence she had come out with, and it was my turn to be taken aback. 'I do envy those that have passports that are accepted by many countries, it must make travelling very much easier.'

'Yes, it must.' Anja replied.

The conversation had just been about myself up until that moment, but I asked how she was getting on. 'As you know, after my graduation, I quit my old job and I'm now a full-time researcher, and already I've uncovered many valuable artefacts.' My brain was racing. I was sure she was sending me a coded message, but what should I read into it?

'Anyway, it pays quite well and the prospects are good. What about yourself, have you discovered anything interesting on your holidays?'

'Yes,' I replied, desperately trying to think of a way of saying something useful, while disguising the true meaning of my words. 'Saw some exciting scripts and took some interesting photos.' Remembering the tourist photographs I had taken on the way south in Iran, which I had fortunately copied to my flash drive. The camera was left in the flat in Bandar, and I have no idea where that ended up.

'You know, the usual tourist trail.' It was difficult to keep up this facade of normality, but I knew I had to. Anja was also struggling to keep the conversation going, but she went on.

'I'm sure that you'll have lots of presents for me when you get home, and I'll make sure you get your Christmas present as soon as possible.' I had completely forgotten it was Christmas coming up, and I thought about my parents in London. They knew I would probably be away for a long time without any contact, but to miss Christmas, that would worry them.

Anja must have read my thoughts as she said, 'And your parents, we mustn't forget them.' It was the sort of chat any young couple would have in a warm London pub with the rain hammering down outside, but it wasn't. I hadn't seen rain for months, and this small, sparsely furnished room on a desert island was as far removed from a London pub as it could be. The red light on my mobile was blinking, and the imminent flat battery was a convenient excuse to end our talk which was beginning to sadden both of us, and with Anja's promise that she would get the best Christmas present I had ever had, we broke the connection.

It was difficult to know if she understood the problems I was facing. Without a visa, I was unable to travel to many destinations with my Moroccan passport, and without my wallet that Ahmet had given me, which had disappeared the night that I had been shot, I was unable to make any credit card transactions. I did have some Omani currency that Samir had exchanged for the Iranian money, but even though I had not used any of it, there was not enough to buy an airline ticket. I decided it was probably best to go to the British embassy in Muscat and tell them of my plight. It meant going against the advice of my boss in London, but I could think of no other solution. If I had said that I was a tourist who had lost his passport, they would ask questions, and the lies could get me into more serious trouble. What a dilemma!

I went to bed feeling very despondent.

Chapter 26

After breakfast the following morning, the elderly patriarch invited me down to the beach again for a talk. He was interested to hear how the conversation went with Anja. Without divulging any details, I told him it went well, which I thought it did. He was genuinely pleased for me, so I thought maybe he could be approachable for ideas on how to leave Oman. I was still not sure how much he knew about me. He had been told that I was English, that I gathered from our opening exchanges, but since then we had conversed in Arabic.

'You and your family have been very kind to me.' I began, 'But I cannot stay here forever, and I wondered if you had given any thought as to my best way of leaving.'

He put a large hand to his grizzled chin. 'I understand it can be difficult for you here.' He replied slowly, 'I think the best you can do is go to Muscat and visit the British embassy.'

It was not what I had hoped to hear, but he was probably right, there was no other course of action left to me.

'My son will be back from his fishing trip in about three weeks, and he can take you to Muscat the next time he goes fishing.'

'You're very kind.' I said, and then resigned myself to a long wait on this sunny island.

In fact, it wasn't sunny all of the time. One morning I arose for breakfast and the sky was yellow without any trace of sunshine. The old man said, it was haze, the remnants of a sandstorm somewhere to the north. When we went to take our morning walk, we could barely see a hundred metres down the street and we quickly returned back to the house with the fine sand irritating our eyes and throats.

'In the old days, we thought days like this were brought to us as punishment and we spent the day praying,' the old man said. It certainly was a strange coloured sky. I spent the rest of that day playing with the children in the yard, and I realised that I was becoming increasingly bored with the routine of village life. I thought about hiring a taxi and visiting the largish town in the north of the island, but the old man quite rightly warned against that. Although he was sure he could trust his own household, there were people that may start asking questions.

At the end of the second week of my confinement, another unpleasant element of desert weather occurred. It became increasingly cold and windy, and even though the sun shone brightly, I was constantly shivering in the dry air, and an added problem was the eddying sand that seemed to penetrate every corner of the house and was an unwelcome addition to every meal. On Fridays there was a special meal, with meat, rather than fish, and it was after one of these meals I received a phone call as I was readying myself for bed. The call I had made to Anja, some two weeks earlier, had ended with an agreement that she should call me next, and I had become increasingly saddened by her silence. That very evening, I was thinking of ringing her, and once again it almost appeared as if telepathy had prompted her call.

She sounded excited, 'Where are you?' I asked, as I heard many voices in the background.

'At a birthday party,' she replied.

Pangs of envy shot through me.

'But it is raining outside,' she said as if capturing the mood that I was in, 'but quick, is it okay for me to talk openly?' She whispered.

'Yes, yes,' I said. 'Go ahead.'

'The Christmas present you were wanting is at the Spanish embassy in Muscat. Can you get there?'

'Yes, I think so.' I replied but having no idea how I could get there before the twenty-fifth.

'Okay,' she continued. 'Let me know as soon as possible when you can be there, and I'll make an appointment for you. Is that clear to you?'

I felt as if she was my boss giving me instructions for a new assignment. I bristled somewhat, but then she said, 'I'm missing you, and I really want to see you at Christmas. Must go now, bye.'

I just said, 'bye' and the phone was dead. I heard the birthday song in the background, and that was probably her reason for leaving. I felt buoyed up, but how was I to leave the island before Christmas, and why the Spanish Embassy?

I didn't sleep well that night as I searched my mind for a way to leave this sandy outpost. As far as I knew, there was only one recognised exit and that was the ferry from Hilf, in the north of the island, to Shannah on the mainland. I knew there was no bus from there to anywhere, and the cost of a taxi to Muscat would be prohibitive. There was an airport, but the chance of a lift to Muscat in a military Hawk trainer was very slim indeed, although it would be quick, much quicker than the captain's fishing dhow which would probably not put to sea again until close to the new year.

The weather had returned to clear blue skies and light winds, so in the morning after breakfast the old man invited me for a walk to the beach. He could tell there was something on my mind, and I told him of my conversation with Anja on the previous evening.

He thought for a while and said, 'I have an idea, but there is a danger to you.'

'Okay,' I said.

'Go ahead.'

'There is a man called Haddad who lives in Hilf. He is a rogue, and I do not like him. It is said, he killed his wife's lover and then smashed her right hand so badly that she couldn't eat and eventually she died.'

'That doesn't sound good.' I replied, knowing that some of the old man's stories tended to be exaggerated. 'Did they die on the island?' I asked.

'No,' he replied, 'Haddad is an Algerian. I'm not sure how he arrived here, but he has a lorry, and once a week he travels to Nizwa to collect things that are not easy to obtain on the island. Mainly furniture and machinery, but he is expensive and sometimes he sells his wares to the highest bidder. He is not very reliable, but it may be your best chance of getting away.'

For me, the decision was easy. I was willing to take the risk, but what about the cost? 'Your idea is a good one,' I replied, 'but I only have a small amount of money, and is it easy to get from Nizwa to Muscat?'

'Hmm, how much money do you have?' The old man looked at me intently.

'Just over a hundred Rials, I think, I haven't counted them properly.'

'Haddad will want more than a hundred for the trip to Nizwa, and then there's the ferry crossing.'

'Is that expensive?' I asked. 'No, less than ten Rials, but he will probably try to get you to pay for his lorry too.'

I was beginning to feel glum. He detected my mood and said, 'Don't worry, I can lend you some money. My son says you are a good man. I will speak with

Haddad this afternoon.' My gloom was lifted, although I wondered if this lorry driver was willing to take me as a passenger.

I didn't see the old man in the afternoon, but he was in his usual position for dinner, and he was smiling when I sat on a cushion next to him. There were some family members close by, and it was probably why he didn't mention Haddad during the meal. No opportunity arose for a conversation after the meal and I went to bed frustrated that from my perspective no progress had been made.

Next morning after breakfast, I was once again invited to the beach. 'I have good news for you, my friend. Haddad is willing to take you to Nizwa. He wanted two hundred and fifty Rials for the journey, but when I pointed out that it was cheaper to go by taxi, he reluctantly put the price down to two hundred Rials. He is leaving on the Sunday morning ferry that departs at nine o'clock. He said, he will buy your ticket. I am not sure that he will, but you can easily get a ticket when you get there.'

'Thank you,' I replied, 'but how do I get to Hilf?'

'Oh, I'll take you on my motorbike,' he replied, and I suddenly felt there could be more danger involved in the trip to Hilf than during the rest of the journey. That evening, I phoned Anja, and in a roundabout way I conveyed to her that I would be at the Spanish embassy in Muscat at nine o'clock on Monday morning.

Sunday arrived and making sure that I had my small quantity of personal belongings with me, and above all the flash drive, I set off on the back of a small Honda motorcycle to Hilf. Fortunately, the road was good, but it took all my strength to remain on the back of his whining machine. It was strange to see the bustle around the port. It had been a long time since I had seen so many people gathered together. There was only one lorry ready to board the ferry and the old man walked briskly towards it with me in pursuit.

I was introduced to Haddad, a large dark man with dishevelled curly hair and a permanent looking two-day growth of stubble. He stared at me through black expressionless eyes and nodded when my name was mentioned. The old man brought out a wad of Rials and counted out one hundred and gave them to Haddad. 'Half now, and half when you reach Nizwa,' as he handed a hundred to me. Nizwa scowled and began to protest, but the old man held up his hand and Haddad fell silent before spitting in the sand and climbing into the cab of his lorry.

I turned to express my thanks to the old man, and to my surprise he grabbed my arms and kissed me on both cheeks. He took my hand and pressed something into it before wishing me a good trip. He then turned and walked briskly towards his motorbike. I put whatever he had given me in my pocket, went around the other side of the lorry, opened the door and jumped in.

Haddad glanced at me malevolently and said, nothing. I asked him if he had a ferry ticket for me. I expected no would be the answer, but he rummaged through some papers by the gear stick and handed me a ticket.

'Ten Rials,' he said.

Trying to keep up a pretence of civility I thanked him and took a note from my knapsack and handed it to him. He snatched it from my hand and put it into a moneybag that he had belted round his waist. He then turned the ignition key and the engine reluctantly sprung into life. The diesel fumes that came through the window were a pleasant change from the smell of stale sweat that I would have to put up with on the journey across the desert.

The boarding of the ferry was rather haphazard but Haddad appeared to know what he was doing, and shortly after nine o'clock we began our trip to the mainland. The ferry was a modern catamaran which sped across the flat calm sea and arrived at Shannah, after less than hour on the water. The port, itself, was about two kilometres from the mainland to which it was connected by a causeway, but apart from a mosque and a few shacks, there was little in the way of infrastructure to suggest any town at all. Just after we left the port, Haddad pulled into a service station and filled the tank with diesel. I was expecting him to ask for money to pay for the fuel, but he didn't, and when he returned from having made his payment he threw two water bottles over to my side of the cab, so perhaps Haddad wasn't as bad as he had been made out to be.

The first fifty or so kilometres consisted of salt flats that appeared to be totally lifeless, and the monotony of the landscape was brain numbing. The colours ranged from sandy yellow, through to brilliant white with the occasional tinge of pink. However, the road had a good surface, and for entertainment there were rows of telegraph poles to count while we drove through this desert wilderness.

As we continued, I attempted small talk with Haddad, but his replies were mostly monosyllabic. He did get animated for a while about football, but my knowledge of that subject was limited and he fell silent again. Eventually, after almost two hours, the odd tussock of grass appeared amongst the sand, and even the occasional small shrub. I remarked on what a harsh climate Oman had, and didn't he find it depressing. I thought the question might elicit a conversation, and it did, but not in the way I expected.

'You're not a Moroccan,' Haddad said, sourly.

'Why did you say that?' I feigned surprise. 'Because your Arabic is not that of a Moroccan.'

It was a statement I was prepared for. 'I grew up in Zag, in the southwest and we spoke Berber at home and learnt Arabic and some French at school.'

It was a gamble. I thought it unlikely that he had been to that part of the country, and it proved to be the case.

He spat out of the open window. 'So, I was right, you're not a proper Moroccan.'

'Have you been there?' I asked, feeling a little braver.

'Yes, several times. I drove lorries to Nador.'

'That's near Melilla, isn't it?' I said, thinking that maybe his cargo dropped off close to the Spanish enclave wasn't strictly legal.

He glanced sideways at me. 'Yes,' he replied suspiciously, 'ever been there, to Melilla that is?'

'No.' I replied, 'Isn't it full of Africans trying to get asylum in Europe?'

'Yes, I believe so.' Haddad said, slowly, and the subject was then dropped.

'Why did you come to Oman?' I asked, partly to keep Haddad awake as he was beginning to appear drowsy. It did seem to make him more alert.

'It was a long time ago. I had trouble with my tax. They wanted to rob me of my hard-earned money and I said no and left.' He laughed, 'They got nothing.'

'So why did you come here, of all places?' I asked.

'I went to Saudi first, but didn't like it, then Abu Dhabi, but they didn't like me.' He roared with laughter, 'and then I came here. It's alright, people leave me alone.'

'Are you married?' I asked, wondering what the reaction would be.

'I was once,' He replied with a hint of bitterness in his voice, 'but no more, no more.' His voice faded into a whisper, and there was no more conversation until we reached Nizwa, some two hours later.

Nizwa was a busy city and the traffic was heavy. Haddad was snorting and grunting at the slow-moving vehicles, and as we approached the centre his mood worsened. I thought it was time to retrieve the money I owed him and leave. There had been no trouble on the trip, and although he hadn't been the best of travelling companions, I decided to give him an extra ten Rials for not trying to double-cross me in any way. He pulled into a coach-parking bay outside one of the many historic buildings that graced the city and I paid him. He was genuinely pleased with the extra ten Rials and we parted on friendly terms. The first half of the journey to Muscat had been completed without a problem.

I would like to have explored the city, it looked fascinating, and I was surprised how many groups of tourists were walking through the streets, but I was eager to continue travelling, and my next task was to find a taxi. I tried a couple of taxis but they were not interested in the trip, others were unoccupied, their drivers apparently having lunch somewhere. It was very frustrating. I wandered the streets, and alongside a river that desperately needed replenishing, before reaching the old fort. There were plenty of taxis outside, and they seemed to be keen to take passengers. The first one I tried wanted seventy Rials, but I thought I could probably find one cheaper. Eventually, I found a little man in a new Toyota that had a meter, and he said that a trip to the centre of Muscat would cost around fifty Rials. He seemed to be a straightforward, honest person, and for once I was relaxed when I opened the door and sat in the seat beside him.

It took a while to leave Nizwa, but once we had left the city, traffic was free flowing on excellent roads, most of which were dual carriageways. The scenery was an improvement too. It remained very dry, although there was an occasional watercourse, but there were rugged mountains with ancient villages nestling amongst them. Vegetation was still sparse, but occasionally date groves added a splash of green to the grey and brown landscape. The driver was a relaxed friendly type who made a point of telling me that he was Omani and the government only allowed Omani citizens to become taxi drivers. He seemed to be a proud man who was earning a good living to feed his wife and five children. He asked me a few questions, but he didn't wait for replies before he carried on talking about his family or the places he had been to in Oman. He was a very good ambassador for the country of his birth, and I must confess, what I had seen of this part of the sultanate justified his positive attitude.

As we neared Muscat, the landscape became somewhat greener, although it was obvious that irrigation played a large part in the greening. The density of the population increased and so did the traffic. The driver asked me where I wanted to go, conscious of the fact that his meter was clicking over and we were making only slow progress. I asked him to take me to an area where there were plenty of cheap hotels, and he cheerfully obliged. He pulled off into a side street and pointed to a hotel and said, it was cheap and he had met a Dutch couple who had stayed there and had said, it was okay.

The cost of the journey was a little more than he had anticipated, but the fifty-five Rials was considerably less than the other quote in Nizwa. I gave the driver a generous tip and walked the few metres to the hotel entrance. The receptionist was a smart middle-aged man with a smiling demeanour, but when I asked for a room he informed me that they were all full. I asked for a nearby recommendation, and he kindly phoned some hotels to see if they had any vacancies. At the fourth attempt, he found one that did. He said it was busy, and to my surprise, he said, it was because it was close to Christmas, and many Europeans came to Oman for their Christmas holiday.

The hotel he found was quite a long walk away, but the receptionist provided me with a street map, and before I left I asked if he would kindly mark the Spanish Embassy for me. He gave me a strange look, but without a word he went to his computer, looked up the address of the embassy and marked it on the map. It took nearly an hour to find the hotel, but with my dwindling money supply, I was reluctant to take a taxi, and anyway, the mid-afternoon temperature was pleasant and, of course, the sky was cloudless.

I was pleased that the new hotel was closer to the embassy, but it was situated on a busy main road and looked rather tatty. The receptionist was a small balding man with a forced smile. He was one of those people who would look untidy in a Savile Row suit, and he was certainly not wearing a suit. He was dressed in a checked shirt and brown trousers, and neither had seen a washing machine for some while. I didn't like him much, but he quoted nine Rials, and perhaps, after my so-called Christmas present waiting for me at the embassy had been collected, I could move to better accommodation. The room I was shown to was facing the main road and I suspected it would be noisy through much of the night. I asked for another room, and for a further three Rials I was shown to one. It was dark and dingy but considerably quieter, so I accepted it.

The bathroom had a western toilet, the first I had seen for many months. It wasn't particularly clean and there was this smell of bleach and sewage. The mattress was stained, but a clean white sheet had been thrown over it, and there was a covered roll of foam on the bed. I lay down and fell asleep instantly, only to be awoken around mid-evening by pangs of hunger. The sun had long set by the time I left the hotel in search of a restaurant. There were plenty of people in the street and I noticed two young couples, who were obviously English, and I asked them if they could recommend a restaurant nearby. They were suspicious of my motives, but when I said that I had only just arrived from Nizwa, they immediately assumed that I was just another tourist.

They had only been in Muscat for three days, but they pointed out an Indian restaurant less than a hundred metres along the road and said that they had been there on Saturday night and that it was good, 'but not as good as those in Manchester,' one quipped. They then wanted to talk, but I used hunger as a valid excuse for curtailing the conversation and left for the short walk to the restaurant. It lived up to its billing, and I would say it was one of the best meals I had eaten since leaving Europe.

After the meal, on the stroll back to the hotel, I began to think about the 'present' that was awaiting me at the embassy. I assumed that Anja had somehow arranged a Slovenian passport for me, or perhaps a Spanish one; she was certainly capable of that. I hoped it was the latter, because my knowledge of the Slovenian language was limited and to enter that country with less than a basic knowledge of the language would arouse suspicions. Perhaps there was some money, and maybe an airline ticket awaiting me, but the more I thought about it the more apprehensive I became.

I didn't have a good night's sleep, and when the early morning call came I felt decidedly groggy. It didn't help that a mere trickle of lukewarm water emerged from the showerhead. I quickly finished dressing and made myself as presentable as possible for the meeting at the embassy. I paid my hotel bill, retrieved my passport, and walked the short distance to the embassy. As I approached the gates a chill ran through me. I suddenly thought, *who am I?* My passport says Rachid Alami, but that's not me and, as far as I remember, I never mentioned my surname to Anja. If I gave my real name to the man at the gate, he would probably ask me to produce identification. It was a problem, and I had five minutes to solve it.

Honesty is the best policy as I introduced myself to a smart middle-aged man wearing a hat and dark glasses. He gave the appearance of someone that could be awkward. He asked for my passport, and on the spur of the moment, I told him that I had lost everything and I was at the embassy to collect new documentation. He asked for my name, checked it on the computer, and pointed to the door that I should enter, and with much relief I entered the Spanish Embassy.

Inside, it was more like a health centre waiting room than my perception of an embassy. There were plenty of comfortable chairs, but no occupants. In fact, the large airy room was deserted. A notice in Arabic, Spanish and English read reception. I waited for a minute or two before pushing the bell on the desk. The sound of footsteps was soon followed by the appearance of a young attractive woman of indeterminate origins.

She smiled and said, 'Mister Boateng?'

'Yes.' I replied, returning the smile. I wasn't sure what to expect, but this was an encouraging start.

'Carlos will be here to see you shortly.' She continued in less than perfect English, 'Please take a seat.'

About five minutes later a fairly elderly gentleman in a creased fawn lounge suit floated into the waiting area and beckoned for me to follow.

He led me through a long corridor and then into a windowless room, brightened by a few pictures that looked like representations of various parts of Spain, including one I knew well, the Alcazabar in Malaga.

He introduced himself and then extracted a leather briefcase from a cupboard. 'We understand you are a very important person Mr Boateng.' Carlos looked me straight in the eyes and smiled warmly.

'Am I?' I was genuinely surprised. He ignored the response and went on in almost perfect English.

'I have been instructed to give you various papers and objects. It is not in my brief to ask you any questions, but I am obliged to relieve you of any passports that you may have, any mobiles, laptops, any money, receipts. Do you understand?' It wasn't a command, more a statement, and I could see that it was sensible to dispose of my Moroccan passport; but why my money, and what about the paper notes and information on the flash drive from Bandar Abbas that nearly cost me my life? I was concerned that all the months of work would be for nothing.

I expressed my concerns and Carlos looked pensive. He seemed to come to a decision and I was invited to leave the room and return to the reception. Carlos watched as I walked along the corridor and re-entered the expansive waiting area. I had a feeling that this was going to take some while so I helped myself to a cup of coffee.

A few individuals were seated in the reception area and they were being dealt with, but it was over an hour before Carlos, looking somewhat flustered, requested that I accompany him again to the room near the end of the corridor. I entered, and to my astonishment all my personal possessions that I had handed over to Ahmet in Batumi were spread out on the table in front of me, and on the floor there was my old rucksack.

'I don't believe this,' I said, spontaneously. 'I never thought I would see these again.' Even my old laptop was there.

Carlos observed my reaction and seemed satisfied. 'It is my brief to ask you to leave everything behind that you came in with and take what you see in front of you.'

'Do you know why?' I asked quietly.

'No, and it's not for me to know.' Carlos replied with a slight note of irritation in his voice.

'But I have some important documents.' I protested, thinking of the scraps of paper that I had taken from the port in Bandar Abbas.

'Those are my instructions.' Carlos appeared resigned to confrontation, and I felt that I would be the loser.

'Okay,' I continued. 'Can I photograph the documents and load them onto my PC, and can I also copy the contents of my flash drive to my PC?'

After a moment's hesitation Carlos said, 'I believe so.'

I could not understand why I was being pressured into this, but it appeared to be the only chance of getting what I thought was vital information back to Europe. It took a long time to take the photographs of the relevant crumpled container receipts, send them to my email account and then delete them from the mobile. The flash drive contents were loaded onto the PC and then to cloud, and eventually I was satisfied that all the important documents were safely duplicated. I also made sure that there were no obvious signs remaining of the documents on my laptop. For whatever reason, my possessions were hot property, but I certainly didn't want to lose them. It was a point made to Carlos, who had stood patiently watching me making the copies.

'Are you instructed to destroy the originals?' I said, with just a hint of sarcasm.

As if he was reading a script, he replied. 'Everything will be stored for a while. It could be several years. That is our policy in situations like this.'

'Have you had situations like this?'

'No.' Carlos replied abruptly.

It was then time to look through my old possessions. Remarkably, everything appeared to be there. I thumbed through my passport, and I was amazed to find an entry stamp into Oman dated earlier in December, but the greatest joy was finding an airline ticket to Ljubljana leaving from Muscat International Airport in the early hours of the next morning. I looked at Carlos with tears of happiness in my eyes. He spread his hands and just smiled. It suddenly occurred to me that the flight could be going via Madrid, and I could be on their wanted list. I doubted it, though, and anyway, when I examined the ticket I could see there was one stop, and the connecting flight was from Frankfurt.

I changed my clothes, discarded the few other belongings that had served me well during the previous few months and after signing the obligatory form, I was ready to leave the embassy as the real me. I could only describe myself as being euphoric. I walked, almost skipped, out of the gates of the embassy, but after about ten metres I was confronted by two men in police uniform. One said, in Arabic 'Mister Alami, you're under arrest.'

Chapter 27

It was probably the most mood-changing moment of my life, to be told that you are under arrest moments after leaving the embassy as a reinvigorated free man. I had to think quickly, very quickly. I saw a navy blue and white vehicle across the road and it had 'Police' in English written on the side door, so I was left in little doubt that these were real policemen. They were armed, so running away was not a sensible option, and anyway, I was intrigued to know why I had been stopped, but firstly, I had to remember how to be an Englishman.

I tried to look fearful, in fact I probably was fearful, and said, somewhat indignantly 'I don't understand.' They spoke to me again in Arabic, and in a manner typical of an Englishman abroad, I repeated 'I don't understand.' but louder.

The first, more senior looking, officer, looked a bit nonplussed, but his younger colleague said, in accented English, 'We are arresting you.'

This was the break I was looking for 'Why, what have I done? You can't do that.' I was proud of my theatrics, and it seemed to weaken the resolve of the first officer.

The other one, however, was more confident. 'We have been ordered to detain you because you have been identified as Rachid Alami.'

'Who?' I said, with a forced smile.

The first officer, who was losing eye contact with me, probably doubted my Moroccan identity. He asked me in Arabic for my passport. I looked blank. There was a long pause before the younger man said, in English, 'Passport.' I opened the front of my rucksack and produced my passport. I handed it to the younger man, who examined it and then handed it to the older man. By this time, they had decided I had no knowledge of Arabic and quite a heated discussion took place between them with my passport going to and fro between the two men.

After a while, the younger man said, 'We would like you to come to the police station with us.'

'But why?' I protested, 'I have a plane to catch.'

The plane was not due to leave until the early hours of the following morning, but it had been my intention to go to the airport as soon as possible. A further discussion ensued and it appeared the younger man was ready to release me and just say it was a case of mistaken identity, but the older officer was not willing to do that, and I gathered from the conversation, that although the first officer agreed with his colleague, he had been told by his boss to bring me in, and that was what he was going to do.

'What time is your plane leaving?' The younger officer asked.

'After midnight.' I replied.

'Come with me.' The older officer pointed to the car across the road.

'But I haven't done anything wrong.' I said vehemently.

'Ask those in the embassy, ask the gatekeeper. They know who I am.' The older officer hesitated, but then said, again. 'Come with me.' It was a strange arrest. I wasn't handcuffed, I wasn't searched, I wasn't bundled into the car like you see in films. It was more an invitation to join these men at the police station, but an invitation that I couldn't refuse.

It was about a three or four kilometre drive to the police station and it was made in silence with the younger man driving and the older man sitting beside me in the back seat. At the police station, it was quiet and I was given curious glances by other officers as I was led along a brightly lit corridor to a small room, but with a window overlooking a grassy area with a couple of trees. At least, I wasn't led away to the cells. The older man said something to the younger man which I didn't quite catch and then left, shutting the door behind him. The younger officer asked if I wanted some water, and when I nodded he went to the cold-water dispenser in the corner and brought me a cup of water. He then sat down by the door and looked at me.

'Do you not want to search me, or anything.' I said, after a while. I thought about saying I might be carrying a bomb, but maybe that would have been the wrong thing to say in the circumstances. 'Have you any idea why I have been brought here?' I asked. I had heard horror stories of people being incarcerated in Middle Eastern police stations, and although this place looked forbidding from the outside, it appeared quite comfortable inside.

The young man thought for a minute and said, 'I don't know why you have been brought here, but if you have done nothing wrong then you have nothing to worry about. We have a very honest police force in this country.' He smiled benevolently, and that made me feel more relaxed.

It was an hour or so later that the older police officer came into the room, whispered something to the younger man, and I was escorted to another office occupied by a man of medium build and wearing a smart suit.

'Mister Alami,' the man said.

'No,' I interrupted, 'Mister Boateng, and why am I here?'

'Okay, Mister Boateng, if you like,' and he introduced himself.

I didn't catch his name but he was an inspector. He seemed a pleasant fellow but his eyes showed a deep intelligence and I was immediately aware that he could prove difficult to lie to.

'That question will be answered in good time,' the inspector replied in perfect English,' but first of all we need you to answer a few questions.' He gestured to the young officer, who had remained standing by the door, and asked him in Arabic to spread the contents of my large rucksack on a large side table.

He then asked me for my passport. 'I understand that you are leaving us today. Are you going back to Morocco, no, sorry England?'

I felt that he was teasing me, and I said, with as much verbal aggression as possible without shouting. 'I'm going to Slovenia to visit my girlfriend for Christmas.'

He appeared to be surprised by the answer. 'We do not have flights to Slovenia.' He looked slightly bemused.

'I'm flying via Frankfurt in Germany. There's a ticket in the front of my rucksack, if you care to look.' Without prompting, the young officer withdrew my airline ticket from my rucksack and handed it to the inspector.

He looked at it and said, 'Are you not spending Christmas with your family?' For me, this was a breakthrough. He now seemed to be accepting that I wasn't Moroccan.

'My parents are probably working over Christmas and I prefer to see my girlfriend.'

'Where in England do your parents live?' He asked.

'North London.' I replied.

'Very nice place.' The inspector replied, 'I know it well. I did some training in Hendon, do you know it?'

I didn't know it very well, but I was now on home territory and I was feeling more confident about how the conversation was proceeding.

'I grew up in Highgate,' I responded, but my father works quite close to Hendon.

'Do you know the Spaniards Inn?' The inspector inquired. I gave him a puzzled look.

'Yes, it's next to the heath, Hampstead Heath, Why?'

'I just wondered,' the inspector commented. He continued 'Would you like a cup of coffee, and we'll see what you have with you.'

The contents of my rucksack were neatly laid out on the table. I regretted taking my expensive binoculars with me to Batumi, because that was the only item that really stood out as an unusual accessory for a holidaymaker in Oman.

The inspector noticed it. 'Nice binoculars you have there, Mister Boateng, good for spying on people I think.' He smiled cheekily and looked into my eyes and beyond.

'That may be,' I responded, 'but they are very good for bird spotting.'

'So, you're an orni, er...whatever it is.' The cheeky smile remained and I was sure that he derived pleasure from this gentle interrogation.

'There are some very good places for bird spotting in Oman. I hear there are many birds to see in Masirah Island. Do you know it?'

'Well, it's strange that you should say that.'

I was beginning to think this was more than teasing. 'I spent some time in Masirah, and yes, there were plenty of birds.' I realised I could get myself into deep water and changed the subject.

'You have lovely weather here in December, not like in London where it's usually grey and drizzly.'

He ignored me, and went on, 'Did you see any Egyptian Vultures? Splendid bird, never seen one myself.' He looked at me expecting an answer, and as it happened I had seen one, in fact I had seen two. They had been pointed out to me by my host on the island when we had been for our morning walks.

'Yes, I did see a couple.' I replied nonchalantly, hoping that he wasn't really that interested. I then took a chance and went on the offensive.

'Have you been bird spotting in Masirah?'

'No, I haven't.' He replied.

'Never been there, I hope to go one day.' I carried on.

'So, you haven't told me what I have done wrong yet. Why am I here?'

'We haven't said that you have done anything wrong, we're just making some enquiries.'

'Have I answered your questions appropriately?' I chose the word appropriately on purpose to see his reaction.

He laughed. 'I can see you are a clever man, Mister Boateng, but so am I. Please pack your bag and my officer will take you to the airport and see you on to your flight.'

'Is that it?' I asked.

'Yes, Mister Boateng, that is it.' I packed my clothes and other items into the rucksack. My wallet had been opened and the contents neatly arranged by the officer on the table but the Inspector had not even looked at them. My passport had remained in the Inspector's hands throughout our conversation, and he had one last thumb through it before handing it back to me. I felt there was going to be one last catch to this, but when I had crammed everything into the rucksack and was ready to go he proffered his hand and I shook it like two friends would do. The officer looked somewhat bemused but opened the door and walked slowly along the corridor.

As I left the Inspector's spacious room, he whispered in my ear, 'The next time you come to Oman Mister Boateng, I hope you won't arrive in a fishing boat. Goodbye, and good luck.'

Chapter 28

The young policeman seemed somewhat resentful that I had changed from being a criminal to something of a VIP, but his brief was to see to it that I left the country, and presumably it was not for him to reason why. Outside the police station, the older officer was talking to colleagues by his car, and when the younger man explained to him what had gone on inside, he looked at me curiously, but with a certain amount of respect. This time, instead of putting the rucksack on the front seat, the younger officer sat on the front seat, and I was politely asked to go into the rear seat with my rucksack.

The journey to the airport was about forty kilometres, but the traffic was heavy and it took nearly an hour to get there from the police station. I thought I was just going to say thank you and make my way through into the departure hall, but I was wrong. I was escorted to the VIP area and quickly processed through passport control and security. I was then ushered into the VIP lounge, where a handful of passengers were sitting.

I felt like a common criminal and somewhat self-conscious having two uniformed policemen as companions, and there were several derisive looks from other occupants in the lounge. There were several hours before the flight was scheduled to leave and I asked if I could have a walk around the modern terminal. To my surprise, my request was granted, but the older officer accompanied me on my walk. It was another splendidly designed airport, complete with palm trees. Many of the shops commonly found in European airports were present, including alcohol in abundance.

I decided to buy a filigree silver bracelet for Anja. She was not one for wearing jewellery, but on a couple of occasions I had seen her wearing a bracelet. I then collected a few souvenirs of Oman, including a small carved wooden camel, a memory of my time in Masirah. It occurred to me, as I was standing in the queue to pay, that my credit card had not been used for months and maybe it had been blocked, but no, it was fine, and with a bag loaded with duty frees, my minder and I returned to the VIP lounge. As the older officer was poor in English, conversation was limited and I thought it prudent not converse with him in Arabic, although I had become fairly proficient in that language. I suggested that we went for something to eat and I made it clear that I would pay for his meal. This was something that pleased him, and he became bolder in his use of English, and our time together passed quicker.

Eventually my flight was ready for boarding, and at the departure gate I said goodbye to the now friendly police officer. The plane was only a few minutes late leaving, but it was with a great sigh of relief that we took to the skies and headed northwest along the Gulf towards Turkey, and then over Europe to Frankfurt. The flight took about seven hours, and apart from turbulence over Turkey, there were no problems. I had an aisle seat and the middle seat was unoccupied. The occupant of the window seat was a middle-aged man of Middle Eastern appearance who seemed to sleep throughout the flight.

In Frankfurt, I sent a short text message to Anja, just to let her know I was now in Europe. The connecting flight to Ljubljana was delayed and I had plenty of time to wander around the busy terminal building, and this time alone. There were the trappings of Christmas everywhere but the main difference to the airport in Muscat was the clothing. Passengers in Frankfurt were either wearing, or carrying, heavy coats, and outside there was drizzle and low cloud, something I hadn't seen for months. I ate breakfast in one of the cafes, and I never thought that I could enjoy toast so much, an item of food that had not graced my plate for such a long time.

Eventually, the 'flight boarding' notice appeared on the departures screen and I made my way to the gate. The short flight of just over an hour was completely full, and I wondered how Anja, or whoever it was, had managed to get me a seat at such short notice. I had a window seat, and next to me there was a German couple, who were excited at the prospect of spending Christmas with their daughter and family in Ljubljana. They did not stop talking the whole flight, and they even brushed aside the offer of tea or coffee so they could continue talking. It actually made the time go quickly, and I was grateful that they did not ask me any questions. I wished them well after we touched down in Ljubljana as they, like almost everyone else on the plane, impatiently shuffled towards the doors in an attempt to leave the plane a minute or two earlier than they otherwise would. I waited until the melee had subsided before grabbing my rucksack and joining the now orderly queue.

I expected no problems at passport control, and there were none, and it was my turn to become excited as I strode towards the green channel and then out into the arrivals waiting area. It was very crowded and noisy and many people were holding sheets of paper with names on. I looked around for Anja but couldn't see her. I continued walking until I reached a quieter area by a car-hire desk and then sent a message. Two minutes later, she appeared with a big welcoming smile.

We hugged for a long while without saying anything, but I then became aware of a man, probably about sixty years old, standing a few metres away looking at us. He had a kindly, but careworn, face, and he just stood there staring.

I whispered in Anja's ear, 'There's someone looking at us.'

'Yes,' Anja said, 'Let me introduce you to my father.'

Franc was his name and for a salesman he seemed extraordinarily shy. He let Anja do the talking, and for me, it was like returning home after a short trip away.

As usual, Anja had decided what we were going to do, and that was to spend Christmas with Franc at his house in Maribor, and then to go to Bled for New Year, unless, of course, I had any objections, which I hadn't. Franc had his car at the airport, and he drove us in his ageing Volkswagen to Maribor. It took us about an hour and a half through the drab mist-shrouded countryside. Even in the heated car, it was difficult to keep warm, but the most noticeable thing was how grey everything appeared without the sunshine. We sat in the back seat and Anja just talked, with only the briefest of interruptions from her father or me. Franc's house in Maribor was actually a small, but neat, whitewashed bungalow set amongst rows of large houses not far from the centre.

Immediately we were inside, Franc began preparing food, and in spite of our protests he insisted we should sit in the lounge and continue to get reacquainted. Up to that point, we had not spoken directly about work, and when I made an indirect reference to it. Anja put a finger to her lips and pointed at the walls, before talking about the imminent Christmas. I felt sorry for Franc, but Anja was quick to point out that he had lived alone for many years and it was best not to disturb his home routine too much, otherwise he was just happy to have us there. I phoned my parents, and they were overjoyed to hear from me. It had been a long time since contact had been made, but they knew months of silence went with the job, and they didn't appear too concerned. They asked when I was coming home again, but that was something I didn't know. I felt a pang of guilt about the neglect, so after the conversation I ordered some flowers to be delivered to them on the following day.

On Christmas Eve, in Maribor, we had the traditional meal of pork roast, followed by Potica, a sweet nut roll that Franc was proud to inform us that he had made himself. It was somewhat dry, but Anja insisted that we had ice cream with it. Needless to say, there was plenty of good Slovenian red wine served with the meal and afterwards we played Tarok, a card game that had been played in households across the country for hundreds of years. For me, it was a steep learning curve as the card pack was different to the ones I had been used to, but with increasing knowledge it became more fun, and it was a jolly finish to the evening.

Christmas Day was the day for exchanging presents. As neither Anja nor I drank spirits, the duty-free liqueurs and whisky were presented to Franc who was very appreciative of the gesture. My gift for Anja was a hit, and she gave me a silver pig on a chain, which she assured me would bring luck. She said, there would be something else but that I would have to wait. In the afternoon, there was a knock at the door. Franc answered it, and a woman of about fifty years old was invited in.

She was introduced to us as Ana. She was very shy and Franc was somewhat embarrassed, but said that she was his girlfriend and they had been seeing each other for over a year. It was obvious that Anja had not met her before, but there was a warm greeting, and it didn't take long before she was chatting freely, although her English was rather stilted. Alcohol improved that aspect of her language and after dinner a few rounds of Tarok, a game in which she was an accomplished player, culminated in a very enjoyable end to Christmas.

Anja suggested that I gave my parents a call before we left on Boxing Day morning as we might not have the opportunity in Bled. I thought that was strange, but rather than question it, I went ahead and called them. They both had the day off work and we had a long conversation, although most of it was from their side. They said, a friend had called round a few times to speak with me but as I had instructed, they hadn't revealed my address in Tooting, nor had they given him my telephone number. They didn't know him but he called himself Bernie, and however deep I went into my memory bank, I also couldn't think who that could possibly be.

After lunch on Boxing Day. Anja packed a large hamper of food from the fridge, and Franc packed us and the hamper into the small Volkswagen and drove us to Anja's flat in Ljubljana. We wished the kindly and generous Franc a good trip home and we were then alone again in the flat, just like we were in the early summer. As usual, Anja had been well organised, and she had ordered bus tickets for us to travel to Bled early on the following day.

For the first time since I had arrived back in Slovenia, the sun shone on the twenty-seventh, and it was pleasantly mild as we boarded the morning bus up to the lake. It was full, and many had brought skis with them, although there wasn't a trace of snow to be seen. Anja's uncle was not at the house, and we had the place to ourselves again, although Anja said, there was a group renting the property in early January, so we could only stay for a week. Only for a week, I thought, but even two days in this beautiful place would be enough for me after weeks of living in a sandy wasteland.

It was still morning when we arrived in Bled, and Anja suggested we take some food and bottles of water to the lake as it would take a while for the house to warm up. Even though the sun shone, it was quite cold, and there were not that many people out walking. We found a bench on the water's edge, and I think we both realised that it was the first time we had been completely alone to safely talk since we had been reunited before Christmas. I had already thanked Anja for her efforts in getting me out of Oman, but she just dismissed it casually by saying it was part of her job. I felt somewhat aggrieved that she regarded my rescue from Oman as 'part of the job' but she said a lot had happened while I had been away, and before I made a judgement on her she wanted to update me. I admired her professional attitude, and I suppose if she was going to tell me what had happened she still trusted me. That was good, so I sat back on the bench and listened.

Anja began by saying, 'I would like you to hear me out because there are things I am going to say that you might not like, and some of them you may not believe.' Her voice was assured, but slightly apologetic. I knew by her tone that this was going to be important news, but about what, I had no idea.

Chapter 29

Anja went on. 'You remember when we talked about governments being complicit in the introduction of these drugs into their countries?' She looked at me, I nodded. I remember the conversation and I think I was fairly dismissive at the time, but since then I had become less sure. She continued. 'Scientists from several countries have produced evidence that the cannabis we have been chasing does have mind-bending attributes, giving a sort of psychosis, and that populist governments are using this for their own political ends and they are having considerable success.' I must have looked somewhat sceptical, because Anja continued 'Yes, of course it sounds like something from science fiction, but well-researched papers have been published, and although most of the media machine, orchestrated by various governments, have tried to discredit the findings, there are some journalists investigating the link, and at least one has died because of it.'

I let out a *phew*, 'Is that true?' I said, blandly.

Anja paused while a middle-aged couple and a dog strolled by.

After a couple of minutes she resumed, 'In Italy, a well-known journalist was shot dead, and in London a young reporter, who was a rising star in an anti-government national newspaper, got run over and killed as he was leaving his local public house. A coincidence, maybe, maybe not. The police report said he was drunk and it was an accident, but the name of the driver of the car was not revealed, to protect his family, they say. There is more, though; the men, and sometimes women and children, that used to sell drugs on street corners, or at large gatherings, have been pushed aside by a more sophisticated type of salesman. All the time, the English media were supporting the government and talking about conspiracy theories, while internet access to certain sites was becoming more and more restricted.' Anja paused while a middle-aged jogger loped by.

After looking around, she carried on, 'It appeared the government-led media had won over the people, and the story disappeared from the news bulletins and the front pages, but then there was, in some ways, a fortuitous accident. It happened in southeast England, on the motorway between Dover and London, in early November, there was a big accident. It was foggy, I think, and several vehicles were involved. A number of people were killed, including the driver of a container lorry. When the local police were clearing up the mess, and apparently it was quite bad, they found that the container, although not badly damaged, had lost a door and a replacement was needed. The company that owned the contents of the container was summoned and they transferred the items to another lorry.'

'What were the items?' I asked.

'I'm coming to that,' Anja replied and continued, 'It was office furniture from Slovenia.'

'Okay,' I said. This was now becoming interesting.

'Yes,' Anja looked slightly irritated by my interruption. 'To allow the motorway to be re-opened quicker, various people had been called in to help. One of those people was a sort of policeman, not sure what you call them?' It was a question, she looked at me.

'It was probably a community support officer, he or she often works alongside the police to prevent crime. Anyway, they do a good job, carry on.' I could see that Anja didn't want a long definition and she immediately resumed talking.

'His name was Tom Scrubs, although that's irrelevant, and it's not a name you'll probably see anywhere. Anyway, he was helping to shift a cupboard and he noticed slight damage to the back. He also noticed that there was, what looked like sacking, the corner of which was leaking something. He smelt it and realised it was cannabis resin. He took a quantity of it and repaired the leak 'as best he could,' they are his words, but instead of going to the police, the clever young man contacted the national newspaper that had been pursuing the government in their drugs investigation.

A reporter then met the youngster, took the drug for analysis and found it to be this bad cannabis that we have been chasing.'

I let out a quiet 'wow'.

'It gets better.' Anja said, smiling. 'The reporter managed to find out where the office furniture went to, and it was an industrial unit in Wimbledon. The company was operating lawfully and had been importing furniture from Slovenia for some time, in fact, about the same length of time that this new variant of the drug had been known in England. The police raided the premises and took away various items, witnessed by the reporter and a cameraman, and next day the national newspaper ran an exclusive about the drugs raid. The strange thing was that only one other paper even mentioned the drugs raid, and nothing was broadcast on television or radio.'

'Why was that, then?' I instinctively asked.

'I'm coming to that.' Anja replied, 'The company that was importing the furniture was one of those secretive offshore ones, but the reporter was not to be put off, and he found out that one of the active directors was a government minister.'

'Wow.' I said, somewhat louder this time.

'Yes, and he had links to the security services where you work.'

'Really,' I replied. I was beginning to think this was becoming a bit far-fetched.

'He is a close friend of Sir Oliver Legg,' Anja continued.

'Are you saying,' I interrupted, 'that the minister and Legg are mixed up with the importation of cannabis?'

'We believe so.' Anja replied.

'But why?' I asked.

'As we've talked about before, your government wants to cling to power at any cost, and to brainwash the young people by allowing these mind-bending drugs into the country is of the highest priority for them.'

'But don't they realise that they will be found out?' I countered weakly.

'And who will find them out?' Anja responded.

'Well, for a start, this reporter and the newspaper he works for.'

'Not anymore,' Anja replied. 'The reporter is dead, and the story has died with him, at least in your country.'

'Really,' I retorted. 'Is the reporter the one that was run over?'

'Yes.' Anja replied abruptly.

'But that's outrageous.'

'Yes.' Anja repeated.

We fell silent. A crow cackled in the tree above us, and it shook us both back to the present.

'What happens next, then?' I asked Anja somewhat despondently.

'The European media continue to run the story, and in Italy, there's a similar sort of scandal that has led to ministerial resignations. We just have to be patient. The factory, in this country, where the furniture was produced is under surveillance, although the chance of any more drugs arriving there are low.' There was a pause, 'How did you get on?'

This was the first time she had asked about my hardships, apart from a brief sympathetic 'Oh dear,' a reference to the ugly scar on my shoulder, noticed during a passionate bout of lovemaking on our first night back together. I was slightly concerned about this almost callous indifference to my sufferings, but her 'walls have ears' mantra was my reason not to doubt her fondness for me.

'I had a few problems.' I began, and I was almost lost for words because the big picture was not about me, and I knew that Anja shared our almost manic wish to bring these drug traffickers to justice. I gave her a precis of what had happened and watched to see her reaction. It was not one of astonishment as I had expected, or even concern, but more like adding information to her case history. I was a little perturbed.

'Did you know if I was still alive before I contacted you from Oman?' I asked suddenly.

She seemed taken aback and stared at me. 'It's just that you don't seem that surprised about what I've been telling you.'

'I'm not.' Anja replied, and it was my turn to be taken aback.

'Why?'

Anja smiled. 'If it is our business to know something, then we find it out if we can. I may appear heartless, but it was my business to know about what was happening to you, you're very special to me.'

Tears welled up in her eyes and I felt incredibly guilty for doubting her.

'Did you know that Ahmet got killed?' I said, after a pause.

'He didn't.' Anja replied, 'He's in prison in Tehran.'

'Well, at least he's alive, but it's not good, is it?'

'He'll be alright.' Anja responded.

'But he killed a policeman.' I added.

'Not killed, just wounded.'

'Okay, that's something. How do you know all this?'

'I work for the intelligence services.' Anja replied, 'You know that.'

'But so do I.' I said, weakly, 'and I don't know half of what you know.'

Anja gave me a wicked grin and said, 'Do go on.'

I did, and she became very interested when I told her about the information gathered at the port in Bandar Abbas, and it was yet to be translated and analysed. 'It sounds exciting.' Her eyes gleamed as she grabbed my arm, got up and dragged me back towards her uncle's house.

'We must find out if it was all worthwhile.' The house had become tolerably warm by the time we arrived back and Anja rummaged in my rucksack for the computer. She set it up on the kitchen table for me, and within five minutes we were sitting in front of the screen, a sandwich and a cup of coffee on either side, as we accessed the Iranian files on Cloud.

There were tingles of excitement in both of us as we extracted the files and copied them into google translate. Most of them were of little interest to us, with intricate details of tonnage, numbers of sacks and their legitimate contents. It took us a long while to find anything about the transportation method, or where the carrier arrived from, but eventually the crumpled-up piece of paper, that had lain in my pocket for months, and that I remembered to photograph in the embassy, revealed the point of departure of the ship, and when we saw it we both let out gasps of amazement.

Chapter 30

'I didn't even know they grew rice commercially in Australia.' I said.

'No,' said, Anja. 'And if they did I would have expected it to be grown in the north where it rains a lot, but that part of Australia, that really is surprising.'

We had forgotten about our rule of not talking about work inside buildings, but Anja said, she was fairly sure that there were no listening devices in her uncle's house.

We then searched for more information about the ship and found out it was a regular conveyor of rice from Melbourne to Bandar Abbas, and on average it took thirty-four days.

'That fits in with what we have observed,' said Anja. 'There always seemed to be around five weeks between active periods when we suspected that the drugs were being distributed, but of course, they were clever, and until recently it had been impossible to break the cycle.'

I searched for rice production centres in Australia, and it appeared that the crop was mainly grown in southern parts of New South Wales. I had always thought that rice was grown in places where it rained on a regular basis, like Southeast Asia, and that a drought-prone country like Australia struggled by with grain and vines in the less harsh areas, and a few large sheep farms. For me it was a steep learning curve, and I only vaguely heard Anja say, 'I suppose you'll be going to Australia next?'

It was a thought that hadn't yet occurred to me, and as the cold wind increased and rattled the shutters outside the windows, it seemed an inviting prospect to head to Australia for their summer. 'You are going to tell Greg, I suppose?'

Anja looked at me with some merriment in her eyes. She knew I was not very keen on him, and probably thought that I was somewhat jealous that she was on good terms with him.

'I wasn't going to, no.' I replied, 'Do you think it is necessary?'

'He is Australian, and I'm sure he knows how to get things done there.' Anja responded, 'But do you trust him?'

I stared at Anja. I was slightly irritated that she had even suggested that I should cooperate with him. 'Yes, I have no reason to doubt him.'

'What part of Australia is he from?' I said sharply.

'I don't know, why?'

'It's not somewhere near Melbourne, is it?' Anja was beginning to get a bit flustered.

I continued. 'You don't think that he may be the so-called Englishman that everyone talks about. Perhaps he's the Mister big.' This was beginning to escalate into a row which I didn't want, and I'm sure Anja didn't want either.

'Okay,' I said after a while, 'but I'd rather do this by myself this time. I know Ahmet was very useful in Iran, and I'm grateful for that, but Australia is English speaking and it should be easier to find out things.' We left it at that, but I could see Anja wasn't particularly happy about the situation. We slowly regained our usual jollity during the evening, and that was complete the following morning when we awoke to see ten centimetres of snow covering the ground outside.

Before going for the inevitable walk in the snow, we had to think through a strategy for Australia. I looked for flights to Melbourne, but the price was very high and the connecting flights meant that it would take me two days to get there. I then looked at Sydney. It was still expensive, and the journey time was almost halved. There were two changes on the way, one in Istanbul and the other one in Kuala Lumpur. The next problem was a visa and the reason for going in a hurry, because normally the visa would take several weeks to obtain.

'Regent honeyeater.' I said, after a long perusal of the internet. Anja looked at me strangely.

'Pardon?'

'It's a rare bird and it could soon become extinct.'

'In the next few days?' Anja seemed concerned.

'No, no, but the dreadful fires they have had in southeast Australia have decimated the population and I had better hurry up before more fires break out.'

Anja laughed. 'Are you going bird spotting?'

'Yes, why not?' I replied, 'I have these very good binoculars, you know.'

Anja shook her head and looked out of the window where the snow was still tumbling down.

My first step was to apply for an emergency e-visa. It said online that around ninety-five percent of approved applications are dealt with within an hour. I filled in the form and sent it electronically. I could see that Anja was keen to go out, and I thought, even if the application was accepted, the Christmas holiday probably meant that there was only a skeleton staff operating. The rest of the morning was ours so we went down to the lake and retraced the route we had taken together many months before.

'Do you remember the last time we sat here?' I said, as we brushed the snow off a bench and sat down and looked out over the unfrozen lake.

'Yes.' Anja replied. I laughed to myself at the revelation Anja had made all those months ago about killing someone. It was shocking. I looked around to make sure we were completely alone and said, 'Do you still carry a gun?'

'Yes.' Anja said, quietly, and with a wry smile, she continued, 'but I haven't used it for a while.'

We fell silent. 'Do you ski or snowboard?' Anja said, suddenly.

'No, never have, always preferred warm holidays.'

'Would you like to try?'

'Okay, but where?' I wasn't that keen, but if it was something Anja wanted to do I was game to try.

'What about equipment?' I was beginning to lose my bravado.

'What size shoes do you have?' Anja said.

'They're tens, I think.'

'But what's that in European units?' Anja countered.

'About forty-four or forty-five, I'm not sure, actually. Why?'

'My uncle has skis and ski boots in the cellar and he won't mind you borrowing them.'

'Are you sure?' I replied, 'I wouldn't like to break or damage them.' I felt that I was being cornered, 'but what about clothes?'

'Oh, he has those, too.' I could see that Anja was enjoying my discomfort, but there was no other option than to accede to her wish.

We spent the remainder of the day ambling round the lake with a long break for coffee and cream cakes. The snow had stopped falling by the time we arrived back at the house and breaks in the cloud suggested a frosty night to come. I went straight to the computer when we were inside, and to my great joy, I found my request for an emergency visa had been granted. The next task was to find a flight.

'How long do you think I should stay there?' I asked Anja, more to judge what her feelings were about me leaving for Australia.

'If you find what you are looking for there, are you going to call the police?' Anja said.

'I wasn't going to.' I replied, 'So, what are you going to do, then?'

'I suppose, I'll report back to my boss and he'll instruct me.' There was a pause.

'Sometimes Sean, you're so naive.' Anja continued, 'There's corruption in your government, there's probably corruption in your intelligence services, and you're going to report back to your boss? Do you know that he's honest?'

I had to admit there had been some strange things going on at work, and Anja was right, if I made the wrong decision I could jeopardise the whole operation.

'What do you suggest, then?' I said it with resignation because I knew, and not for the first time, that she knew a lot more about this business than I did.

'You should contact Greg and talk about what you should do.'

'No,' I said forcefully, 'I don't trust him, and to me it seems strange that he turns up here occasionally. Perhaps just when the consignment of drugs is arriving. No. I'll do this myself and report back to you.'

Anja blushed, 'You're learning fast, Sean.'

I scrolled through the list of flights available and found one leaving on the evening of the third of January and arriving on the morning of the fifth in Sydney. The flight time was over twenty-nine hours with changes at Istanbul and Kuala Lumpur. It seemed like an arduous journey, but if I could get results in Australia we may be able to put an end to this odious smuggling.

'Where are you going to stay?' Anja said.

'Hotels, I suppose. Why?'

'Do you think that the average bird spotter looking for a regent honeyeater would stay in a hotel?' Anja went on.

'Are you suggesting that I camp?' I felt that was exactly what she was suggesting, and I didn't like the idea of it.

'Isn't Australia full of unfriendly spiders and snakes?'

'Oh yes, everywhere you look.' I could see she was enjoying this.

'I thought that you could rent a camper van.' Anja suggested.

'They're a bit big.' I said, weakly.

'You could get a small one, unless you were thinking of sharing it with someone else.' I held up my hands. Anja's ideas appeared sound, again, and I booked a small camper van to be collected at Sydney airport on arrival.

When we had completed all the necessary preparations for the trip, we went to the cellar to look for ski gear. I was hoping that the boots were too small or the skis were broken, but Anja pointed out enthusiastically that there was a good shop in the town where I could hire ski equipment, and I soon realised that I was in a corner with no escape. As it happened, the ski boots were too big, but an extra pair of socks solved that, and on the following morning we set off for the slopes.

The sun was shining from a clear blue sky, and although a chilly wind was blowing, it was uplifting weather. Anja was obviously a competent skier, and she said that she had been skiing since she was a child. It took lots of patience from her to teach me, but there was some progress amid plenty of laughter. I was a little worried about breaking a leg before my trip south, and I did proceed tentatively, but after a couple of days I had mastered the basics, and on the third day I went up the chair lift to try the main slope.

It looked terrifying to me, but Anja said, it was a blue run, the second easiest, and we would stop half way where there was a ski tow on a green run which was very easy. She was very confident in my ability, I wasn't.

We stood together in the queue awaiting our turn on the chair lift. We edged forward, and all of a sudden we were side by side waiting for the chair to sweep us off the ground and upwards. I looked behind and watched as it came menacingly round the corner. The seat hit me just above the knee, and in a very short space of time we were at tree level above the snowy landscape. My knees were trembling at the prospect of exiting the chair at the other end, but I observed what the couple in front did, and apart from a gentle nudge from the chair, the departure was relatively elegant.

Although we were not that high, the views were stunning. Anja let me take in the scenery, but after a while I could see she was becoming impatient and I had to try and negotiate the slopes safely. It was quite busy, with a mix of snowboarders and skiers, but people seemed considerate towards each other. I asked Anja if she had any good tips and what the etiquette was on the slopes. Her main concern was the trees, and there were many of them bordering the piste, but she also said, if you go into the trees you'll upset the bears. That did worry me a little.

To my surprise, I did manage to return to the bottom of the slope without injury, and I was confident enough to try again on the following day, and by New Year's Eve I was actually enjoying the sport. There was a tinge of sadness as we celebrated the New Year. We were going to part again, but neither of us spoke about the future, and to cap it all, low clouds shrouded Bled, and the firework display at midnight was rather muted. It was drizzling on New Year's Day so we decided to go back to Ljubljana a day early. It wasn't possible to change our bus tickets from the second to the first, but Anja found someone who was driving a minibus of Spanish tourists to the airport, and we managed to squeeze in, and at the airport we were able to take a taxi into the centre of Ljubljana.

'Have you changed your mind about Greg?' Anja said, as we walked from the station to Anja's flat.

'No,' I replied, 'I think I'm safer alone.'

'As you wish.'

And those were the last words she said, on the subject. For some reason, the atmosphere in the flat was a bit tense, and we decided to eat out in the evening. Some levity returned after a shared bottle of red wine, but I detected worry in Anja that I hadn't seen before. It didn't really lift on the following day, and on the evening of the third, as I waved goodbye to Anja at the airport, I felt quite alone in the world once again.

Chapter 31

The two-and-a-half-hour flight to Istanbul was uneventful. It was a full plane and the passengers were very mixed with international tourists, Slovenians, who appeared to be returning to Turkey to work, and Turks, who had taken advantage of the holiday break in Europe to visit relatives. These, of course, were assumptions, but the young Slovenian family that were gathered around my seat, were definitely going back to Istanbul to work, and to my surprise, their children were going to an English-speaking school in the city. They were all communicative, and that leg of the flight passed by quickly. Not so the second leg from Istanbul to Kuala Lumpur.

It was a flight that took over ten hours, and although it wasn't full there were not many spare seats. I was sitting next to a surly woman dressed in black with a young girl, presumably her daughter, sitting in the window seat. I tried to initiate polite conversation, but my attempts were met with increasing hostility, and after only a short while I resorted to watching a series of documentaries and a couple of banal films. I tried to sleep, but soon loud snoring came from the seat next to me and useful sleep was impossible. I was very tired by the time we arrived at Kuala Lumpur, and I had almost three hours to wait before my connecting flight to Sydney was called. It was another stunning airport with its interior jungle area. However, the departure terminal was very crowded, mainly with young Australians.

The eight-hour flight was full, but it was not long before many of the passengers were asleep, and I think I probably slept for around four hours because I felt reasonably awake when we landed at Sydney. There was a long queue for passport control, and an even longer wait to get my trolley case, which I had been asked to put in the hold on the last leg of the flight. When I eventually retrieved my case, there was another long queue.

When I reached the end of it, I was confronted by a large, uniformed man who demanded my passport. No please, no politeness. He looked through the passport, and with steely cold eyes fixed on mine, he said, 'You get about Mister Boateng, or would you rather I call you Sean?'

'Whatever you like.' I replied.

'Ever taken drugs, Sean?' There was a hint of cynicism in his voice.

'No, not to my knowledge.' I retorted.

'Not even at school?' He didn't wait for a reply and went on in a soft voice. 'What brings you to our shores?'

'Bird spotting.' I replied.

'Bird spotting!' The official repeated loudly. He turned to the security man who was sitting behind the x-ray machine waiting for some luggage to pass through.

'Did you hear that Lou, Mister Boateng is a bird spotter. Didn't think your sort did bird spotting.'

'And exactly what sort am I?' I replied sharply.

'I ask the questions Mister Boateng. So, you're in sunny Australia, in the summer, bird spotting. Any particular bird?' He asked sarcastically.

'The regent honeyeater, it's a very rare bird, you know.' I was trying hard to keep my cool, but this man was testing me to the limit.

'The regent honeyeater, eh. Ever heard of that Lou?'

'Vaguely.' Lou said. He didn't seem to want to get involved in this conversation.

'And were you bird-spotting in Oman, Mister Boateng?'

'Yes,' I replied.

'As a matter of fact, I was. Are you interested in bird-spotting?' I was almost enjoying this word chess.

'As I said, earlier, Mister Boateng, I ask the questions. So, did you have any drugs in Oman? Oh, forgive me, you've never taken drugs. You were just there to spot birds of course. Your employer must be very generous to allow you all this time off to spot birds.'

'He is,' I replied succinctly.

'Who is your employer?'

'That, sir, is none of your business.' I did not want to lie, and I knew that government service would probably elicit deeper probing.

'He's a bit cagey this one, Lou. What do you think, drug runner or bird spotter?'

Lou looked up slowly, stared at me briefly, and then let his eyes drop back to the computer. He said nothing.

'Open your suitcase Mister Boateng, and let me see what goodies you've brought from Kuala Lumpur wasn't it?'

I suddenly had this awful feeling that my small suitcase had been taken from me and put in the hold for the last leg of the journey, and I'd heard stories of drugs being planted on people.

'Can you remove the items and spread them out here?' He pointed to the table next to where we were standing. 'Wait, leave those boots there.'

I had a pair of old hiking boots in the case, but I knew the Australians were strict on the import of soil into the country, and I had given them a thorough clean before I had left Ljubljana. The official donned a pair of plastic gloves and picked up the boots and examined them thoroughly. He appeared to be disappointed that he couldn't find a trace of mud on them. He plonked them heavily onto the table, and without a word gestured that I should continue to empty the case.

There wasn't that much to be emptied as I expected it to be hot and the clothes that I had were light. It was a point the official made.

'Travelling light Mr Boateng, are you going to do some busking to make some money for new clothes.' He thought the statement was outrageously funny, but Lou did little more than raise his eyebrows.

'Where are you staying, Mister Boateng?'

'I've hired a camper van,' I replied.

'*Phew*, expensive. Wouldn't have thought you could afford that.'

'And why's that?' I said, with more than a hint of anger in my voice.

'I said, no questions, Mister Boateng. No questions, understand?'

'I don't like your tone Mister Official,' I was very tired and getting irritated.

'Can you call your supervisor, please?' I didn't want to draw attention to myself, but his line of questioning was aggressive and it was one of several times in my life that if I had possessed a lighter skin and was wearing a suit I would have been treated differently.

'Of course, Mister Boateng.' He replied, as if this was an everyday occurrence.

'Can you call Brian?' The comment was directed towards Lou, who mumbled something into the phone and resumed looking at his screen. After about five minutes, an older man appeared and my interrogator walked over to him and they talked together in low voices.

Brian came over to me, and with a cold smile introduced himself and then in a deliberately slow voice said, 'Max tells me that you're unhappy with your treatment. What's the problem?' Max stood in the background smirking.

I felt that this was a battle that I wasn't going to win. 'I appear to have been singled out for a grilling.' I swept my hand around the almost empty arrivals concourse and continued.

'No one else seems to have got this treatment.'

'Mister, Boateng, isn't it,' Brian interrupted, 'We monitor arrivals and randomly pick people to question about their journey, that's all.'

I suspected he was lying. 'How about telling the truth, you pick out people that you think look suspicious, and for some reason I fall into that category.'

'Before you go on, Mister Boateng, making false allegations to government officials is an offence.'

I knew I was beaten. 'Okay, just go ahead and finish the examination, but not from that goon, he's not good at customer care.'

Max's triumphant smile vanished and he glared at me icily. 'You are not a customer, Mister Boateng, you are a visitor to our country. Open your rucksack.' I took the contents out. The space inside had mainly been taken up by a laptop and my binoculars.

'What are these for?' Brian pointed at the binoculars.

'Spotting birds.' I replied. Brian looked bemused until Max explained about my reason for being in the country.

Brian turned back to me 'You won't need binoculars here; all the birds are big.' He thought his comment was very funny.

Max laughed, but I didn't, and Lou didn't even look up. Brian called out to a girl who was manning an X-ray machine two rows along and said, 'Can you swab these, Lucy darling.'

Lucy was not someone I would ever call darling, but she lifted her mighty frame from her seat and waddled over to use swabs for the inside of both my trolley case and rucksack. It occurred to me that I had been wearing my hiking boots in Morocco when we visited the fields of cannabis but I had cleaned them several times since then. After a couple of minutes Lucy shouted, 'All clear.' from her distant seat, and an obviously disappointed Brian asked me to gather my items and put them in security trays ready to pass through the x-ray machine.

Lou became somewhat interested as the items passed slowly along the conveyor, but there was no obvious excitement when the last item, my trolley case, emerged on the other side of the unit. Next it was my turn to be examined. Max fetched a stick from Lucy and I was swabbed from head to toe. Brian took the stick from Max and walked across to Lucy to get an analysis. He looked across and shook his head.

I tried hard to suppress a smug smile, but it was a relief that they had failed to find anything wrong with me or my luggage.

Brian continued talking to Lucy and Max, now obviously annoyed, said, 'I believe you are staying in Australia for two weeks. Please make sure you don't miss your flight home Mister Boateng, we would hate to have to detain you as an over-stayer. Goodbye,' and with that he turned and walked over to join Lucy and Brian. I looked at Lou. He shrugged his shoulders and smiled and then continued to blankly look at the screen in front of him.

Outside the airport terminal I was hit by a wall of heat. It had been grey and cold when I had left Ljubljana over thirty hours before, and I estimated the temperature in Sydney was in the mid-thirties. I took a free shuttle bus to where the camper vans were parked and I was shown to a new, very colourful, van. I had hoped for something less conspicuous, but it was the size I wanted, and after some brief instructions and a lengthy spell of form filling, I drove out onto the main highway towards Melbourne. The traffic soon became quite light, and the air conditioning made the driving pleasant enough, and for those that appreciate eucalyptus trees and dusty yellow fields, the scenery was not too bad either.

I thought it would be foolish to attempt to drive to Melbourne in one day, so I decided to stop at a campsite roughly half way. It so happened that the nearest large town was Wagga Wagga, a name that had fascinated me since I was a child. I had read somewhere that the original meaning of the town name was 'many crows' and I was a little worried that I would have my early morning sleep terminated by their crowing. I laughed to myself that a collective of crows is not called a flock, it's called a murder. There was no murder, though, in fact I didn't see many crows, but the campsite by the river had even noisier birds, hundreds of them, that I later found out were Sulphur Crested Cockatoos. They even screamed at night, and I was glad to leave the following morning still feeling very tired.

The drive to Melbourne on the motorway was not scenic. A diminishing number of eucalyptus trees was replaced by increasingly large fields. Some contained yellowing pasture, while others had been used for growing grain, most of which had been harvested, rolled and wrapped in white plastic. There was one large dead animal beside the road, which I assumed was a kangaroo, otherwise there seemed to be little wildlife apart from a few crows.

The sky was dusty blue and the temperature gauge on the van showed an outside temperature of forty by lunchtime. I was very glad to have the air conditioning. Apart from a short stop to refuel and have a snack and a bottle of water, I continued driving until I reached my destination, a small campsite near an industrial area to the west of the city. I had hoped for a cooling sea breeze, but instead there was an almost unbearably hot wind from inland. The kindly manager of the campsite assured me that the following day would be much cooler, and he was right.

I had dinner at a service station a short walk from the campsite, and I hoped that I might get into a conversation with one of the lorry drivers that was eating there. I tried a few opening lines, but I don't know if it was the searing heat outside, but no one appeared to want to converse and I ended up enjoying my fry-up alone. Overnight, it became very gusty for a while and there were some rumbles of thunder, but in the morning, the weather was completely different. It was fresh, just like a summer's day in London. It buoyed me up, and I hummed to myself as I strode off to the bus stop with my newly acquired transport payment card in anticipation of a trip to the centre of Melbourne.

The bus stop stood alongside a busy dual carriageway and I was somewhat concerned that it was a relic from the past, but after about fifteen minutes a cream and orange single-decker appeared and I waved frantically to make sure it stopped.

'I saw you, mate, 'the driver said, grumpily. 'It's my job to pick up passengers.'

My earlier good humour evaporated as we hurtled through the streets towards the centre of the city. I alighted before we reached the centre because my destination was a hotel close to the port. I was hoping that I may be able to obtain some information about containers, or at the very least get an idea of the layout of the port, although I was lost for a good plan of action.

It was just after eleven when I entered a rather dingy looking inn that I had picked out from the google maps. It smelt of stale beer and sweat and it was just the sort of place I had been looking for. Two youngsters were sitting by the door with two soft drinks having an earnest discussion, an elderly man with long grey hair was sitting behind a large beer, and the middle-aged woman behind the bar, presumably the landlady, was sitting quietly watching daytime television.

'G'day, how're yer doing.' was her standard greeting.

'Fine, thanks, can I have a small beer?' was my reply.

'Sure, on holiday?'

'Yes, sort of.' I answered, but I didn't really want to get into conversation with her, and she was quick to read my mind.

The youngsters resumed talking after briefly stopping to look at me. The man in the corner was also looking at me. I nodded a greeting in his direction and he responded but continued staring. My beer was plonked on the bar and I made a contactless card payment. I decided to approach the man in the corner, perhaps he could help me to formulate a plan.

'Hi, I'm Sean, can I join you?'

'Don't see why not, are you a cop?' The man looked vaguely curious.

'No, I'm new to Melbourne, and I thought you might be able to give me a few tips.'

He smiled, revealing an uneven set of white teeth. 'I'm not cultured, you know, but I can tell you some things. I'm Monny, by the way.'

I put out a hand to shake, but it was ignored.

'I've worked here since I was fourteen, and I am sixty-eight now, but no more work.'

'Have you retired?' I asked. On close inspection, I would have thought Monny was closer to eighty than seventy, but maybe life had been unkind to him. He emptied his glass and looked at me. I took the hint.

'Another drink?'

'Yeh, a beer, Paula knows what sort.'

Paula had a full glass of beer waiting on the bar by the time I had reached it. 'He'll have a couple more before lunch, I bet. One for yourself?'

'Just a half, please.' I wasn't going to match this man, and I didn't want to spend the rest of the day in a daze.

Monny nodded thanks. 'So, have you retired Monny?'

'Yeh, got too complicated, all this computer stuff.'

'What did you do for a job?'

Half his beer disappeared before he replied. 'I worked in the docks. They call it a port now, but I still call it the docks.'

I suppressed a shudder. This chap might be useful. Monny continued. 'In the old days, I was one of those that used to release the cargo from the cranes when they were unloading. It was a dangerous job, but the money was good. One of my mates was killed, a crate of car parts fell on him, the cable broke, you know. When they took the crate off, he was completely flat. Like one of those cardboard cutouts.' He crossed himself, 'Poor old Pete.' He paused, as if reliving the moment, and then went on. 'Then the containers came along. Much easier to unload, so they didn't need us.'

'So, what did you do then?' Monny was happy to tell his tale to the appreciative audience of one, and he continued.

'Paperwork, that's all I did paperwork, and then the computers came along and they tried to sit me down in an office. That wasn't for me, though.'

'What was the job with the paperwork then?' I interrupted.

'Still in Melbourne, I presume?'

'Oh, yeh,' Monny replied, 'Still at the port. I was logging the containers and matching them up with transport, you know, lorries and wagons, that sort of thing.'

'It sounds interesting.' I said, and I definitely was interested. Maybe Monny could solve my problem at the first attempt.

'So, you got to know all the containers and where they came from and where they were going to?'

Monny looked smug. 'If anyone wanted to know anything about containers, they would ask Monny.' It was at that point I realised that I had hit the jackpot at the first attempt.

Chapter 32

Monny drank the rest of his beer and looked at my half-empty glass and said, 'Are you getting another?'

Anyone else saying that I would have considered it to be rude, but Monny seemed to have fine-tuned his ability to coax a drink out of someone. I turned around, and Paula was already pouring the beer into a glass.

'I'll bring it over,' she shouted. 'One for yourself?'

I shook my head. She sauntered across with the glass.

'I need the exercise, you know.'

I swiped a payment on the small machine she had with her and turned back to Monny.

'So, I suppose you know the numbers of all the containers?'

This was a defining moment for me and Monny didn't disappoint. 'Yeh, s'pose so, but what use is that, and then the new containers come in, and then they change the codes and that. It's all on computers now, and I never got into that.'

I waited for Monny to finish, and then said, 'I remember when I was in Europe, there was a container from here, someone said, and I still have the number in my head.'

'I know,' Monny replied, 'It never leaves you.'

'Okay,' I said. I could see that Monny was getting a little drunk. 'Can you tell me about this container?'

Monny looked alert. 'Try me.' He said.

'The number is two zero nine four.' He looked blank.

'Is that it?' He asked.

'Why?' I responded.

'They all have six numbers, no container has four numbers, at least, not the ones here.'

'Are you sure?' I didn't wait for a reply, his eyes gave away the answer.

'Okay, if there were two numbers on the back, can you come with two zero nine four on the front?' He ran a set of dirty fingers through his long hair.

'There's the one from up north, what was it, now. A bright blue fella. Two zero nine four four six.'

Before he had finished the six, I had said, 'Yes, that's it. And what can you tell me about that one?'

Monny thought this was a good game. 'It was packed with rice, came down on the train from Deni. Don't know why they grow it there, dry as a dead dingo's, you know the rest,' He laughed, 'I'm told they make a fair packet up there, so something's done right.'

'Yes, that must be the one, how interesting that you know all that.'

I didn't want to arouse his suspicions about my motives, and after seeing him good for another large beer, I bade him farewell and walked out into the pleasantly warm sunshine of a Melbourne lunchtime.

It was difficult to contain my excitement, but I really thought that I was closing in on in the place that was causing so many problems in the world. I wanted to tell Anja, but I thought an exuberant me at two in the morning might not be to her liking. I would wait until evening. I spent the rest of the afternoon walking into the centre of Melbourne, and managed an hour in the splendid botanic gardens, before finding a Mexican restaurant for dinner. While I was waiting for my meal to arrive, I did a search for Deni to see how long my drive would be. To my surprise, and just a little concern, I couldn't find any reference to Deni in Australia, and before I had a chance to delve further into this mystery, my phone indicated 'low battery.' I put my worry to one side and enjoyed an excellent meal in an almost empty restaurant.

I then took a taxi back to the campsite, put my phone on charger and called Anja. I couldn't get an answer, so I assumed she was working, but I sent a message to her that would leave her in no doubt that I was on to something. I continued to search google for Deni without success, then I typed 'Train to Deni' and it came up with Deniliquin, and from there it was possible to work out that 'Deni' was what the locals called Deniliquin. It was only a three-and-a-half-hour drive from Melbourne and on the following morning I left the campsite early for the trip north. It was hectic driving for the first hour, and it was obvious that Australian drivers were not happy to see a camper van poodling through their city during their journey to work. Eventually, I reached the countryside with yellowing fields of grass populated by grey sheep. A few creeks offered eucalyptus trees and some shade, but it was obviously the place where wild animals gathered, evidenced by road kill, some of which was large enough to seriously damage a vehicle.

In Echuca, a town on the border between the states of Victoria and New South Wales, I stopped for lunch. It was an interesting historic place alongside the Murray River and boasted the largest collection of paddle steamers in the world. The water in the river was low, and I remembered Monny's observation of why would they would grow rice in that area. It was a good place for a rest, though, before I continued north through even drier countryside to Deniliquin. It was late afternoon before I arrived at the campsite which was set in trees by the Edward River. The elderly manager was very welcoming and we were soon chatting freely about many subjects. He assumed that I had arrived for a spot of fishing, but when I said I was bird spotting he became very interested. I said that I had come to see the Regent Honeyeater, and he almost swooned and began telling me all about the bird, and how one had not been seen in Deni for twenty years. Fortunately, he did all the talking, and he was very knowledgeable. I could have been found seriously wanting on the subject of honeyeaters.

He gave me a recital of the campsite rules, and warnings about creatures to avoid, and then asked whether I would like to rent a bike. I hadn't thought of that, but it could be a useful way to explore the area as long as the heat didn't increase too much. There was a large well-stocked supermarket not very far from the campsite and I purchased enough food to last me for several days, and then parked the van in a shady spot close to the river in the almost half-empty site. It felt like being on holiday, but it was quite lonely, and on purpose I wanted to keep a low profile, as I now realised my limitations as a bird spotter.

The following morning the camp manager knocked on the van door and gave me a photocopy of the names of all the birds he had seen at the site in the last year. He was very enthusiastic, and I pretended to match his ardour, but I told him I wanted to explore the town first, before it became too hot. He laughed and pointed out that if I was to explore the town I would be back in time for lunch. He went on his way, sweeping a few leaves into corners, only for eddies of wind to relocate them.

I cycled to the end of the railway line. The station had long since vanished but there were some trucks in a siding, and there, to my great joy, were some sky-blue containers. I moved closer and quickly took a photo of the back of one of the containers with my phone, and then cycled on towards the centre of town.

Deniliquin had been built using a system of blocks, and it was difficult to determine where the centre was. Nevertheless, there was a pretty ornamental lake with shaded seating areas, and many waterfowl to observe. I sat down and looked at the photo I took of the container, and yes, the serial number was the one I had hoped to see. It was a satisfying moment, and I spent the remainder of the morning taking photographs of birds with my expensive binoculars. A few people came to the small park to eat their lunch, but otherwise it was almost empty. It was very relaxing and gave me ample time to think ahead.

I was pleased that Anja had suggested I should stay for two weeks, because even at this early stage I was feeling the pressure of time. I wanted to take a close look at what was going on at this industrial complex, and I thought the camp manager may be able to help me. He could. He told me all about the rice production, and how it was the best rice in the world and exported to Michelin star restaurants in Europe. He also said that he would drive me up to look at the fields of rice.

'You don't want to tidy up the van just to go up there,' He said.

And so late in the afternoon, the hottest part of the day, he took me in his car to see where the rice was grown. He was impressed by my binoculars, and I managed to take some good photos of the bird life in these unusual paddy fields. But there were no signs of cannabis plants. I asked the manager if there were any other rice fields in the area, and he was adamant that we had seen all of them. It was a bit disappointing, but I knew that the cannabis must be produced somewhere locally and it was just a matter of finding out where.

That evening, after dark, I cycled down to the factory and positioned myself behind some discarded machinery and took out my binoculars. If challenged, I would say that I was looking for a plains-wanderer, a rare, almost flightless bird that I had found out was occasionally seen in Deni. It was very quiet. There was no wind, and after a while, the only lights to be seen were those on one of the silos and alongside the factory walls. There were no obvious security cameras, and I wasn't aware that the site had any security guards. However, at a little after midnight, a uniformed man, carrying what looked like a truncheon round his waist, came out from a door in the silo, lit a cigarette, and walked slowly alongside the factory wall. He made a complete circuit of the factory complex, taking about half an hour, then lit another cigarette and did some texting. He then had a cursory look around before re-entering the silo and shutting the door.

I waited for another hour to see if anything else happened but it stayed quiet and there was no movement that I could see, in or around the factory. I silently crept back to my bike, which I had left locked to some railings in some public gardens, and then cycled down to the river to take a few photos of roosting birds with my infra-red binoculars. I had a feeling that the campsite manager would be aware of my return in the middle of the night and may ask some awkward questions.

The following morning, he did ask some awkward questions, but fortunately I did manage to take some very good photos, and I felt that he believed I was an avid ornithologist. I repeated my cycling trip on the following two evenings, and at the factory the same procedure was followed, although on the third night it was a different man that emerged from the silo and he didn't appear to be a smoker.

On the fourth night, I made up my mind to see what, if anything, I could find in the factory. I reasoned that if only two men were looking after the premises at night, I should be able to avoid them, but if necessary, overcome them, and perhaps find papers indicating where the cannabis was being grown. Maybe Anja was right, I should have worked with Greg on this mission, but my doubts were soon quashed. I didn't trust him and that was that.

I left my binoculars in the van when I cycled to the factory on the fourth evening. In fact, apart from my phone, which I had in a pocket of my light fleece, I had nothing with me apart from the keys to the camper van and my bicycle lock. I thought it would be best to leave my rucksack and wallet at the campsite, just in case I ran into any trouble. I locked up the bike in the gardens and, keeping in the shadows, made my way to my hiding place some thirty metres from the silo door. At midnight, the man who smoked came out of the door and immediately began texting before sauntering along by the factory wall, and then out of sight around the corner. This was my cue to walk briskly forward and enter the silo.

I was expecting to be confronted by some kind of office with a man sitting at a computer, or perhaps watching television in the corner, but instead, there was a vast, poorly lit, empty silo with an uneven floor. A square manhole cover had been pushed to one side, and two rounded posts jutted out of the space vacated by the cover. I walked quietly over to the hole and looked down. There were steps down to what looked like another empty area, but it was poorly lit, and it was difficult to distinguish any features. I climbed down and found another room, this time rectangular, with a matching manhole cover pulled aside in one corner. Quite strong light was emanating from the hole in the ground and there was a slight hum, perhaps from air conditioning, also coming from below.

I carefully looked down. There was another set of steps with a platform about three metres below. There was a conventional security door standing half-open on one side of the platform, with more steps disappearing off to the left. I chose the door. A glance inside showed a long table or desk with a couple of computers and what appeared to be gauges set into a low sloping panel attached to the desk. There were two chairs in front of the desk, but neither were occupied, the room seemed to be empty. I slowly pushed the door further open and it revealed a large room similar to those found in an airport control tower, but what was astonishing, was the view through the darkened glass that fronted the office. Row upon row of brightly illuminated green plants were laid out under a structure resembling an aircraft hangar, but probably much bigger. I estimated the hangar was as much as two hundred metres long, and as much as fifty metres wide.

I knew immediately that these plants were not destined for the local nursery. I had finally reached my goal.

'Who are you?' A harsh voice came from the back of the room. A man, who I recognised as the non-smoker from the night before was standing glaring at me. 'I repeat, who are you?' He pressed a button on the wall, and a tired-sounding voice came through.

'Yes, mate.'

'I think we have an intruder in control,' the man said.

'Geez, not another.'

As I was wondering who 'the other' was, I sprang into action. I left the control room, pulled the door shut and ran to the steps.

As I reached the top a man's measured voice said. 'Back down, my friend, or I'll shoot.' I could see a gun pointing in my direction, and the tone of his voice suggested he meant what he said. I backed down, and the non-smoker was standing in the doorway, also with a gun in his hand. It was not the time for heroics.

I was told to sit down on the swivel chair by the desk. The men stood at a distance either side of me not allowing me any chance to seize their weapons which were both still pointing in my direction.

'So, who are you?' The non-smoker looked at me with menace in his face.

'Just a curious tourist,' I replied nonchalantly.

'A blue heeler, I reckon.' The other man said. The smoker appeared in the doorway.

'We've got a visitor, Baz, he says he is a tourist. Any ideas?'

'Feed him to the plants,' the other man said.

The other two looked at him with disdain. 'Big G will want to know where he's come from, you can't just kill him like that.' My life was being discussed in front of me as if I wasn't there, but there was nothing I could do about it.

'A nice nursery you've got here.' I said, trying to play the simpleton, but it just produced three looks of contempt and they resumed talking.

'Don can give Big G a ring in the morning, I'm not calling him.' The non-smoker, who seemed to be the leader of the three, was talking and continued, 'We can put him in Big G's office until then.'

'What if he wrecks the place?' The third man interrupted.

'He won't.' The non-smoker raised his gun and pointed it at my head. 'Will you, Mister Tourist?'

I shook my head.

'It's the only room with a lock, and there's a dunny, so he'll get water and won't die.'

'Why don't you just kill 'im?' The third man obviously wanted blood.

'You know, Big G was livid when that jack was chopped up, and he was a local lad, no we've got to keep him.'

They turned to me. The non-smoker waved his gun at the door and said, 'Through there, third door on the right, and no funny stuff.'

I could see there was no point in resisting against three armed men and walked off into the corridor. I halted at the third door, and the non-smoker said.

'Right, that's your home for the weekend. Open the door, take the key out from inside and throw it to me.'

'Aren't you going to check to see if there's anything personal in there?' The third man interjected.

'There ain't, been through it already.' The non-smoker then laughed. 'He doesn't leave any of his fancy rings here. In.' He waved the gun. 'The light's on the right by the door.'

I switched the light on, walked further into the room, and the door slammed shut behind me, and the key was turned sharply in the lock. There was a musty smell with just a hint of aftershave and it was warm. By the light switch, there was an air conditioning control panel, and to my relief, it worked. A gush of dusty air came from a grill above a door at the other end of the room. The desk was made from cheap-looking wood and had been poorly varnished, but the large swivel chair behind it looked very comfortable. I sat down in it and took out my phone. I thought I would send a text to Anja and apologise to her for not taking her advice about working with someone else on the mission. I thought my foolishness was about to cost me my life. It soon became apparent that there was no signal in this underground complex and I began to feel that my chances of escape were minimal.

The campsite manager would probably think that I was on one of my night excursions, so as the camper van curtains were drawn, he would probably think that I was sleeping during the day. He may not become concerned until the following day, but even then, if I didn't reappear he could think I had fallen in the river and drowned, and of course the police would search for me, but they would have no reason to suspect that a crime had been committed. I just sat back in the chair and looked around me. The walls were painted white, and there were several paintings and framed posters adding colour to the room. The paintings were mostly landscapes. One looked as if it could be the Alps, another was a rural scene, possibly in England, and another suggested a tropical paradise with palm trees bending towards the sea. The posters were of vintage cars, and there was an enlarged photograph of the American president shaking hands with the prime minister. That was a strange one I thought. The collection didn't appear to be valuable, but they were carefully chosen by someone, and I assumed that Big G, whoever he was, influenced the choice.

I remember the non-smoker mentioned a bathroom, and across the room there was a closed door. I went over and opened it, and indeed it was a bathroom, complete with a shower unit. He was right, I would not die of thirst. I returned to the office and went through the cupboards and drawers. There was no paperwork to be found, although there was a laptop which I booted up. Unfortunately, it required a password, and after trying a few of the obvious ones I gave up. One of the drawers in the desk was locked, but it was so flimsy, that I managed to pull the back off and expose the contents. It contained a key, attached to a ring with number seventeen on it, and there were a few receipts, all of which I stuffed into my pocket.

The only other object was a gun. My heart beat faster as I pulled it from the drawer. It was small and I found out that it contained four small calibre bullets, but I felt much more confident that I could get out of this mess with a firearm, and I sat back in the office chair again waiting for the door to open.

It didn't happen. I must have fallen asleep, because I suddenly became alert to the sound of muffled explosions. I soon realised it was gunfire. Just a few pops at first, but these were replaced by the *rat-a-tat* of automatic gunfire. This went on intermittently for about twenty minutes and then there was silence. I was mystified. Was this an argument between the men that had imprisoned me? I doubted it. Their guns looked like standard pistols. Was it a rescue attempt for me? That was highly unlikely as no one knew I was here. I just sat thinking what I should do next. If I shouted, or fired a gun, it might attract attention that could worsen my plight. I stayed quiet.

At about five in the morning, close to an hour after the fracas took place, I began to smell smoke. I thought maybe it could be a fault in the air-conditioning, so I switched it off, but the smell worsened, and then I saw little wisps of smoke coming from under the door. I shouted out for help, but none came. I then tried to force the lock on the door, but it was stronger than I had expected, and got nowhere. I had seen in films that locks could be opened using bullets. I tried once and missed, a spiral of smoke came through the hole in the door. My second attempt was no more successful. The bullet hit the target, but instead of shattering the lock, the bullet just ricocheted around the room and embedded itself in a palm tree in the painting of the tropical paradise. I left the remaining two bullets in the gun.

The smoke got thicker, not helped by the hole I had created in the door. I went to the bathroom and stuffed some wet toilet roll in the hole, and that helped, but smoke was still drifting in from under the door, and it also began to come through the air-conditioning vent. After a while, it was becoming difficult to see the other side of the room and my eyes were streaming. I had read somewhere that the best thing to do in a fire was to soak a towel in water and breathe through it. Whether it was true or not I didn't know, but it was my last chance.

I soaked the towel and stood under the showerhead and tried texting again. I tried and tried but to no avail. Thick smoke was now coming in under the bathroom door even though I had placed wet towels at the bottom of the door. My eyes were smarting from the smoke and tears were running down my face, but they were now being joined by real tears as I realised that there was no escape.

Chapter 33

I was not religious, I had no prayer to offer, but like most of humanity there was this overwhelming desire to survive. The soaked towel on my head felt like a barrier from the ever-increasing amounts of smoke, but I needed more. I lifted the lever on the shower, expecting a gush of water to descend on my head, but instead there were just a few drops dripping onto the floor tiles. With a feeling of utter defeat, I looked down and rubbed my trainers in the blobs of water on the ground, and I then noticed the faintest of arcs etched on to the tiles. It looked like a scratch mark emanating from a corner of the shower area. I tapped the wall. It appeared to be hollow. I checked. The other wall was solid, but this one wasn't. I banged on it aimlessly, but then thought, perhaps it was a hidden room. I felt around the soap container for a release catch. There was nothing, and in frustration I ripped it from the wall. My heart pounded as my act of aggression had uncovered a small bolt set neatly into one of the tiles. I pulled the lever to one side, and there was a click as a newly found door partially opened.

A gust of cool air entered the bathroom with the swirling smoke making a temporary retreat. I opened the door to its full extent exposing what looked like a pipe with a diameter of about two metres. The bathroom light only illuminated a few metres of pipe, but it seemed to offer a better alternative to staying in the bathroom. A further increase of smoke helped to make my mind up. I walked through the door, illuminated the pipe with my mobile, and pulled the door shut behind me. There was a bolt on the inside and I pulled it across. It wasn't fresh air in the pipe, but it was a lot better than the air in the bathroom. I walked along the pipe, and even though I wore trainers, each step I took echoed along the corridor. A scurrying noise in front suggested that I wasn't alone, but if rats could enter this area, then there was a chance that I could get out of it.

I walked on for what seemed ages, but in fact it was only for a few minutes. Occasionally, there was a shallow puddle of stagnant water that smelt putrid, otherwise the pipe was dry and clean. It was surprisingly cold, and the temperature, combined with the fear that I was feeling, made me shiver almost uncontrollably. Eventually, after what seemed like, a hundred and fifty to two hundred metres, I was faced by a rough concrete wall that blocked up the whole pipe. Fortunately to the left of it was a spiral metal staircase that disappeared upwards. I switched off the light on my mobile and put it in my pocket ready to climb the stairs.

Stygian darkness descended upon me and the fear increased, but I began the ascent. With each step, a metallic ping rang out, but I continued upwards, and it gradually became warmer. I slowed my ascent to make sure that I didn't crack my head on whatever was awaiting me at the top. Occasionally I stopped and put my hand up, feeling for a ceiling, and eventually the handrail gave way to what felt like a metal cage on a platform. My knees were trembling, and I was very cautious as my hands padded around my new surroundings. I crawled around the platform on my knees and when I had confirmed it was a safe place to be, I took the mobile from my pocket and used the light to see where I was.

A pipe, obviously much older than the one that I had made my escape from the bathroom in, ran straight down from a relatively small metal cover above. It appeared to be some sort of storm drain, as there were traces of mud around the cover, as well as on the platform. The staircase was much newer, and I marvelled at the ingenuity of the person that had created what was obviously a means of escape for Big G, or whoever it was that occupied the office I had been imprisoned in. I smiled as I thought how smug the non-smoker appeared when he suggested to the others that the office was the best place for me. I swiftly returned to the present as I tried to lift the drain cover. It was just over a metre above the floor of the platform, but lifting the cover proved to be difficult. It was hard to get leverage, and I suspected that mud or something may have accumulated on the top.

I had got so far and I wasn't to be thwarted. I knelt down and tried to use my head and my hands to force the cover open, but although there was a ripping sound, which suggested grass above, there was very little movement. I sat and thought. Perhaps my legs would be better tools for releasing the cover. I lay on the ground and edged my feet up the side of the cage until they were resting on the cover. I then bent my legs and inched my body closer to the cage side. Then, after taking a deep breath, I sprang my legs upwards and the cover clanged to one side, and the outside air rushed in.

I smelt smoke, and momentarily I thought that my travails had been in vain, but I poked my head out of the drain and saw to my immense relief that I was in, what appeared to be, a wooded area. I replaced the drain cover and tried to get my bearings. The air was quite smoky, and I could see through the trees that flames were shooting many metres in the air from a massive fire. The flames illuminated some local landmarks, and to my utter amazement, I realised that my bicycle was less than ten metres away, locked to the sapling, as I had left it many hours, and many emotions, before.

I wheeled the bike out of the garden and cycled towards the fire. A crowd of people, some in nightclothes, were strung along outside a taped off area manned by several police officers. The seat of the fire was probably over two hundred metres away, but the police were adamant that no one should enter the cordoned off area. There were several fire engines in attendance, and two more arrived as I stood watching.

A police officer wandered along in front of the cordon and stood almost next to me looking at the blaze.

'Do you know what happened?' I asked in a concerned voice.

'It's a big fire.' He replied. 'Reckon it's the biggest we've had in Deni.'

I asked again, 'Any idea what caused it?'

'No. Someone along there,' and he pointed to his left. 'Said it could be fertiliser for the fields. Pretty bad blaze, though.' On cue, a jet of flame shot high into the air, followed by a muffled explosion. 'That's why we keep everyone so far away. Goodnight, and sleep well.' He walked off towards a group of young people, two of whom were leaning against a tree on the wrong side of the tape. I could hear him reproaching them as I mounted my bike for my ride back to the campsite. The smoke was drifting towards the campsite as I rode and it was unpleasant, but I could not detect any smell of cannabis, although I was happy in the knowledge that those plants had surely been engulfed by the flames. I hummed as I cycled, the trauma of the early part of the night forgotten as I took pleasure in knowing that it would be a long time before any cannabis would leave that factory again. When I reached the van, the first thing I did was send an obscured message to Anja which I was sure she would interpret as mission accomplished.

It was dawn when I finally lay down to sleep in the camper van, and I slept into the afternoon, only to be woken by loud knocks on the side of the van. I immediately became alert and pushed the curtain to one side. The campsite manager was standing outside with a police officer. I asked them to wait a moment as I quickly donned a pair of shorts.

The campsite manager smiled and said, 'Don't worry, Sean. You haven't done anything wrong, the officer's checking to make sure you weren't burnt alive last night.' The officer scowled.

'Did someone die, then?' I looked at the policeman.

'We think there may have been fatalities.' The officer replied sombrely.

The campsite manager went on. 'Jim in the next rig.' He pointed at the dirty-looking caravan next to my van, 'He worked night shifts at the factory, and he hasn't shown up today.'

'I'm sorry to hear that.' I said, trying to muster as much conviction as I could, whilst thinking that one of the men that wanted me dead was now a small pile of ash.

The officer, satisfied that I was alive, moved slowly off towards another caravan. The campsite manager gave me a friendly wave and said, 'See you later,' before leading the policeman to the next pitch. I then sat outside the van eating brunch and going over in my mind the events of the previous night. It had been a close call, and I silently thanked the person, or persons, who had engineered the escape route. But what about the shooting? I was sure they were gunshots that I had heard, and automatic weapons. I had only seen pistols in the control room, and what about the fire? I couldn't believe it had started accidentally. It was a mystery, but after I had eaten I went to the river and took photographs of birds, a hobby that I was rapidly growing to like. In the late afternoon, I cycled to the supermarket to stock up on food, and on the way I rode past the site of the factory. The blackened silo still stood but had been warped by the heat and was leaning dangerously. Elsewhere, there was nothing to be seen above ground level, and plenty of smoke was rising from the ground, with fire crews still in attendance.

For three days, smoke issued from the area, but a change of wind direction helped to take most of the smoke away from the town. On the fourth morning, the campsite manager came and knocked on the side of the van, and with gushing enthusiasm told me that his mate had spotted two plains-wanderers on a farm just outside Deni, and would I like to come that evening to try and see them. I was genuinely keen, and just after sunset he drove us out to the farm, a dusty, austere-looking place to the north of the town. I was introduced to Mac, a small, friendly man whose face suggested many years of exposure to the Australian sun.

He had a powerful torch with him and he led both of us out into one of his impoverished fields. It was a long walk, but he seemed to know exactly where he was going. He paused and said, to wait, as he slowly walked forward. I had my night binoculars out and I followed him to a corner of the field where there were piles of stones and a few saltbushes. He turned and signalled with his torch to proceed. We reached him and he said, 'Over there.'

He shone his torch at a patch of ground just ten metres from the fence where two birds were standing. The quail-like birds, almost as small as robins, seemed oblivious to the light as they pecked at the ground without any fear of our presence. I managed to obtain excellent film and photographs of them and Mac was obviously pleased that he had made a bird spotter so happy. As we drove back to the campsite I felt the worries of my mission lift from my shoulders.

I had seen two plains-wanderers, what more could a man want? The campsite manager was also pleased as we chatted away about ornithology, a subject that I was becoming much more knowledgeable about. As he dropped me outside the van he said, 'By the way, I forgot to tell you. Someone came to the office asking after you. I asked him if he was one of your bird spotting mates and he said he was. Have you heard from him?'

'No, I don't think so.' I tried to sound calm, but I was deeply worried that this visitor was one of the villains that I had encountered in the factory.

'What was he like?' I asked.

'A respectable type, if you ask me,' the manager replied. 'Was he Australian? Did he leave a name?' I threw the questions at him in quick succession.

'No, he didn't leave a name, he said, he'd catch up with you, but he was Australian alright, from around these parts I guess.'

Chapter 34

I didn't sleep well that night. It was hot and sultry with not a breath of wind and I was very alert, jumping wide awake each time an animal or bird rustled the leaves outside. I was pleased when the sun rose in a powder-blue sky, but I was tired, very tired, and although I thought long and hard, I could think of no one, other than Anja, that knew of my presence in Deniliquin, so I decided it was best to leave as quickly as possible. I made the excuse that the heat was becoming difficult to cope with, which it was, and shortly after mid-morning, I bade a fond farewell to the campsite manager and set off along the shimmering road towards Sydney. It was over seven hundred kilometres away and I was too tired to make the journey in one day, so I chose to have another night in Wagga Wagga. This time I booked into the air-conditioned comforts of a hotel.

In the morning, I was totally refreshed and completed the trip to Sydney, arriving there in the middle of the afternoon. I took the van back to the rental centre and then took a bus into the centre and found a hotel close to the World Square shopping centre. It was cloudy and breezy, a pleasant change from the torrid heat I had left behind in Deni. When I had departed from Wagga that morning, it had been my intention to try and change my ticket and get an earlier flight to Europe, but there was something about the vibrancy of Sydney that made me want to stay, and I did, spending the remainder of my time in Australia seeing the sights of Sydney, and thoroughly enjoying the vitality that the city had to offer.

So, it was with reluctance that I left the hotel for the airport almost two weeks after my arrival in Australia. There were no problems with the flights back to Ljubljana apart from the thirty-two hours it took to reach there. Fortunately, the flight from Kuala Lumpur to Istanbul was less than half-full and I was able to sleep for much of the flight into Europe. After a weather-related delay, I staggered into the arrivals hall at Ljubljana Airport well over a day after I had left Sydney. Anja was there to greet me, and after a long embrace I was dragged to the car park.

'I've taken over my father's old car,' Anja said. I don't think I even knew that she had passed her test, but she confidently drove away from the airport and within half an hour we were searching for a parking space close to her flat. On the way, we just talked about the trip, and other trivial matters, but as we got out of the car she said, in a serious voice 'So much has happened, we have to have a walk in the woods and I'll tell you all about it.'

I was intrigued. Surely, her two weeks had been less interesting than mine, but the couple of times I tried to start talking about my venture she managed to interrupt and change the subject. It was one of those rare winter days when the sky is cloudless, and with no wind it felt mild, well, at least it did to Anja, because compared with the temperatures I had experienced in Australia, it was icy cold. In the flat, Anja prepared a thermos flask of coffee and she filled some baguettes with tuna and cucumber. Meanwhile, I freshened up, before we took the car to the woods on the edge of the city.

'Since you've been away,' Anja began, as we walked arm in arm along the track through the woods, 'We raided the furniture factory where we suspected the drugs were collected for onward distribution. They were concealed in high-quality office furniture which were destined for various parts of Western Europe. Coordinated police raids led to the arrest of many prominent people, and papers seized both here and abroad, produced evidence implicating well-known politicians. Of course, in England, the media were instructed not to report some of the arrests, but social media can be useful in such situations, and the young people took to the streets demanding a change of government. There followed the usual fight-back from the powerful people in the country, and that's where we are today.' Anja turned to me and said, 'Did you know of any of this?'

'No, nothing.' I replied, trying to take in these new developments. 'When did it happen?' I asked.

'Last week. We had to make sure all the big criminals were in position to be caught.'

'And did it work?' I asked, 'Did you catch them?'

'Almost all of them, we think,' Anja replied.

'Even in the UK?' I retorted.

'Some, yes, but others no. We know who they are, and we will get them, if your government allows it.'

I smiled ruefully, 'So who is, or should I say, was, the big boss?' I was thinking of the office I was imprisoned in at the Deniliquin factory, 'I was wondering if he was the Englishman everyone seemed to mention.'

'No, we still don't know who the Englishman is, but I think I know where he lives.'

'Really?' I replied.

'Yes. It was my task to look through the papers we recovered from the furniture factory, while someone else was running through the computer files. Most of the documents related to sales in big cities in Europe and we successfully raided those places, but there were also a few sheets of paper that didn't fit with the usual receipts and invoices. The common theme was a road near Villach.'

'That's in Austria?' I interrupted.

'Yes, not far from our border.'

'So, what did you make of that?' I asked.

Anja continued, 'We know the Englishman lived somewhere in north Slovenia, or most probably across the border in southern Austria, and I think the papers related to his house, or a shop he used, near Villach.'

'The evidence is a bit thin.' I suggested.

Anja looked at me blankly and went on, 'I think it is worth investigating, and I've taken a holiday to go and have a look. Are you coming?'

'What do your colleagues say?' I was a little taken aback by the fervour she was beginning to show.

'I haven't told my colleagues, only you know this.'

'Okay.' I tried to gather my thoughts. 'So, you want to check out a house in Austria, and then what?'

Anja confidently put her case forward, 'I don't know what house, but a few enquiries should be able to establish where he lives.'

'Isn't it likely his neighbours would warn him? It could be dangerous.'

Anja smiled, 'Yes, there is a risk, but we need to get this man.'

'When you say get this man, what exactly does that mean?'

Anja looked around the deserted woods and whispered in my ear, 'He has to be eliminated.'

'Bloody hell!' I said, loudly, 'That's murder!'

'No, it's not.' Anja protested, 'He's responsible for the deaths of thousands of people, and in Austria I wouldn't trust the police to arrest him.'

'But you can't just go to another country and kill someone.' I was worried that Anja was losing it.

'I can, and I will. Are you coming?'

I thought for a minute of the implications and then said, reluctantly 'Yes, I'll come, but can we not kidnap him or something and bring him back here?'

Anja gave me one of those glances. 'If he would like that option, maybe you should ask him.'

I felt the blood rush to my face. It was not a task I was looking forward to, but as much as anything, I wanted to protect Anja from herself.

'I have a week to succeed, shall we start tomorrow?' She concluded.

Anja had already planned ahead and was confident that I would join her on the mission. I had many misgivings, but once Anja begins a project, she takes it on with fervent enthusiasm. And this one was no exception. We drove back to the flat, and Anja immediately started packing. I was instructed to empty the fridge and throw some tins from the cupboard into a holdall. I collected some winter clothes from the wardrobe and added them to my suitcase, and within half an hour we were ready to head north. Anja had arranged with her uncle that we could stay in his house in Bled, and that left Villach less than an hour's drive away.

It was usually an easy journey to Bled, less than sixty kilometres away, but that evening it was very foggy and it took nearly two hours to reach our destination. I was tired, and still felt uncomfortable about our reason for heading into Austria. Anja detected my mood, and after a quickly prepared supper we went to bed. In the morning, I awoke with a start. I could smell smoke. Anja was not beside me, and I quickly pulled on some clothes and rushed down the stairs to the kitchen. She had lit the wood-burning stove and was in the midst of preparing breakfast. I then realised how much I had been affected by the fire in Deniliquin. I mentioned to Anja why I got up so quickly, but she remained uninterested in my Australian exploits, and over breakfast she talked about the plan for the day ahead.

We pored over a google street view map of the road she thought the Englishman lived in. It was long, very long, and she had no idea what house he lived in. 'It's a problem, Anja, you can't just knock on every door in the street until you find him. The police would probably arrive to find out what was going on, don't you think?'

Then, as I was thinking back to the fire in Deni, I remembered the key I had found in the drawer in the factory office. I rushed upstairs to the suitcase where my light jacket was lying, and in the side pocket there were scraps of paper and the house key. It was a long shot, but I ran back down the stairs and threw the key on the table.

'That may be his house key.'

Anja looked up at me with incredulity and a certain amount of sympathy, 'Of course, my dear. Where did it come from?'

'Australia.' I said, strongly. 'I suppose Australia and Austria look a bit similar when written.' She gave me that wicked look that made me veer from love to hate and back in seconds.

'It was in a drawer in an office that he may have used in Deniliquin.' I tried to be clear and sound confident, but I knew that Anja was right, the link was tenuous.

'Anyway, it does say seventeen on the keyring, so why don't we look at number seventeen on the google map?' Anja agreed, probably just to humour me, but after careful scrutiny we did find number seventeen, and following breakfast we took the car to visit the address.

The route passed through hilly and wooded countryside. It would be pleasant enough in the summer, but on a dull day in winter it was uninteresting. The border crossing was unmanned, and in less than an hour we were in Villach looking for the road and number seventeen. It was easy to find but looked totally different from the google street view which had been photographed during the height of summer. The leafless trees and shrubs made it easier for us to observe the house which was unassuming and actually smaller than the neighbouring properties. There was a swing and a trampoline in the garden but it looked as if they hadn't been used for a while. That was not surprising, though, it was winter.

I was all for giving up at the start, but Anja said she wanted to stay, and we did, for the rest of the day. We had some snacks with us, which we ate as dusk fell. We had seen nothing in, or around, the house all day, but just as darkness fell a light appeared in a room at the side of the house. No further illumination occurred and at around ten o'clock I persuaded Anja to return to Bled. Just as Anja started the engine on the car in readiness to leave, a light appeared further up the side of the house, the lower light was extinguished, and another light appeared in a front room, presumably the bedroom. Within ten minutes, all the lights had disappeared, and although we waited a further half an hour, nothing happened.

I thought the day had been disappointing, not helped by Anja's suggestion that I paid the toll charges on the motorway with my credit card because if anything happened I would be more difficult to trace than her. Anja was much more optimistic. She thought the house was occupied by just one person, because there would have been more lights being switched on and off if it had been a family. Even so, I thought the evidence for this being the home of the Englishman was very flimsy.

A buoyant Anja cooked dinner and from the cupboard produced a bottle of wine. During dinner, which spanned midnight, we discussed the future strategy. It was decided that we should return to Villach in the afternoon and see if anything interesting occurred. It was cloudy and cold when we left Bled, but after we crossed the border it started to snow. It was not particularly heavy, but it covered the countryside in a thin white shroud, although the roads were just wet. There was no movement in the house, but after dark a light came on downstairs, and at around ten o'clock lights appeared on the stairs, and then the front room upstairs.

'I think the lights are on a timer.' Anja said, 'We'll come back tomorrow afternoon and see if there are any footprints in the snow.'

The following day was crisp and sunny, but the snow showed no signs of thawing in Bled, and the same was true for Villach when we arrived there in the early afternoon.

'Okay.' said Anja, 'Let's go.'

'Wait!' I replied. 'What about a burglar alarm? There's bound to be one. And I can see they have cameras, look,' I pointed at the two cameras, one on the side of the house and one above the front door. 'They could be programmed to go to a security firm, or even the police. And don't you think the neighbours will be suspicious?'

I thought my arguments were sound, but Anja dismissed them. 'I think it's unlikely he'll have a burglar alarm. If it sounded while he wasn't there it would attract attention and he wouldn't want that. The same with the cameras, they're probably just for show, and as for neighbours. Have you seen any?'

'Okay, you win.' I said reluctantly, 'But you seem more confident that this is the right place than I am.'

'Come on.' Anja opened the car door and I followed suit. We were dressed for winter, and as we walked along the road our faces were only partially visible to anyone looking in our direction. We halted by the gate and looked up towards the front door. The snow had partially thawed, but it was clear that no one had used the path since the snow had fallen. Without speaking, we opened the gate and walked briskly up to the door. My hopes were raised when I saw a Yale Lock, and I reached into my pocket for a key.

It fitted perfectly, and with a tingle of anticipation I opened the door. As soon as we were inside, Anja pulled out her gun from a side pocket.

'Hello, anyone at home?' She shouted in English, 'It's only the cleaners.' I admired her coolness. She would make a good Bond girl, but I continued to realise my limitations as a James Bond figure. There was no sound in the house, and significantly there was no heating on. Anja continued 'I think we have the place to ourselves. Where shall we start?' I detected disappointment in Anja's voice. I am sure that she had hoped to find the Englishman and mete out justice to him, but she was eager to search for clues as to his whereabouts.

We began with the attic. It was typical of any attic in any house, containing a few cardboard boxes, plenty of insulation and copious amounts of dust. Below the attic there was an empty room with neither furniture nor fitted cupboards. The landing next to this room had bare wooden stairs leading down to the first floor which had a bathroom and three bedrooms. I quietly followed Anja into the bedroom where we had seen a light on the previous evening. It was furnished with two dark oak wardrobes and a matching bedside table. There was a chest of drawers, also in dark oak, and a double bed. It was very old-fashioned and my first impression was that it belonged to an elderly man.

Two watercolours hung from the wall. One was a landscape and the vegetation suggested it could have been anywhere in central Europe. The other one was more intriguing, because it bore a striking similarity to the palm tree picture in the factory office in Deniliquin. It tipped the balance for me and made me certain that we had found the house belonging to Big G, and that Big G and the Englishman were the same person.

Anja was methodically searching through the wardrobes and drawers. I left her to it and went into the bathroom. It was also old-fashioned but, like the bedroom, it was clean and tidy. I noticed an electric razor on the shelf in the bathroom cabinet, along with a toothbrush and toothpaste. There was nothing to suggest that more than one person used the bathroom. I looked in the cistern for anything hidden, and I even tapped the back of the shower area in case there was a door to somewhere. There was nothing out of the ordinary there and neither was there anything of interest in the other two bedrooms, except that one of the bedrooms had a single bed and it appeared that he used that room, as the contents of the drawers were less arranged. In fact, both the drawers and the wardrobe seemed to have items missing, suggestive of a rather hurried departure.

The idea of a hasty exit was confirmed in the kitchen where the kitchen stove had been crammed with the ash of burnt papers or documents. I hauled out the burnt contents of the stove and put them in one of the empty drawers of the freezer which was switched off with the door standing open. Anja, who was now becoming quite miserable, looked at the pile of ash, and silently moved on to the larder. Almost everything had been completely incinerated, but there were just a few stamp-sized remnants. From them, I could see that at least some of the writing had been in English and there was one incomplete telephone number. I slipped that in my pocket and after putting the drawer of ash neatly in the freezer I resumed the search.

We ended up in the basement, which was considerably more untidy than the rest of the house but yielded no clues. Reluctantly, we decided to leave. Anja was deeply frustrated that we had not found anything, and she barely spoke as we drove back to Bled through the mist and drizzle. We stopped off at the supermarket for provisions, but my suggestion of a candle-lit dinner was met with a stare of disapproval. Anja said that we should watch a documentary on television about the drug seizures and after dinner we settled down on the sofa to view the programme. It had been hastily put together, but although I struggled to understand some of the Slovenian, the graphics starkly showed the impact that the psychosis-inducing drugs had had on young people in certain European countries, and the worrying veer to the right of the young electorate.

France and the UK were not mentioned by name, but the increase in drug-related crime and localised riots brought about by draconian policing policies were cleverly illustrated. We watched in silence, apart from my occasional request for translation. At the end Anja said, 'Now perhaps you understand why I want that Englishman.'

We sat in silence for a while. Outside, it was raining heavily and the splashing from a broken drainpipe was the only sound we could hear. I still detected a mood in the house, and I wondered what I had done wrong.

As I prepared some coffee, I said to Anja, 'Since I've been back you have not asked me about Australia, and every time I try to talk about it you carefully change the subject.'

Anja looked sullen. 'I was worried about you, and I did something that would make you very angry, and I thought it had led to your death.' She looked at me with those big blue eyes and said, 'I'm sorry.' And burst into tears. They were tears of frustration, anger and love all in one and lasted a long while, but after some time I managed to comfort her, and when I felt the time was right I gently asked her to explain.

'After you left for Australia,' Anja began, 'I contacted Greg.'

I bristled, but said nothing.

Anja paused, but then went on, 'I said, that you had left for Sydney, and as it happened, he was on holiday visiting his elderly parents north of Melbourne. I told him you were renting a camper van. You were followed from the airport and the vehicle you rented was tagged when you stopped at a service station.'

'What do you mean tagged?' I interrupted.

'It was fitted with a tracking device,' Anja looked up to see my reaction.

I felt like a naive idiot, but quietly said, 'Go on.'

'We followed you.'

'We?' I exclaimed.

'Yes, Greg kept me informed.' Anja replied coldly, 'Greg grew up in Echuca, you know, not far from the town you went to.' Anja said, brightly, but her attempt to lighten the mood failed, and after a pause she went on, 'We tracked you to Melbourne, and then to Deniliquin. We thought you must have found something, otherwise, this was what Greg said, you wouldn't have gone there. He sent a couple of men to follow you, and they saw the blue containers that you talked to me about. Greg managed to get the Army special forces mobilised.'

'Wow,' I interrupted. 'That's amazing, I didn't realise he had that much confidence in me, I'm humbled.'

Anja ignored my comments and went on. 'The night you went into the silo, the man that was following you alerted Greg and his team, and after an hour or two, they decided to send the specials in. There was resistance and the criminals were eliminated.' Anja said, eliminate without emotion as if she was talking about a computer game, but she continued. 'They obviously discovered the cannabis production plant and were instructed to totally destroy it, which I believe they did.' Anja looked up and gave a weak smile. She appeared drained, but relieved that the tale had been told.

'Did anyone search for me?' I asked.

Anja shuddered. 'Greg told me he didn't think anyone was left alive in the factory after they had gone.'

'So, you assumed I was dead?'

Anja nodded her head, 'I was prepared to accept that, yes.'

'But you didn't seem to be that surprised when I contacted you afterwards.' I was confused by Anja's reactions and saddened by her emotionless portrayal of events as they unfolded.

'I thought there may have been a chance that you had survived, and I asked Greg to go himself to the campsite to see if you were there.'

'I didn't see him.' I said, somewhat aggressively.

'No, you were shopping or bird spotting or something.' Anja was back to wicked looks and I could feel the atmosphere thawing. 'How did you get out?' Anja said, after a pause, and finally I told her the story of my escape.

'It was good that I gave you that silver pig at Christmas.' Anja said, after I had finished, and I really think she thought that lucky pig had saved my life.

'What shall we do next, then?' Anja had recovered her usual *joie de vivre* by the following day, and as rain continued to tumble down outside, we endeavoured to come up with ideas. I remembered that I had some pieces of burnt paper in my pocket, and it also occurred to me that there were scraps of paper in my light jacket pocket purloined from the factory office in Deniliquin. I assembled all the fragments and spread them out on the table. Careful examination of the burnt paper from Villach, only produced one clue, and that was fairly obscure. It was part of a telephone number. Fortunately, it was the first part with plus, then the numbers one four seven three followed by three fours. We searched on google for any clues, but the best we could do was a tenuous link to a taxi firm in eastern England. We then sifted through the pieces of charred paper from Villach again, but apart from the partial telephone number, there was no further progress.

Next, we looked at the scraps of paper I had gathered from the drawer in the office in Deniliquin. It looked as if they had been lying in a pocket for some time and had been hurriedly placed in the drawer. In all, there were five pieces of paper, three were unreadable, one of the others was a receipt from a restaurant, but the last one was the most interesting. It was a receipt from a computer repair shop and the name of the customer looked like Mr G Spence.

Could that possibly be Big G we thought, but of even more interest was the telephone number. The first part matched the number found amongst the ash in Villach, but it wasn't eastern England where this computer repair business operated, it was in the Caribbean, on a little island called Grenada.

Chapter 35

It was Anja that suggested we should call the other number and add permutations of the last three digits and see if we could get an answer. It was an arduous task, but with the rain continuing to pour down outside, the job felt somewhat less tedious. It was after lunch before the 'Sorry, the number you have reached is not in service,' was replaced by a ringing tone, and a woman answered. I had got through to a police station, and the friendly voice at the other end informed me that she was in the capital of Grenada, St George's.

'Would you like a working holiday in the Caribbean?' I asked Anja.

'Of course.' Anja replied. 'But no guns, please.' I was constantly aware of this little weapon that she carried, and I could see that it could become a problem on this tropical island.

'Do you really think he could be in Grenada, Sean?'

'I think there's a good chance.' I replied. 'It's not just the telephone numbers, but do you remember the picture with the palm trees in the house in Villach? Well, there was a similar one in the office in Australia. So, I reckon it would be a good place to run and hide.'

'Always wanted a winter holiday in the tropics.' Anja said flippantly, and we spent the remainder of the afternoon looking at tourism in Grenada.

That evening, we drove back to Ljubljana through the rain and sleet and had a much more romantic candle-lit dinner prior to an early night. In the morning, Anja said, she would like to go to her office and get permission to fly to Grenada and complete her assignment, and that included having the leader of the drugs syndicate brought to justice. I waited in the flat during the morning, peering out on the street I had come to know well. What next, I mused, and it was with those thoughts running around in my brain that I heard the outer door slam and scrambling at the lock. Anja came in, slammed her bag on the table, and with eyes blazing told me that her request to go to Grenada had been refused. Their reasoning appeared sound and I could only comfort Anja in her frustrations, but for me it would be another expedition alone.

It was surprisingly easy to obtain tickets. This time, we thought that a week should be enough to track him down, if indeed he was there, put a case to the local police, and then have him arrested. It was with that in mind, when Anja took me to the airport early on Saturday morning. The roads were quiet, and it was clear and cold with twinkling stars when we walked into the terminal building at Ljubljana. For some unexplained reason, I was very reluctant to leave, and Anja, probably sensing my mood, was quite emotional when we said our goodbyes. The flight to Gatwick was uneventful, but it felt strange to walk along the corridors of the airport, on English soil again. I wondered if I would be stopped and questioned, or even prevented from travelling onwards after all that happened in the past months, but just over three hours later, the large comfortable aircraft that was taking me to the Caribbean lifted off from the runway, with the green patchwork of English fields soon disappearing as the aircraft became enveloped in clouds.

I was in a window seat of a half full plane with plenty of time to plan my week ahead, as there were no fellow passengers ready to engage in idle chatter anywhere near me. I had booked a hotel not far from the capital, St George's, and from there I intended to make discreet enquiries to find the whereabouts of the so-called Englishman. The plane made a scheduled stop in Antigua before continuing on the short flight to Grenada. Although it was early evening when I wheeled my trolley case through the green customs control at the airport and out into the main concourse, I was struck by how intensely hot and humid it was. I was immediately bathed in sweat, and it was very uncomfortable standing in the queue waiting for a taxi.

One eventually arrived, and the driver was disappointed to hear that my destination was only a ten-minute drive away. The hotel was made up of several small semi-detached bungalows with comfortable furnishings and, most importantly, efficient air-conditioning. They were set in beautifully manicured gardens and I could understand how generations of writers had described these tropical islands as paradise. Although I fully appreciated my accommodation, my brain was occupied searching for ways that I could accomplish my mission.

I had the foresight to bring insect repellent with me, and as I walked to a local restaurant in the evening, I was grateful for that. There were many insect and animal noises to be heard, topped by dozens of frogs that inhabited the ditches at the side of the road, presumably built to distribute the heavy downpours. The restaurant I found was little more than a beach bar, but the food was plentiful and the locals very friendly and we had an enjoyable evening discussing politics and sport.

After dinner, I returned to the hotel with the idea of talking to Anja, but it was the early hours of Sunday morning in Ljubljana and I thought a phone call would be inconsiderate, so I just sent a short text and then went to bed. In the morning, after a delicious fresh fruit breakfast on a covered terrace, I ordered a taxi and went exploring in St George's. It was a Sunday, and several shops and market stalls were closed, and surprisingly to me, many people were dressed up, with churches assembling much larger congregations than I had ever seen in London. There were plenty of tourists meandering around in the heat and many took the signposted route to the rather dilapidated early eighteenth-century French fort set on a promontory with good views of the sea, the harbour and much of St George's. I looked through my binoculars and took several pictures of the luxurious properties on the hillside around the town, and silently wondered which one, if any, belonged to the Englishman.

After returning to the town, I managed to locate the restaurant that produced the receipt I found in Australia. It was an interesting place right next to the harbour, and the management encouraged customers to write their names, with messages, on the walls or furniture. I resisted the temptation, and I also thought it was prudent not to ask about the Englishman in that restaurant. The food was spicy, very tasty, and reasonably priced, but even at the water's edge it was uncomfortably hot. After lunch I sought out the computer shop that Big G appeared to have used, but of course it was closed. I then spent the rest of the afternoon sitting in a shady beach bar, absorbing the coolness offered by the sea breeze and texting Anja until the low battery message appeared on my phone.

On Monday morning, I decided to walk into St George's via the beach. My destination was the computer repair shop. It took me longer than I thought it would. Great Anse beach and it's fine, almost white, sand, leading down to a turquoise sea with gentle wavelets, was a photo opportunity I didn't want to miss, and it was close to twelve o'clock before I reached the shop. A bell clanged on the door as I entered but there was no one there. I waited for a couple of minutes, but still no one, then the door to the street opened and a man entered carrying a bag of hot food and a bottle of soft drink.

'Sorry,' he said, 'Wanted to get some food in before the rush. How can I help you?'

'Just looking to buy a memory stick for my camera, that's all.' I replied.

The man said, 'That's something we do have. A choice.' He smiled, 'On holiday?'

'Yes,' I replied, 'from England.' I thought that was the best thing to say. 'Ever been there?' I asked.

He seemed like a man who enjoyed a chat, and the shop was more like a workshop than a place that could be overrun with customers, so I thought we could probably have some time together undisturbed.

Nathaniel, his name as I soon found out, had never been out of Grenada but he had aspirations now that his computer repair business was flourishing. He said, 'One day, I would like to own one of those big houses up in the hills.' And he slung his hand in the direction of the hills behind St. George's.

'I bet those big ones are owned by foreigners, rich Americans.' I ventured.

'Yeh, some are.' Nathaniel said, with a hint of disappointment in his voice.

'Any English?' I asked casually.

'None that I can think of.' He replied, 'There's a Scottish gentleman, for sure, but English…' I could see that Nathaniel was thinking hard.

'That's a shame,' I proffered. 'There was an old friend of mine that used to live here, but he's probably left now.'

'What was his name?' Nathaniel asked, his curiosity aroused.

'We used to call him Big G.'

'Oh, that must be Mister Spence. Yes, I'd forgotten him.' My heart beat faster. 'He has a big house at the top of the hill.' He gesticulated towards the hill. 'He ain't there very often, you know. He's some big businessman in Europe. They say he's a very important person.'

'You don't have his address, by chance?' I asked casually.

'Sure do.' The smiling Nathaniel went to a computer and scrolled through a list of customers. 'He spends a lot of time away, you know. He might not be there. Yep, here it is,' he said, after a while, and he read out the address and telephone number.

'I'll give him a ring if you like, to let him know you're here.' Nathaniel said.

'No, no.' I replied, 'I would like it to be a surprise.'

'Okay,' Nathaniel seemed disappointed. 'I'll let him know how helpful you've been, though.' I smiled at Nathaniel, and indeed he had been more helpful than he would ever know.

After leaving the shop, I went along to the harbour for lunch and then had a walk around the covered market. It was busy with locals and tourists alike, and a sudden shower added to the claustrophobic feeling of the place as people rushed in from all sides to shelter from the rain. Within five minutes, it was dry again, but it had cooled the air a little and I decided to walk up the hill to find 'Rosada', the name of the house I was looking for.

The road was in a state of disrepair, but the houses either side of it were not. Luxurious villas with expansive gardens looked out over the town, and the higher I walked, the grander the properties. The last one had a red and white sign reading 'Rosada'. I had reached my goal. There were security cameras above the electric gate which had an intercom set above the mailbox. I took a few photographs, to make it look as if I was a tourist admiring the grandeur just in case anyone was monitoring the cameras, then I turned and walked slowly back down the hill.

I was totally convinced that this property housed the man security forces in many countries had been looking for, but what should I do? He wasn't on any wanted list by name, as far as I knew, and to just go to a police station and ask an officer to arrest him would probably prove difficult. I needed more evidence, and to get that I needed to be able to take photographs of him and compare them with the limited shots of him that Anja had managed to obtain. I went back to the hotel, had a shower, and examined the photographs that I had taken of the property. Although there was a security gate at the entrance, the fence around the garden was irregular and could be easily breached. That evening, with sunset rapidly followed by darkness, I set off up the hill towards 'Rosada' to find Big G.

The road was dimly lit and I was worried about getting mugged, but there were neither cars, nor people, to be seen, and after several minutes of hard uphill walking I arrived close to the entrance. I could see light filtering through the thicket that marked the boundary on the roadside of the property, and I was encouraged to think that my adversary was at home. On the adjoining property, I had noticed from my photographs that some drainage work had been carried out, and that had necessitated the removal of some shrubs and trees. The resulting gap was large enough for me to gain entrance to Big G's property. I hoped the fence had not been electrified, but I had seen no evidence to suggest it had been, and I grabbed hold of it and swung myself through into the gardens. The lush vegetation still proved to be a difficult barrier to penetrate, and the whirr of insects and the rustle of unknown creatures added to the discomfort.

I heard some voices, and as I moved closer to the edge of the shrubs, I could see, across a sloping lawn, two people sitting on a terrace playing cards. I was too far away to see them clearly, but by creeping stealthily behind the shrubs I was able to move closer to the terrace. And then had a much better view of the people. One was a uniformed police officer, and from the stripes on his blue short-sleeved shirt, I assumed he was a sergeant. He sat with a bottle of soft drink and a glass, with his hat and a handgun on a low table beside him. He was dealing cards to a white man dressed in beige long trousers and a neatly ironed white shirt that just about contained the corpulent person within. The man was balding slightly, with small eyes and a pug nose that supported a pair of horn-rimmed glasses. His hands were adorned with silver jewellery and as soon as I heard his affected English accent I knew that this person was not just the Englishman, not just Big G, it was George Spence, the awful person that I once had to share a classroom with at school.

I stood and stared in disbelief, but yes it was him and he was drunk. A half empty bottle of rum was standing on the table in front of him next to an ice bucket containing a couple of large plastic cola bottles. The policeman was talking quietly whilst George was loud and vulgar. I thought long and hard about my next move and probably made the wrong decision. Rather than go to the police station in the morning, I decided to confront George there and then. It was probably the shock of seeing him that fuelled my idea, so I just walked onto the grass with my hands in the air and said, 'George, do you mind if we have a few words?'

The policeman grabbed his gun, and George momentarily looked startled, but he quickly regained his composure and said, 'How nice to see you, Sean isn't it? But you could have rung the gate bell.'

The policeman appeared confused, but he was using two hands to keep his gun firmly pointing in my direction. I was surprised by George's initial reaction and my pause allowed him to continue.

'We were at school together, William. How about that, all those years ago. We haven't seen much of each other since, although he visited my house in Austria just last week, didn't you Sean?' He glared at me and there was more than a hint of menace in his voice.

'What would you like me to do with him, Mister Spence?' William asked, still obviously wondering what was going on.

'You can shoot him if you like, or you can invite him to play cards with us. What do you think?' George had a malevolent smile on his face directed at both me and the policeman.

'Are you sure that he's a friend?' William said, coldly.

'What do you think?' George repeated in a patronising manner, 'Shoot him.'

A cold sweat broke out on my forehead. I realised I had handled this badly and my life was in the balance.

'This is one of the most wanted men on the planet.' I said, strongly. 'Can you arrest him please and take him to the station.'

George guffawed. 'Always had such a good sense of humour, Sean.'

'Mister Spence, we really ought to go to the station and sort this out.' William said, weakly.

'Yes, please do.' I said, quickly. 'I have a pass in my wallet to say that I am working for the British government and I can get that fact verified.'

I noticed a look of doubt in George's eyes and his lips tightened. 'Search him William, I'm sure he's bluffing. It's just part of his warped humour. Give me the gun and I'll cover you in case he makes a wrong move.

William was a big man, roughly the same age as me, but not a person I would like to have a fight with. I told him where my wallet was and he removed it and threw it towards the table. He then frisked me and removed my rucksack before throwing that towards the table. When he decided that I was free of weapons he returned to the table with my possessions. First of all, he went through my rucksack, which only contained my precious binoculars, two bananas, which I had taken from the breakfast table, and a bottle of water. In my wallet there was the usual array of cards which William meticulously examined, until eventually he came to my security pass.

'He's right, you know.' William said.

'I had better call the station.' William made a movement to release his phone, but George, his eyes flashing angrily, turned his gun towards William and said, 'Stop!'

William looked askance across the table. 'Come on, Mister Spence, you can be in serious trouble for pointing a gun at a police officer. I'll let you off this time. Give the gun to me.'

I saw an opportunity to interject. 'You can see now that this man is just a common criminal.' George glanced at me with hate in his eyes as I continued, 'He is responsible for the deaths of many thousands of people and…'

Before I could continue, the policeman bravely made a grab for the gun but George was too quick for him. He pulled back and fired a shot at close range into the chest of the officer.

Instantly, I lunged towards the gun, but George was slow on this occasion, perhaps realising the enormity of what he had just done, and within a minute I was stepping back and pointing the gun at George. William was already unconscious and his laboured breathing quickly subsided. Blood dripped quietly on to the terrace and it was obvious that the police sergeant was dead.

'You're in big trouble now, Sean.' George whined in his irritatingly false accent. 'You've just shot a police officer, and the punishment for that on this island is death.' George poured some rum into a glass and topped it up with cola.

'What do you mean?' I said, thinking that I may have misheard him.

'You came to burgle my house, was disturbed by the policeman that I pay to protect me, grabbed his gun and shot him. You can make your escape if you like, but I'll call the police and you'll be hunted down. It will be a pleasure to see you hang. I'm not sure who you are working for, but my business interests, well let me say, have been disrupted recently and I'm not too happy about it.' George took a large gulp of rum from the glass and continued.

'One of the neighbours may have heard the shot and called the police. Failing that, my caretakers will be here in the morning, and when they see you, they'll call the police. Unless you want to shoot them as well.' George laughed malevolently. 'You could become a mass murderer.' George laughed again. 'I'll call the police and have you arrested.'

'I haven't killed anyone.' I protested.

'As you wish,' said George. 'But I know this island well, and it's me the authorities will believe, not you. You're finished, Boateng. You can be hunted like a fox, or quietly give in and get hung by your neck until your legs stop twitching.'

'There is an alternative.' I said, 'I could kill you and there would then be no one to contradict my story, and I would be free to go home.'

I detected a brief look of fear in George's face before he went on. 'Now that's something you lily-livered communists would never do. You were pathetic at school and you're pathetic now.'

It was at that moment that I shot Big G in the stomach.

He looked down at his white shirt, which was rapidly turning red, then up at me with pleading eyes. 'You needn't have done that, Sean, we could have worked something out.' He grimaced with pain, then began a tirade of racial abuse followed by his full repertoire of other invectives. It ended with him retching, inhaling deeply and slumping forward on the chair. Like the policeman beside him, he was obviously dead.

Chapter 36

I stood for a couple of minutes looking at the corpses, before placing the gun on the table and gathering up my possessions and placing them in my rucksack. Apart from a background noise of croaking frogs and a dog barking in the distance it was quiet. There was no sign of any police arriving, so I walked down the gravel drive and let myself out of the electric gate. I had hoped it would remain open to allow access to the police, but as I walked down the hill I could hear it gently closing. I had a feeling of utter relief, almost euphoria, that the job had now been completed. I was trying to justify in my head why I had killed George. Was it revenge for the taunting he had given me at school? Was it for the death of Anja's mother, a woman I had never met, or was it because I felt he had the power and the money to get away with murder and live as a free man. I didn't know, but although it was the middle of the night in Ljubljana, I sent a message to Anja saying, 'Job done.'

I reached the red painted building housing the police headquarters, and for a moment I thought it was closed as the lights were low, but there was a uniformed woman on the front desk and she calmly asked how she could help me. There was a woman with two young children sitting not too far behind me, so I just whispered to the officer, 'I've come to report a very serious crime.'

She looked up with widening eyes, and in a soft voice said, 'What sort of crime, sir?'

'Murder.' I mouthed at her.

'I see,' she said calmly.

I was not sure if she was taking me seriously, or I was being placed in the category of unhinged. Anyway, she pressed a button, and almost immediately a very large officer appeared, and after the desk officer had succinctly explained my reason for visiting, I was asked to accompany the large officer to an interview room.

It was on the first floor and after the lights were switched on it revealed an almost bare room, apart from a table and two chairs. The windows opened inwards and metal bars were attached to the outer wall. The officer went back to the door and switched on the ceiling fan which gently squeaked as it erratically revolved. A small laptop was produced from under the table and after a few notes were typed into it, the officer looked up, and with an expressionless countenance, asked for my name and a few other routine particulars.

'I understand you would like to report a murder,' the officer began.

'Two,' I interjected, 'Well, two deaths anyway.'

'I see,' the officer continued blandly, 'Can you tell me what happened in your own words.'

I thought that was a strange sentence to use, but I then began an account of the evening's proceedings. The only part where I veered away from the truth, was how I waited before shooting George, but to me it was irrelevant. If I hadn't grabbed the gun he would have killed me. It was me or him.

After I had finished speaking, there was a very long pause. 'Is that it, Mister Boateng?' The officer looked at me intensely and not in a friendly manner.

'I think I've said everything, yes.'

The officer rose, and as he stood towering over me, he said, 'Would you mind showing me the contents of your rucksack, and as it is such a serious crime that you are reporting, I have to do a body search on you.'

'Fair enough.' I replied, 'Go ahead.'

Not for the first time in recent months, the contents of my rucksack were carefully laid out on the table.

'This is an expensive piece of equipment you have here, sir.' He was pointing at my binoculars.

'Yes they're for bird spotting, and spying on villains.' I smiled, and immediately regretted that I had mentioned spying. Although I had alluded to my work for British Intelligence in my statement, my reply was met with a frosty look. After my possessions had been listed, I was asked to pack them away.

He roughly took the rucksack from me and slung it over his shoulder, and with the laptop gripped in one giant hand he said, 'I'll be back later. There's water over there,' pointing to a dispenser in the corner, 'and if you want a toilet, just lift the phone and speak to the front desk.' With that, he opened the door, glided into the corridor, and gently locked me in the room. I was tired from the evening's events and it wasn't long before I fell asleep.

I was awakened by the sound of a key in the lock and voices. Four men entered the room. The first man was middle-aged, short and stocky and wore a crumpled dark suit. He immediately introduced himself as detective chief inspector, and I can't remember the name, and sat down behind the desk. The second man was also wearing a suit, but this one looked more expensive and he introduced himself as Paul Benyon, a local solicitor who appeared to be in awe of the chief inspector. The other two men were policemen that had been assigned the task of bringing in chairs and a full array of recording equipment.

The chief inspector had a business-like, bordering on aggressive, manner as he fired a quick succession of questions at me. Mister Benyon, who had positioned himself next to me with notepad in hand said, 'You don't have to answer these questions.'

'But I want to,' I replied, 'I want to help as much as possible.' I felt that I was becoming the criminal, and as the questioning went on, I realised that was exactly what the thinking was, that I was the murderer. Of course, the death of the policeman was much lamented, but what I was unaware of was that George Spence was a well-respected member of Grenadian society and was close friends with the elite on the island. My protestations that he was nothing but a common criminal, not only fell on deaf ears, but fuelled the increasing animosity that was building up towards me.

In my original statement, I had mentioned my connection to the British intelligence services, but preliminary enquiries had failed to confirm that, and the telephone number in London that I had provided them with was unobtainable. At the very best, they thought I might be a private detective, and at the worst, a would-be burglar who was unexpectedly caught out. It was not good, and Benyon shook his head gently on a number of occasions when my statements appeared flawed. The interrogation, because that was what it was, went on for the rest of the day, although I had toilet breaks and some very good food was served up for me.

Without a goodbye, the chief inspector left late in the afternoon, and although I had not been charged with any offence, I was taken downstairs to a cell. I protested vehemently, but it made no difference, and after another good meal for supper, I was left to sleep on a hard bed in a clean, but very stuffy cell. In the morning, another detective came to visit me, along with Paul Benyon, and I was charged with a double murder, and driven to the local prison.

My head was buzzing as the nightmare continued to unfold. My solicitor was very good, but when I asked him for access to a phone, a computer, or even writing paper, it was refused; the excuse being, that the crime was so bad that I was not allowed any direct contact with the outside world. My first night in prison filled me with utter despair. Where were my colleagues? Where was the support when I really needed it?

I spent two weeks in that cell. The food was adequate and apart from the extreme heat and humidity I had no cause for complaint. However, it was crushingly boring. Benyon visited me every other day and brought with him a few books, but they were lightweight novels and observing the various insects that entered the cell was a more pleasurable experience. To my intense frustration, Benyon seemingly was unable to verify my existence. Even my bank account had mysteriously been closed and as I understood it, I was now destitute. This Kafkaesque situation I found myself in, was made worse by the lack of contact from Anja. I did manage to get Benyon to send a message to my parents, and that gave me hope, because I knew my father would not rest until the perceived injustice had been righted.

Although Benyon was a thoroughly nice man, and listened to my pleas with patient empathy, I felt that he could do more to get me released, and I politely asked if he would contact a lawyer in the UK I knew personally. To my surprise, the request was turned down, and just over two weeks after being remanded in custody, my trial for murder began. Normally, the wait for a trial would be considerably longer, but apparently the local media had clamoured for justice to take place. I asked Benyon to see what the media in the UK had said, about my arrest and the pending trial, and he did so diligently. However, although the initial double murder was widely reported, the consensus of opinion was that it was a local man who had committed the crime, and my name had not even been mentioned. He also said that the murder had been reported in the European media with a somewhat different slant, and that gave me some hope that this sorry episode would be resolved in my favour.

While on remand, I had access to my own clothes, and on the first day of the trial I tried to look my casual best. The judge was an elderly man with thick-rimmed glasses, and the lawyer for the prosecution was tall, thin and exuding intelligence. My confidence as I entered the courtroom evaporated quickly. The jury looked like a fair cross-section of Grenadian society, and their looks at me were more of curiosity than hatred. That encouraged me somewhat, but my positive feeling was short-lived after the prosecution lawyer began to outline his case.

He expressed himself eloquently, and if it wasn't me he was talking about, I would have admired him considerably. As it was, he told my version of the story in a way that would make any one sitting on a jury think that the defendant was guilty. Benyon was then invited by the judge to clarify any points that the prosecuting counsel had glossed over. His presentation was slow and stilted, and although he put over the main points, which were, 'Why didn't I carry out the burglary after the murders? And why did I go to the police station rather than make my escape?' I could see from the reaction of the jurors, that Benyon was not holding their attention, and I could feel myself gently shaking my head.

Over the following three weeks the trial continued and at the end of each day my prospects looked bleaker. Every morning, on entering the courtroom, I scanned the public gallery for friendly faces. Where was my father? Surely, he must believe my innocence, or perhaps he hadn't been told about the seriousness of the case. I looked around and there were many hostile faces, and just a few curious ones. I tried to get Benyon to call a variety of telephone numbers in Britain, and I tried to get references from my university, and even my old school, but either Benyon was not making the phone calls, or persons unknown had made a thorough job of wiping out my history.

It came as no surprise to me that at the end of the trial I was found guilty of the murder of the police sergeant and the popular local philanthropist, George Spence. What did surprise me, however, was that I was sentenced to death by hanging for, in the judge's opinion, 'the most heinous crime the island had ever seen.'

Chapter 37

I was bundled out of the courtroom without a word from anyone and put in the back of a waiting police van. Instead of returning to my old cell in the prison, I was taken to another, which was less clean and even more bare than the previous one. Benyon visited me the day after the trial and his demeanour made me think that he expected me to be angry with him personally about the verdict. But no, it wasn't him I was angry with, nor was it the jury who believed the very clever prosecution lawyer. No, it was the friends, colleagues and family, who had let me down. And no, it wasn't anger, it was extreme disappointment.

An appeal was immediately lodged, but no new evidence was forthcoming, and it was quickly rejected. A crumb of comfort was that no hanging had taken place on the island for many years, and as Benyon put it, 'Your sentence may be commuted to a whole life tariff in prison.' He meant it in a positive way, and I believe he knew I was innocent, but I had no access to money to pay him and he had every right to disappear. However, he didn't, and once a week he came to visit me and told me about some of the happenings in the outside world.

It was probably these afternoons with Benyon that kept me sane. He allowed me to ask him many questions to which, with his widespread and up-to-date knowledge of current affairs, he was usually able to provide an answer to. I had given up on those that were close to me, but I kept up an interest in England, and over the weeks, the news from that country became increasingly grim. The internet had become heavily censored, and news correspondents from the foreign media were hassled or had visas and accreditation revoked. Civil unrest was rife, and the European Union, along with many Commonwealth and Latin American countries, had imposed sanctions on the country. I worried about my parents, but despite the efforts of Benyon to contact them, nothing had been received in reply.

After his visits had ended, I sat on my bed and watched the insects scuttling up and down the cream and green walls. I tried hard to work out the reasons why these flies and beetles behaved the way they did, and if I understood them, maybe, just maybe, I could understand what was happening to my country.

My cell was in the old part of the prison, and although there were no windows, there were missing bricks high up on the wall that allowed light in, as well as the insects and occasionally some rain. It was never cold, but when it rained heavily, there were often refreshing gusts of wind. I was expected to keep my own cell clean, and a mop and bucket were provided for that purpose. Once a week, I think it was on Monday, a prison officer, usually a burly individual who introduced himself as Mister Wood, came to inspect the cell.

He never said anything, just looked around and left. Otherwise, food and drink were pushed through a slot in the door onto a shelf three times a day and I was left alone. For me, in the condemned cell, there was no formal exercise, but I kept fit by pulling myself up to where the bricks were missing for ventilation, and I had the added bonus of seeing the view towards the sea and freedom. To the right, I could just see some big houses on the hill, and I could not help feeling a pang of envy at the luxury some of the owners might be enjoying.

One Friday, it was probably about four months after I had been incarcerated, Benyon arrived with some exciting news. A snap general election had been called in the UK as a means to prevent further mayhem occurring. Although I was as far removed from the troubles as one could be, the thought of a change of government delighted me. I knew that the media, and other vested interests, would try all they could to maintain the *status quo*, but I felt confident that the British people would finally oust the appalling populist regime that had brought the country to the edge of ruin. I had to wait another two weeks for the election results, but a smiling Benyon arrived to tell me that a change of government had occurred and many arrests of high-ranking officials had taken place. I was worried that there would be a military coup, but Benyon assured me that it was unlikely. The change was welcomed in Europe and it looked as if sanctions were going to be lifted.

The following week, Benyon was uncharacteristically gloomy, and although he said nothing to suggest that he was hiding anything, I became a little concerned. Day after day I sat in the cell. Counting insects, composing songs in my head, and listening to the steps outside in the corridor and trying to imagine the person or persons making them. Usually, it was the food trolley that took an age to reach my door, having many stops on its journey from prisoner to prisoner. The warder that inspected my cell was surprisingly light footed for a big man, whereas Benyon took little noisy steps in his polished leather shoes, but that was the sound I really longed for every Friday.

The week after Benyon had presented himself in a gloomy mood, he failed to arrive. This made me seriously worried. He had not hinted at an absence, and prior to that he had been so reliable. I received no message of explanation, nor did I expect one, but many thoughts went through my mind, the main one being, was it now my time to go to the gallows? My ears became extra keen, picking up the faintest sound of footsteps outside. Apart from the regular supply of food and water, and the cleaning inspector, there was one other event in the week that merits mention, and that was the laundry man. He brought a fresh set of prison uniforms, underwear, and a towel. He was a fellow prisoner, who must have been under strict instructions not to speak to me, because all attempts to engage him in conversation failed. I tried to interact with the guards that let him in, but there were no responses.

I was beginning to think I was going insane as my thoughts were becoming rushed, jumbled and often irrational. On the Monday after Benyon failed to arrive, I actually thought it was Tuesday at the time, a testimony to the state of my mind, I heard the slow approach of footsteps along the corridor. I estimated that there were more than two pairs of feet, and I heard a low murmur of voices. If it was anything to do with food or inspections, there would be pauses while each prisoner had his needs dealt with. I was last in line and had been since the beginning. These footsteps, however, were not stopping and my head began to pound as I was gripped by fear. Was it irrational? I tried to take control of myself. All these emotions manifested themselves in a very short space of time as the footsteps came ever closer.

Chapter 38

Eventually, it seemed like an hour, but it was probably less than two minutes, the footsteps stopped outside my cell door and the rattle of keys was quickly followed by the turning of the lock. The door opened, revealing a prison guard, who I had seen before on several occasions, Paul Benyon, who was as immaculately turned out as ever, and a man, also in a suit, whom I thought I vaguely recognised. I was shaking with fear by this time and my head was humming. It was difficult to take in the three people in front of me. My eyes flitted from face to face, but their expressions were not of hate or sympathy. The guard just stared at me blankly, the other man seemed to view me with curiosity, while Benyon was smiling.

The older man introduced himself as the prison governor and was the first to speak. 'We have some good news for you, Mister Boateng. You are to be released.'

'Released?' I said, much louder than I wanted to, and I automatically said, 'Why?'

This last question seemed to take the governor by surprise, and as his eyebrows lifted he appeared lost for words. Benyon quickly came to his rescue. 'A lot of new information has emerged since the government changed in the UK, and as a result, your conviction has been declared unsafe, and in due time it is likely that it will be quashed.'

I must have looked totally bewildered. 'So, what happens next?' I asked.

It was a question that Benyon was prepared for. 'You will be formally discharged and released into the care of the British authorities.'

'So, I'm not free to go, then?' I interrupted.

'You are a free man, Sean.' It was the first time I had heard him use my first name, and that one sentence was enough to make tears well up in my eyes.

I sat on the bed with my head in my hands and took in the enormity of what he had just said. Apart from the distant sound of prison life, there was silence, until the governor quietly said. 'Are you ready to come to my office, there are a few formalities we need to go through. In your own time, though.' I possessed nothing, so after a cursory glance at a gecko I had befriended, sleeping by the window I led the others out of the cell.

The governor then strode briskly along the corridor followed by Benyon and with me taking up the rear. Even though I had tried to maintain fitness, I found myself struggling to keep up speed, and even the short walk to the governor's office left me breathless. A man was sitting in the office, his back to me, hunched over a laptop into which he was rapidly typing something.

'Here's your man, Peter.' The governor addressed the man with the laptop. Peter turned around, and I was amazed to see it was Peter, the person that had interviewed me at Cambridge, Peter, the person that had interviewed me for the job in the S.I.S.

'Hello,' I said, with a weak smile. 'What are you doing here?'

There were forms to fill in and I sat down at a corner table while Peter and the governor chatted amicably. When the paperwork had been completed, I was handed my suitcase, presumably taken from the hotel many months before and kept somewhere. In it were some clothes that I had not used whilst I was on remand, and toiletries that I never expected to see again. After I had checked through that, and the remaining clothes, my wallet, rucksack and binoculars were placed on the table. I checked through it all, and lastly, in a side pocket of the rucksack, I found the silver pig on a chain that Anja had given me for Christmas. I put my head in my hands and wept inconsolably. I was emotionally drained.

After a while, Peter put his hand on my shoulder, and gently said, 'I think we should go now.'

'Where?' I retorted.

'We are taking a flight to St Lucia where you will be debriefed. Do you think you're up to it?'

'Yes.' I replied in a whisper. I knew it was policy to have a debriefing session after a mission with the aim of discussing problems encountered and how to improve technique. I apologised for my emotional outburst and gathered my possessions together. In a much better frame of mind, I left the prison and felt a stiff wind across my face for the first time in months. There was a driver waiting for us outside and Peter, my solicitor, and myself were driven to the airport. Once there, I thanked Benyon profusely for standing by me, and told him he would be well remunerated for his loyalty, and then, with a minimum of airport formalities,

Peter and myself were escorted to an old Cessna that was sitting on the runway. I had never been in a light aircraft before, and my brain, swimming with mixed emotions, soon had just one concern, the hope that this flimsy looking aircraft would manage to take us the two hundred odd kilometres to St Lucia.

We were met at the Airport by an official from the high commission, who introduced himself as Toby, driving a battered land rover. He was a young, jolly and enthusiastic young man who had the ability to make anyone feel at ease, but his prowess with the steering wheel on his ancient vehicle wasn't the best.

However, the hour-long trip to his home outside Soufriere on the west coast, was filled with such interesting scenery, that the occasional excursion off the side of the road almost went unnoticed. The house we arrived at was typically old colonial, mostly made from wood, and with some extravagant architectural features. It was set on the hillside and offered beautiful views towards the sea. I was introduced to Toby's wife Angelique and two young children who were totally underwhelmed by our arrival.

Toby quickly made tea for us and produced a bowl of banana chips and coconut balls, but it was the tea that I enjoyed the most. I had not been able to ask any questions on the flight, it was too noisy, and the trip across the island had been too absorbing for me to spoil with trite enquiries, but now I felt it was time to begin.

Turning to Peter, I asked, 'How did you manage to get me out, then?'

Peter replied. 'I'm not sure how much you got to know about current affairs, Sean, but times have changed, and there's a new order in much of the world, and eventually it included the UK. But it's not my place to go into detail. If you feel like it after your snack, we can go to the garden and start the debrief. You probably know the procedure, and you'll have ample opportunity to put in some questions. Whether we can answer them, goodness knows, there have been some strange times.' And with that enigmatic answer I was left to finish my banana chips.

In the heat of the afternoon sunshine, Peter and myself ambled down the sloping lawn towards a shaded terrace where a cooling wind was blowing in from the distant sea. It was a very relaxing place, and Peter helped me to wind down. There were four carafes of water on the table that we sat by, and also four upturned glasses. I commented on that fact and Peter just smiled and casually said that we were to be joined by two others, and with a wry smile he said, 'I think you might know them.' My immediate thought was that it must be Anja, but who could she be with, and if this was a debrief, surely foreign agents would not be invited. As these thoughts were going through my head, I noticed two figures emerge from between some shrubs at the top of the garden. The loping stride of the person on the left I instantly recognised and it didn't make me happy. The one on the right, I thought I knew, but I wasn't sure until he was just a few metres from me.

It was my line manager from London. He shook my hand warmly and said, 'Good to see you Sean, it's been a long time.' The other man, in his customary wide-brimmed beige hat was Greg, the Australian, who had almost got me killed in Deniliquin. I turned away from my boss, and with cold eyes staring into his, I said to Greg, 'I see the grim reaper has arrived. Have you come to collect me?' There was not much humour in my voice, and not much intended.

Greg looked embarrassed. He tried to lighten the occasion with a couple of banal quips, but the others could see that me and him were not the best of friends.

Peter poured out four glasses of water and we sat down waiting for him to open the proceedings. He reached to one side and took a laptop from the shelf.

'Okay, Sean, once upon a time you took a flight to Ljubljana. Please carry on.'

I then gave him an outline of what had befallen me on my travels. Occasionally, he sought clarification, and other times he asked me to pause while he typed something into the computer. My boss and Greg just sat impassively while I was speaking, and probably, after about three hours, I ran dry.

'What can I say,' Peter said at the end. 'You were given a job and you completed it. I think all of us are grateful for what you did.'

The other two nodded.

'And I suppose you now have a few questions for us?' They looked at me as if I was a ticking bomb that was about to explode, but by telling my tale I had expunged the bitterness and resentment that I had felt, and now I was just glad to be alive.

'Peter, there has been one thing that has puzzled me for a very long time and I wonder if you have an answer? The placement I had in Spain when I did my degree. Was it connected to the drugs fiasco in Malaga after I had started working for SIS?'

'Yes.' Peter replied.

The other two looked bemused. There was silence.

'Can you elaborate, please?'

Peter gave my boss a shifty look. 'Okay. As you know, we trawl the universities for likely candidates for our line of work, and you seemed to be suitable, but somewhat naive, if I may say.'

'You can say. I think I'm totally naive.'

Peter ignored the comment and went on, 'At the time, we believed that the source of the psychotic cannabis was either Spain or Morocco, and we knew that the clementine farm that you were placed on was probably exporting drugs to the UK. Our agent there was convinced that the cannabis was nothing out of the ordinary.'

'Your agent didn't happen to be called Youssef?' I interrupted.

'Yes, that's the one.' Peter said, and I noticed a slight smile appear on my bosses' face. I let out an expletive and shook my head.

'So, what happened after I came to work for SIS and was sent to Spain looking for drugs?'

This was getting interesting. 'Can I take over here, Peter?' My boss looked at me with pleading eyes. 'Although it's bad policy to shift blame, we were led in completely the wrong direction by Ollie.'

'Sir Oliver Legg?' I interjected.

'The same,' my boss continued, 'As you may, or may not, know, he is in prison now, and for years he, along with members of the last government, had been making fools of us, and yes I sent you to Malaga on his recommendation, as he considered you "to be the man for the job". Before your head gets too big, he basically wanted to get you out of the way, and to disappear in Spain was a good solution.'

'*Phew.*' I exclaimed, 'So he set me up to be shot by the Spanish police?'

'Yes and no.' My boss replied, 'Ollie tipped off the intelligence services in Spain that the UK was sending a spy to disrupt the drug running business from Morocco, so that the psychotic version of the cannabis could become dominant. Confused? So was I, and so were the Spanish authorities. They sent an intelligence officer in to meet up with you'

'Jose,' I interrupted, 'Yes, and unfortunately you killed him.'

'Hold on,' I said. 'He was about to kill me.'

'Yes, and another of their men was shot by the Spanish police.' My boss continued. 'It was a sorry affair and best forgotten, but no blame is attached to you by the way.'

'So, what happened next, then?' I asked. 'I should imagine that Sir Oliver was none too pleased.'

'A correct observation, Sean, and it was about that time that Greg appeared on the scene. Over to you chum.'

Greg, who had been sitting, arms folded, listening intently, cleared his throat and began, 'We had a notion there were some bad eggs at the top in your organisation, and as I knew your boss from college days and trusted him, we arranged a meeting, as we had a hunch that the drugs were not coming from North Africa, but from the Middle East or beyond. I asked if there was a reliable young bloke that could be sent out to central Europe to try and find the route for importation. We were sure we were on to something when he disappeared in Slovenia or Hungary, that sort of area.'

I thought of the chap that Anja had shot in Bled, but I said nothing.

Greg continued. 'Anyway, you were next in line, and we kept it very quiet in London, because if Ollie had got wind of that, you would probably have disappeared too. There were only four people who knew what you were up to in Slovenia, and three of them are sitting around this table.' Greg had a triumphant air about him, and while Peter looked away sheepishly, I felt somewhat indignant.

There was an awkward silence until I confronted Greg with, 'You left me to die in Deniliquin, you knew I was in there.'

Greg's eyes narrowed. 'No one is indispensable, you know that. We went in to eliminate all traces of the cannabis factory and we succeeded. The folk of Deni thought it was just a big blaze in a semi-derelict factory. They didn't know anything about drugs or criminals, and they still don't. We're grateful for the job you did, and we are, but in the big picture your life is of minimal importance, it's in the small print of your contract.'

And as an afterthought Greg finished by saying, 'And anyway, I personally checked out at the caravan site to see whether you were still alive because your dear girlfriend asked me to. That's the trouble when you have women in this sort of business.'

'Come on Greg, that wasn't called for,' my boss abruptly interposed.

I glared at Greg and said nothing. There was a prolonged silence before I continued. 'Can I ask a few more questions now?'

'Yep. Go ahead,' Peter replied.

'What happened to Ahmet, the Iranian Turk?'

My boss answered, 'He was Iraqi actually, but he's okay. He has just been released from prison in Tehran and he's back with his family.'

'Why couldn't Benyon contact my family?' I looked individually at the three faces around the table.

Peter answered. 'Er, they were difficult times. We did get a message to your parents to say that you were okay, and from what I've heard, your father accepted that you were doing a difficult job in difficult times.'

'So, why couldn't I access my bank account?' I continued, 'I think that's probably something to do with your conviction. Your assets were frozen in case the families of the deceased wanted to make a claim.'

'Oh, I see, of course, I hadn't thought of that.' I replied. Finally, I said, 'Will I be able to call my family and friends now?'

The three men at the table looked at each other before Peter replied. 'I think we've covered everything of importance. Where would you like to make the call?'

'Here would be nice.'

'Okay, then let us adjourn to the house.' And with that, they arose and strolled up the garden towards the shrubbery.

I phoned my parents. My mother was on a night shift and my father was already in bed, but we had a long father-son conversation. I was mildly reproached for not contacting them, but he could understand that my top-secret work had made it difficult for me and he slowly became lighter and started telling me about the family. I had hoped to call Anja, but I noticed the window on my phone saying that my battery was low, and inwardly cursing, I had to cut short the conversation with my father. After the call had finished, I wrote a short message to Anja, 'Flat battery, everything is absolutely fine, speak to you soon. Love you.' Moments later, the phone went dead.

I sat watching the sun over the western sea and marvelled at how quickly it set in the tropics, but just as the last rays of orange played across the water, I heard a rustle behind me. I turned sharply and a voice said, 'Got your message, love you too.'

Ingram Content Group UK Ltd.
Milton Keynes UK
UKHW021928220623
423799UK00003B/21